Vessel of Power

by

Michelle O'Leary

This is a work of fiction. Names, characters, places, and incidents are either the product of the author's imagination or are used fictitiously, and any resemblance to actual persons living or dead, business establishments, events, or locales, is entirely coincidental.

Vessel of Power

Contact Information: info@thewildrosepress.com

Cover Art by *Debbie Taylor*

The Wild Rose Press, Inc.
PO Box 708
Adams Basin, NY 14410-0708
Visit us at www.thewildrosepress.com

Publishing History
First Fantasy Rose Edition, 2016
Print ISBN 978-1-5092-1134-0
Digital ISBN 978-1-5092-1135-7

Published in the United States of America

This is it.

Heart thumping hard, Eylee'ai slipped over the rail of the ship, flowing into the shadows like a piece of liquid darkness. She kept her skin black as the night and body supple but shifted her hands into long talons, hard enough to rip out a man's heart.

Or a prince's.

Eyes fixed on her prey, she slunk closer, concealing herself behind barrels. Three men formed a triangle on the deck, one of them the elemental prince. She knew the prince by description but didn't recognize the other two. If she was fast enough, they wouldn't matter. All she needed was time to get her claws in the prince's throat. After that, her death was an acceptable price for the safety of her family, if it was the gods' will.

She drew a deep breath, eyes flicking over the trio, seeking the best approach. *For my mother and sister,* she thought. *May the gods preserve them.* Her muscles drew taut, thrumming with violent purpose. She'd never taken a life before, but with so much riding on it she wouldn't hesitate. She could not hesitate.

The prince's voice rose, ringing with steel and cold fury. "Is that a challenge, Uncle?"

She hesitated.

Did he say uncle? Mother of All, two royals? The gods must not be feeling merciful. She stared from one to the other, wondering if she could take them both.

Dedication

This book is dedicated to my family,
whose staunch support and generous encouragement
has kept me going through cloudy days.
And most especially to my son Dominic,
who is my sunshine, more joy and adventure
than any story,
and the very best thing I can and will ever create.

Chapter 1

This is it.

Heart thumping hard, Eylee'ai slipped over the rail of the ship, flowing into the shadows like a piece of liquid darkness. She kept her skin black as the night and body supple but shifted her hands into long talons, hard enough to rip out a man's heart.

Or a prince's.

Eyes fixed on her prey, she slunk closer, concealing herself behind barrels. Three men formed a triangle on the deck, one of them the elemental prince. She knew the prince by description but didn't recognize the other two. If she was fast enough, they wouldn't matter. All she needed was time to get her claws in the prince's throat. After that, her death was an acceptable price for the safety of her family, if it was the gods' will.

She drew a deep breath, eyes flicking over the trio, seeking the best approach. *For my mother and sister,* she thought. *May the gods preserve them.* Her muscles drew taut, thrumming with violent purpose. She'd never taken a life before, but with so much riding on it she wouldn't hesitate. She could not hesitate.

The prince's voice rose, ringing with steel and cold fury. "Is that a challenge, Uncle?"

She hesitated.

Did he say uncle? Mother of All, two royals? The

gods must not be feeling merciful. She stared from one to the other, wondering if she could take them both.

The older man raised his voice to match his nephew's. "If a challenge is what it takes to teach you respect, boy, then so be it!"

The third man stepped between the combatants, holding up a hand to each. Anxiety edged his features as he looked from one to the other, his voice low and careful. "Wait, please, let's not be hasty. May I speak with you, cousin?"

Three royals? Eylee'ai sent a glare to the heavens, wondering what she'd done to deserve this twist of fate. On the other hand, the two younger men were moving toward her, coming within easier reach. Her muscles tensed and teeth sharpened. Shifting back into the shadows, she went still, poised for a lethal leap as they approached.

"Soul brother," the cousin said with low urgency, "don't do this. He's been baiting you since he came aboard. He wants a fight, wants to remove your claim. With you gone—"

"For gods' sake, Rune, I'm not daft." The prince's stony features eased with a hint of amusement. "Uncle Storm wouldn't know subtle if it struck him between the eyes."

"Right," Rune muttered with a wry tilt of his head. "No king of cleverness, that one. So why take his challenge?"

"Uncle Storm's aboard to root out all I know about the Vessel, and then find it first. I can't have that. He has to go."

"But a fight, Des?" Rune asked, expression growing anxious again. "Why risk it?"

“No risk. I won’t lose. And it’s good reason to keep him off my ship.”

“There’s always a risk! He’s—”

“Rune, I won’t lose because I can’t fail. Father gave me this mission and I won’t fail him again. Last time I did, he gave me this, if you’ll recall.” He made a sharp gesture toward his face to a scar cutting across his cheek and marring the curve of his upper lip. “That was just for losing a hunt. What do you think he’ll do if I don’t bring him the Vessel?”

The two young men stared at one another, grim and silent.

Eylee’ai swallowed hard, holding still with an effort. It dawned on her she wasn’t going to attack. Rune’s concern for the prince and the companionship between them had startled her. It was so unexpected from a people she’d always believed heartless. Their revealing conversation had also distracted her, but the prince’s scar unsettled her the most. She knew something of violent fathers and the consequences of defying them.

Gods curse it, why does he have to be human? She bared her teeth, yearning for a hatred that wouldn’t come. If she let him live, he would destroy everything she held dear. The uncle had made a challenge, though. She’d never seen an elemental duel, but maybe one royal would do away with the other and save her the trouble.

Rune sighed, his shoulders slumping a little. He reached out and rested a hand on the prince’s shoulder. “I suppose you’re right, Des. Take an extra swing at him for me, would you?”

The prince snorted, though she couldn’t tell if the

sound was humor or irritation. His face had settled back into a stony mask once again. They returned to the third man without another word.

Eylee'ai sagged against the bulkhead, covering her face with shaking hands. What was she doing? How could she risk so much because of a scar? *I can still do it,* she told herself. *If he's still standing after the challenge, I'll end him.*

Stomach in fiery knots, she peered around the barrels again. They were moving, heading for an open space at the prow of the ship. She moved with them, flowing along the lines of shadow with heightened caution. The three royals seemed too involved to notice her, but the stealthy movement of curious sailors behind her was too close to avoid for long.

Cursing silently, she headed for the rail and the safety of the water, then changed course when she noticed a small dinghy tucked against the side of the ship. It was still a risk, with enough light she would be exposed to view, but with luck no one would even look in her direction. Flattening on the surface of the little boat's canvas cover, she blended her body colors to the cloth and settled to watch.

The three men paused in the open space, facing each other in a tense triangle. Then the uncle said in a loud, stiff voice, "Crown Prince Destin, I cry challenge for the right to lead this expedition to retrieve the Vessel of Power for High King Stern. What say you?"

"Accepted."

The older man hesitated as if he'd expected more. Then his expression hardened and he spun on his heel. The prince mimicked him and they stalked away from one another for a few paces. Rune backed away until he reached the rail not far from Eylee'ai, hands fisted at his sides and form tense as a bowstring. He muttered something through his teeth.

A long moment held suspended in the darkness.

Then the two opponents spun to face one another and fire bloomed. Shock ran through Eylee'ai like lightning. Most elementals needed a source for their fire, just as they used the air around them and whatever water or earth they could reach, but a few, like these two combatants, could create their own fire. No one had ever told her it wouldn't look like ordinary flame.

The uncle turned his initial spin into a lunge, fists punching out to produce twin hammers of blood-red heat. The roaring blast never reached its target, though, deflecting away from the prince with a whistle of wind. At the same time, sinuous ropes of white light spun out from the prince's fingers, dancing toward his opponent.

The older man's face flickered with surprise, but he didn't hesitate, shifting back and sweeping his arm in a grand gesture, creating a scythe of fiery red. Eyes on the delicate filaments spinning toward him, he moved to step forward again with an aggressive slice, but his foot didn't touch down before the other one slid out from under him.

The uncle yelped as he landed on his back, his fire splashing around him in a shower of bloody sparks. Before he could scramble to his feet, a wave of water flowed over the rail of the ship, slapping him flat to the deck, then froze over him in a solid block.

The night turned dark and quiet again. Eylee'ai blinked, trying to clear the light streaks from her eyes. She was breathing too fast, heart banging like a trapped bird in her chest.

The prince approached the downed man. "You always were too proud of your fire, Uncle. Your challenge is done. Now get off my ship and go home. If I catch even a whiff of you in my wake, I'll bury you at the bottom of the ocean."

"Your father will hear of this," the man snarled.

"Yes, he will. From me." The prince made a scooping gesture with one hand and the ice became water again, balling around the older man and lifting him off the deck. Flicking his fingers with no more effort than shooing away a pesky bug, the prince sent his uncle flying far out over the water.

Eylee'ai tried to track his path, but her eyes still held traces of dazzle, losing sight of him in the night. A faint splash sounded in the distance.

The prince turned to look at his cousin.

Rune gave him an engaging grin, relaxing against the rail with his arms folded. "Never doubted you for a moment, soul brother."

The prince snorted. "And I was so inspired by your confidence in me. I need a drink," he added in a sour tone, heading away. He paused when Rune didn't move. "Are you coming?"

"My frail heart is still going pitter-pat," Rune drawled, teeth flashing in another grin when the prince snorted again. "Some fresh air will do me wonders."

The prince moved away, muttering something derogatory, and the shadowy forms of sailors scattered ahead of him. With a low chuckle, Rune looked down and crossed his booted ankles as if he meant to stay a while.

Eylee'ai glared at his bent head. She couldn't twitch without drawing his attention. She couldn't go after the uncle or the prince. Maybe she could just kill this cousin. But then she would eliminate the advantage of surprise and he might not even be a threat.

She chewed on this, furious at her lost opportunity and horrified she might have given up her one chance to save her family. *The uncle is in the water,* she told herself. *And there will be other nights, other times when the prince is alone. If this idiot would just...*

"Quite a show," Rune said in a thoughtful tone.

She blinked, staring at his profile, a tingle of alarm running along her spine. Who was he talking to?

He turned his head, eyes locking on hers with a faint, wry curve of his mouth. "Wouldn't you say?"

Her muscles contracted, hands becoming talons, gouging the canvas beneath her. But for some reason she didn't leap on him, even though her entire body quivered with leashed violence. "How did you know I was here?" she hissed, curling her lip to show him the razor edge of her teeth.

"Ah." His eyes slid away across the empty deck. "I felt you. I thought I sensed you earlier, but I wasn't certain until the duel. Are you about to snack on my liver?"

She shifted in place, studying him. "I'm thinking about it," she muttered, though her hands were already back to normal. "You're a spirit weaver."

With a rough sound, he tipped his face up to the night sky. "Not quite. I haven't mastered spirit yet, but my family has always been more sensitive to that element." He paused, clearing his throat. "You're probably already aware of this. But you happen to be spectacularly nude."

"I'm a changeling. Clothes don't come along for

the ride," she responded with a dry look. "Does it bother you?"

He snorted, mouth twisting with sly humor. "Not at all. I've been thinking about thanking you but didn't want to offend." He slanted a quick glance at her. "And I'm not certain my liver is safe yet."

"So why aren't you screaming for help? Or blasting me off the ship?" she added with a gesture at the scorched deck.

"I'm no fire weaver. And I've sense enough not to chase away a gorgeous, unclad female. Especially a mysterious, gorgeous, unclad female."

She sighed. She hadn't a ghost of a chance of sneaking up on the prince now. Even more depressing, a part of her didn't want to. Rising in a quick, fluid flex, she slipped over the rail, ignoring his swift indrawn breath to scan the deck. "Is calling me mysterious your sneaky way of asking why I'm here?"

"Would you repeat the question when I'm done fantasizing? I'll be just another moment or two." He was studying her slim form with a bemused smile on his face.

Eylee'ai swallowed a sudden and surprising urge to laugh. After her monumental failure, she should be thinking about drowning herself at the bottom of the ocean. None of this should be funny. Shaking her head, she drew closer. "You're a strange elemental. Shouldn't you be calling me a beast and covering your prudish eyes before I corrupt you with my wiles?"

He met her gaze, face brightening. "Say, could you? I haven't been corrupted in far too long."

She covered her mouth, but a snicker slipped out anyway. He flashed a wicked grin, eyes twinkling. A sudden suspicion narrowed her gaze and she whipped out a hand with blurring speed, talons closing on his throat. "Are you sure you can't weave spirit?"

It was the only explanation she could think of for her odd reaction to this elemental. Spirit weavers could influence thoughts, change emotions, even control actions if the weaver was strong enough.

His smile gone, Rune unfolded his arms, lifting one hand in an open-palmed, placating gesture, touching the fingertips of his other hand to her wrist. "Even if I could, I would not," he whispered. "To bend your will with mine is a violation, one I would only practice in the most extreme circumstances and only on my enemies. Are you my enemy?"

She sighed again. His touch held not a hint of hostility and his eyes, soft golden-brown shot with streaks of green, were direct and sincere. She let him go with a grimace. "I guess not today," she growled.

His chest rose with a deep breath, but his voice remained steady. "Nor am I yours. Our people may have their differences, but I prefer to judge each person by their own actions. So far you've done nothing but enrich my fantasy life."

She tossed her head and began to pace. "Well, I was going to kill you."

"That would've ruined my night. Thank you for refraining."

"Not even going to ask why?" she snapped, flashing him a dark look.

"I assume it's my sparkling personality. Des wants to kill me for it at least once a day."

"I can see why." She paused by the rail, folding her arms and brooding out over the water. "I overheard you. What's the Vessel of Power?"

He was quiet for a moment. "I think you know," he said.

"Why would you think that?"

"Changelings avoid us. They don't seek us out, especially not days out to sea. You meant to kill Des, didn't you? Why? Are you after the Vessel yourself?"

"No," she breathed, a well of sorrow pooling in her chest. She swallowed hard and took a deliberate breath, letting it out in a slow gust before turning her head to look at him.

Strange, he seemed so normal. If she passed him on the street, she wouldn't know him for an elemental. Somehow she'd thought her instincts would know them for the enemy, see the danger written on their faces. But he was just a handsome young man with messy, dark hair and pretty lashes around his calm, hazel eyes. She couldn't even tell he was high-born, judging by the plain cut of his clothes. "You're not what I expected."

He smiled with disarming openness and a hint of mischief. "A compliment at last. I hate being predictable. You, on the other hand, are everything I could ever wish for in a changeling. May I play host and offer you something to eat or drink?"

She lifted an eyebrow with a wry twitch of her lips. "I notice you didn't offer clothes."

"I'm not that daft," he responded with a wink.

A small laugh snuck out before she could stop it and she glowered at him to compensate. "You think flirtation and charm will make me not want to kill you?"

"It's currently my fondest hope." His expression sobered as he studied her face. "What made you want to kill Des?"

She looked away, watching the quarter moon slip from behind a cloud and shimmer on the restless water. The night was gentle, the ocean busy but not wild, the breeze cool but not biting. Odd how the world could be so calm while her emotions were in such upheaval.

"I heard a rumor. Prince Destin, the High King's only son and heir to the elemental throne, is looking for the fabled Vessel of Power for his father. That's all I knew before I came on board. Now I know the rumor is fact and the prince is not the only elemental searching. I know the prince was scarred by his father." She shifted, a shudder running down her back. "And you're some kind of cousin. What's your line to the throne?"

"Not direct. My mother and Destin's mother were sisters. My name is Rune, in case you missed it. I'd be honored to know yours."

"The Ephemerals believe names are power."

"Is that what you believe?"

She shrugged. "At this point, it doesn't much matter. My name is Eylee'ai."

"Lovely. Lots of vowels, I assume."

Her mouth curled in a small smile. "You can call me Lia."

"I'd be delighted," he answered with a smile of his own. "Is there anything I may do for you, Lia? Some state secret I might spill perhaps, something to make you cry off your plan to end my cousin?"

She made a rude noise in the back of her throat. "As if you'd tell me any royal secrets."

He held up a hand with a solemn expression. "I will be as honest as I can. If I can't answer, I'll tell you I can't answer when I answer."

"Do you ever trip over that slippery tongue of yours?"

He leered. "Would that be an invitation?"

She slapped a hand over her mouth to contain a burst of laughter and shook her head, then rolled her eyes when his face fell. "Gods have mercy on everybody around you. How does anybody know when you're serious?" He opened his mouth, but she made a slicing gesture with her hand and said, "Don't answer. Let's check your honesty instead." She paused, gnawing on her lower lip a moment before snapping her fingers. "I've got one. What is the point of the squiggly thing the king wears on the top of his head? The pictures of him always show it but I've never seen a reason."

"Ah, yes, the squiggly thing, better known in the elemental court as the king's ceremonial headdress. It's supposed to represent the five elements and his mastery over them."

"Uh-huh. Well, it makes him look like an overstuffed rooster."

Rune nodded in solemn agreement, though his lips compressed as if he held back a laugh. "Hmm, I've often thought so, too. Anything else you'd like to know?"

She turned away, shivering a little as the wind strengthened. The moon had slipped behind a cloud and the night was thick with darkness. "Why did his father scar him?"

There was a short silence. When Rune spoke, his voice turned low and serious, tight with some emotion she couldn't identify. "Our king is a hard man. Not easy to please and not forgiving of mistakes. They were on a hunt and Destin missed the kill. In a moment of anger, the king backhanded him, laying open his cheek with a stud on his glove. Des wouldn't allow anyone to tend it. He had so much blood on him when we returned to the palace, I thought my mother was going to faint dead away."

"You were on the hunt?"

"Yes."

"You called him 'soul brother.'" She turned as she spoke, watching uneasily when his shoulders lost their stiff tension and his expression warmed into a crooked smile.

"His mother died when he was young. After, he spent a great deal of time in our home. We've been together much of our lives." He shrugged, ducking his head a little. "He's as dear to me as a brother."

She spun away again and resumed pacing to walk off her distress. This wasn't going well. Instead of discovering reasons to hate these royals, she was suffering from increasing sympathy. "Why does he want the Vessel?" she asked in a sharper tone. "Is he so eager for the king to destroy the world? Or does he want the power for himself?"

Rune didn't answer.

With a hiss of impatience, she rounded on him, crowding him against the rail. "Well?"

Face sober, he studied her. "Neither. Lia, what do you know of the Vessel?" Voice soft, expression earnest, he leaned toward her with disarming openness, inviting her to lay bare all her secrets.

Time to go, she thought. Before this odd royal got her to say things she shouldn't. "I know it was sent by the gods to test us." She swung onto the rail, balancing there for a moment. "And I know we're failing." With a sickness in her stomach and a clenching around her heart, she leapt off the rail, plummeting into the black water.

Chapter 2

Rune let himself into his cousin's cabin. The prince was bent over a map, ancient tomes and charts piled around him, a glass of wine left neglected at the edge of the table. Rune strode to a nearby chair and sat, both embarrassed and amused by the weakness in his knees. Their little changeling visitor had made quite an impact.

"Well, Des, we appear to have a problem."

Destin grunted, not looking up from the map. "Did Uncle Storm find his ship already?"

"Probably, but that's not the problem. Remember the old joke that ends, 'But the changeling followed me home. May I keep her?'" Rune said. "Well, I do believe the jest is on us."

Destin lifted his cool gaze from the map to stare at Rune without expression. The scar gave his angular features a dangerous edge. This particular hard stare was known to send servants scurrying, make veteran courtiers stammer, and cause even the most intrepid lady to pale and turn away.

Rune was none of those people. He smirked and settled lower in the chair, stretching his legs out and crossing them at the ankles. Linking his fingers across his stomach, he lifted his eyebrows and waited.

"I'm in no mood for your games, cousin."

"Oh, this is no game, soul brother. A changeling came aboard tonight to kill you."

Destin straightened. "Tell me."

Rune described his encounter with Eylee'ai and their conversation as accurate as possible, knowing the prince needed unembellished detail. He waxed a little poetic over his description of the girl, but who could blame him? He didn't meet such a stunning example of female every day and certainly not one as unabashedly nude, or as enigmatic.

When he finished, Destin lifted a dubious eyebrow. "Are you certain you weren't dreaming? Or hit your head?"

"I'm certain." He sat up and leaned forward, tipping his chin back to expose his neck. "She had her claws on me. See the puncture marks?"

"If you poked holes in yourself just to play me—"

"No," Rune interrupted, dropping his chin and meeting Destin's grim stare. "No games, no play. This is real. She's real and I don't know why. She knows you're after the Vessel of Power and she doesn't like it. That's as much as I could glean from her."

"Will she return?"

"Well, I did try to make you look a sympathetic character, but I don't think she fell for it. My guess is we'll see her again. Let's just hope it's not at the moment when she rips your head off."

"Nice. First you fret and flutter over a duel with our uncle, now you think I can't handle a single changeling? Grow a pair before you change into your mama for good."

Rune smothered a grin and tried to look offended. "My lady mother, your devoted auntie, charged me with the chore of looking after your reckless hide. I take my chores quite seriously."

"Right. The day you take anything seriously, the gods will fall out of the sky in shock." Destin lifted his wineglass and settled back in his seat, the harsh lines around his mouth and eyes, lines he was too young to carry, easing into wry amusement.

Rune concealed his satisfaction behind a cocky grin. As the crown prince, Destin carried enormous weight on his shoulders, the responsibility of a nation and the harsh expectations of his father. Rune had watched his friend suffer and struggle all his life, watched helpless as he was beaten and forged into whatever shape the king required.

His cousin would be shocked to know the depths of Rune's fury and hatred toward their sovereign.

Early on, Rune had learned guilt for his simpler upbringing and sorrow for his adopted brother, though Destin had never shown a hint of resentment. He had everything Destin didn't, an easy, fulfilling life, little responsibility, and the guarantee of parental love. Rune had made it his mission to be sure the prince enjoyed life a little, even if he couldn't find happiness in it.

"Oh, I'd love to take that changeling seriously." He cupped his hands with a leer. "Or at least get my hands on her sweet, tight little—"

"Eh, don't have one of your sick fantasies in front of me," Destin interrupted, turning his face to the side with an exaggerated grimace. "My stomach can't take it."

Rune chuckled, linking his hands behind his head and rocking the chair back on two legs. "Don't throw me that prissy face, Des. I've seen how many girls slip in and out of your princely chambers."

"Fool, you're thinking of your own chambers.

Remember, ladies pick your pretty face over mine every time."

"Well, if you'd stop scowling at them, they might reconsider." Rune eyed his friend for a moment before flashing a wicked grin. "You know, I do believe I'm looking forward to seeing the changeling again. I can't wait to see what she does to you."

Destin raised an eyebrow and took a swallow from his glass. "So, now you want her to rip my head off?"

"Not what I meant, brother. If she doesn't bring you to your knees and make you drool like a starved dog, I'll be utterly amazed."

****

Eylee'ai watched the sunrise streak the sky with vibrant color and called herself nine kinds of idiot. Because only an idiot would be sitting up on a boom, freezing her rear off while she waited for the man she'd been planning to kill to get out of bed so she could talk to him.

Gods help her, she knew he wasn't going to stop chasing the Vessel. She had to stop him, for the sake of her sister, for her whole race, and for the sake of the entire thrice-damned world. Yet here she sat, not stopping him. Maybe the problem wasn't him at all. Maybe deep in her soul she was too much a coward to take a life.

She frowned, huddling closer to the mast as the wind snapped her damp, salt-stiffened clothes around her. She didn't like to think she was too weak to do what needed to be done. She was a fighter. She'd had to be, to protect her sister and mother. Only circumstance had kept her from killing anyone before, not cowardice.

She sighed, hating this uncertainty, this self-doubt.

She'd always been decisive, setting a course and seeing it through even when it terrified her.

So why couldn't she just kill this power-hungry prince and be done with it? *Because Rune made you doubt he was power-hungry,* she answered herself. If he wasn't the one who wanted the Vessel, then her real target sat beyond her reach on his throne in the center of the elemental nation.

She ran rough fingers over her eyes, longing to curl up someplace warm and let sleep take it all away for a while. Changing into a sea mammal might have kept her from freezing in the ocean, but she hadn't been able to do more than doze in order to keep the shape and not return to human form. She was thinking about a quick nap when the sailors, a sickeningly jovial bunch this early in the morning, fell silent. *Nobody shuts up a sailor better than a prince,* she thought with a grimace and rose to pace down the boom on silent feet.

Crouching around a billowing sail, she watched the prince and his cousin saunter across the deck, deep in conversation. Rune was eyeing his cousin while the prince scanned the horizon with an intensity suggesting he was looking for something in particular. His uncle's ship? She didn't doubt Rune had told the prince about her, but his sharp gaze was cast too far out to be looking for a lone changeling. She'd gone hunting for the uncle after leaving the prince's ship, only to find he'd forgone the water for his own flotilla.

Yet another wasted opportunity.

Determined not to waste any more, she stepped off the boom and dropped to the deck. Ignoring a surprised shout from the nearest sailor, she moved to intercept the royals.

They caught sight of her at the same time and Rune groaned, handsome face falling into tragic disappointment. "Clothes! By the gods, where did you get clothing?"

She squashed the urge to snicker with an impatient toss of her head. "From the bag I brought with me, you rude royal."

He pouted. "If you're taking suggestions, I prefer you unclothed. I was looking forward to the sight in the light of day."

"Yeah, I'm starting to prefer it, too. Saltwater makes fabric chafe." Bracing herself, she turned to the prince. "Prince Destin. Your cousin told you about our meeting last night?"

"He did," he said without infliction. In contrast to his cousin, the prince showed not the slightest bit of emotion, looking her over with cool, calculated assessment. Some family resemblance appeared in the hue of their dark hair, the golden caste to their skin, and the angle of their faces, but their differences stood out the most. The prince's eyes had more gold and green, giving them a colder, more predatory gleam. His mouth was thinner and had faint, bracketing frown lines, unusual for somebody so young. His hair smoothed back into a short club at the nape of his neck and the angles of his face were sharper, harder, made fierce by the scarred ridge running across his left cheekbone to his mouth.

Nothing in his face gave her cause to doubt he would pursue the Vessel of Power to the ends of the earth. *Yeah, I really should kill him.* With an inner sigh of despair, she asked, "So, any chance I can get you to drop this quest of yours and take a holiday instead?"

His eyes narrowed, head tilting like a predator preparing to strike. "No. I will retrieve the Vessel for my father if I have to go through your entire race to do it." Both of them ignored Rune, who slapped a hand to his forehead with a groan. "What's the Vessel to you? Do you know where it is?"

"No one knows where it is," she said in a stiff tone, trying to remain calm. "It was last seen a thousand years ago, so I think your quest is doomed anyway. But let's say you manage it. What do you think your father will do with it?"

He said nothing, gold flashing in his eyes like the prelude to fire.

"He will destroy everything," she answered for him with slow emphasis.

"You've no right to malign my father," he growled. "You don't know him."

She folded her arms across her chest, suppressing a shudder. "The Vessel contains ultimate power and will ultimately corrupt. Nobody can use it without causing the ruin of the world. That's the gods' test. Are we wise enough not to use it?"

"Vessel lore has many interpretations. Others say such power shouldn't be left uncontrolled or it will destroy on its own."

Eylee'ai curled her lip in a sneer. "Others like your father? Is he so selfless?"

She couldn't break eye contact. The green and gold storm in the prince's eyes made looking away impossible. She had a feeling he'd pounce if she did, like a raptor waiting for the prey to make a run for it. A shiver of anticipation slid down her spine.

"You two are making my head ache," Rune

interjected. "Why don't we discuss this over breakfast? We can come to an understanding about Vessels and quests, and how much better we'd all feel if Lia were nude."

As if Rune hadn't spoken, the prince said with low menace, "Get off my ship, little changeling spy, before I decide you'd look better in chains."

She supposed she should be afraid. Instead, the fire in his eyes made her want to go toe-to-toe with him and bare her teeth. While she battled this unexpected urge, an idea bloomed. Her mouth curved in a pleased smile. "I'll leave, but fair warning, your highness. I plan to stop you from reaching the Vessel, any way I can."

The fire spread to his hands and she backed away. Flashing him a challenging grin, she spun and sprinted for the rail with white flame at her heels. This wasn't the precise stream of fire he'd used in the duel with his uncle. The blaze roared and crackled, a wall of heat at her back, and she laughed as she leapt onto the rail and over without pause.

Twisting in midair, she watched the white explosion fan out across the morning sky with fascinated exhilaration. When she hit the water and sank into the depths, she was grinning.

****

Destin stared at the scorched, smoking rail and did his best to hide his chagrin. Not easy, with the changeling's laughter still burning in his ears and Rune braying like a donkey next to him. Before the crew could do it and make him feel worse, he called a bit of water from the ocean with a flick of his fingers and soaked the wooden rail.

"Gods love her," Rune gasped between guffaws,

bending over to brace his hands on his knees. “You should’ve seen your face!” He bawled a fresh round of laughter, covering his red face with one hand.

“Quiet, Rune,” Destin muttered. He didn’t have to look to know they had the rapt attention of the crew. “They’ll think you’re daft.”

“No more than you,” his cousin responded, straightening to wipe tears off his cheeks and blink watery merriment at Destin. “Setting fire to your own damn…ship…” Clutching his stomach, he brayed again.

Destin did the only sane thing and stalked away. Much as he would love to clunk his fool cousin on the head, he had to maintain some scrap of royal dignity in front of the crew. And any further show of emotion would only fuel Rune’s softheaded humor.

With purposeful strides, he crossed to the ladder leading to the upper deck. Ascending the rungs, he paused at the top to scan the horizon again. They appeared to be alone on the water, but he knew it was an illusion. Uncle Storm wouldn’t let go of his search for the Vessel so easily.

Approaching the captain at the wheel, he nodded to the man’s respectful bow. “Captain Trough, any word from the crow’s nest?”

“Good rising, your highness. I’ve got my best eyes up there. She says she saw a sail at first light but nothing since.”

Destin nodded. “Uncle Storm has an experienced crew on his ships. They’ll know how to stay hidden in our wake. Tell your eyes to stay alert.”

“I will, sire.” The man hesitated then asked, “Was that a stowaway you chased off the ship, your highness?"

Unexpected heat flushed up Destin's neck but he kept his face expressionless. "A changeling has decided to be a nuisance. Should you or any of the crew see her again, report it to me immediately, captain."

The man's weathered face twisted into lines of disgust. "Phah, a changeling? Don't worry, Prince Destin. I don't allow filthy little animals on my ship. She won't concern you again."

Destin studied the captain with a spurt of surprise. Many elementals held a prejudice for the changeling race, but he hadn't known his captain felt the same way. "I will handle the changeling, Captain Trough. No one is to take action, only report her presence to me. Understood?"

"Understood, sire," the captain responded with a deferential dip of his head.

Destin glanced down at the lower deck and cleared his throat. "I believe I weakened the rail. It may need repair."

The captain's mouth lifted in a faint smile. "I'll assign a detail to fix it. Ship's still afloat and the creature's gone, so no harm done. Impressive fire, my prince."

He supposed the man was giving him a compliment, but it stung like a reprimand instead. *Setting fire to your own damn ship.* Lack of control was a weakness his father had taught him to abhor and abolish. He had no idea why he'd reacted so strongly to the changeling, why her words had infuriated him into fire, but it was a humiliation he didn't mean to repeat. Clenching his jaw, he turned away from the captain without a word and headed for the lower deck.

A nice, quiet breakfast and another look at the passage in the Ephemeral history would settle him. The Ephemerals were an ancient race, long-lived with long memories. His own people had no record of the Vessel, but the Ephemerals made reference to it with a kind of awe and evasive description that both tantalized and frustrated.

Something about the wording of this particular history gnawed at him. It suggested the Vessel was different each time it resurfaced. Or were there multiple Vessels? The stylized and cryptic Ephemeral writing seemed like a labyrinth. Deciphering it was painstaking work, but Destin knew it held the answer to finding the Vessel of Power.

When he reached his cabin, he had to forgo the nice-and-quiet aspect of his breakfast. Rune didn't bother to lift his gaze from his plate, just waved a hand and mumbled something unintelligible through a mouthful of food.

With a sigh, Destin joined him at the small dining table. It would do no good to chastise his cousin for entering his cabin, eating his food, and acting like a pig with no manners. Rune was Rune, there was no changing him at this late date. And though he'd never tell his soul brother, he wouldn't have him any other way. Rune's cheerful irreverence pleased him to no end. His life was so structured he didn't have the simple freedom of speaking his mind. Watching Rune ignore every convention and rule gave him a deep sense of satisfaction.

Sitting across from his cousin, he loaded the second plate the galley crew had supplied; eggs, hot mush, and biscuits again this morning. Pouring a hot drink, Destin watched his cousin shove an enormous spoonful of mush in his mouth. "If you choke, all I'm going to do is laugh and toast the irony of the gods."

Rune gave a nonchalant wave of his spoon and swallowed the entire bite with an impressive gulp. "The gods love me too much to kill me with breakfast." He sank the spoon deep in his bowl then paused, slanting Destin a sly smile from under his brows. "So how did you like our little changeling?"

Destin had been expecting the goad and didn't even blink, taking a slow sip of his drink without answering.

Rune's smile broadened into a grin. "You don't fool me, cousin. I know you too well. She's just your type, with rich brown hair like a mink's pelt."

"If you like salt-crusted rats' nests."

Rune's grin faded, eyes narrowing. "Obstinate bonehead. I suppose you'll tell me you didn't notice her sweet little body either."

"How was I to notice anything under those baggy rags?"

"They weren't that baggy. And you could still see how she moves, how flawless her skin is."

"She's a changeling, Rune. They can morph right out of acne."

"You're starting to irk me. I know you noticed her sinful mouth and those fantastic gray eyes. You stared at them long enough."

"All changelings have gray eyes. That doesn't make her special, cousin. What I noticed was the threat. Her plan to stop us by any means necessary, if you'll recall."

Rune scowled. "She got to you. I know she did. I

haven't seen you flame like that since our training days."

She went straight to my gut, curse her. But he didn't say it aloud. Instead, he forked some eggs onto a biscuit and took a meditative bite. "She struck a nerve," he said after a moment. "She questioned Father's integrity. I lost my temper."

Rune snorted and sat back in his seat, features riddled with disgust. "Only you would think about your father's integrity at a time like that. You're hopeless, Des."

"If she were elemental, her words would have been treason."

"Oh certainly, because no one can disagree with the king." Rune rolled his eyes. "Brother, if that were the case, I'd have been tossed in the deepest dungeon to rot a long time ago."

"Father excuses you because you're addled."

Rune met his steady gaze, blinked, then threw back his head and laughed. "Gods, I hope he does believe it. Think of all I can get away with as the court loony." He paused, rocking on the rear legs of the chair and gazing into the distance with a dreamy smile. "Oh, what mischief and pandemonium."

Destin smothered a grin. "Hate to ruin your happy little world, cousin, but you are addled."

"Hmm," Rune responded, smile still in place and eyes unfocused.

Shaking his head, Destin finished his breakfast in satisfying silence. At some point, Rune would notice how he'd distracted him from the subject of the changeling, but for now Destin meant to enjoy the peace and quiet. A sudden, unsettling memory of the girl's smile destroyed his peace, though. The curve of her lips had lit her face and made her eyes glow like mist in the morning sun. *Eylee'ai.*

He swore silently, taking a deliberate gulp of his drink. Setting the cup down with a sharp clunk, he forced his thoughts away from her and onto his mission. Leaning over, he dragged the tome of Ephemeral history off his desk and opened it to the tantalizing passage, studying it with absorbed concentration as he finished his meal.

Chapter 3

Ettie would love this, Eylee'ai thought with an inner grin. Her sister was fascinated with the natural world and Lia's ability to mimic it. Just changing shape didn't mean a changeling could pass for a specific animal, but Lia had an uncanny instinct for how to move and how to act in whatever creature she became.

At the moment, she was a mottled whale. A female mottled whale in season, calling mournfully for a mate. She'd attracted a bevy of interested, excitable males, just the thing to create serious havoc.

Avoiding the attentions of an aggressive male, she rose under the prince's ship, rolling and coating the hull with her scent. Then she shifted shape, leaving the whale suitors with a wooden mate to woo.

Snickering to herself, she swam to the surface, climbing the hull to the bag she'd left dangling off a hook. The leather was drying out, but the clothes she'd stashed inside remained stiff and damp. With a grimace, she went through the rigorous process of yanking on her clothing while hanging off the side of a boat. The alarmed cries of the sailors made the effort worthwhile.

Grinning, she ascended the hull to the prow, touching respectful fingers to the small, graceful figurehead of Shenoh the water goddess, before she pulled herself over the rail to the forecastle. Chaos ruled the main deck, sailors scattering everywhere, hampered by the rocking and bucking of the ship in the whale-infested waters. Chuckling to herself, she scanned the deck looking for her nemesis and found him striding across the unsteady surface with Rune in his wake. His narrow eyes fixed on her.

Pasting a grim smile on her face, she jumped down to the foremast and leaned a shoulder against it with arms folded in a casual stance. "Afternoon, your highness," she called over the noise. "Having a little trouble with the local wildlife?"

"You did this," he said in a low, dangerous voice, not slowing his approach.

She had to skip backward to keep from being run over but compensated with a toothy, humorless smile. "Yup."

He fisted a hand in the front of her shirt and hauled her up onto her toes. "Undo it," he growled.

Heat baked off his fist and she wondered if he was scorching her shirt. The gold in his eyes flared like the sun, streaked with menacing green.

She supposed she ought to be afraid.

"Sorry, highness, not gonna happen. Before you fry me, think on this, I can make them go away, but if I'm dead, no telling how long they'll hang around."

He shook her once with a black scowl. "Fine, I'll do it myself." Shoving her away, he stalked to the forecastle.

Eylee'ai frowned in concern, following on his heels. "If you kill them, you'll have to sail through a lot of whale carcasses. It'd be a horrible waste. And you might have more to deal with soon."

He swung around, the hard lines of his face filled with ferocity, but it was Rune who asked, "What did you do?"

She answered without looking away from the prince's hot green-gold gaze. "I coated the underside of the ship with the scent of a female mottled whale in season."

Rune spluttered. Then he burst into laughter.

The prince blinked at her, the heat of his gaze tempered by surprise. "You can do that?"

"So there's a group of males down there wanting to mate with us? Holy gods, girl, you're a mad genius!" Rune swept a hand out to capture hers and sank down onto one knee, face filled with glowing hilarity. "I'm deeply in love with you, Eylee'ai of the changelings. Marry me."

She held her composure with an effort but had to admit she was starting to like this royal. "You're an idiot."

Hazel eyes twinkling, he opened his mouth to respond, but a new cry interrupted. "Sails! Blowing in fast!"

Eylee'ai pulled her hand from Rune's and stepped to the rail in tandem with the prince. She sighted the incoming vessels with hair prickling the nape of her neck. "Your uncle?"

"Yes."

"What will he do when he gets here?"

"Attack," he snapped and thrust his hands out over the water, over the pod of innocent whales.

Lia grabbed the elemental's wrist, imagining the bloody massacre he could unleash. "Wait. I'll take care of it. For a price."

He stared at her grip on his wrist, his expression impossible to read. "I won't stop looking for the

Vessel."

"We can work up to that. For now, how about just a hot meal? And maybe a bath and a place to sleep for a while." He flashed a curious look and she shrugged. "Raw fish is gross no matter what shape I take."

He pulled out of her hold and pointed at the big bodies below them. "Get rid of them and I'll consider it."

She scoffed and folded her arms. "No maybes, Prince Destin. It's either yes or no. Hurry up, your uncle's coming."

His eyes narrowed to glittering slits, but Rune responded before he could speak. "We would be delighted to offer our hospitality. Perhaps even a change of clothing, if you insist on wearing them. It would be our pleasure, right Des?"

"I don't bargain with—"

Rune stepped between them, shouldering his cousin and flashing Lia a charming smile. "He says yes."

She grinned in response, swinging onto the rail and balancing there as it rocked hard beneath her. Meeting the prince's fuming gaze, she asked, "Is it a deal?"

He hesitated, glancing at the oncoming ships, then gave her one sharp nod. With a curl of anticipation in her gut, she launched off the rail, diving for the water with visions of hot food and steaming bathwater dancing in her head. The ocean was a mass of enormous, heedless animals, swamping her with water and threatening to crush her. She stripped and dove, hoping she'd be able to retrieve the clothes later. In a moment she was a whale again, huge and graceful as she cleaved through the ocean.

Singing to her bevy of suitors, she led them away from the prince's ship. She changed her tune, calling alarm with a slap of her tail on the water. Wailing a song of fear, she sounded, and the group of males sounded with her, moaning their confusion as they dove deep into the darkness. When she judged they were far enough not to be drawn back to the scent on the ship, she morphed into one of the few predators of the mottled whale, an enormous razor shark.

It was a risky move. The mottled whale was a dire beast when riled and a good number of strong, healthy males swam in her wake. She had to be threatening enough to make them scatter without triggering an aggressive response. Instead of heading straight for them, she swam in a wide circle with the lazy power of a predator considering its next meal. With rumbles and whistles of alarm, they scattered.

When they were gone, she shot for the surface, thrilling at the speed of her new, muscular form. Sharks might be violent eating machines, but she had to admire the efficiency of their design and she enjoyed this form's easy power. But she didn't like the lack of clear vision. She sensed the vibrations of the surface vessels but couldn't pinpoint them.

She broke the surface and shifted back to human form, only to duck below again with a squeak of alarm as a splash of red fire danced over the water. The ocean heaved around her in an unnatural spin. She flailed and cursed the elementals for warping the natural order. Why couldn't they just use the ship's cannons?

The rogue wave dragged her weak human body above the surface, requiring her to change back into a shark. She'd seen, when drawn up in the curve of the wave, how his uncle had surrounded the prince's ship. Five vessels with elementals on each. She gnashed her shark's teeth and swung her head back and forth, fighting conflicting emotions.

The uncle cheated and that made her mad. He couldn't win in a fair duel, so he gathered overwhelming numbers to take his nephew down. *Coward*, she sneered.

On the other hand, the uncle was providing the perfect solution to her problem with the prince. All she had to do was sit back and the uncle would end the prince's quest for the Vessel right here and now. She didn't have to kill him or spend all her time and energy fighting to slow him down and distract him.

Two glaring problems with this strategy, though. Once the prince was gone, she'd still have to deal with the uncle and his five ships chasing the Vessel. Plus, she'd have to let the uncle kill both of his nephews. Even though they were royals, she was starting to like Rune. And she had a hot meal, bath, and full night's sleep to look forward to on their ship. If the ship was still floating by nightfall.

With an inner sigh of resignation, she changed to the whale again, noted the location of each ship, and then sounded into the dark depths. When she thought she'd gone deep enough, she reversed her course and thrust for the surface with her enormous tail, feeling the resistance of the water with a moment of doubt. It didn't seem possible to get this much animal out of the water, but she'd seen whales breach before. They managed it somehow. With a quick prayer to Kel the Hunter, she thrust harder with her tail, watching the surface loom closer with both exhilaration and anxiety.

This was going to hurt.

A moment later, she burst out of the water past her flukes, arcing into the air in amazing, improbable flight. Then she lost all grace and mobility, crashing down onto one of the uncle's ships like a stone.

It hurt, all right.

Worse, the form so buoyant and fluid in the water was now an uncoordinated, crushing weight, stunning her into thoughtless panic. She thrashed, pain and a horrible suffocating sensation blinding her. The surface under her gave and bobbed. She could sense water beneath and writhed in a desperate burst of energy.

With a simple suddenness that left her blinking, she slipped back into the ocean. In the water's calm and buoyant embrace, the haze of panic cleared and Eylee'ai took a deep breath of relief. With a sheepish slap of her flukes, she dove beneath the floundering ship, embarrassed she'd lost control when she could have just shifted shape. And her entire right side hurt. The water reverberated with her long, low whale moan. No more breaching. The first ship was sinking, but she couldn't do that again.

A moment later, Eylee'ai winced and dove deeper as the water turned hot enough to scorch. Some fire weaver was trying to boil her out of the ocean. *Yeah, well, I don't like you either,* she thought and considered her next move. They would fry her the moment she came to the surface. She needed to stay out of sight.

Rising high enough in the warming water to locate the prince's ship, she paused in amazement as the surface lit with a wreath of white flame around the vessel. He was still busy fighting his attackers. Did he think he could take on all five ships himself? She meant to give him his chance to run, but it was up to him to take it, if he could swallow his pride long enough.

Not filled with much hope, she picked her next target and dove deep so the humans on the surface couldn't track her, placing herself below the ship. She barreled toward it, though without as much power as her previous breach. At the last moment, she dropped her nose, her back coming in contact with the wooden structure. Something cracked and she hoped it wasn't anything of hers. This attack didn't hurt as much as her crash onto the other ship, but her back now throbbed in concert with her side.

With a groan, she rolled away and down, shifting her form to heal her injuries and decrease the pain. Muttering seal obscenities, she wriggled her new, agile body and shot for the surface. At first glance, her second target seemed unaffected by her attack, still afloat, all sails up, no obvious wreckage. Disappointment stabbed through her until she noticed the sailors running below. The bellowing orders of the captain proved they were taking on water. Lots of it.

With a little yip of triumph, she turned her sleek head to find the prince's ship. Wonder of wonders, he was taking advantage of the opening she'd made in their trap, his vessel sailing into open water. The sails stretched taut and quivered as if riding a gale. Somebody must be weaving air to speed their escape.

At first triumph surged higher, but as she watched the ship cleave through the water, her heart sank. The prince's ship was moving fast. He was trying to leave her behind, too. With a bark of outrage, she dove, shifting and stretching into the razor shark again. She lunged through the water with a powerful twist of her streamlined body, following the royals' wake with ease. But she'd shifted many times today, healed herself, and just plain worked hard. Her muscles quivered with weariness.

Gritting her teeth, she poured on speed. If she didn't catch them soon, she'd lose them for a while. Who knew what kind of mischief the blasted prince would concoct while she wasn't watching? Besides, she had a hot meal and bath waiting for her on their ship. She was not going to let them sneak away. Cursing the royals, she powered through the water, focusing on closing the gap between her and the ship and not on her fast-depleting energy.

By the time she reached astern, she was acting on will alone, mind ignoring the screaming pain and weakness in her muscles. In a last burst of determination, she shot upward, shifting and driving long talons into the hull as she slammed against its unforgiving surface. Gasping, she dangled, helpless against the rough motion of the ship.

For a long moment she just hung there, trying to recover enough energy to climb. Flume chilled her body and sprayed her face, making it hard to draw air into her burning lungs. Consumed with the need to breathe, she didn't brace when her body twisted then slapped into the harsh planks of the hull.

Crying out at the sudden flare of pain in her bruised right side, she made talons of her feet and scrabbled at the side of the ship for purchase. Finding a grip, she clung to the hull and rested as best she could, trying to find the will to ascend. *Hot bath,* she bribed her aching body. *Warm, soft bed, lots of sleep.* Panting with her forehead tucked in the crook of her elbow, she imagined the look on the prince's face when he had to honor his bargain with a barbaric changeling.

Yeah, that's worth it.

Drawing a deep breath between clenched teeth, she thrust upward and fixed her eyes on the rail above her. It looked impossibly far, but she refused to give up, to allow her quivering muscles to falter.

An eternity later, she grasped the rail and wiggled up and over. Strength gone, she slipped off the rail and collapsed on the deck, groaning in relief. She'd landed in an awkward sprawl across part of the rigging, but the rough rope and hard deck seemed like a featherbed. She closed her eyes and just lay still, breathing in and out.

Paradise.

Chapter 4

Rune stood at Destin's elbow and worried. He was a solid air elemental, but he was growing weary keeping the constant flow of wind in the sails. Destin had battled their uncle with every element available to them, and now wielded both air and water to speed their passage in the waves. Rune was afraid his cousin was running on pure willpower at this point.

"Des," he murmured, flicking a glance at his cousin's grim profile, "isn't this far enough?"

"The more distance we put between us and Uncle Storm, the better."

"I know, but…"

A shout interrupted. A crewman scrambled up to their deck. Breathless, the wiry young man sketched a quick bow, keeping his gaze lowered. "My prince, I don't mean to bother, but you said if we ever spotted her, if she ever came on board, we should come to you."

Destin's head snapped around, fierce gaze pinning the sailor to the deck.

Rune winced. The crew would see only Destin's implacable will and unbending determination, but Rune knew him better and read the burn of exhaustion in the lines of his face, in the grim tightness around his eyes and mouth.

Destin's gaze flicked to Rune before returning to

the sails and the ocean view. "Handle it," he growled.

Rune hesitated but could say nothing in front of the crewman. With an inner curse for stubborn cousins, he let his air weave falter and die, turning toward the sailor. "The changeling is aboard?"

"Yes, sir." The young man glanced up, spare face anxious. "She seems hurt, sir."

Rune stiffened, Destin's sudden tension pressing along his backbone. "Show me."

The crewman led Rune aft, to a tangle of rigging with a nude female draped across it. Rune would have taken a moment to admire the stretch of sleek, well-formed flesh if she'd shown any sign of life. Her limp and awkward sprawl alarmed him. So did the bloom of angry bruises down her side.

"Lia?" He touched her shoulder, wincing at the icy feel of her skin, but drew a relieved breath when she groaned. To the ring of watching sailors, he said, "A blanket, please. Hurry." Turning back to the changeling, he brushed strands of wet hair away from her face. "Lia, can you hear me?"

She was lying face down, head twisted at an uncomfortable angle against a loop of rope. Her eyes stayed closed and muscles lax, but she mumbled, "Hot bath and food. Warm bed. You promised."

"I did and you may have all of that and more. But I need to know how badly you're injured. Is anything broken, Lia? Can you move?"

She opened one misty gray eye and looked at him with a great deal of disgust and a slice of hostility. Both went a long way toward relieving his anxiety. "I'll move when I'm good and ready. Don't rush me."

"I wouldn't be so foolish. You have a whole

regiment of bruises, Lia. Do you have any serious injuries we must tend?" At the tail end of his question, a sailor passed a thick blanket over his shoulder. Rune took it and shook it out over her limp form.

She sighed, eyes closed. Then she untangled from the rigging and pulled her limbs under her. Rune clasped her elbow, helping her to sit on a flat spot of the deck. She huddled in a sorry-looking ball, forehead on her knees and blanket wrapped around her.

Rune crouched in front of her, frowning with concern at her bent head. "Lia, I want to help. What do you need?"

"About a year of sleep," she grumbled behind the wild, dripping curtain of her dark hair.

Rune looked around at the still watching crewmen. "Will someone fetch a hot drink? And please bring a meal and bath to the guest cabin."

No one dared mention the guest cabin was his. None of the crew would question a member of the royal family, but they exchanged glances as a few of the crew went to follow his orders. Rune looked down at the top of Lia's head with a wry twist of his lips. These sailors gossiped worse than old women. By the time the sun went down, the entire crew would believe he was having a torrid affair with the changeling.

"Eylee'ai, thank you for your help with our uncle. I've never seen anything like you leaping out of the water and crushing his flagship. You nearly broke it in half."

The young sailor who'd brought Rune aft, knelt by her side with a steaming cup. "My lady, you were a right marvel," he said in a low voice, brown eyes alight with hero worship, or infatuation.

Eylee'ai lifted her head, eyes fixing on the hot drink, before she reached for it with a shaking hand. "No, I was stupid. I almost broke myself in half, too." Wrapping both hands around the cup, she took a long gulp then closed her eyes with a shudder. "And I'm nobody's lady. Call me Lia."

The sailor blushed and ducked his head. "Pleased t'know you. Name's Cleave," he mumbled to the deck.

"Thanks for the drink, Cleave. You're a lifesaver."

He muttered something Rune couldn't hear. The poor boy seemed to be strangling on his blush. To rescue the sailor, Rune leaned forward. "Are you able to walk, Lia? Or will you allow me the great pleasure of carrying you?"

She gave him a look as dry as desert sand. "Give your slippery tongue a rest, Rune. My legs work. I just need to sit for a bit." She paused, flashing a cool glance toward the upper deck. "Where's his highness?"

"Putting us out of reach of our murderous uncle, I hope."

She had fine features, as delicate as any well-bred lady of the elemental court, but a feral quality in her erased any sense of fragility. This was not a pampered female who needed to be sheltered. She reminded Rune of a vixen when she met his gaze and her face hardened, sleek and graceful beauty merging with quick and dangerous cleverness.

"Why didn't you run?" she asked with a hiss of temper in her cool voice. "Even for thickheaded royals, five-to-one odds should've been enough reason."

Rune smiled with as much charm as he could muster, hoping it would blunt her temper. "Uncle Storm surrounded us before we could flee. Why did you help us? He could have ended our quest for you."

Her expression soured. "I thought of that, but I would just be switching one annoying royal for another with more ships. Besides, we had a deal."

"Yes we did," he murmured and held out a hand. "May I help you rise?"

She took another long gulp from the cup before handing it to Cleave with a word of gratitude. He took the cup, bobbing his head with a dopy smile and shining eyes. Rune almost winced in sympathy. This changeling was dangerous on several levels.

Gathering the blanket close, she rose to her feet in a quick, smooth motion, but her first steps were slow enough to concern him. Rune cupped her elbow without asking, feeling a strange turmoil in his chest when he touched her. She affected him in ways he wasn't sure he understood. He shouldn't feel so drawn to her. She'd threatened to kill him and his soul brother, after all.

At least she didn't refuse his help. They made their way past curious crewmen and into his small cabin. Inside, a round wooden tub occupied most of the extra floor space, the water a steaming invitation. She made a moaning sound and shrugged off his hand along with the blanket.

Rune blinked and shut the door while she climbed into the hot water. He watched her settle into the bath and cleared his throat. "Well. You're not bashful."

"You've already seen me naked. What would be the point in getting all prissy about it now?" She closed her eyes and rested her head on the edge of the tub.

The girl had a point, and who was he to argue? The view was spectacular. "Does this mean you'll allow me to help you bathe?"

"Don't push your luck, fancy boy. You can stay and talk, keep me awake. Be a shame to waste a hot bath by drowning in it."

A grin of delight tugged at his mouth and he stepped around the tub to sit at his small table. She was so refreshing, natural in her skin and more straightforward and practical than any female he'd ever met. Were all changelings this way? If so, he might consider an extended stay in their territory.

"How did you find us, Lia? We're not traveling on the royal barge with a full military entourage."

"Luck," she mumbled then straightened with a deep breath, lifting her head and opening her eyes with what looked like serious effort. "At Churling Bay, the last port where you docked, someone recognized your prince and spread the word." She scrubbed her face hard then sent him a stern glance. "You can stay, but you're not watching me wash."

He went for full drama, but she didn't relent. With many a deep and dreadful sigh, he turned to straddle his chair, putting his back to her. "The last port was days ago. Are you saying you've followed us from there? How did you survive?"

"I stayed in animal form most of the time. I can't sleep that way, though, so sometimes I'd hang off the side of your ship. Rigged some ropes to hold me and my things."

He blinked, trying to imagine it. "You slept on the side of the ship?"

"Yes, but not very well. That's why I made our deal." There was a splash and her voice hardened. "But don't get the idea you can get rid of me by just staying out to sea and waiting for me to drop. I won't stop,

Rune. Not until he gives up the Vessel."

Her word choice was revealing on a few levels. A smile curling his mouth, he rested his arms on the back of the chair and his chin on his fist. "Why won't you stop? What is the Vessel to you?"

There was a moment of stillness. Then she said with bitter emphasis, "What it is for all of us; elementals, changelings, humans, even Earth Keepers and Ephemerals. It's the path to the end of the world. Somebody has to stop it."

He considered this while he listened to her splash, a frown pulling at his brow. The smell of sandalwood rose in the air, along with the subtle fragrance of warm, mysterious female. "You seem too practical to be so dramatic and self-sacrificing."

"You think I'm making more of it than it is? I suppose you agree with your prince that somebody has to contain the Vessel, to control it. But it can't be contained, Rune. It can't be controlled. Anybody who tries will be the destroyer of everything we know."

The passion in her voice tugged at him, working on him in ways both disturbing and exhilarating. His frown deepened. "Someone trying to save the world is either a lunatic with a hero complex or a desperate soul with a personal stake in the outcome. What aren't you telling me, Eylee'ai?"

She snorted and didn't answer. A moment later, a knock on the door drew Rune's attention. He rose, edging around the tub and opening the door. A crewmember stood outside with a tray of food. With a word of gratitude to the stone-faced woman, he took the tray and closed the door, trying not to smirk. Keeping his eyes on the tray, he moved to the table and deposited the food. "You're doing wonders for my reputation, Lia. You should've come aboard days ago."

She made a rough sound like a smothered laugh. "You want a reputation as a lecherous pervert who romps with animals?"

"I defy anyone to label you an animal, my lady, but I'll admit I enjoy being a lecherous pervert." She snickered and he grinned to himself. "Are you ready for your meal?"

"Just about. Need a towel… oh, here it is."

Though it strained his willpower, he kept his gaze averted while she dried off and shrugged into his robe. With a courtly bow, he positioned the chair at the table for her and ignored the rolling of her eyes. Sitting on the edge of his narrow bunk, he studied her while she ate. Her eyes were swollen and red-rimmed with weariness, movements slow even though she had to be half-starved, judging by what she'd told him. Her hair was a wet, tangled mass down her back.

"Don't fall asleep in your noodles, now." She gave him a dirty look but didn't comment. He watched her for another moment before venturing, "Would you allow me to dry and comb your hair? I don't think you should sleep with a cold, wet head. It'll make you ill."

She lowered her fork and gave him a direct stare that would have rivaled Destin's if her eyes hadn't been so bloodshot and droopy. "Why are you being so nice? I threatened to kill you both. And I already told you I won't stop."

He shrugged, coating his smile with charm once again. "I'm just contrary." When she continued to stare without blinking, he let his smile fade and answered honestly. "I'm intrigued by you. You're the first changeling I've interacted with outside diplomatic circles. You've taken me by surprise more than anyone I've ever met and you're more mysterious than I can stand. I like that. I like you."

She blinked. Then she took another bite, studying him with a thoughtful expression. "Huh. That is contrary."

He nodded then gestured to her crown. "So, may I be of service?"

"Sure. But you try anything and I'll rip your throat out."

The casual surety of the threat unnerved him a little. He hesitated a second before rising to his feet and giving her a gallant bow. "I will be the soul of propriety."

She muttered something insulting under her breath.

He pretended not to hear as he retrieved a comb and stepped behind her. The thick, dark brown silk of her hair was wet and cool in his hands and quite snarled. He began winnowing his comb through it, weaving warm air in and around the mass as he worked. He remembered brushing his mother's hair a time or two when she wasn't feeling well. He'd been a child then and recalled feeling like it was a chore, hurrying through it so he could move on to better entertainment.

Untangling Lia's hair was different from his childhood experience, holding a strange kind of fascination, meditative and almost hypnotic. Under his hands, the wild strands smoothed into waves of dark and shiny silk of an amazing length and fine texture. And the way Lia relaxed under his touch, like an animal learning to trust, was just as fascinating.

By the time he was finished, she'd fallen asleep,

slumped in the chair and in danger of tumbling to the floor. Rune put away the comb and turned down the bedcovers before crouching by her side. "Lia? Lia, I'm going to lift you and put you in bed now. Please don't slice me in half." When she didn't respond, he slipped his arms around her and rose. She was a limp weight, light and smelling of his soap.

He settled her into his bunk, covered her, and then stood by the bedside studying her for a long peculiar moment. It gave him a lurch, her tucked in his bed, hair spread across his pillow, but not in the way he'd expected. She looked small and fragile, and he was feeling more protective of this girl than seemed sane, since she truly could rip his throat out.

With a baffled shake of his head, Rune backed away and left the cabin, stepping across the hall and into his cousin's cabin without knocking. Destin should have been sleeping off his overexertion, but he was sitting, a wine glass in hand, and his eyes closed.

"Waiting up for me? How sweet."

"Don't start," Des answered without opening his eyes, voice raspy. "What'd you do with her?"

"It's not polite to ask for the sordid details."

Rune was hoping for a glare at least or a snappy retort. He grimaced when all Destin did was sigh. His friend must be worn to nothing.

"She had her hot bath and her meal and is sleeping soundly in my cabin," he answered his prince in a quiet voice. "She was almost as weary as you are. Go lie down, Des, before you fall down."

"You're too young to be a mother," Destin muttered in response, cracking one eye open. "Was she injured?"

"Bruises only when she came aboard. Most of those had faded by the end of her bath. Changelings heal fast."

Destin opened the other eye a fraction and stared at Rune, green glitter shot with gold through the screen of his lashes. "You watched her bathe?"

Most people would not have heard anything other than morbid curiosity in his question, but Rune knew his soul brother. The devil in him smiled with slow mischief and watched the prince tense by degrees. But he couldn't keep his friend skewered for long. "She allowed me to stay in the cabin with her, to keep her awake until she'd bathed and eaten, but she didn't allow me to watch. Of course, I begged and offered my services, but she brushed me away like lint."

Rune crossed to the second chair, snagging the glass from his cousin's lax grip and taking a sip. "You should consider letting her stay. She knows something, Des. She lied to me when I asked what the Vessel was to her. She's personally invested, and we need to find out why. She could lead us right to it."

Destin made a growling sound in his throat. "She wouldn't. You just want to keep her in your bed."

"Naturally, though I'd be much happier if I was in bed with her." He followed this flippant response with a shrug. "Of course she wouldn't tell us outright, but I'm hoping she'll divulge as she did earlier. She followed us from Churling Bay, slept off the side of the ship and dogged us in animal form. She's too sure, too adamant when she speaks of the Vessel. And when I asked what she wasn't telling me, she was conspicuously silent."

"You're reaching. You like her."

"I do like her, Des, odd as it sounds. But I'm not

reaching in the dark. I felt her, sensed the truth of her. I'm beginning to read her, and you know how rare that is."

Destin closed his eyes with a creased brow. Like his father, Destin could weave all five elements, but his spirit weaves were blind, like grasping a cup with numb hands and closed eyes, apt to go astray more often than they worked. The proper path to weaving spirit began with an intimacy with the element, a sensitivity Rune and his family line possessed. But Rune had discovered while he could sense spirit in all living things, he could connect or resonate with only a few.

Destin had been his first, and why Rune had named him 'soul brother,' closer than blood. The others had all been family, with some notable exceptions; the king for instance and their bloody-minded uncle. He'd never been able to read a stranger, not without serious effort. Eylee'ai was proving to be more of an enigma with each passing hour.

"You sure you're not just seeing what you want to see?" Des asked, brow still creased and eyes closed. His voice not only rasped but slurred.

Rune shook his head and rose to his feet. "There's no point talking to you. You're falling asleep sitting up. Get in bed, Des, or I'll drag you there."

Destin lifted his head and looked at him from under heavy lids. "Nag."

"Bonehead," Rune responded with a grin.

Destin rose and staggered to his bunk, falling onto it with a muffled groan. "Get out," he muttered and ceased to move.

"Dolt," Rune scoffed. Yanking a blanket out from under the prince, he draped it over Destin and muttered,

"You know she needs to stay…" *For more reasons than just the Vessel,* he thought but didn't say aloud to his stubborn, sleeping cousin.

Disregarding his prince's order to leave, Rune dug a hammock out of storage and hung it in a corner. Rolling into it with practiced ease, he studied the back of his friend's head with a thoughtful frown for a moment. Then he sighed and flicked his fingers at the lanterns, blowing the flames into darkness.

Chapter 5

Destin leaned on the rail of the upper deck with folded arms and studied the sky. A storm loomed to the north, white towering mountains of cloud underscored with dark menace and flashes of lightning, but it appeared to be moving more east than south and shouldn't cause them trouble. He kept his eyes on it all the same, watching the play of morning light over the billowing clouds and feeling the restless energy of the storm even at this distance. He refused to consider it might be his own restless energy moving through him.

"She's sleeping late."

Rune's knowing looks and smirks wore his patience. He kept his gaze fixed on the clouds and didn't glance toward his fool cousin. When Destin didn't answer, Rune chuckled, grating on his nerves. It was inconvenient, having someone around who could read him right down to his soul, especially when someone didn't know the meaning of the words tact and discretion.

The captain approached, his stiff disapproval a welcome distraction. "My prince, no sighting of your uncle's ships yet. We have clear sailing for now." He nodded toward the distant storm. "The squall may bother us later this eve, if we stay on this heading."

"We'll navigate around if we must but only if it becomes necessary."

"Very good, sire." The captain hesitated, gaze flicking over the rail to the lower deck.

"Is there something else, Captain Trough?"

"Sire, about the changeling—"

"Her name is Eylee'ai," Rune interjected in a helpful tone that didn't fool Destin for a moment. He sent his cousin a quelling glance, but Rune only grinned.

"She's distracting my crew," the captain said in a firm voice, shoulders straightening. He met Destin's gaze with a directness the prince had to admire.

"Understandable, after she saved us yesterday—"

"Rune," Destin growled, watching the captain's face darken and back stiffen. "Unless she is interfering with the functions of the ship, leave her to me, Captain Trough. I'll handle her."

The captain gave him a sketchy bow and stalked away. Destin turned to level the full force of his displeasure on his cousin. Rune gave him a sunny smile, eyes wide with feigned innocence.

"Stop stirring up trouble, cousin."

"It's not me doing the stirring, Des. I'm just looking trouble in the eye instead of pretending it doesn't exist. Shall we go wake her?"

Destin stared at him for a moment, keeping his face expressionless with an effort. "You'd drive a devil to drink."

"Everyone has a special skill." Rune's gaze flicked over his shoulder and his smile widened into a grin. "And some of us have quite a few. Good rising, lovely Lia."

Destin turned, trying to ignore the coil of anticipation in his gut. She was a hindrance, an obstacle and threat to his mission. He disagreed with Rune. Whatever knowledge she might possess of the Vessel of Power wasn't worth the distraction and problems she would cause aboard his ship. When he caught sight of her, his own uncontrolled reaction only underscored the point. She was trouble. And as soon as he got his breath back, he'd tell her so.

She should have looked ridiculous. The court had conditioned him to expect female beauty in dresses and robes from demure to sultry. Female workers wore practical clothing for their chosen field, like the sailors who wore pants and tunics to cover without hampering their work. But Eylee'ai wore a man's white shirt and dark slacks, too fine to be from any of the crew.

They were undoubtedly Rune's, a fact that sizzled in the back of his mind like acid, though he did his best to ignore it. The clothing was too large on her, so she'd rolled up the sleeves and cuffs and tied the tail ends of the shirt in a knot under her breasts. This showed a disconcerting amount of skin at her midriff and upper chest. Her hair hung in a sleek, shiny braid down her back and her feet were bare.

The effect should have been foolish or crass, but she moved in her borrowed clothing with confidence, unselfconscious and natural as though she wore the same every day. Another woman might have flaunted the exposed skin, using her considerable feminine advantage, but Eylee'ai didn't seem aware of it. Moving across the deck with easy grace, she flicked Destin a cool glance before giving Rune a faint but warm smile. "Thanks for the loan."

Destin's contrary cousin captured one of her hands in both of his with a too-charming smile. "My clothing looks much better on you than on me. I'm putting my entire wardrobe at your disposal."

Her eyebrows rose, but her hand remained in his cousin's. "You're kidding. After all your talk about me being naked?"

"Ah. Good point." His smile changed to a scowl. "Return my clothing immediately, you thief."

A grin flashed across her face and went through Destin's gut like lightning. He gave thanks it didn't last. When she turned her head to look at him, her expression became cool and guarded. "Prince Destin, thank you for honoring our deal," she said with stiff formality.

For some reason her tone grated on his nerves. So did her hand still clasped in Rune's. He folded his arms over his chest and responded in the same tone, "You are satisfied all terms of the bargain have been met?"

She faced him, chin lifting. Rune turned with her, giving Destin a warning frown and small shake of his head.

"I am."

"Good. Now get off my ship."

She made a rough sound in her throat and Rune closed his eyes with a heavy sigh. "Such gratitude," she sneered. "No thanks, your highness, for saving you yesterday?"

"We saved ourselves," he bridled. "And we would have done so without your interference."

"Interference?" She stepped toward him on stiff legs with hands fisted at her sides. Rune groaned and shielded his eyes with one hand. "You arrogant ass! You were overrun. You were stuck without my help."

"I can handle my uncle. Now get off my ship."

She folded her arms and narrowed her eyes, sparkling gray challenge framed by dark lashes. The coil of awareness tightened inside him, deep and insistent. "Not until I get a thank you. I took out one ship, maybe two. I deserve a little gratitude."

He took a slow step toward her, the heat of potential flame flowing up his spine and down his arms. "Your stunt with the whales allowed my uncle to surround us in the first place. You deserve to get thrown overboard."

She bared her teeth, which looked a lot sharper than he remembered. "Just try it."

Rune stepped between them, hands raised in a warding gesture. "Stop. Take a breath, if you please. Agree to disagree and so forth."

She hissed like an angry cat and stalked away, snarling over her shoulder, "My father was right. You can only trust an elemental to stab you in the back."

Destin watched her slide down the ladder and stride across the lower deck toward the prow. Sailors stopped to watch her as well, but she didn't seem to notice them. She leapt up to the forecastle and then over the rail without hesitation in a breathtaking display of animal grace.

He was waiting for the crew to return to their duties when Rune punched him hard in the shoulder. "Gods bless it, Des, what is wrong with you?"

Destin rubbed his aching shoulder and stared at Rune. His cousin's face was red as he paced back and forth with violent energy. Destin had only seen his affable cousin this angry a handful of times and it never failed to astonish him. Rune was so easy-going, it always seemed as though he didn't have a temper.

Disturbing he'd lost it now over a changeling.

"She was beginning to trust me. Now we'll be lucky if she doesn't strangle us in our sleep!"

"She's the enemy." Rune made a rude noise, but Destin continued, "She made herself my enemy by threatening this mission, the king's mission. Your king's mission. Try to recall which side you're on, cousin."

"I'm on your side, Des. No one else's."

It was treason for him to say it, but Destin ignored the insult to his father. What was said between them was private. He would never betray his friend's trust, honesty, and loyalty by crying treason, but he wouldn't let Rune get away with warping the truth, either. With a scowl, he retorted, "My side, right. You're fawning all over our enemy for me?"

"So it's jealousy that's making you blind and thickheaded like our gods-forsaken uncle? You're a prince, Destin! You used to think like one. I don't believe she has to be our enemy, but even if she is, it's better to keep the enemy in sight. Instead, you rile her and dump her overboard! Nice work, brother," he said with uncharacteristic scorn, then turned his back and stalked away.

Destin resolutely faced forward, trying to ignore the burn of dismay and anger in his face. *Is it jealousy?* The idea horrified him. He'd never before been jealous of Rune's success with the fairer sex. Sometimes he'd envied his cousin his handsome, unscarred face and the freedom to pursue any attraction, but he'd never resented him for it. They couldn't change the circumstances of their births. No sense getting bitter over it. But now, instead of being amused or disapproving of Rune's overt flirtation, he was conflicted.

He tried to view his own reactions in an objective light. Yes, he was attracted to the changeling. She wasn't beautiful in the traditional sense but lovely in her own way, and the silky, effortless way she moved would threaten any man's sanity. Aside from the physical, she faced him with a fascinating, fearless challenge, her conviction and point of view on the Vessel intrigued him. He could admit, if he wasn't constricted by his duty, he'd want to spend more time with her, learn more about her. But his duty was to his father and his father had given him a crucial task. He couldn't fail to complete his task, and she was standing in his way.

It wasn't jealousy, he decided. Just regret over the circumstances. And he was angry with Rune for complicating matters that were complicated enough already. If the changeling knew something about the Vessel, then others did also. He'd find information elsewhere without endangering his ship, his crew, and his mission.

His decision to eject the changeling was sound. Rune's judgment was skewed by a pretty face.

Nodding to himself, he turned from the rail and headed for his cabin. He'd told the captain to set a course for the nearest port, to resupply the ship. He also wanted to glean more detail on their destination, the last known location of the previous millennium's Vessel of Power. While he had a moment not involving fending off his uncle or the changeling, he wanted to refresh his memory on the sanctuary where the Vessel was last seen. According to legend, it was still in use by an obscure sect of monks, but the more knowledge he had of the place and its inhabitants the better.

He poured over ancient text for hours in the blissful peace of his cabin, memorizing all the information he had available on the place. Sometime later, his stomach pulled him from his research with a plaintive growl. He glanced at the port and frowned at the long light of evening.

As if surfacing from a deep sleep, he realized his little world had been too quiet. No one had come to inform him of the changeling's return. The captain hadn't sent word of the storm or his uncle's ships. And Rune had never gone this long without pestering him. Had he been so furious, then? The thought gave him a pang. His soul brother was the one person he could rely on to be by his side through anything.

With a sense of impending doom, he left his cabin and strode out onto the deck, scanning the surrounding area. Everything seemed serene, but he wasn't reassured. He climbed to the upper deck and approached the helmsman. "All is well?"

"Yes, my prince," the man answered with a deferential bow abbreviated by the wheel. "The storm is a safe distance and no ships sighted."

"Where is the captain?"

"Supping in his cabin with Lord Rune, sire."

Destin schooled his expression before he winced at the alarming news. The two men had radically different viewpoints and Rune wasn't known for holding his tongue. If his cousin didn't get tossed overboard, it would be a miracle. "The changeling?"

"No sign of her, your highness."

The man's tone and expression stayed neutral, so

Destin couldn't tell if this sailor shared his captain's view of changelings or not. He nodded and moved away, scanning the horizon. The storm seemed less ferocious but still thick with rain off to the east. To the northwest, a small fog bank captured the evening light. Other than that, the horizon was clear with nothing but dark blue rolling waves in sight, heralding a calm night and smooth sailing for their ship. If they kept to this pace, they would sight land by morning and be in port before noon.

With some of his anxiety eased, Destin headed back down to the lower deck, intending to check on the captain and Rune. If neither had shed blood yet, perhaps he'd stay for supper. He'd only taken two steps toward Captain Trough's cabin when a sailor raised the alarm. He glanced around as they tacked to the northeast and dropped sail to slow, then noticed the fog bank looming much closer all of a sudden.

Destin grabbed the arm of the closest crewmember, halting her flight across the deck. "What is that?" he demanded, pointing a finger at the fog.

"Sea serpents, sire," she answered breathlessly, eyes wide and body yearning away from the billow of white. "Dragon snakes. A whole swarm of 'em. Should pass by if we can slow enough…" She tugged on her trapped arm with a pleading look.

Destin let her go to her duties. Moving to the port rail, he studied the fog. The serpents weren't visible, but it didn't look as though the fog would pass by. It looked on a direct course for his ship. "Eylee'ai," he growled under his breath and a hot shudder slid up his spine.

"What is it?" Rune asked, appearing at Destin's

side.

"Steamers," he answered, not bothering to voice his suspicions. They'd find out soon enough.

The captain bellowed orders to drop all sail and turn the ship, to come to a full stop, but his efforts would be in vain. The fog, more steam than mist, flowed toward them. As it neared, humped shadows became visible within, a coil here and a spiny head there. The serpents' undulating cries echoed across the water, accompanied by whistles and whooshing blasts of steam from their vents.

Sailors named them dragon snakes because of the steam they produced. They couldn't breathe fire, but they could heat water inside their bodies to the boiling point and expel it at a dangerous velocity from their vents and mouths. The cloud of steam served as both protection and hunting camouflage.

Even if the serpents did no overt damage to the ship, their portable fog bank would make it almost impossible to navigate. They answered Destin's question of whether or not Eylee'ai was involved when the sinuous bodies swarmed around the ship, and stayed.

Destin swore under his breath and headed for the bow with long, hard strides. Rune paced him, snickering, but Destin ignored his cousin. When they reached the forecastle, the changeling was just swinging over the rail, her face glowing. Her bright eyes met his for a moment and his heart hitched in his chest, infuriating him even further. She wore inexplicably dry clothes, the same outfit as this morning. He recalled Rune telling him she'd slept on the side of the ship, which meant she kept supplies there.

"Darling Lia!" Rune exclaimed on approach. "The steamers are absolutely inspired. Run away with me and have my children."

Destin halted a few paces away and folded his arms across his chest to contain the sudden, ferocious urge to beat his cousin senseless. His struggle kept him silent while she smothered a laugh and gave Rune a horrified look. "The gods would strike me dead for even thinking of making more of you."

Rune seemed undaunted, claiming one of her hands and bowing over it in a dramatic sweep. "But my sweet, how will we know unless we try?"

"Get rid of the serpents or I will," Destin gritted between clenched teeth.

Eylee'ai pulled her hand free of Rune's and turned to meet Destin's gaze with a tight, challenging smile. "Go right ahead and try. They love fire and anything you do with water will mess with your ship, too."

He narrowed his eyes on her. "Then I'll just chain you in the brig and wait for them to leave."

She leaned against the rail in a casual stance, giving her nails a studious inspection. "Well, that's one way to go. But I'm not easy to chain and…" She turned her head, letting out an eerie, almost alien cry, the echo repeated among the serpents. "I made myself their leader. They won't go anywhere without me."

Rune gave a bark of incredulous laughter, watching her with sparkling eyes. "That is amazing! However did you manage?"

"Sea serpent swarms are led by the largest, strongest female, the queen. I made myself larger and stronger and fought her for leadership."

"You fought?" Rune's delight faded, his eyes

coasting over her.

She shrugged. "Not for long. She backed down quick. Death matches don't happen often in nature."

Rune shook his head. "Lia, you're incredible. How many shapes are you able to assume?"

Through his seething, Destin noticed her sudden tension. She flicked Rune a wide-eyed glance before looking down with another shrug. Her reaction tugged at him, but he couldn't think around his fiery temper.

He growled, "They'll leave if their leader dies."

Her features stony, she locked silvery eyes with his. "You can try," she said.

Destin's entire body tensed and heated with the prelude to fire, but Rune stepped between them, hazel eyes anxious. "Please, I thought we'd gone beyond this killing each other business. There must be a less drastic solution. Perhaps another bargain?"

"Actually," Eylee'ai drawled from the other side of Rune, "I'm pretty happy with how things are."

She sounded so smug, Destin had a moment when he thought he'd go through Rune to get his hands on her. Rune's eyes widened as he stared at Destin, though he didn't move out from between them. "There must be something you want," Rune said, casting a sickly smile over his shoulder at the changeling. "You've been away all day. Are you hungry?"

"Nope. I ate with the snakes. Gross, but filling."

"Hot bath?"

She smiled and spread her arms through the warm mist and gathering early twilight. "Not cold in the slightest. No, I think this time I'll hold out for this ship turning around and going back to the royal port."

"Lovely Lia, you know that's not going to

happen," Rune told the infuriating female in a gentle, reasoning tone.

"Then I guess we sit," she responded, folding her arms across her chest and looking from one to the other with calm confidence, driving needles in Destin's already raw temper.

Destin let the fire straining against his control ignite on his palms, glaring at her through the threatening glow. "We won't be sitting," he growled. Beneath his fury, he was startled by how much effort it took to restrain the flame, to shape and contain it to just his hands.

"Des, wait…" Rune began, but the changeling shouldered him aside, stepping into the flickering pale light of Destin's flame. Her eyes seemed to glow, face growing feral and dangerous, sleek body sliding into a hunting stalk.

"I'd love to dance, your highness, but you need to know the only reason the dragon snakes aren't breaking your ship is because I'm on it. If they think I'm in danger, though, they won't play nice. Are you willing to risk it?"

His entire body thrummed with the urge to take her challenge, to pit his strength and skill against her own. It was difficult to resist the primitive male need to battle her, to prove himself and exert dominance.

But his reasoning self couldn't ignore the threat to his ship and crew from the serpents. He fisted his hands with a snarl, white flame slipping between his fingers and dancing across his knuckles before he was able to smother it. Still his entire being hummed with heat. "All right, changeling," he conceded with guttural fury. "What'll it take?"

Her eyebrows rose in cool, aggravating amusement. "You're willing to deal?"

"Yes," he snapped, muscles flexing with thwarted violence. "But I won't end my search for the Vessel. Anything but that."

"Anything?" she repeated with a smirk.

"Within reason." His clenched teeth and stiff lips garbled the words, but she must have understood them.

"The proud prince is ready to deal," she murmured, folding her arms and narrowing her eyes as if she didn't believe him.

"Get on with it, changeling. What'll it be?"

She tossed her head, meeting his gaze with a slow, taunting smile. "A kiss."

A kiss. He stared, waiting for the words to make sense. She had him in a corner and they both knew it. His ship was going nowhere. Though he could chase her off and battle the sea creatures, he wasn't willing to risk the ship and crew when they had another alternative. She had the advantage, slowed or even stopped his search for the Vessel. And to undo all of this, she wanted a kiss? "What?"

Chapter 6

It wasn't nice to rub it in. Eylee'ai's mother would disapprove and her sister would be disappointed in her. But if anyone deserved to have his pride stomped on, it was this arrogant prince. She didn't expect him to agree to the deal, which was the point. Even when he had a way out, he would never take it. Not when it meant lowering himself to touching a barbaric changeling.

She had to revel in his stunned expression, though a tiny, guilty part of her sent an apology to her mother. Rune seemed even more delighted than she was, choking on his laughter until tears beaded his lashes.

"What?" the prince said, as if he'd never heard anything so horrifying.

"A kiss. You've heard of those, right? Two people putting their lips together…" Rune distracted her by falling at her feet, his face red with silent laughter. The only sound he made was a faint wheeze. "I don't think your cousin is well."

"Why?" the prince demanded.

"Ah, because it looks like he can't breathe."

"Why do you want a kiss? It makes no sense."

"Sure it does. It's my price. You have to kiss me, a real one, no granny pecks, for a believable length of time. Then I'll take the snakes away." She looked down and frowned at the man rocking at her feet, nudging him with a bare toe. "Rune, stop it. You'll make yourself sick."

"What do you really want?" Destin asked in a hard, impatient voice, propping hands on lean hips.

She met his hot, green-gold stare and gave him a grim smile. "That is what I really want, your highness. So is it a deal?"

"No, it is not a deal! It's senseless. What's wrong with you?"

She smirked. "Is the price too steep for you?"

He stared at her, scarred face blank for a moment. Then his brows came together. "Is this a jest to you?"

She frowned back at him. "No, chasing elementals across the ocean is not my idea of fun."

"Then make a different bargain."

She folded her arms across her chest and glared at him. "No."

He spun on his heel with a muffled roar and a sharp gesture, stalking away into the thickening mist. She watched him disappear in a swirl of fog, wondering how safe she'd be if she stayed on the ship.

Then she remembered Rune, alarmed at his silence. Looking down, she found him sprawled on his back, gazing at her with an adoring smile on his damp face and a bright glow in his hazel eyes. "I really do love you," he told her. "You're everything I've ever wished for in a woman."

She crouched, tilting her head to study him. "Did you hit your head as a child?"

"Repeatedly," he answered without losing a bit of his smile.

She nodded. "That explains it."

He sat up, leaning on one arm and resting the other on an upraised knee, his handsome face sobering. "Are you able to control the snakes, Lia? Sailors avoid them for a reason, you know. I don't want anyone harmed."

She lowered her eyes with a guilty pang and sank into a sitting position, crossing bent legs at the ankles and wrapping her arms around them. "Control is an illusion, Rune, especially with nature. They're wild animals and I can't make any promises. But every animal has a pattern to how it'll act. As long as no one attacks them, the ship should be safe."

"You seem to have some sort of rapport with animals, first with the whales and now these serpents. I didn't realize changelings had such ability. I had the impression they just changed their shapes."

She twitched with embarrassment, flicking a quick look at his earnest face. "Not everybody can be the shape they change into, act like the animal. But I'm not the only one who can."

"You were a whale, a shark, a serpent. Were you raised on the coast? Is that why you're able to change into so many different sea creatures?"

She shrugged, trying to hide her growing discomfort. "Everybody has different levels of talent. Not all elementals can use every element, can they? You said you're sensitive to spirit. What else can you weave?"

"Air," he answered. "But I'm sluggish with water and earth, and I couldn't spark a flame if I was standing in a bonfire. I understand what you're saying, Lia, but I've never known a changeling to shift as fast as you or be able to take so many different forms. Isn't it unusual?"

"No," she lied, watching her toes instead of him. "You must not have been around too many changelings."

"Hmm."

When he said nothing else, she peeked at him. His mouth curved in a wry smile, eyes patient and knowing. *Spirit,* she reminded herself. Rumor had it some spirit weavers could tell if a person was lying. Clearing her throat, she changed the subject. "What do you think the prince will do now? Am I gonna be barbequed, or is it safe to spend some time on deck?"

"I'm sure he wouldn't want me telling you what I think he'll do, but you're safe for now." He flashed a delighted, conspiratorial grin. "Did you see his face? Lady, you make him lose his temper like no one I've ever met. You're the best thing that's happened to us in a long time."

She quirked an eyebrow. "It's a good thing I make him mad?"

He sighed, waving a hand through the warm fog with a pensive expression. "Des was taught to always be in control. The discipline is so much a part of him now he doesn't even consider it, doesn't see how it cages him and limits him. As a prince, it is a dangerous blind spot. As a man…well, it's not living at all." He caught her eye and his expression warmed. "Yes, it's a very good thing you knock him off balance. And it's quite entertaining for me." He chuckled and flicked a finger at the end of her nose. "A kiss! That's priceless."

She batted at his hand. "I can't be the only person who's ever made him mad."

"But none as gorgeous as you," he said with a sly smile, leaning closer. "When will you ask me for a kiss?"

"Only in your dreams," she replied in a dry tone. A

questioning whistle from the ocean drew her to her feet and she stepped to the rail, giving an answering croon repeated by the swarm.

Rune joined her at the rail, looking down with an expression of intense fascination. Not much could be seen through the fog and early twilight, but every once in a while a long, scaled, and shadowy hump would rise. "Did you just tell them all is well?"

"Pretty sure."

"How in Shenoh's name do you know how to do that?"

She shrugged uncomfortably. "Instinct, I guess. I don't know. I just do it."

"I've never seen a steamer. What do they look like?"

"Like big lizards without legs. Their heads are a little scary with a spiked crest on top and big black eyes. But they have pretty swirls in black, white, and gray down their sides. They use a blowhole like a whale to breathe and blow steam when they're in the water."

"They use the steam to attack?"

"When they're hunting or fighting with each other. But now they're using it for cover to protect the swarm. They have young down there."

He turned his head, studying her with the same fascinated expression. "I almost wish I could join you in your world, see what you've seen."

"Almost?"

He ducked his head with a self-depreciating smile. "I don't believe I'm brave enough."

She snickered and said without thinking, "You sound like my sister." She froze, staring into the fog, hoping he didn't notice her reaction.

No such luck. "You have a sister?" he asked in a tone too somber for the casual question.

"I'm not talking about my family."

"Why not?"

She sighed and sent him an impatient look. "We're on opposite sides, in case you hadn't noticed. Anything I tell you, you'll tell mister crabby prince, who'll find some way to use it against me."

"You're not my enemy, Lia." He seemed to mean it, hazel eyes warm and sincere.

"You don't have a choice, Rune." He started to shake his head, but she interrupted with a sharp gesture. "No, you don't. Who will you choose if it comes down to it? Some stranger you just met or your soul brother?" Brushing a drying strand of hair off her cheek, she faced the roiling fog, avoiding his troubled gaze. "I can't trust you not to do what's in your and the prince's best interest."

He was silent for a moment. "What if we discussed my family?"

"That's an easy offer. I can't get close enough to hurt them."

"You think we'll harm your family?"

I know you will, she thought. She pressed her lips together and didn't answer. He touched gentle fingers to the back of her hand. She was gripping the rail tight enough to whiten her knuckles. She loosened her hold with an inner curse. *I'm sorry, Ettie. I betray you even when I'm trying not to.*

"I don't have a sister," Rune said quietly, fingers still on the back of her hand. "Or a brother by blood. I believe my parents would adore you."

She looked at him with a crease between her

brows. He seemed sincere, offering her an undemanding smile. He was either the nicest man or the best liar she'd ever met. She didn't know what to do with him. "I don't understand you."

His smile took on a mischievous edge. "No one does."

She stiffened, resisting his strange charm. "If you go anywhere near my baby sister, I'll kill you." Her flat tone and stare emphasized the promise.

He lost his smile in a hurry, face paling a little as he removed his touch from her skin. "I would never willingly harm you or those you love."

"Rune." She sighed and shook her head in despair. "You're a royal. You can't be this green. Willing or not, we do what we have to do. Do you really think I want to be here?"

"Well, that is an arrow through my heart, darling," he said with a smirk. "And here I believed we were coming along so nicely. But you do have a point." He paused, glancing over his shoulder toward the interior of the ship, his smirk deepening. "I wonder how long it'll be before my cousin does what he must do?"

Chapter 7

Destin took a deep breath, curbing the urge to throttle the captain. It wasn't Captain Trough he wanted to strangle, but the man didn't make it easy to remember. "A little fog is no reason to stop dead in the water," he growled.

"I can't risk it, your highness. Just drifting is dangerous enough. No telling how far off course we're getting. And too much activity might stir up the snakes." The captain's tone remained deferential enough, but disapproval etched the lines of his face. His dark eyes brimmed with blame as he stared at his prince, and Destin couldn't fault him for it. If he'd just dealt with the changeling when she'd first become a threat, none of this would be happening.

Turning away from the captain, Destin folded his hands in the small of his back and stared down into the drifting steam, working hard to suppress his fury. "This is your area, Captain Trough. There must be a way to discourage the serpents, to drive them off."

"Without great risk to the ship and my crew? No, sire." There was a pause while Destin ground his teeth and tried not to snarl. "My prince, if this is the changeling's doing, perhaps she can be persuaded to undo it. If she won't listen to reason, I know more effective methods."

"No!" He spun to face the captain. "I told you to

leave her to me. Are you having trouble understanding such a simple command?"

The man stiffened, chin lifting in defiance, though his eyes slid away. "No, sire."

Destin drew a hissing breath. The thought of the captain taking violent action against Eylee'ai triggered a wave of protective dismay, which was stupid, considering he'd thought about killing her himself. And because of this stupidity he was alienating the person in charge of his ship and their safe voyage. "I trust your judgment, Captain Trough. Do you think fire would discourage the animals?"

After a moment's pause, the captain answered in an easier tone, "More like the opposite, sire. We could try freezing the water, but I've seen steamers melt icebergs, so I don't know if it would do us any good. It might provoke the beasts instead of chasing 'em away."

Destin nodded, brooding down into the deepening twilight. Across the ship, faint gleams of light came and went, lanterns fighting the foggy gloom. Controlling his voice with an effort, he said, "Thank you, captain. Carry on."

Without another word, the man moved away and Destin allowed himself to grip the rail hard enough to knot muscles in his arms and across his shoulders. Anger was a living thing inside him, as hot and destructive as fire, alarming in its immensity. Like a dark wave, fear rode underneath the anger. Never in his life had he been so out of control, unable to restrain his emotions. Not even when his father had ripped open his cheek and left him scarred for so little reason. Then he'd responded with a dull, sick anger, blunted by a morass of other painful emotions, nothing like this white-hot burst. She shouldn't be able to affect him so strongly when his own father couldn't make him lose his hard-won control.

Part of his frustration lay in not knowing why she'd made such a ridiculous demand. What would she gain from it? She couldn't know what she did to him could she? He considered this with furious dismay. Had she been able to read him, when no one else could have except Rune? Did she mean to humiliate him? Or was her motive even more devious?

His anger chilled, his experience with the intrigues of court leading him down different avenues. Her goal was to prevent him from finding the Vessel. She'd already admitted she'd do anything to keep him from it. If she'd divined his attraction, she might use it to cloud his mind, to distract him from his mission. Distraction must be her motive.

It made sense to him, giving her actions structure and calming him. His anger turned cold, calculating, and rational.

They couldn't remain as they were. He'd just begun his search for the Vessel and couldn't afford the time spent finding another solution to the changeling's stumbling block. He could kill or imprison her, but it wouldn't solve the serpent problem. It might, in fact, make it worse. The fastest and most viable solution would be to agree to her terms.

Knowing a trap was the first step in avoiding it. He refused to react to her, to allow her to influence him. *Just an obstacle,* he told himself with grim resolve as he straightened and headed for the lower deck. *Remove the obstacle*. With their bargain completed and the snakes gone, he would find a more permanent solution to the changeling problem. Tossing her overboard wasn't effective enough.

He entertained himself with a satisfying image of clapping shackles around her wrists while he pushed through the moist, opaque air. It was so thick now he couldn't even see the rail, though he knew he was only feet from it. He breathed brine, tasting salt on his tongue as if the air was turning into ocean. The odd, warm touch of fog on his skin repulsed him, like the brush of a sun-heated reptile.

He slowed, finding his way through the steam by moving from one recognizable object to another, coils of rigging, the trap doors leading to the hold, the foremast, until he found the forecastle. He stood alone at the bow, though dim glows shifted and disappeared around him like apparitions, accompanied by the shuffling and muttering of uneasy sailors. Hesitating, he cocked his head to listen, straining his eyes through the gloom. Where was she?

Then Rune's soft laugh drifted through the gloom. Sudden, shocking anger flared hot again. He battled it with a bewildered kind of determination, heading in the direction of his cousin's humor. Destin knew Rune would be with the girl, which bothered him almost as much as her insane bargain.

Just get it over with, he thought when their shapes formed out of the mist. He didn't pause, though the changeling's eyes widened and she tensed into a defensive stance. Stalking up to her, he fisted a hand in the front of her borrowed shirt and lifted her to her toes, ignoring the sudden, vice-like grip she had on his wrist.

"It's a deal."

He meant to be merciless, punishing. She hadn't

said it had to feel good and she deserved a little punishment for trying to manipulate him. If he could hold onto his anger, he could avoid her trap.

But somehow it all went wrong.

Her lips were softer than he'd expected, with a fullness he could feel even under the brutal pressure of his mouth. The sensation intrigued him, luring him into relenting just a little, just to absorb the feel of her. She was smooth, silky, and luscious.

Heat slammed into him, erasing all thoughts of traps, distractions, and missions. He moved his lips over hers in slow, greedy exploration, excruciatingly aware of each tactile sensation, every slide and brush and twist. Her mouth fit his so perfectly. He breathed in her scent, a mix of ocean and sweet, a mysterious spice making his tongue tingle with the need to taste. A vague unease kept him from deepening the kiss, but he couldn't recall why he shouldn't. And he was starving. He wanted to dive into her and never surface, never stop.

With shocking abruptness, she broke free, stumbling backward. Rune caught her elbow, steadying her. Destin took an involuntary step toward her before his mind cleared and he halted, assessing the stunned disbelief in those wide gray eyes. Heat was churning through him like wildfire, his palms itching with the beginnings of flame.

Oh, gods. He was close to losing control over his ability to create fire, something that hadn't happened to him since he was a child, an added humiliation to the thunder of his heart, the gasp of his breath, and the hot ache in his gut.

Destin fisted his hands and tucked them behind his

back, scowling at her as he battled for control. "Our bargain is complete," he rasped, trying to ignore the wry grin on Rune's face. "Now undo it."

Eylee'ai couldn't feel her legs. They seemed to have been replaced with limp noodles, but she couldn't look away from golden fire long enough to check. Rune was the only thing keeping her upright. She'd thank him later when the shock wore off. When her heart stopped battering against her ribcage and she remembered how to breathe.

He'd kissed her. The prince had stooped to touching her, setting aside his pride for one long, stunning moment. As she would've expected, he'd started hard and angry, but then he'd… She raised the back of her hand to her mouth, shivers chasing themselves over her skin at the remembered shock of his lips moving with such thorough deliberation over hers. He'd kissed her and somehow managed to suck all the strength out of her muscles at the same time.

"W-what?" she whispered.

"Undo your mischief," he snarled, his scar standing out with the predatory tightening of his features. "Take the serpents away. Do it now, changeling."

Oh, right. The dumb deal she'd made. But who knew the prince would agree? And how was she supposed to undo anything when she couldn't even stand up? "Uh-huh," she breathed, sending Rune an urgent glance. "I'll, uh, get right on it."

Rune was grinning, the beast, but his support stayed steady. He transferred his hold to an arm around her waist. "Surely it can wait until after my kiss."

"You don't get a kiss," she said without much attention, trying to be discreet about testing her wobbling limbs.

Rune pouted. "But darling, aren't I your favorite?"

The prince made a rough sound and Eylee'ai flicked him a wary glance. He looked out of patience and ready to fry them both, if his narrowed eyes and fierce snarl were any clue. Plus, the mist glowed behind him as if his backside had caught on fire.

"My favorite what?" she responded with an acid edge and a firm elbow in Rune's side.

He let her go. Her legs still quivered, distant and watery, but held her upright. "I'd be your favorite anything, sweetheart," Rune crooned with a charming smile.

She rolled her eyes and turned toward the rail. "A deal's a deal," she said over her shoulder to the prince. "Just give me a moment." She paused, cocking her head to listen.

"I said now," he growled behind her.

She held up a hand to forestall him. "Wait, there's something…" She closed her eyes, focusing on the sounds below them. The serpents were restless, edgy, their anxious calls rippling through the swarm from aft to bow. With a frown, she moved starboard with the men trailing her, trying to pinpoint the source of the animals' nervousness.

"What is it?" Rune murmured.

She shook her head, holding up a hand again for silence. She looked into the blinding fog, listening hard. The mist echoed with the creak of a ship, the call of a sailor, the slap of water on wood. Not the prince's ship.

She spun and met his fire-laced eyes. "Destin."

"I hear it," he said in a low, grim voice. "Rune, warn the crew. No light. No sound. Tell the captain to be ready to sail hard."

Rune nodded once and sprinted away, the slap of his feet muffled by the fog. Eylee'ai flinched anyway at the noise, hoping the serpent cries would drown it. Shifting closer to the prince, she hissed, "Your uncle is a huge pain in the ass."

His dark lashes swept down in a slow blink over his fantastic eyes and his mouth eased in what could have been the beginnings of a smile. A strange fluttering bloomed in her stomach at the sight, but she squelched it. She might have believed a smile on any face but his. "We need cover."

She didn't have to ask what he meant. "I can keep him busy with the swarm."

His neck stiffened and his jaw tensed, gaze slipping past her to the impenetrable cloud. "At what price?"

She chewed on her lip, thinking fast. She couldn't afford to waste such an opportunity, but how far could she push him? "Let me stay on the ship."

"No." He didn't even hesitate or look at her.

She sighed, shifting in place and listening to the increasing wild whistles of the snakes. They hadn't heard from her and they were reaching the point when they'd act without her. What they would do without her direction was a worrisome mystery. "Just at night," she compromised. When he didn't answer right away, she whispered, "Come on, it's not such a bad deal."

"One night."

"Stingy," she scoffed. "I could take the swarm away right now. No telling how long the fog would last, but it wouldn't be long before your uncle spots you."

His jaw flexed as if he was grinding his teeth. "If you stay on this ship, you'll be sleeping in the brig," he gritted in what was clearly meant to be a threat.

She grinned. There wasn't a jail in the world that could hold her. "No problem. I'll take the bargain." Not waiting for his reaction, she whirled and sprinted for the rail at the bow. Climbing down to her bag, she crooned reassurances to the swarm as she stripped and secured her clothes, before pushing off the side of the ship and diving into the water.

It was scalding hot. With an involuntary scream, she writhed into her new form, blowing gusts of relief through her vent as her serpentine body adjusted to what now felt like gentle bathwater. She should have remembered the dragon snakes could sustain such heat within the swarm, especially if they stayed in one place.

Whistling in sharp command, she undulated her long body under the prince's ship and headed in the direction of the other vessel. The swarm followed, crooning their relief at the return of their leader. They might also be relieved to be on the move again and she flinched under a wave of guilt. She shouldn't be using them like this. It made her no better than the elementals, warping the natural order around them. It was an act of desperation, a poor excuse, but she couldn't bring herself to turn the swarm loose.

She found the other royal's ships much too close, though there were only three. Either she'd done permanent damage to the fourth one or it had fallen behind. Slithering between the vessels with the swarm on her tail, she considered her options. She refused to incite a full out attack of the swarm. Many of the animals would be injured or killed in a fight. The gods would know who was responsible for such unnatural bloodshed and measure it against her soul. But any overt aggressive move on her part would encourage the rest of the serpents to do the same. There had been only one time they hadn't acted in unison, when she'd challenged their queen.

Blowing a great gout of steam across the bow of one ship, she measured the hull with a sinuous brush of her long body, wondering what the snakes would do if she acted out a queen challenge against these vessels. They weren't serpents, so would the beasts consider them prey and join her?

A harpoon cut through the water next to her head, and she made her decision. Calling a warning to the swarm, she herded them away to a safer distance. Then she raised her spiny head out of the water and mimicked the booming challenge of a queen serpent to a rival. If the swarm tried to attack, she'd just have to lead them away. Most of the steamers lifted their heads out of the water with her, curious as cats to see the new queen. When no new serpent appeared, questioning whistles and bewildered cries rose from the swarm. But they didn't attack.

Eylee'ai weaved her great head in a queenly threat at the ships as she undulated closer. The dragon snakes tangled together in a confused bundle of sinuous coils without following, blowing protective steam into the air in reaction to a threat they didn't understand. Perfect. The thickening fog would blanket the three hostile ships while the swarm stayed safe beyond their bows. She moved faster toward the royal's flotilla.

Vision was strange and murky in this body, but as she drew closer to the lead ship, Eylee'ai could sense the shapes of its crew, the bundles of blood and flesh calling prey to her reptilian instincts and glowing with heat like steady candles. She hissed and butted the hull with her spiny head, listening to the flat human outcries; the sounds didn't vibrate across her senses as they would in water. *I'll have to remember this for Ettie,* she thought. Ettie would find the life of a sea serpent to be enchanting.

Fire distracted her and she flinched, diving under the wooden vessel before she realized it hadn't hurt. The heat radiated through her scales with invigorating warmth. She hunched her coils and bumped the ship, rising on the other side with a showy plume of steam.

Then they tried ice.

It hurt in a way she'd never felt before, strange flashes of pain driving deep in her body like lightning strikes. With a shocked bugle, she writhed against the burning grip of ice, shattering its hold. Reptilian rage stoked her internal fire and she circled herself with boiling water, producing clouds of steam to hide her from the ship. It couldn't hide them from her, however. She could still sense the dead planks of wood and the bags of warm blood and flesh, her prey. The instinctive urge to strike, to sink her fangs into those sources of heat and food was almost overwhelming.

Eylee'ai shuddered and slammed into the ship's hull instead, aiming her predatory fury at their safe haven. She ignored the pain and new bruises, battering against the wood until it weakened, water flowing into the ship.

Then she paused to catalogue her wounds with an internal groan. *This is not healthy.* Shifting into a shark again to heal the worst of the injuries, she headed back toward the swarm at a slow swim. She was done. If the prince didn't have sense enough to flee in the time she'd given him, then so be it.

Before the swarm could recognize her as a threat, she changed back into their queen and called to them, weariness thickening in her muscles like a dark disease. This had been a really long day. The fast shape changes, the battle, and her new injuries took an enormous toll. She wished she could just leave the swarm here, but she didn't trust the royal uncle to leave them in peace.

With a sharp whistle of command, she led them away on an angle she hoped would keep them out of the path of the royals. When they'd gone a few leagues, she shrank her size and presented herself to the previous queen, showing her belly in a sign of submission. Without hesitation, the female boomed a challenge, swelling in the water with hostility. Eylee'ai crooned her submission to the new rule and slithered into the depths, changing back into the shark and leaving the swarm as she'd found them.

She didn't expect it to erase her sin, but she hoped it would count in her favor when her soul and earthly actions were weighed by Benon, the Eternal Judge.

Now, she had to go back and find the prince again. With an internal sigh of bone-deep weariness, she went hunting.

Chapter 8

Rune stared into the night, knowing it would do little good to search for Lia but unable to stop. The memory of her scream still drove needles of horror into his skin. But the swarm had moved away. Had Lia led them or had they lost their leader? He fretted over his inability to weave spirit in an effective way. If he could, he might have been able to tell if she was alive. The most he could sense after the scream was a great deal of serpents moving with sudden purpose.

Destin had declared the serpent exodus proof she was alive and leading them, even though Rune could read his inner turmoil. The prince had told the captain to sail without even looking for her. They'd been streaking across the ocean, wind- and water-weave powered, away from Lia ever since. Rune swore he was going to punch his cousin right in the mouth.

Rune spared a glare over his shoulder toward the night-shrouded upper deck where the prince weaved their escape, before he turned back to the dark ocean. If the girl was dead, it was going to take him a long time to forgive his soul brother. Destin might be in denial, but Rune grew more certain of his own feelings for Lia by the day. His attraction to her was the least of it, he'd have to be dead not to react to her natural sensuality. The rest of his feelings, though, were going to take some getting used to, but he knew she was important to him, to them both.

He strained his eyes in a useless effort to pierce the darkness, stretching his sense of spirit to the point of pain as he combed their wake for some sign of her. The ocean teemed with life, radiating vitality from the infinitely small to the immense. He wasn't sure he could separate her spirit from the rest, their connection still tenuous and her trust still a delicate, nebulous thing.

You can only trust an elemental to stab you in the back. He frowned at the memory of her words, at the hurt and strange alarm they pulled from him. He also hadn't liked the way she'd said *my father* with venom in her tone and pain in her eyes.

He shook his head, gripping the aft rail hard. *Gods, please let her be safe.* The ship lurched under him and he tightened his hold on the rail, startled. Had the gods answered him? Or was he just getting dizzy with effort? He let his senses falter for a moment, closing his eyes and breathing deep to ease the tension in his shoulders.

When he opened his eyes and heart again to the night, she was there.

"Lia!" he gasped, leaning over the rail and peering down. He saw nothing, but her fierce determination and wild spirit flowed upward through the night. She was a shark again. He sensed the power in her streamlined form, and her weariness. He swore, looking around for some way to help her. A line, a floater, something. There had to be some way for the sailors to get over the sides to rescue someone who'd fallen in. Then he remembered seeing a ladder.

Scrambling along the port side, he fumbled through the rigging, muttering to himself. Where had he seen it?

Hadn't it been right here? It should have been in easy reach, a rope ladder with hooks for the rail, a simple expedient for cleaning the outer hull, lowering into skiffs, or retrieving something lost from the ocean. Like a gorgeous, exhausted changeling.

Rune stumbled over something in the dark, fell with bruising force to his knees, and nearly slammed his face into what he was looking for. With a swift and breathless prayer of gratitude to the contrary gods, he snatched the ladder from its cradle and sprinted back to where he'd sensed her. She was there, now a pale smear in the darkness, dangling from the hull. He wasn't sure what she was holding on to, but she wasn't moving. Weariness spiraled along their connection like a poisonous vine.

"Lia, hold on!" he called to her, juggling the ladder. If most of the crew wasn't fast asleep at the other end of the ship, he'd have a sailor do this. His inexperienced hands made more work of the thing, tangling it once before he managed to hook it on the rail and toss the rope ladder over the side.

Swinging a leg over the rail, he gritted his teeth and hoped he wasn't about to make an end of himself in the dark, frothing sea. Muttering curses and prayers, he made his slow way down the twisting, slippery ladder. Spume and sweat soaked him until his entire body dripped by the time he reached her.

"Lia, do you hear me?" The darkness hid her features and the way her pale body swayed with the movement of the ship frightened him. "Lia!" He reached for her and almost fell off the ladder before he wrapped a rope around one arm. Cursing and fumbling, he managed to get his other arm around her waist, then had to pause, stymied. How was he going to get her to the deck?

While he was thinking, a shudder ran through her and she slipped an arm around his neck. She was ice cold, as soaked as he but without the meager protection of clothing. Twisting into him, she released whatever she'd been holding on to and wrapped her other arm around his neck, their bodies aligning on opposite sides of the ladder. Rune clutched her tight as they swung.

When they steadied, bumping to a relative standstill against the hull, Rune took a deep breath and rasped in her ear, "Lia, will you be a dear and rescue me?"

She chuckled, the sound and warmth of her breath infinitely welcome. Tremors of relief and cold shuddered down through his limbs and he shifted his grip to hold her and the ladder steady.

She shifted with him, bracing her feet on a rope rung, lightening her weight. "Just give me some time," she husked so low he strained to hear. "Then I'll climb."

"No, you're exhausted. You should hold onto my back. I'll climb."

She made a rough sound, disapproval or disbelief. Either way, she had a point. He'd barely gotten down this far on his own. With a weight on his back, he might dump them both in the ocean.

He acquiesced with a sigh. "So will you carry me, then?"

She gave another soft chuckle. He smiled as they dangled there in the wet dark, the cold wind whistling and plucking at them with greedy fingers. He curved his body as best he could to provide shelter for her, some protection from the wind and icy spume. She pressed her cold face to his throat, and a great surge of protective tenderness shocked him.

How could she mean so much to him in so little time? He knew almost nothing about her, yet imagining a future without her in it was painful. How could he love someone he didn't know? It seemed ridiculous, but he couldn't deny his connection to her. Her spirit spoke to him more strongly by the moment, the warmth of her affection and gratitude almost enough to chase away the night's chill.

"Much as I love holding slippery bare women, I have to say I'd prefer doing this in a hot bath."

She nodded, her torso expanding with a deep breath. Then she began unwinding her arms from around his neck with aching slowness. He grimaced in sympathy, supporting her as best he could while she started to climb the ladder. He followed, disconcerted by the extra twisting of the rope from her movements. They both climbed at a snail's pace, though he guessed if she was at her full strength she could shimmy up and down this ladder as though it was nothing. He pressed on, doing his best to ignore the bone-deep ache in his fingers. It would be worse for Lia.

When he stumbled over the rail, gasping his relief, he found her curled in a fetal position at his feet, body rigid and muscles locked with cold. Taking a few deep breaths to recover from the climb, he crouched and lifted her into his arms without a word. She didn't protest, which worried him, but he didn't have the breath to ask if she was all right.

He staggered to his cabin without seeing a soul. After setting her on a chair and wrapping her in a blanket, he lit a lantern and stripped off his wet clothes with clumsy speed. She said not a word, and he only thought of the impropriety after he was nude and rubbing warmth into his flesh with a towel. With a mental shrug, he yanked on warm, dry clothing.

Turning to her, he rubbed a towel over her hair and weaved hot eddies of air around her. He could tell he was making progress when her body relaxed enough to shiver, but he didn't like how much she shuddered. "You pushed yourself too hard," he said with a frown.

"No choice," she mumbled in reply, face buried in the blanket over her knees.

"I'm unable to give you a hot bath."

"I know."

"But you're still chilled."

She made a rough sound of amusement in her throat. "Let me guess. You want to come to bed with me and keep me warm."

He grinned, his worry easing a little. "I'm only thinking of you, darling," he said in a lascivious tone.

She snickered and raised her head. She was smiling, misty eyes tilted and glowing with good humor and trust. The sight made his heart lurch with simple happiness and a smidgen of terror. "Thanks for the rescue, but I'm not sleeping with you."

"Sleep is just what you need," he responded with an earnest frown. "Which you won't get with your teeth chattering away and your limbs shaking to pieces. What if I promise to stay clothed?"

She stared at him, smile fading. "Are you serious, Rune?"

His face heated with an unexpected blush and he broke eye contact, focusing on winnowing his fingers through her tangled hair. "You need heat. That's all I'm offering. Wild passion should wait until you have the strength for it."

She snorted, quiet for a moment. "I believe you. It's the nicest offer I've ever had from a man. You amaze me, Rune."

His face grew hotter. He said nothing.

"Can I ask you…?"

He stopped fussing with her hair and met her troubled gaze. "What is it?"

"Would you kiss me?"

Rune's eyebrows lifted off into the stars. That was just about the last thing he'd expected.

Her mouth twisted with humor. "I know, not fair. But when he, the prince I mean, when he kissed me, it was…different. I'm just wondering if it's a royal thing."

He wanted to smirk and tease, but it wouldn't be healthy or wise. Keeping his voice even, he asked, "Different in what way?"

Her gaze flickered, features settling into discomfort. She looked down with a jerky shrug. "It wasn't what I expected," she muttered.

"So now you'd like to compare techniques?"

"I was just curious, Rune. Never mind, it was a stupid idea." Bad temper and embarrassment colored her tone.

Rune bit the inside of his cheek hard to stop any further mischief. It went against his nature, but he refrained in the interest of keeping his body parts intact. Cupping her chin, he raised her face as he bent toward her, hesitating a breath away to read her eyes. Seeing no resistance, only curiosity, he pressed his lips to hers.

Rune wasn't sure what he thought would happen. Watching Destin kiss Lia had been a revelation, a confirmation of what he already knew of his cousin's passion. He'd nearly cheered when his soul brother lost control and felt without restraint for the first time in memory. He'd also experienced a pang of what could only be called worried jealousy when Lia responded to his cousin with equal fervor. So, he was as curious about this kiss as she.

He didn't expect the sudden burst of warm affection across their connection, a resonance of spirit like the dawning of the sun. Contentment and comfort flowed through him. He basked in the warmth and easy happiness for a moment before lifting his head.

She smiled and it reached her eyes, lighting the misty gray with tenderness. "That was nice," she murmured.

He realized he was also smiling. "Yes, it was."

Then her smile began to fade, a faint crease appearing between her brows. Twitching her chin out of his light clasp, she narrowed her eyes. "Why was it so strange?"

He straightened, trying to look innocent. "My kiss was strange?"

"No, and that's what's strange. What did you do to me?"

He chuckled and shook his head. "Nothing," he soothed, clasping her elbow and urging her to her feet.

"Horse dung," she snapped, though she allowed him to lead her to his bunk and tuck her under the covers. "You're a spirit weaver. What did you do?"

Rune knelt next to the bunk, brushing her hair back from her face and tucking it behind her ear. "Nothing,

Lia. It's not something I'm able to control. Every once in a great while, I will connect with someone, form a bond of spirit, but it's not deliberate. It usually means they're someone very important to me." He brushed his lips against her forehead and smiled down at her. "Will you sleep?"

She scowled at him. "Stop being so nice. It's creepy."

He chuckled again and rose to his feet. "Goodnight, Lia. Sleep well." She muttered something he couldn't hear, sounding disgruntled. He grinned, blowing out the lantern and heading for the door. When he reached it, he stepped out into the corridor, shutting the door behind him.

Then he let himself laugh, in sheer delight and wonder. He'd never had a soul sister. This was going to be interesting.

Rune waited in Destin's cabin. He'd considered heading for the upper deck to let the prince know Eylee'ai was alive and sleeping in his cabin. But he was in a mood to punish his cousin a little, let him flounder in the quicksand of his own making.

When Destin dragged his weary self through the door, Rune squelched a twinge of sympathy and met his look with raised eyebrows. "Finally had enough?"

"You could have lent a hand," Destin grumped, stumbling to a chair.

Rune linked his hands behind his head and sent the hammock into a gentle swing, staring at the ceiling. "I wasn't looking forward to getting thrown in the brig for punching my prince in the mouth."

Destin grunted. "Still feel like hitting me?"

"No."

"Why not?"

Rune swung the hammock and studied the planks above his head. One boasted an interesting knot, the shape resembling a woman in sensual motion.

Destin sighed. "All right, I'll ask. Have you seen the changeling?"

"Her name is Lia, you dolt. She's alive, though she has more bruises. Right now, she's fast asleep in my bed." He said the last with malicious emphasis.

Destin made a deep sound like the rumble of a waking volcano. But he said nothing.

Rune let him stew for a little bit before he added, "She was frozen solid. I offered to sleep with her, but all she took was a kiss."

Destin exploded to his feet, knocking the chair to the floor with a crash. "Damn it, Rune."

Rune launched out of the hammock and stalked up to his soul brother, ignoring his furious expression and balled fists. When they were standing toe-to-toe, Rune said in a low, determined voice, "You are not driving her away. She's too important. Agree to her bargain, Des. She'll use my cabin at night."

Destin fisted a hand in the front of Rune's shirt and gave him a rough shake. "You want me to harbor an enemy just so you can have a bedmate?"

Rune's hands balled and he took a deep breath, working hard to control his temper. "Gods above, you try my patience. I'm not the one who wants her, cousin."

Destin let him go with an angry shove, pacing once around the small room then pausing at the desk. Placing his hands flat on its surface, he leaned there, staring at the stacks of histories with his shoulders knotted. Rune watched him, feeling another twinge of sympathy, but he waited in silence. His anger had faded, but not enough to keep him from making it easier on his soul brother.

"I can't have her aboard."

"Look the other way. I've already had the crew stow her things in my cabin."

Destin whirled, glaring at him.

Rune shrugged. "They believe I'm smitten. If she slips aboard and into my cabin at night, they'll blame me, not you."

Destin settled a hip on the desk, his scarred face conflicted in a way Rune rarely witnessed. "Are you, Rune? Are you smitten?"

He studied his cousin, measuring the trouble in his eyes, reading the conflicting concerns in his brother's soul. No, he wasn't ready to hear all of it. Rune gave him what he needed without creating other crises. "I do care for her, Des, but not in that way."

Destin looked down, but not before Rune saw relief rush through him, followed by dismay. Rune sighed, aggravated for a dozen different reasons. A flare of old rage caught him by surprise, hatred for what the king had done to his son. What he was still doing. Not for the first time, Rune wondered if he was capable of regicide. But he'd never known if that would open the cage door and set his soul brother free, or fuse the cage shut forever.

"You kissed her," Destin said in a careful tone.

Rune pursed his lips, then decided on the truth. "She was curious."

"She was?"

Rune grinned. "Apparently your kiss was different,

not what she expected. She wanted to know if all royals were the same."

Destin was still looking down, but a flush darkened his skin and tension stiffened his muscles. "And are we?"

"Afraid not," he said with deliberate cheer and headed back to his hammock. "Goodnight." Rolling into his blanket, he faced the wall with a silent snicker. The quiet behind him spoke volumes, burning curiosity and unasked questions thickening the air. But if Destin was ever going to leave the cage, he would have to take the first step himself.

Silence reigned for a long moment. Then Destin extinguished the lantern and shuffled to his bed. *Poor Des,* Rune thought, all humor lost.

Chapter 9

Destin dreamt of fire, of hands buried in rich, dark silk and bodies twined in aching perfection, of spice on his tongue and softness on his skin, a conflagration of senses. He dreamt of Eylee'ai and woke to scorch marks and despair.

He sat up, staring at the burnt edges of his blanket and the streaks of ash on the wall, evidence of his humiliation and weakness. He'd never lost control like this in his life. Never once had he suspected he could weave fire in his sleep or lose control of it. He was falling apart piece by piece, destroying his sense of self and failing his father. Why was this happening now?

Rune interrupted his dim horror, stepping into the cabin with a tray full of food. "Ah good, you're awake." His gaze went from Destin to the burn marks and he paused, eyebrows lifting. Destin's despair multiplied and unfolded in him like a grim disease. His weakness was no longer a secret. He waited for the recriminations, but Rune only said, "Must've been a good dream."

With a waggle of his eyebrows and a smirk, Rune continued to the small table and set down the tray. Whistling through his teeth, he fixed himself a plate and sat down, pausing with a fork in his hand to glance over at Destin. "I'm not waiting for you, brother. I'm starving." Cutting an enormous bite of flat cake, he stuffed it into his mouth and chewed with enthusiastic difficulty.

Shaking his head, Destin rose to his feet and moved to stand by the table, staring at his cousin with a frown. "I almost burned down the cabin and you have nothing else to say?"

Rune sent him a comical look, all wide eyes and bulging cheeks. Swallowing with obvious effort, he muttered through the remaining bite, "Don't be a dimwit, Des. You mastered fire when you were only twelve and put your own teacher to shame. You're not going to burn down anything in your sleep."

His cousin's easy dismissal didn't reassure him. He could still feel the heat of the dream, could still feel how much he'd wanted the burn. "I should have better control," he protested, sinking into the seat opposite Rune.

His cousin paused in his attack on the flat cake, eyeing him with uncharacteristic seriousness. "Control is an illusion, so I've been told," he said with a peculiar half-smile. "Be easy, Des. There was no harm done, was there?"

Destin scowled. "Not this time."

"Well, next time I promise to wake you before you reach the best part." Rune cast him a taunting grin, then stuffed another huge bite in his mouth.

Destin folded his arms across his chest and glanced at the porthole. The light was strong, the morning already well begun. "Is she off my ship yet?" he asked in a hard tone.

Rune smiled and didn't answer.

Shoving to his feet, Destin stomped to the door and slammed his way out of it. For some reason, Rune was determined to make his life miserable. It gave him a vague sense of panic and loss to think his cousin had switched sides, Rune acting on the changeling's behalf now instead of Destin's. Stalking past the guest cabin without a glance, he made his way to the upper deck and found the captain at the helm. The captain informed him the changeling had left the ship early in the morning.

Hiding his relief, Destin turned to the thread of shore in the distance. "When do we land?"

"Late morning, sire. You put us ahead of schedule last night."

He didn't respond to the approval in the captain's voice, turning aft to search the horizon. "Any sign?"

"None, your highness."

Destin nodded and left the captain, returning to his cabin to wash and change before scrounging what little breakfast his cousin had left him. Rune had disappeared and Destin took a moment to imagine his cousin mooning over the rail after the changeling before he dismissed them both from his thoughts. He had much larger concerns, like what he would find at the sanctuary and what to do about his uncle.

He spent several hours compiling his thoughts, memorizing information, and planning before a member of the crew came to inform him they were about to weigh anchor. With a sense of anticipation, Destin left his cabin and strode out on deck, lifting his face into the wind and taking a deep breath.

The day was clear, sunlight strong and the air fresh with salty hints of fish and earth. The ship drifted in the gentle waters of a bay, a sheltered nook shaped by a finger of land jutting out into the ocean. The port lay in the sheltering curve of the promontory, a small fishing village with no docking accommodations for such a large ship. But they could skiff to shore, purchase supplies, and ask after the sanctuary.

Destin lifted his eyes to the horizon and the craggy edge of a mountain in the distance. If the Vessel sanctuary was there, as the histories indicated, he could either sail further up the coast to shorten the distance across land or set out from here. The advantage of going to ground at this point was to reduce his uncle's strength and level the playing field. He didn't doubt Storm would follow him across land. From the probing questions his uncle had asked in the past, Destin knew Storm had no idea where to look for the Vessel. He was unaware of the existence of the sanctuary, so he would have to follow Destin wherever he led.

Studying the gray and cloud-shrouded edges of the mountain, Destin calculated the supplies and necessities he would need for a fast trek across country, while a part of him marveled at the enormity and power of the jagged spikes of rock. His home was a low, rolling fertile land. He hadn't been to a mountain range since he was a child. Had they been on a holiday or a state visit? He couldn't recall.

"Amazing," Rune murmured, appearing at his elbow. "Look how the clouds part and give way. Amazing to think Earth Mother could touch Father Sky in such a way."

"You were with us," Destin said, still thinking of the long ago trip to cold reaches and incredible amounts of snow.

As usual, Rune didn't need an explanation to follow his thoughts. "Yes. The Earth Keepers had demanded an audience of our king. Do you recall the flat slider made of bark? I've never been so cold or excited, sliding on it off a cliff."

"It wasn't a cliff, just a foothill."

Rune grinned, eyes far away and gleaming. "It felt like a cliff."

"It felt like a fast slide into a tree. Didn't you crack your head?"

"Only a little."

Destin snorted but didn't comment, content to let his cousin enjoy the memory. It had been fun, until he'd seen blood on the snow. He'd had to drag his cousin back to their camp on the sled after he'd passed out trying to climb the hill for more. "This mountain has snow only on the top. I wonder how far up the side the monks live."

"Are we going to find out?" Rune glanced at him with a curious tilt of his head.

"We'll head over land from here," Destin confirmed. "Let's leave Uncle Storm behind." *And the changeling,* he thought but didn't add aloud.

With a strange little smile, Rune looked across the landscape to the mountain. "Well, this ought to be interesting."

Destin's brow contracted and he smoothed his expression with an effort, studying his cousin. "Rune, did you speak with the changeling this morning?"

Rune turned to stare at him with a tightening of his features. "Say her name, Des," he snapped.

Blinking a little at this sudden hostility, Destin decided he needed answers more than he needed to argue with his cousin. "Did you speak with Eylee'ai this morning?"

Rune's expression eased and he turned to the view again with a nod. "She was awake early. We spoke over breakfast."

"And? What did she have to say?" When Rune's face shifted into furtive humor, Destin sighed and pinched the bridge of his nose. "Gods, Rune, swear to me you didn't tell her where we're going."

"It wasn't necessary," his cousin said. When Destin dropped his hand to stare at him, Rune met his gaze with solemn intensity. "She already knew."

"What? How?" he barked.

Rune shrugged. "As I said, she knows more than she discloses."

"But the sanctuary of the Vessel isn't widely known."

"Perhaps she reads," Rune responded in a dry tone, his hazel eyes cutting. "I hear some changelings know how."

Destin folded his arms over his chest and tried not to glower. "What else did she say?"

"She doesn't want you to go there," Rune answered with a reluctance that made Destin's chest tighten. His cousin looked down as though ashamed. "So I assume something critical to finding the Vessel lies at the sanctuary."

"Why do you trust her?" he asked, voice harsh with a sense of betrayal. "This could be another distraction, a way to lead us off the right path."

Rune shook his head and turned away. "She can't lie to me," he said over his shoulder. Then he walked aft.

But you can lie to me, Destin thought with a sudden spear of pain through his chest. No, he wouldn't start suspecting his soul brother. It would be like suspecting his hand of rebellion.

He looked at the port and the rising land beyond. Eylee'ai was out there waiting to thwart him. A wild surge of anticipation took him by surprise and reminded him of his silken dreams and scorch marks. "Damn you," he muttered into the wind. But he couldn't be sure if he was damning her or himself. With a grim clench of his jaw, he went to find the captain.

Several hours and a heap of aggravation later, Destin started on the road to the sanctuary. The beast under him had come from a farm but wasn't a draft horse. He was a barely broken stallion, gray and feral as the changeling. The farmer had made a show of reluctance to sell, but relief gleamed in his eyes when he took the gold and handed over the reins. The man had fought much harder to keep the mare Rune now rode, a slim, brown beauty with far more manners than her rider.

Destin made the decision to set out on his own without the contingent of men he'd first thought to bring. They were sailors not soldiers, and with a small party he could move fast enough to stay well ahead of his uncle.

The only other person in their little traveling band was a young sailor named Cleave, who had begged to join them with solemn promises not to slow them down. He now bounced along behind the horses on the back of a sprightly donkey. The sight was pure entertainment, but Destin hoped the boy wouldn't be more trouble than he was worth.

"When someone says you can't miss it, you know they're leading you down the garden path, right?" Rune called from behind him. The villagers had given them information about the road to the sanctuary, a little-used trail leading into the foothills. No one in the fishing village seemed to know the place was still populated. They didn't understand why he wanted to visit the ruins. Destin had pretended to be a scholar and historian, gaining them cheerful, if vague and somewhat contradicting, directions.

"We'll find it," Destin answered, tightening the reins as the gray danced under him and pulled at the bit. "Here, you devil," he growled, thumping the stallion's flexing neck with rough affection. "Want to run, do you? Now's your chance." Turning in his saddle, he called to his cousin, "I'm off ahead. Don't fall too far behind. Keep the boy moving," he added, nodding to Cleave.

Rune gave him a salute and a wide grin, which he returned in a rush of energy. He'd always loved to ride, to feel the power and speed in the animal beneath him and revel in a kind of freedom. It had always ended too soon even if he'd been riding all day, and a part of him grieved to dismount and return the horse to its stall.

Crouching low over the gray's neck and grabbing a fistful of mane, he whispered, "Go," and dug in his heels. The stallion laid back his ears, screamed a triumphant challenge, and leapt into a full-out gallop. The landscape blurred into green and brown, power flowing under him and through him, exhilarating and breathtaking.

Still Destin urged the gray faster, controlling only his direction to stay on the hard-packed road, allowing him the joy of speed, the delight of freedom. Allowed himself a moment to forget he was a prince with a duty and a mission, and a life that was not his own. He simply existed, breathed and flowed with the motion of the animal under him, not hearing his own laughter.

As always, it ended too soon. The gray slowed on his own and Destin settled back in the saddle, reining the big stallion to a trot and then to a walk. The stallion was blowing hard and his skin gleamed with sweat, but his neck arched and his gait held a strut that made Destin grin. "Still ready for more, eh?" The gray flicked his ears and nickered, a companionable sound. Destin patted his neck. "Yes, it was a good run. You were fast as the wind. That's what I'll call you," he decided. "Wind."

The gray tossed his head as though in approval and Destin chuckled, casting a glance behind him. He had the road to himself, Rune and Cleave nowhere in sight. The sun spread warmth in patches over him through the trees. The forest was thickening, with fewer fields and more pine, and the road had begun a steady incline. It would take them over a day to reach the mountain, perhaps two, even on a horse as fast as Wind. An unexpected, peculiar happiness swept over him, a joy and contentment he was having trouble identifying.

He was alone.

He couldn't recall the last time he'd been so isolated. Shouldn't this make him lonesome? Perhaps even concern him a little, since this was a strange land with unknown dangers? Instead, he was happy, excited. He was free.

He swallowed hard, guilt needling him in a thousand places. *No, that's wrong,* he thought with a determined shake of his head. *I'm not escaping. There's nothing to escape. I'm proud to serve my people, proud my father entrusted me with this mission.* It was the truth, yet somehow rang false in this place with its earth smells and rustles of life, with the strong motion of the animal under him.

Frowning, he raised his eyes to the jut of snow-capped rock in the distance and reached back to touch the shape of the books in his saddle bag. *What do you suppose your father will do with the Vessel?* The memory of Eylee'ai's voice taunted him. "He'll save the world from people such as you," he muttered in furious response, then went still. It was the truth but it also sounded wrong. He meant fanatics, people who destroy what others create. But was that what his father meant?

He shook his head again and nudged the gray into a trot. "He's my king," he snarled through clenched teeth, ignoring the flattening of the stallion's ears. "My father. He'll do what's right for his people."

He rode on, ignoring the small voice in the back of his mind asking what was right for his people.

The sun had settled on the rim of the world when Destin found Eylee'ai's first obstacle. He stared at the mound of trees collapsed across the road and the surrounding thick forest for a long moment, then sighed and dismounted. Well, they'd needed a fire for the evening anyway.

Leading Wind a distance back the way he'd come, he secured the horse next to a small stream with plenty of grass to keep him occupied before returning to the road block. Calling fire was too easy. Thoughts of Eylee'ai brought it to the surface of his skin. He would burn away the block of trees, trying not to set the forest on fire at the same time.

Ordinarily, he wouldn't worry about control, but as of late, it hadn't been his strong suit. With a frown of concentration, he let flame spring to life on his fingertips and dance white in the air, fueled by the energy at his core. Laying his hands on a fallen tree trunk, he gave the fire other fuel, encouraging it to feed and spread.

The fire turned lively orange, crackling and smoking as it consumed the still-green trees. Destin stepped back and watched, focusing hard on the fire's roaring energy. Whenever it crept toward the forest or sparked into the air, he turned it or absorbed it, containing its destruction to the road block.

He was so intent on the blaze he wasn't aware of his cousin at his shoulder. Only when he sensed wind eddies did he realize Rune was beside him, helping to contain the raging fire.

"Eylee'ai?" Rune called over the roar of the flames.

Destin nodded.

"What in the name of the gods did she change into?" Rune gestured to the toppled, uprooted trees.

Destin shrugged, wishing his cousin would drop the subject. Bringing her to mind wreaked havoc with his control. Thinking cold, sane thoughts of mountain reaches and ancient history, he focused the fire's heat at the center of the road block, urging the flame to consume the wood to ash in a wide enough path to allow them passage. Then he dampened it, pulling its energy into himself and allowing it to flow down into the earth, until only one tree, small enough to be left alone, was still ablaze at its end.

"All right, let's set up camp."

Rune frowned at the burning trunk. "In the road?"

"Worried we'll get trampled?" Destin gestured to the deserted road. He hadn't met a single traveler all day. "Where's Cleave?"

"Back where you left your nasty beast. Ill-tempered nag, that one."

Destin contained a ferocious smile with an effort and started back toward the horses. "Wind has his own mind."

"Wind? You named him?" Rune grinned in the growing twilight, teeth flashing. "I named my girl, too. Take a guess."

Lia, he thought but didn't say. It revealed too much about where his mind wandered. "Brownie?" he guessed instead.

"Insulting," Rune sneered. "Her name is Sugar, because she's sweet as."

"Very inventive," Destin said with a somber nod.

Rune punched him in the shoulder and called him something rude. He would've responded in kind, but Cleave's curled form and moaning distress distracted him.

"Sorry, your highness. Muscles all cramped up on me. Ain't much of a rider," the boy gasped when Destin knelt by his side.

"You should have mentioned that back in the village," Destin growled, stretching the youngster's limbs out with no regard for Cleave's whimpers.

"You'da left me behind."

"And I may still send you back."

"Please don't, sire. I'll be right in the mornin'."

"Why do you want to come along so badly?"

Cleave didn't reply, looking at Destin with wide,

pleading eyes. Rune gave a discreet cough at his elbow and pressed a small container into Cleave's hand. "Rub this everywhere it pains you. The prince and I will be down the road at the fire when you're able to join us."

Destin frowned at his cousin but decided to hold his judgment until morning. If the boy was unable to ride, he'd be on his way back to port, at a walk if necessary.

Rune gathered Sugar's reins and turned the gentle mare toward the glow of the fire, but when Destin reached to do the same with Wind, the stallion snapped at him. Quick as a snake, Destin grabbed hold of the horse's tender upper lip. The big gray went still, ears coming forward.

Destin looked into a dark, equine eye and said calmly, "Now, I'll have none of that, you devil. Remember who has the grain." Letting go, he took hold of the reins and led the horse toward the light, gratified when the animal followed with no more protest than a soft snort. Yes, he and Wind were getting along just fine.

With the ease of long practice earned through plenty of hunting trips, Destin and Rune tended to the horses, laid out pallets, built a makeshift lean-to in case it rained, and fixed a quick, cold dinner of salted meat, biscuits, and fruit. Cleave took a long time to join them, limping along with the disgruntled donkey in his wake. Rune ordered the boy to sit while he took care of the animal. Cleave huddled close to the fire with his head down, the picture of misery and shame.

With a sigh, Destin handed the boy food and watched with some amusement as he gulped it down like a starved wolf. "I require someone to help carry the load, to tend the animals and take a turn keeping watch at night. I do not need an inexperienced boy with blisters on his behind."

"Yes, sire. I'm very sorry," Cleave whispered to the ground, his face turning ruddy in the firelight.

"If you are unable to sit the saddle in the morning, tell me. No sense crippling yourself for a bit of adventure. Understood?"

Cleave nodded, clutching a piece of biscuit in one white-knuckled fist. "I won't let you down, my prince."

Destin sighed again. "Lie down. You'll feel better for it. I'll take first watch."

The boy cocooned himself in a blanket and lay down with a muffled moan. Rune flashed Destin a grin. "Bets?" he mouthed, tipping his head toward Cleave. Destin gave his cousin a quelling frown. Rune responded with a careless shrug and reclined on his pallet. Ankles crossed and hands tucked under his head, Rune stared up at the sky in silence.

Destin knew his cousin. He wasn't preparing for sleep. He was waiting. Destin waited with him, listening to the night and wondering if he expected the changeling. Apparently, he was only waiting for Cleave to fall asleep.

At the first soft snore, Rune lifted his head to study the boy, then propped himself on an elbow to grin at Destin. "I'll tell you why he wanted to come with us. He's head-over-heels in love."

Destin schooled his face to show only mild interest. "With you?"

"Amusing. No, he's utterly gone on our tree-toppler. Which is incredible, by the way," he muttered, glancing past the fire at the mass of half-burnt wood and ash. "You should have seen him mooning over Lia before she left. So, will you bet on whether he'll still want to come with us in the morning?" Rune's grin was sharp.

Oh, terrific, Destin thought, eyes falling to the tuft of sun-bleached hair sprouting from Cleave's blanket. *Another one.* Another conquest for the changeling, another defector to the dark side, another body he might have to go through to remove her from the picture. He should have brought the captain. At least he wouldn't have stopped Destin from doing whatever he needed to do to the troublesome female.

"You look thrilled," Rune said with a snicker.

"Go to sleep. I'll wake you when it's your watch."

"Jealousy adds such a pleasant green sparkle to your eyes."

"Still your tongue and go to sleep, Rune."

Rune complied, chuckling as he rolled into his blanket. When the night was quiet, Destin brooded into the fire and thought about things he'd never consider in the light of day.

Chapter 10

Ash covered everything. The wind had strengthened sometime in the night and tossed the stuff around with wild abandon. They were all covered in dark streaks and dusted with flecks, and Destin was profoundly grateful. The streaks and ash camouflaged scorch marks from yet another fiery dream.

His sleeping mind had conjured Eylee'ai, her silken limbs and silkier hair wrapped around him, gray eyes dark with urgent need as she whispered his name. Each time he recalled the dream, he lost his breath and had to pause to get it back, to steady the tremors rolling down his spine to his extremities. He had to squelch the fire roiling in his gut.

Cleave hadn't noticed anything, too focused on being the perfect helper this morning, but Rune sent Destin several odd looks. His cousin held his tongue, though, and they broke camp with a minimum of bother. Cleave had insisted he could ride the donkey, but Rune shook his head and burdened the smaller animal with his pack so Cleave could ride Sugar with him.

Destin turned a blind eye to the new arrangement. He should be sending the boy back to the village, but the ship might have left by now and he was preoccupied this morning with his own concerns, with his own weakness. How could he chastise Cleave for slowing them down when he was a fiery explosion waiting to happen? He mounted Wind and set out in grim silence.

Rune followed with Cleave, the donkey's reins tied to Sugar's saddle. The little beast protested this arrangement until Sugar turned her head and nickered at him. Then he trotted by her side as though he'd turned into her foal. When Rune laughed, it eased Destin's tension somewhat. Rune had a clear view straight to Destin's soul. If he was in any danger of erupting into flame, his cousin wouldn't be so relaxed.

The day was windier and grew colder as they progressed further into the foothills. They retrieved thick coats and gloves out of their packs when the sky clouded over and stole the warmth of the sun, but Destin wouldn't allow them to pause. He ran Wind when the stallion grew restless, though he didn't enjoy it as he had the previous day. He was too distracted by the end of his night and the mountain looming closer. By midday, they found what had to be the path to the sanctuary. It was small but well-worn, leading toward the mountain while the road curved to stay in the foothills. A neat pile of stones marked the junction.

"Well, I suppose this is clear enough," Rune commented.

Destin cocked an eyebrow at his cousin. "You can't miss it."

Rune made a face at the reminder. "If we find ourselves at some little witch-house in the woods, we're stopping for dinner."

"Fair enough," Destin muttered and urged Wind onto the new path. He hoped they'd be dining with monks once night fell.

As pines gave way to scrub clinging between rocky

ledges and boulders, the mountain's shadow seemed to swallow the world and dim the air. Twilight was fast approaching when they encountered Eylee'ai's second obstacle. Wind snorted and danced beneath him while Destin studied her handiwork with a measure of admiration. She'd chosen her spot well. The pile of stones obscured the path. With a wall of mountain on one side and a sheer drop on the other, they'd have no choice but to go over the pile or go back.

However, Destin was a master of earth. This obstacle wouldn't slow him long.

"How did she manage this?" Rune called behind him.

"I would assume she started an avalanche."

"Seems too deliberate."

Rune was right. There was no spillover or rush of smaller stones, just a pile of medium-sized boulders precisely where he couldn't slip around them. Had she carried them here, one by one?

"Gods have mercy, she must be worn through." Rune's voice brimmed with sympathy and Destin scowled at the rock.

"Are you talking about L-Lia?" Cleave stuttered.

Destin scowled harder. Instead of answering, he closed his eyes and sent his earth sense into the pile, questing for weakness. If he pushed there and there… The pile shuddered, groaned, and shifted toward the sheer drop. When the key stones fell, the entire mass disappeared over the edge in a rush of movement and a roar of sound. A few base stones remained, which Destin lifted into the air and tipped over the drop after the rest.

Rune snickered. "Don't tell her how easily you

cleared it. She'll tear your throat out."

Destin hid a triumphant grin. She'd hardly slowed him down this time. Triumph gave way to foolishness, though. It was dimwitted to feel so proud of something almost any earth weaver could accomplish. Clearing his throat, he nudged Wind into motion.

When their path darkened too much to see, Destin wove a ball of fire to light their way. Wind shied at first, rolling his eyes at Destin, but calmed after a few words of reassurance. His ears flicked back and forth, though, and his proud head stayed up and alert like the lead stallion in a herd.

Destin gritted his teeth and dismounted, suspecting the changeling of yet another surprise. All she would have to do is panic the horses enough to bolt and they'd all end up at the bottom of the mountain. "Walk from here," he ordered, wondering how far they'd have to climb before they reached the sanctuary. So far, he hadn't seen a good place to camp. It would be a long, weary night.

The path grew steeper then disappeared between cliff faces. Destin stepped into the narrow space, staring upward into darkness with a sense of foreboding. Was she there? Would she tumble rock down on them? Sending his earth sense questing along the cliff faces, he tugged Wind into motion and led them upward. They hovered in the claustrophobic space for an eternity, every sound magnified and echoing, until it seemed they'd entered the throat of a huge and hungry beast, ready to devour them at any moment.

When Destin stumbled out into open ground, it was a shock to his senses. He swayed, blinking bleary eyes and fighting to understand what he was seeing. The flat ground under foot was springy with tough grass. A well-lit wooden structure stood beside a jumble of leaning stone. Cliffs of rock surrounded the whole area, rising high to end in jagged peaks against the open sky. The clouds had broken, giving him glimpses of stars. The wind gusted cold and sharp against his numb face.

"What is it?" Rune mumbled at his side.

"Sanctuary," he rasped in response and plodded forward, too tired and sense-shocked to discuss it.

It seemed to take forever to cross the flat plain to the alluring lights of the wooden building. When they reached it, the double doors opened in a blinding flood of warmth and light, spilling a mass of people out onto the stone stoop.

"Welcome! Welcome your highness, young sirs," boomed a jovial voice. Destin focused through the light on a short, tubby figure with twinkling, dark eyes and a wild mass of gray hair. "This is the Bre'anah'met Monastery. You are cold and weary. Please enter and be welcome."

Destin stared at him, numbness fading on a surge of alarm. "You know who I am?"

"We've been expecting you. Please, your mounts are also in need of warmth and rest. Young Ebreck'an will care for them."

A young man darted forward but skidded to a stop when Destin jerked up a hand. "How do you know us?" he asked, gazing over the crowd to assess them for hostility. He didn't find any overt signs, but their thick tunics could hide many weapons.

"Eylee'ai told us of your visit, of course. Won't you come in? I am Elder Yel'estya and this is my flock." He gestured to the surrounding monks before noticing Destin's tense form with a crease between his brows. "We are a peaceful people, Prince Destin. You will come to no harm here."

"He's telling the truth." Eylee'ai appeared, sliding between monks like a cat, disgust in every line of her face and form. Her hair was still braided, but now she wore a long gown, elegant and even stranger in this place than her other outfit had been. "He won't hurt you. He won't even tell you to leave. The gods know I tried, but the fool means to welcome you with open arms no matter what I say." She cast the monk a seething glare then sighed and turned back to the open doors. "You might as well come in and make yourselves at home."

He believed her, the defeat in the slump of her shoulders convincing him more than the acid in her tone. He followed to keep an eye on her, asking the monk as he passed, "This is the sanctuary of the Vessel of Power?"

"This is the Sky and Earth monastery. The sanctuary lies beyond. But surely you would rather eat and sleep now? Morning is soon enough to see it."

Destin tore his eyes from Eylee'ai's retreating back to glance down at the round monk, measuring his honesty. "You wouldn't try to keep me from it?"

The elder smiled, eyes sparkling. "On the contrary, you must see it. When the light is good and you are rested, yes?" His round cheeks bobbled when he nodded.

"We would be grateful for your hospitality," Destin answered with grave respect. He wasn't sure he believed this good fortune, but he wouldn't start questioning it until he ran into trouble. Stepping across the threshold of the monastery, he looked around the interior.

The double doors opened into a great room filled with many tables and ending in an enormous fireplace. Stairs rose to either side of the double doors, leading to a second floor ringed with railing and doors. Destin assumed those were the sleeping quarters. Of the dozen or so monks, most were older with a handful of men Destin's age or younger. All of them wore rough-spun tunics in various earthy shades, thick and heavy in deference to the cold weather.

Eylee'ai stood at the fireplace, staring down into the flames with her arms folded, the feminine elegance of her form and dress contrasting with the residents. Her gown was pale blue and simple, long-sleeved and high-collared, the hem trailing behind her. Destin suspected another borrowed outfit but couldn't deny the draw of her slim back, the curve nestling into her small waist before swelling into the rise of hips and bottom.

His palms itched with the urge to trace that curve and he turned away, facing the elder. "Do you have stables?"

"Nothing so formal, but we have a small barn to keep your animals warm and dry, plus hay enough to feed them. Will you honor us at our table? Our food may be simple, but it is filling."

"Thank you. We are most grateful."

"Excellent. Roust the cook! Tonight we feast!" the elder bellowed, to the amusement of his fellow monks. One grizzled man rolled his eyes and stomped toward the end of the great room past the fireplace. Eylee'ai watched him go, her mouth pinched, before returning her attention to the fire.

Hopelessly drawn, Destin succumbed and crossed the great room to join her at the fire, keeping his itching palms at the small of his back. She ignored him, lips pressed into a tight line. "Eylee'ai." Her head snapped up, eyes wide and mouth softening. This was the first time he'd called her by name. "Do I have you to thank for the deadfall and the rock pile?"

She shifted, wary eyes flickering. "I had to try. Guess they didn't hold you back for long. I didn't think you'd get here until tomorrow."

"They were good tries," he murmured, surprising himself with his conciliatory tone. What was he trying to do, comfort her? He must be more exhausted than he thought. "What did you say to the monks?"

"Does it matter?" she said with a little jerk of her chin. "You'll get what you came for."

"The Vessel isn't here."

She shrugged then sighed. "I'm so tired," she breathed, and he nearly took her into his arms. Swallowing hard, he kept his hands behind his back, clutching a wrist tight enough to grind bone. What was wrong with him?

She made an aimless gesture before touching fingertips to her forehead. He noticed for the first time how she trembled, how pale her skin was against the dark circles under her eyes. His throat tightened, almost choking him with dismay.

"Enjoy your stay, prince," she muttered, turning away from him.

She took three steps and bumped into Rune, who did what Destin had struggled so hard not to do, and wrapped his arms around her. "Lia, are you all right?" his cousin asked with palpable tenderness.

It ripped something in Destin, this proof of what he'd suspected. No matter what Rune said, he was enamored, as lost to her as the hovering Cleave. His cousin, his soul brother, was in love with their enemy. It hurt more than he'd expected, startling him into stillness and silence. He could only stand and watch his truest friend betray him.

Rune lifted his head, blood draining from his face when he met Destin's gaze. And still he spoke gently to their enemy. "You're exhausted, Lia. Go lie down. Cleave, will you see her to her room?"

The sailor leapt forward, even though Lia said she was fine. They moved away, but Destin didn't watch them go. He stared into his cousin's pained eyes and let his anger grow. Anger was easier than hurt.

"Don't, Des," Rune said in a low, tight voice when they were out of hearing range. "I haven't betrayed you. I never would."

"You love her. What have you told her of us? What have you given away while you stroke and croon over her?"

Rune's hands snapped into fists. He stepped close enough for them to be almost nose to nose. "I would never betray you. But yes, I do love her. She and I have a spirit bond. Not just a connection but a bond. She's my soul sister, Des. You and she, you're both a part of me. Stop forcing me to choose."

While Destin was still absorbing the shock, Rune spun on his heel and stalked over to the monks. After a moment of conversation, one led him upstairs. Staring after his cousin, Destin realized he could no longer feel his hand. Releasing his wrist, he held the numb appendage out in front of him, flexing clumsy fingers and waiting for the pain. The other pain, the one in his chest, grew larger, eclipsing anger.

He was losing Rune, bit by bit, to something far more serious than an affair of the flesh or the heart. Spirit weaving was a gift from the gods. How could he fight a bond the gods had forged for his friend? Should he fight it? Why had the gods chosen a changeling, and his sworn enemy, to be Rune's soul sister?

He stared at his waking hand, needles of sensation pricking his fingers. He had no answers. But even more frightening, he wasn't sure he would ever find any.

Clenching his hand into a fist, he moved to the tables and sat with the monks, nodding with absent attention to their comments and eating without tasting a thing. When a monk offered to show him to a sleeping chamber, he followed without a word and dropped down on a cold cot in a sparse little room. Mind as numb as his hand had been, he let chilly sleep swallow him whole.

Chapter 11

"You know I hate being cold," Lia muttered, wrapping the woolen blanket tighter around her shoulders and sending the elder a narrow look.

He gave her his usual bland smile. "You are a young lady, Eylee'ai, not a monk. You must dress like a young lady."

"Your clothes are warmer, Yel. And where did you get this dress? It smells like yak."

His smile didn't falter a bit. "I don't believe I've ever smelled yak."

Flipping the blanket off one arm, she held the sleeve out to him with a pointed lift of her eyebrows. "Be my guest."

He threw back his head and laughed the same old laugh, right from the belly and loud enough to wake the dead.

Lia grinned and huddled under the blanket again. If that didn't get the prince out of bed, nothing would. If they were going to go through with this farce, then she wanted to get it over with as soon as possible. "Explain to me one more time why you can't just tell the prince no."

"Because he must see it, my dear. He among all of them knew where to begin. That makes him the one who must search."

"But he's on the wrong side! Why can't you

choose to stop him?"

Yel'estya gave his head a mournful shake, jowls drooping. "We cannot interfere in the test of the gods."

"Why not? You're part of this world whether you want to be or not. And you know which side should win. It sure isn't his side. So why can't you choose to protect the Vessel?"

"Because we were told not to."

She growled her aggravation, thumping a fist on the table. "By who? The Earth Keepers and Ephemerals? Who made them the score keepers?"

"The gods, of course."

Looking into his troubled dark eyes and seeing the pain swimming in their depths, she sighed and relented. "Always throwing the gods at me," she grumbled with a sour grimace and a shiver.

"Never listening when you should," he countered with a weak chuckle. "Tell me more about the young man who touched you so familiarly. You said he was the prince's cousin. You didn't mention you knew him quite so well."

She snickered at the disapproving pucker of his mouth, wondering what he'd do if she told him Rune had seen her naked. "You want the icky details?"

He shook his head at her, the prissy expression on his face priceless. "You have no shame, Eylee'ai. I would like to know if his intentions are honorable."

"Rune? Honorable?" She burst into real laughter, remembering a few of Rune's more colorful comments. "Oh, Yel, he's about the furthest thing. But don't worry," she added. "Rune and I are just friends."

"Darling, I'm crushed," Rune drawled behind her. When she turned to look at him, he slapped a hand to his chest and staggered. "I may never recover from the rejection and pain."

She snorted. "You just need breakfast. Sit down."

"Breakfast?" He sat with a hopeful look.

Yel chortled. "A rascal with an appetite! You remind me of myself at your age. Be careful you don't grow to be my size." He winked and patted his rotund midsection.

"Yipes!" Rune said with a dimpled smile. "Warning well taken, sir."

While Yel chuckled, Cleave joined them with respectful nods and an unsure smile.

"Good rising, Lady Lia. Are you well?"

"Well enough to smack you if you call me a lady one more time," she retorted but smiled to ease the reprimand. "I'm guessing you're hungry, too." At his nod, she continued, "Then somebody should get the prince out of bed or he'll get a cold breakfast."

"Oh, he's already at the ruins," Rune said in a casual voice, though his eyes skipped away from hers.

"What?" She launched to her feet, shoving the bench back in the process. "When? I didn't see him leave."

Yel cleared his throat, looking no more comfortable than Rune. "He rose before the sun. I fear he did not sleep well."

"Oh, poor man," she drawled, climbing over the bench with a toss of her skirts and stalking toward the door. "Let's go."

"But what about breakfast?"

"Move it, Rune."

The moment she stepped outside, the cold cut right through the blanket and her dress as though the cloth didn't exist. Sucking in a shocked breath, she clenched her jaw and scurried for the ruins, wishing she could change into a wolf or a bear, something with lots of fur to withstand the cold. But that would destroy this gods-cursed dress and upset Yel. And she was not stripping naked in this wind. Muttering to herself, she darted into the darkened interior of what used to be a great, columned entryway. The leaning stones cut the wind somewhat, but she was still freezing.

"Curse all princes and their…" She broke off with a little cry when she ran into something a lot warmer than stone.

"And our what?" Destin asked, hands clasping her arms to steady her. It had the opposite effect, her knees wobbling with an alarming weakness.

"Ah…great fashion sense?" she ventured, staring at his warm coat and backing out of his grip. "You wouldn't have another one of those, would you?"

"A coat? No."

"Blast," she said with a grimace. "If you h-haven't noticed, it's c-cold."

Fire bloomed on his palm, white-hot and delicious. She gasped and almost fell into it, shuddering at the pleasure of its warmth. "Why aren't you dressed properly?" he snapped, as if this was a criminal act.

"Go ask that crazy monk." She wanted to fall into him. Snuggle into his warm coat and wrap his heat all around her. She kept her gaze on the flame. It was so beautiful, white and dancing, as fierce and dangerous as the man who created it. "Have you seen what you need in there?"

"I have questions. Where is that, ah, crazy monk?"

She looked over her shoulder. Not a soul in sight.

Maybe none of them were as crazy as she to bolt out here without ten layers of extra clothing. "I guess he's with the rest of the smart people inside. Let's go be smart, too." But she moved closer instead of walking back the way she'd come, drawn to the heat of his fire.

"You should have at least worn a coat," he growled.

As if she hadn't thought of that already. She rolled her eyes. "Nobody likes a know-it-all. Could you just…?" She froze when he lifted a hand toward her face, gulping the rest of her words. What was he doing? Gaze flashing to his, she couldn't move, couldn't speak. His eyes glittered golden fire streaked with dusky green, his face intent and absorbed.

When his fingertips touched the side of her neck, she gasped and leaned closer. His touch wasn't just warm, it was hot, as if fire writhed just under his skin. And she craved his heat with everything she had. He slid his hand around the back of her neck, spreading warmth down her spine like seductive fingers. Her eyes drifted closed on a long, sighing, "Ahhh," of pleasure, prickles of gooseflesh running all the way down her body to her toes.

"Gods," he whispered and all of a sudden there was more heat, achingly close.

Lia dragged her eyelids open, gasping at his closeness, at the sudden driving need to have him even nearer, to press herself against him. She wasn't cold anymore. Yet she still craved his heat, his touch. The strength was running out of her legs again, melting her toward him.

His mouth was a breath away when someone called, "Prince Destin," in a firm, no-nonsense tone.

He released her so abruptly she staggered, catching herself against a leaning column with a wince at the bitter cold. It was like a slap in the face, a dose of cold reality jolting her mind back into working order. She stared at the prince, aghast. *Holy Mother, was he about to kiss me? On purpose?*

"Just what do you think you are doing with my goddaughter?"

Lia flinched and cast a despairing glance toward the bristling monk, wishing him mute. The man was going to make this way too easy for the elemental prince.

"Goddaughter?"

"Yel, can we talk about this later? The prince says he has some questions for you."

The elder glared at the younger man for another moment before he harrumphed and folded his arms across his puffy chest. "Ask."

The prince had his hands behind his back, a crease between his brows. He cast a swift glance at Lia and cleared his throat. "There is a mural. It tells the story of the last Vessel of Power when it appeared a millennium ago."

"I know of it." Yel'estya's tone said this was going to be a painful, drawn out interview.

Under any other circumstance, Lia would enjoy watching Yel stonewall the prince, but they were still outside in the cold. She sighed. "If we aren't going back to the monastery, could we at least get inside the sanctuary? Where it's a little warmer?"

The prince flicked another glance at her, this one so full of fire her knees wobbled again. "You don't need to be here."

She clenched her jaw until it hurt and stared hard at Yel, but when the monk didn't relent, she sighed again and stomped toward the sanctuary opening. "Yes, I do. Let's just go take a look at the mural and chat. It'll be great fun. There might even be a cave-in to make my day complete."

"Eylee'ai," Yel admonished.

She rolled her eyes then flinched when fire bloomed beside her. Giving the prince a reproachful look, she waved him ahead. Instead, he clasped her elbow and ushered her along, keeping her close to his heat. She was having trouble breathing when they reached the mural. The fantastic piece of art had once stretched as high as a three story building. Now it was reduced to a fraction of its former glory in the rubble.

As the prince lit torches, Lia stared at the mural with a sour twist of her mouth. Of course, the gods would preserve the most revealing section of the piece.

A young woman, almost life-sized, sat cross-legged with her hands cupping the rim of a chalice. Light shone down on her bowed head and poured out through the chalice, the cup glowing with artistically rendered power. Lia tried not to stare. This part of the mural always made her chest hurt until tears stood in her eyes.

"Elder, this mural is an incredible work of art. This isn't all of it?"

Yel thawed under the prince's respectful tone and contained enthusiasm. "I'm afraid this is all that's left, it once was a much larger work. The mountain has claimed most of the sanctuary, though we preserve what we can." Warming to his subject, Yel spread his arms and looked at the great slab of rock over their heads. "This room was once the centerpiece of the sanctuary, a soaring testament to architecture and art."

"Oh, here we go," Lia mumbled and huddled next to a torch for warmth, ignoring Yel's frown at her interruption.

"The Vessel's history was depicted here for all to study and marvel, from its appearance through the great tragedies and triumphs of its age to its disappearance. The smaller, more personal rooms of the sanctuary have long been crushed, but this large wedge of stone holds back the mountain for us. You can imagine, though, how this glorious room must have appeared to visitors. See the base there…"

Lia stopped listening to the familiar lecture. Instead, she studied the prince, who looked strangely interested. He was good at schooling his expressions, she had to admit, but there was a gleam in his eyes while he listened and looked about him as though he could see the phantom structure Yel described. He even asked questions, gods forbid, driving Yel on to greater heights of enthusiasm. He also touched, palm absorbing the massive patience of the leaning slab protecting them, fingers questing along the base of a shattered column, fingertips tracing the seams between sections of mural while Yel explained how the artist had rendered the work of art one piece at a time.

A polite, patient listener might allow Yel to yammer on, might even ask a question or two just to keep on his good side. Only a true enthusiast would stroke the stone as the prince did. The man was either a closet architect or a true-to-life scholar and historian. It was strange, to think of this hard-faced prince with his rough scar and predatory eyes as a lover of words and knowledge. But when he went to a shadowed corner and retrieved a saddlebag full of books, she had to start believing.

Yel's chubby face lit like a child on his birthday when the prince pulled out a tome as thick as her arm. "Ephemeral histories?" The silly man clapped his hands together, almost dancing on his toes.

Lia groaned. "Yel, you're embarrassing me," she muttered.

"Don't be foolish, child," he responded, leaning over the book with an avid gleam in his eye. "Nothing embarrasses you."

She smirked. "I don't know, I thought it was pretty embarrassing when I found you in the bathhouse with…"

"All right!" Yel cut her off, dark eyes wide, color flooding his face. "You've made your point, you little heathen." Clearing his throat and shuffling his feet, he carefully did not look at the prince while he gestured to the tome. "You've read it, your highness?"

It took Lia a moment to realize the prince was staring at her instead of the monk. She stopped smiling and turned her face away, feigning a deep interest in the shattered end of the mural, a section depicting a bloody, catastrophic battle. The part the Vessel had played was lost in the rubble, but she could imagine it. She'd had nightmares about it.

"Yes, I've read this and several others." The prince stated it matter-of-factly, but Yel made a sound of appreciation and amazement. Lia wanted to gag. "There is a passage in this one, a difficult wording I've been attempting to decipher. Would you consider helping me? Are you familiar with Ephemerals?"

Lia held her breath and waited, heart tripping in her chest. But Yel was still drooling over the book and must not have noticed the opportunity to stab her and her family in the back.

"I would be delighted to consult with you. I assume the passage is the one related to this mural?"

"Yes, it's quite tantalizing."

Tantalizing? Lia lifted her eyebrows, watching him with skeptical interest. She wouldn't have expected anything to tantalize this stone-faced man.

The prince opened the tome and then flicked his fingers in the air. Fire flew from his fingertips and condensed into a ball of white light hovering just over his shoulder. Ignoring the monk's muffled gasp, the prince riffled through the pages until he found what he was looking for. "Here, now, you see?" he asked the monk, holding the book for him as Yel leaned in.

The elder hummed as he read, tapping the page with a chubby finger now and again. The prince waited with what seemed an extraordinary amount of patience. Or maybe he was reading along with the monk. Either way, this was not what she'd pictured when she'd thought of the prince reaching the sanctuary. Her imagination had drawn pillaging and plundering, demands and torture.

Who would have imagined study partners?

Shaking her head, she pulled her blanket closer and stared at the little ball of flame over his shoulder with a helpless kind of longing. Her body stayed in one long, endless shiver and her jaw was starting to ache from clenching it to keep her teeth from chattering. The torch next to her burned with normal fire and didn't put out as much heat as his white flame. Maybe she could pretend an interest in the blasted book and stand at his elbow, absorbing delicious heat from his flame, from his long body. *Why was he about to kiss me?*

Yel interrupted a short fantasy about crawling into the prince's clothes while he was still in them. "You are wondering what the Vessel looks like," he said in a mild tone.

Her shivering stopped as every muscle in her body snapped taut.

"Yes and whether there is more than one. You see how they refer to it here…" The prince pointed at the page and waited for the monk's nod before he continued, "This seems to indicate it changes forms or becomes something new every time it appears. Yet this mural consistently shows the Vessel as a chalice. Can you explain this contradiction?"

Lia held her breath, staring at Yel hard enough to bore through his skull. *Don't, you old fool. He would end us, end everything. Or at least his father would.*

Yel clasped his hands, studying the mural with a thoughtful expression. His eyes darted her way once, but he didn't meet her intense gaze. Stepping forward, he placed a pudgy hand on the mural and said with infinite calm, "The Ephemerals are not a literal-minded people. They don't mean to be obscure, though it may seem that way. They simply think in much different terms than we fleshy mortals do. This part of the mural shows only the last Vessel's era, not those that came before. There is no contradiction, only a piece of the truth."

"Ah." The prince frowned at the mural. "You're saying the Vessel is different every time. So if I'm not looking for a chalice, what am I looking for?"

Yel nodded. “Yes, that is the challenge you must face.”

The prince sent him a sharp glance, eyes glittering with a shrewd light. He closed the book and let his arms drop to his sides, holding the tome in one hand. “You know what it is.” It wasn’t a question.

Lia’s heart pounded so hard she was sure both men could hear it.

“I do.”

“But you won’t tell me?”

“I can’t.”

Lia gasped for air, leaning all her weight on the mural before sliding down to sit on the rock-strewn floor. Relief had stolen her strength.

The prince flicked a stern glance her way before returning his attention to the monk. “Why can’t you?”

“Because I cannot interfere in the test of the gods.”

Lia let out a weak laugh and covered her face with her hands, trembling from more than cold.

“What do you mean?” She could hear the frown in the royal’s rough voice.

“You are being judged and measured, young prince, as we all are every day. The Vessel of Power is a tool the gods use to bring out the best in us or the worst. It was sent here to teach us, to humble us. We are their children and children must learn if they are to grow. So it was with the Ephemerals, with the Earth Keepers. So it will be with us. My own test is to stand aside. Do you not believe I would do anything to choose, to work my own will in this largest of challenges? But I was ordered to stay my hand. And stay it I will,” Yel finished in a murmur, sending Lia a sorrowful glance.

She sighed and climbed back to her feet. "You could've told me."

"Then you would not have had a chance to yell at me and argue with such passion."

She gestured at the prince without looking at him. "He could still torture you for information."

"I trust the gods to know when to end my suffering."

"I can't believe you said that with a straight face."

The conflict on his features said he wasn't sure whether to laugh or censure her for blasphemy.

The prince interrupted. "I could torture you instead," he said to Lia in a hard voice. She turned her head, met his glittering, fire-shot gaze. His mouth was set in a grim, straight line, the very picture of an unhappy prince. "You're his goddaughter. You know this place. You know what he knows." He took a deliberate step forward, the hand not holding the book clenching into a fist. "So you also know what the Vessel is."

Lia let the blanket fall and took the two strides necessary to stand on his toes. Lifting a hand between them, she changed it, lengthening the fingers, hardening the nails to razor-sharp points, and settling them over his heart. He didn't move, didn't blink, and didn't break eye contact for even a moment. "Torture isn't an option," she said in a warning tone. But she was the one who blinked first, glancing down. "Can I borrow your coat?"

He made a sound low in his throat, like a muffled laugh, mouth easing at the corners. "If you tell me what the Vessel looks like and where it is."

She scowled at him, backing away to swipe her

blanket off the floor and around her shoulders again. “Not in this lifetime. And I don’t know where it is.” That much at least was the literal truth.

Yel clasped her arm, looking her up and down with a frown. “Why aren’t you wearing a coat, young lady?”

She stared at him. “You just noticed? What kind of a godfather are you?”

She’d meant to be funny, but the elder shrank a little into himself, his jowls sagging. “A poor one. The gods should have chosen better protection for you, my dear.”

“Yel, I can protect myself,” she protested.

“Even from those you love?”

The words froze her, then filled her with unreasoning anger. She swallowed hard, once, twice, struggling for control. Yel didn’t deserve her anger, no matter how guilty he looked. “You aren’t responsible for the choices other men make,” she said with care.

“Eylee’ai—”

“Elder Yel’estya,” she interrupted. “Let it go. I’m going back to the monastery and the great big fireplace. I might even climb in it.”

They watched her leave, neither man saying a word.

Chapter 12

Destin leaned on the railing and stared down into the great room, watching the activity with brooding discontent. The monks had good reason to look cheerful and so did Eylee'ai. The changeling, he amended when her name caused his muscles to tighten with kindling fire. He'd badgered the monks all day to no effect. They all seemed to know what the Vessel was, what shape it took in this age, but none of them were willing to give him the slightest hint. Strangely enough, the monks' refusal to cooperate held no hostility, only a kind of gentle regret. A few even wished him luck in his search. It all seemed quite bizarre.

He knew he was going about this wrong. Somehow he was missing something. A critical clue to solving the Vessel riddle was here, right in front of his eyes. But it continued to elude him. He rubbed a hand over his eyes, trying to ease the scratchy ache in them. He needed sleep. If he were more alert, his mind working as it should, he would understand the situation more clearly. He was so weary but dreaded sleep, afraid of the fire in his dreams.

He looked down again, watching Eylee'ai laugh at something his cousin said with a sick hollowness in his gut. Rune's face was open and full of mischief, smiling the way he did when he was most relaxed. It could have been the drink, trust monks to have a stash of potent liquor handy, but Destin had to admit most of his cousin's good cheer was no doubt due to the changeling.

Soul sister. It shook him, angered and troubled him. Rune would not be so easy with someone devious or malicious, and he could not make a bond with evil.

It doesn't matter, it doesn't change anything. He sighed. The defensive thought was both true and false. His cousin's bond and the changeling's inherent decency didn't change his duty. But it did make doing what he needed to do so much harder. When he retrieved the Vessel for his father, it would hurt Rune by hurting Eylee'ai. He gripped the rail hard, his complex fury flaring high, but it burnt itself out without a target to decimate. The ashes of anger left his interior landscape gray with pain and despair.

Rune sensed it, of course. His cousin's smile faded, face turning up to Destin's, eyes dark with reflected pain. Eylee'ai glanced up as well, a crease forming between her fine eyes.

"A song!" one ruddy-faced monk called as he rose, distracting the group below. He was unsteady on his feet, sloshing liquid from his cup, his lined face creased in a wide, sloppy smile. "Lia-girl, you've been out in the world. You must have a new song for us." Laughter and enthusiastic agreement echoed in the great room, the cry of "new song!" repeated with gusto.

Destin shook his head. Drunken men were the same the world over, no matter if they were monks. Most women he'd known would have been offended by their behavior, uneasy with so much male attention, but Eylee'ai grinned and rose to her feet. "Settle down, you troublemakers!" They laughed with as much gaiety as children at a fair. When they'd quieted down, she asked, "Have you heard *My Almost-Perfect Love?"* Rune chortled and she turned to him with a sly smile. "I guess you have. You can help me remember the words." Then she turned back to the monks, soliciting their approval.

Destin shook his head again. He couldn't think of a less appropriate tune for a bunch of secluded, pious monks.

She began singing, the words sketching a young woman's excitement and lament over her new lover. The first stanza extolled the man's courtly virtues, the adoring look in his eyes, his attentive nature, how well he listened. His only flaw, he couldn't dance.

Eylee'ai brought the song to life with her dreamy smile and the sparkle in her eyes, with eloquent gestures and the provocative sway of her hips as she moved among the monks. She created the blush of young love with a secret taunt buried within her smile.

Her new love was always there, never strayed or looked at another woman, always ready to hold her, but how sad, he couldn't dance. Sharing a conspiratorial grin with Rune, she skipped over the stanza about the man's sexual endowments and stamina. Then she sang the young woman's complaint to her mama over her lover's single flaw. Hands on hips, Eylee'ai settled into the impatient stance of a put-upon mother and said, "Baby, statues can't dance." As the monks began to snicker, she became the sly young woman again, hand patting her chest as she sighed and crooned, "Yes, my almost-perfect love."

Guffaws echoed through the great room and she flashed them all a wicked grin, a look that went through

Destin like lightning. He sucked in a deep breath, hands tightening again on the rail. The female challenge in her look tugged at him as though she had a claw sunk deep in his guts, or further south. She might as well have for all the control he showed around her.

His mind flashed to the moment he'd touched her, the moment he'd snagged any flimsy excuse to put his hands on her. Oh, yes, must warm the frozen girl, he jeered as the memory of her heavy-lidded pleasure and moaning sigh stole his breath. Gods, if her plan was to seduce him into forgetting his search for the Vessel, he was making it far too easy for her.

Just as difficult to forget was her warm smile when she'd teased her godfather, her quicksilver changes in mood from wariness to feral threat, from easy humor to baffling fury. He didn't want his enemy to be so intriguing and endearing. He wanted to hate her. It annoyed him to discover he couldn't.

The monks carried on with their impromptu celebration, singing their own songs and playing lively notes on ill-tuned instruments. Destin watched them, watched the changeling and his cousin revel with them, and ached inside with a strange pain he couldn't identify. It was utter silliness, undignified and juvenile, but he couldn't turn away from it, or stop listening to the charming cacophony.

He thought at least Cleave had more sense than to join in, until he caught sight of the sailor in the shadows collapsed across a table with a cup cradled in his hand. *Lightweight,* he thought with cynical amusement. As he studied Cleave's drunken sprawl, he caught sight of Eylee'ai heading for the stairs with a purposeful stride. But not the stairs leading to her chamber.

With a frown at the anticipation tightening his gut and hard thump in his chest, he turned to watch her flow up the stairs and across the balcony toward him. Gods, the maddening creature moved like every man's hottest dream. She had to know it, had to be using it. He would have called her on it, too, would have driven her away, except her expression wasn't challenging or seductive but wary.

She slowed as she neared, a crease forming between her eyes. In the dimness they were dark as an ocean storm and as fraught with trouble. Pausing an arm's length away, she nodded a greeting, hesitated, then leaned against the railing to look down into the great room without a word. As though her whole purpose had been to join him, to keep him company.

He frowned harder. "Are you drunk?"

She ignored his harsh question, watching the antics below with a little curl of her lips. After a moment, she said without looking at him, "They'd welcome you, you know. You don't have to stay up here." When he said nothing, just stared at her in baffled silence, she shifted. "It hurts Rune," she continued in a soft voice. "You hurt him when you do this to yourself. I thought it was just princely disdain, but he says you'd like to be down there. You'd like to relax and let go, but you won't let yourself. You stay isolated and it hurts him."

She seemed to feel his hard stare. Folding her arms, she shot him a glance out of the corner of her eye. "Well, that's what he said," she muttered.

"Rune's sloshed."

She gave a sharp twitch of her shoulders. "So liquor loosens his tongue. Doesn't mean he's lying. Besides, whatever the truth, you're still hurting him by lurking up here. It might sound stupid, but I like him. I think of him as my friend—"

"Yes, that sounds incredibly stup—"

"And," she interrupted with a glare that amused him for some reason, "I don't like it when he's hurt. So fix it already."

"Is this why you came here? To be Rune's advocate?"

She frowned at his dubious tone then sighed and faced him, arms still folded across her chest. Her grim expression warned him he wasn't going to like what she said next. "Why did you try to kiss me?"

His brain skipped a few essential functions, leaving him mute and staring.

When he didn't answer, she made an exasperated sound. "Don't try to deny it. You couldn't have fit a blade of grass between us. I just can't figure out why. You didn't find out I knew about the Vessel until later. Unless you already suspected I knew things and you were trying to get it out of me. Is that it?"

He blinked. "You think I was trying to seduce you for information?"

"Well, for gods' sake, it wasn't me getting so close," she muttered, looking uncomfortable. "I know it's weird. That's why I can't figure out why you did it."

The strangest sensation of ice and heat chased itself over his skin, prickling his face and numbing his tongue. He'd never, in his life, been so befuddled by a woman. He'd think she was playing a game, except she looked thoroughly out of sorts. It was as if she truly couldn't understand why he'd touched her.

"Eylee'ai…" Her name on his tongue struck fire

along his bones, heat racing up his spine and out to his fingertips. He had to swallow hard before he could continue. "How much did you have to drink?"

She sighed, resentment settling into the lines of her face. "I should've known I wouldn't get a straight answer from you. Gods-cursed elemental." She poked a stiff finger to his chest. "Just so you know, I don't like people who don't play fair."

"Nor do I," he growled, fighting the urge to nip her slender finger and full, expressive lower lip.

She snorted as though he'd said something ridiculous. "And get some sleep. You've got huge shadows under your eyes and it's making your cousin worry."

"I'll take that under advisement."

She glowered at the sarcasm and spun on her heel, stalking away. After three steps, though, she stopped and cursed. She turned and stalked back, staring at him with hands on hips and a dark frown. "I have had too much to drink," she announced.

He should have known it was a warning, but she blindsided him. She clasped his face between cool hands, rose on tip-toe, and pressed her soft lips to his in heart-stopping, clinging contact. Heat raced through him like wildfire.

Before he could catch hold of her and bring her back for more, she spun around and left him there. Over her shoulder she said in an odd tone, "The rail is smoking," without meeting his gaze.

He looked down. Tendrils of smoke curled from between the fingers of a hand so clenched around the wooden railing his bones showed white under the skin. He let go, staring at the black handprint in dismay. It was getting worse and worse. Not only was he burning in his sleep, but now he was scorching things without knowing it while awake. His gaze flashed down into the great room, meeting his cousin's dancing eyes and wide grin. Of course Rune had seen everything.

With his ears ringing and mouth tingling, Destin glanced along the balcony, but Eylee'ai was nowhere in sight. Ignoring a sharp pang of disappointment in his gut, he stomped down the stairs and marched straight to where his cousin lounged against a table. "No more of this for you," he growled, snatching the cup out of Rune's hand.

"Only if you drink it for me," Rune said in an easy tone, his smile wide.

Destin didn't argue, lifting the cup in a silent toast and draining it. Then he shuddered and sat next to his cousin. "Gods, that's horrible. It's burning a hole through my insides."

"It's made from dandelions and sweetened with honey. It grows on you."

"No need for threats." He turned his head and met Rune's gaze. "Why did you set her on me, Rune?"

Rune shook his head, holding up a hand. "Oh, no! You're not blaming me. I had no part in her going to you. And how did you manage a kiss from her?"

Destin ignored his question, still teetering on the edge of fire and straining for control. "She said I was hurting you."

Rune sobered for a moment, studying him with uncharacteristic seriousness. "She's awfully blunt. But she's also right. It does hurt when you lock yourself away."

His heart sank. "I'm not locking myself anywhere.

Stop being so dramatic."

"So why weren't you down here with us?"

"Princely disdain, of course," he drawled.

Rune threw back his head and laughed, slapping him on the back. "She cut you with that one, didn't she?"

Destin didn't respond, just grabbed the vile-looking bottle on the table and poured more into his cup. He was being reckless. His control was uncertain enough without adding the loosening effect of liquor. But she'd told him to fix it. For once, she was right. He had hurt his soul brother and he couldn't stand it.

"Ah, Lia," Rune murmured, snickering as a monk reeled by, bellowing an incomprehensible tune. "She's extraordinary. So determined. So driven. She reminds me of you." Destin swore and Rune chuckled. "Watching the two of you clash is a pleasure. I wonder what you'd do if you didn't have the Vessel to fight over?"

Destin tried not to think of it but couldn't quite keep his memory from sliding through his dreams and scorching him from the inside out.

Rune chuckled again. "I thought so."

"Get out of my head, brother," Destin growled, shooting him a warning look.

Rune held up his hands in surrender, though his mouth twisted in a smirk. "Apologies, my prince." He dropped his hands, face sobering. "Have you forgiven me yet for making a bond with a changeling?"

"There's nothing to forgive." Destin shook his head, taking a deep swallow of the disgusting brew. Grimacing, he added, "You aren't able to weave a bond on purpose and her being a changeling isn't what concerns me. The gods must have a reason, but a bond with an enemy? There will be a price."

"There always is with divine gifts. But Lia isn't my enemy."

Destin jerked, meeting his cousin's gaze with pained shock. "Have you switched sides, then?"

Rune made a face. "I'm trying to say I'm not on a side. If it was my decision, I'd forget the Vessel and go home. I certainly have no use for ultimate power."

"I have a duty."

Rune snarled with a slash of his hand. "To hell with your duty. Did you ever wonder why King Stern, master elemental and sovereign of all he surveys, sent you after this Vessel he wants so badly?"

Destin frowned at Rune's disrespect. "Someone must rule our land."

"So why didn't he place you on the throne and pursue the Vessel himself?"

"Father's the king. It would be too dangerous."

"Oh, yes. Too dangerous to risk his precious hide, but he has no trouble risking his son and the only direct heir to the throne. You know why, Des. You just don't want to admit it. He's guarding his position and power. He couldn't risk putting you on the throne even for a short time. You'd be a much better ruler than he. He sent you on this ridiculous journey because he wins either way. Either you bring back the Vessel and he gains ultimate power, or you die in the attempt and he's rid of his most potent rival."

Destin stared at his cousin in stunned disbelief. Rune was often rebellious but he'd never been this hostile. "Rune, that's treason," he said in a low voice.

"So throw me in the dungeon when we get home.

Just think about what you're doing, Des. Is the Vessel really worth it?"

"The Vessel's worth doesn't matter. It's my responsibility to find it." He paused, searching Rune's bitter features with sudden suspicion. "You know something, don't you?"

"I know this search is going to cost us both more than we could ever imagine." Rune sighed, rubbing a hand over his face. "Lia is the key. The monks know more than they say, but it's her they watch. She's too involved not to be a keystone. She believes we'll hurt her family, Des."

He frowned. "You're saying her family has the Vessel?"

Rune shrugged, lines bracketing his mouth, shadows swimming in his eyes. "From what I understand, an average changeling learns to shift into a small number of forms over the course of their lifetime. I've seen Lia change parts of herself as easily as blinking, and she's become half a dozen different animals since we've met her."

Destin's breath caught in his throat. "She's come in contact with the Vessel."

Rune leaned forward, bracing elbows on knees and burying his face in his hands. "It's a reasonable conclusion," he said in a rough voice. "She's too personally invested and she's more powerful than any changeling we know. I've been waiting for you to think of it, but you've been too intent on pushing her away."

Despite his treasonous words, Rune was proving he was still on Destin's side. But it was shredding him in the process.

He settled a hand on Rune's shoulder. "You're

right. I should have seen it. I let her distract me."

Rune dropped his hands, staring down at the floor with the faintest of grim smiles. "You didn't let her distract you enough. She's more vulnerable than you know. And I feel her as deeply as I feel you. For my sake if not hers, let the Vessel go."

Fissures of pain cracked all through Destin, a battle of conflicting necessities. He would do anything for his lifelong friend, for his soul brother. Anything except betray his father and king. He wove spirit, wove emotion and need into words, and cast it blindly. *Rune, my brother, I would have been lost without you. I still would be.*

Rune barked a humorless laugh then slanted Destin a pained look out of the corner of his eye. "Well, it's true," he muttered, his expression relenting. "You would have been a humorless toad with no sense of fun. And you need constant reminding. You're a great deal of work, Des."

"I know," Destin murmured, squeezing his cousin's shoulder. "We both need sleep before we start weeping on each other like old women."

Rune shook his head. "I'm warning you, I'm not going to leave this alone. I'll hound you until you give in."

"I'll forgive you since you can't help yourself. You're a natural born nag." He set the horrid drink aside and rose to his feet. "Will you make it to your bed or do I need to carry you?"

Rune scowled. "Have you become my mother? I haven't drunk enough to brave one of those frozen chambers yet, but you go right ahead and enjoy the ice."

Destin chuckled, giving his cousin a little salute and heading for the stairs again. Behind him, Rune's voice rose in song with the monks. Destin shook his head with a relieved smile. One good thing about his cousin, he didn't hold a grudge or brood for long.

His little bare sleeping chamber was bitter cold and his cot icy, but the moment he laid his head on the pillow, sleep claimed him with dark insistence.

Chapter 13

Destin woke to fire, the wall and cot rippling with flame. At first he stared at it without comprehending, his body arching in an agony of desire. *Eylee'ai.* When he realized her hands and mouth no longer tormented him and he couldn't hear her maddening little moans, he lurched up with a harsh groan and silenced the flames on the wood. He couldn't extinguish the fire writhing between his fingers, though.

Rolling off the cot, he paced the small confines of the room and tried to think icy thoughts. Hard to do when his heart still thundered in his chest, breath sawing in and out of his throat. His body ached and throbbed with a lust strong enough to fog his mind.

The dream had seemed so real, Eylee'ai following him to the sanctuary where they'd argued about the Vessel, where she accused him of being heartless, her teeth chattering and lips turning blue. He'd meant to warm her, to show her he had compassion, but his good intentions flew away with the first touch. She'd responded to him so wildly he'd lost all control, lost himself in savage passion. A tormenting dream-image of sultry gray eyes and slick little body writhing against him made him shudder, fire flaring from his hands to light the room in dancing white.

Cold thoughts. He grimaced, trying to focus on anything but silky skin and soft lips. They'd argued about the Vessel. That part of the dream was much more realistic than her responding to him with such fierce abandon. An element of the exchange teased him, though he couldn't remember the exact sequence.

Why heartless? He frowned, puzzling over his dream-Lia's choice of words. Was his sleeping mind just worrying this search for the Vessel would cost him as much as Rune said it would? Or was he trying to tell himself something, remind himself of something he'd forgotten?

White flame guttered and died as his passion cooled into concentration. Something about the Vessel, about what Rune had said last night. A sudden, urgent need to see the mural struck him. After washing from an icy bowl, he yanked on his coat and strode out of his chamber. Many of the monks lay draped across the great room's tables, though Rune wasn't among them. Neither was Eylee'ai.

Destin glanced at the closed door to her chamber but looked away at the tightening in his gut. *Focus on the Vessel,* he admonished himself, turning his collar up as he headed for the front doors. The early morning was dim and gray with a crisp cold stinging his eyes and nose. He didn't try to warm the air or ignite flame. The cold honed his control and sharpened his thoughts.

He moved through the dark ruins by memory, groping along the stone, trying to clear his mind. He wanted a new view of the mural, a fresh perspective he wouldn't get if he looked at it the same way. Stumbling through the dark, he felt the stone until his fingers encountered carvings. Orienting himself in the blackness, he eased backward until he had enough space. Then he spread his arms and called fire.

The mural came to life in the white light. At first it was the same, a piece of the bloody tale of the last Vessel, the early sections lost in rubble and ancient memory. The same battles, the same power struggles, the same chalice… Then he saw it. The same person. He looked from section to section, from image to image. Every time, the chalice was carried by the same female, aging over the timeline of the mural. It seemed impossible the Vessel wouldn't have changed hands multiple times in its age.

Destin studied the mural with care, heart speeding as he became more certain of what he was seeing. The Vessel of Power was the woman, not the chalice. The chalice was a bit of art representing the gift of power from the gods. Now the Ephemeral passage made perfect sense to him, the gods choosing a different person every millennium to house their limitless power.

Destin let his flame die and stared into the darkness, mind racing. So who was the Vessel? *Eylee'ai.* She was more powerful than any changeling he'd ever seen. Could she be the one? He considered then rejected it. She didn't act like someone afraid for her life and freedom. She risked herself as though she was protecting something. Or, he now realized, someone. Rune had said she was afraid they'd hurt her family. If someone in her family was the Vessel, it would explain why she was such a strong changeling, having absorbed their divine power.

She knew who it was. She knew where they were or how to find them. Rune was right. Eylee'ai was the key.

Destin called fire to light his way and ran out of the sanctuary. Sprinting for the monastery, he burst into the great room. The place remained quiet, monks still strewn all over. Launching up the stairs two at a time, Destin headed for the sleeping chamber the changeling had chosen for her own. He had a premonition she'd flown and stolen away in the night.

But when he beat on the door with his fist, she opened it as if she'd been waiting for his knock. Her frown was the furthest thing from welcoming, though. "A little early to be breaking down doors, isn't it?"

"I need to speak with you."

Her frown deepened. "You know, for a prince you have zero manners." But she backed away, opening the door wider to admit him.

Destin hesitated. "You wouldn't rather speak out here?"

"They all need to sleep it off," she said, nodding down into the great room. "And I'm not going outside again in the cold if I can help it. Are you afraid to be alone with me?"

She said it without a hint of seduction, but he still reacted, heart kicking and breath catching. Afraid wasn't exactly the word. Keeping his expression stony and tightening his control on the fire lurking in his bones, he stepped past her into the room, as sparse and chilly as his without a single object to personalize it. Yet it held her fragrance, her light exotic spice teasing him when she shut the door and closed them in together.

"What did you want to talk about?"

"The Vessel is not a thing. It's a person. Who is it, Lia?"

Her eyes went wide, face paling. "I don't know what you're talking about," she breathed.

"Yes, you do. You know the Vessel well enough to risk your life to protect him or her. Is it your father or mother? Sister or brother?" He watched her swallow hard, a strange lurch in his chest.

"I'm the Vessel," she whispered.

He shook his head. "No, you're not. You've been changed by it, but you don't fight like someone with divine power."

"That's a stupid thing to say. You haven't seen everything I can do." The words were defiant, but her voice was almost inaudible.

"You're not the Vessel, Lia. Who is it? And where are they?"

Her eyes faded to liquid-gray desolation. Fisting her hands in the fabric of his coat, she tried to shake him. "Take me to your father. Let him decide if I'm the Vessel."

He covered her cold, shaking hands with his own. "I won't harm your family. I give you my word. But I have a duty to my king. I must know where the Vessel is, Lia."

"Don't you understand?" Her voice broke. She reached up and touched the scar on his face with disconcerting gentleness. "I know about fathers who beat their children for not being what they want them to be. So do my mother and sister. Even if you could get my mother to let Ettie go without a fight, your father will crush my baby sister."

Between the tender stroke of her fingers and the quiver of fear in her stark words, Destin's chest constricted until he could hardly breathe. *Fathers who beat their children.* The thought of any man laying a hand on her ate at him like acid, virulent and ravaging.

"Lia," he husked, hands stealing around her shoulders, pressing her closer in unconscious protection. "I wouldn't let it happen. I would give my life to keep her from harm."

Her face crumpled and she dropped her forehead to his chest with a sob. She clutched his coat again, slim form trembling. "I should have killed you," she whispered. "Why can't I kill you?"

The words hurt him, needles of pain in unexpected, vulnerable places. "No, Lia," he murmured without knowing what he was saying, slipping his arms around her, drawing her into the curve of his body, under the sheltering bow of his head. "No." He brushed her hair with his scarred cheek, absorbing silk and inhaling sweet spice.

"Destin, please, I'm begging you." Her voice shook and shredded him from the inside out, pooling sickness in his stomach.

"Oh, gods, don't. Don't beg. Fight me, Lia."

"Fight you?" She tipped back her head, eyes full of darkness and tears. "Destin…" She shook her head with a sound like surrender, rose up, and molded her lips to his.

She was forever taking him by surprise. But his surprise lasted only a heartbeat, just long enough for all thought to crash under a wave of sensation and desire. After that, he could do nothing but feel. Too many nights of too little sleep and erotic dreams took their toll. He had no control. With a groan, he cupped the back of her head and dove into her mouth, her sharp, sweet flavor blooming on his tongue, an instant addiction. He had to have more, needed it more than breathing, and delved deeper, learning her from the inside out.

Her response devastated him. Matching him move for move, she twined her tongue with his in a slick little dance, kissing him back with just as much ferocity. Slipping her arms around his neck, she tunneled her fingers through his hair to grip with an urgency that sent heat shooting straight down his spine to his groin. She was making a soft sound in her throat, a cross between a growl and a purr, driving him wild. When she leaned into him, her soft curves pushed him close to madness. He splayed a desperate hand in the small of her back, pressing her closer, growling in fierce possession and burning need at how perfectly she fit against him.

Then her soft moan rose to a muffled cry and she twisted in his hold, shoving away from him. He released her and stared uncomprehending when she stumbled back and sat abruptly on her cot. Gray eyes wide, she touched fingers to reddened lips and made a sound like a choked laugh. “Am I still on fire?” she asked in a husky voice, twisting and glancing over her shoulder.

At the small of her back, thin smoke curled from blackened edges of cloth. Beneath a charred hole, her skin showed angry red in the shape of a handprint. With an inarticulate sound of horror, Destin looked from the red mark to his hand. Small flames still flickered around his fingers. “Oh, gods, I burned you,” he rasped. Illness surged in his throat, nearly gagging him. The room shifted beneath his feet.

She said something he couldn’t hear, couldn’t understand through the ringing in his ears. He had to get away, yearning for fresh air and cold to snap him back to reality. Illness and panic swelling like a tide, he staggered out the door.

Chapter 14

"Oh, gods, I burned you," he said like it was the worst thing he'd ever done. Far from stone-faced now, he looked horror stricken and sick as he stared at his fiery fingers.

Lia blinked at him in startled dismay. "But I'm fine," she blurted. "It's just a scald, I heal fast. Destin?"

But he was gone. Staring at the closed door, she sat still and waited for the world to start making sense again.

The prince had discovered her secret. She'd told herself to expect it and not hope he wouldn't figure it out, but there must have been some hope hiding in her soul to feel such loss. She also should have known better than to try and reason with him, to ask for mercy. There was something in him, though, that pulled unexpected reactions from her, something under his cool exterior called to her.

His fire was definitely part of it. The man had a wild heat that drove her to distraction, a passion expressed in elemental flame despite his efforts to hide it. A shocking revelation, to discover she could call it out of him in spite of his rigid self-control. This was the amazing, thrilling answer to his puzzling actions, the prince wanted her.

But desire was only part of what drew her. The obsessed scholar lurking beneath his royal skin fascinated her, along with the flashes of humor that came and went like heat lightning. She was intrigued by the curious vulnerabilities hinted at in Rune's laments of him, and the uncertainty in his eyes when she touched his scar. She even admired his confidence, dedication, and iron will, though those qualities also aggravated her to no end.

The astonishing tenderness in his touch, the gentle, protective shelter he'd offered in his arms, had seduced her into begging for mercy. She knew she shouldn't trust it, shouldn't trust him, but she'd been unable to stop herself or resist the golden warmth in his eyes and pensive curve of his mouth.

She'd kissed him seeking comfort and reassurance. What she found was wildfire.

Her breath caught and eyes closed, fingers touching tender lips. She could still taste hot ginger on her tongue, still feel the brand of his hungry mouth. She'd never had a man kiss her with such ravenous need, and she'd never responded to any man with such reckless abandon. Her body was still aching and weak, yearning for a man who could destroy her world.

This is crazy, she thought but couldn't control the trembling of her limbs, the flood of heat deep inside when she remembered the imprint of his taut body, his hot, desperate hand in the small of her back.

The pain of the burn mark was almost gone, her changeling skin already working to heal and erase it. On impulse, she paused the healing process and rose on shaky legs, moving to the little wash table and small mirror. Turning and twisting until the small of her back was visible, she studied the hole in the dress and the red handprint beneath.

Seeing Destin's mark on her skin did something savage to her insides. Lust rippled down her body, tightening her muscles. She breathed carefully, a little alarmed. She shouldn't like a man's brand on her skin. Her father had taught her distrust and a feral need for independence. But this mark had been unintentional, proof of the passion she aroused in him. Proof she could make him lose control. It gave her a wondrous sense of feminine power and satisfaction, a new experience for her.

She, Lia, barbarous changeling of lowly birth and no particular station in life, could make the elemental prince catch fire.

Staring at the mark, she decided she didn't want to lose it. With a small, smug smile, she began to work on the handprint, exerting control over the color of her skin.

A knock on the door broke her concentration and made her heart jump. Had Destin come back? Mouth going dry, she stepped to the door and opened it.

Rune stood there, frowning at her. "Are you all right?" he asked in a tense voice. "What happened? Where's Destin?"

She lifted her eyebrows, trying not to show her disappointment. Of course Destin hadn't come back. Holding up a finger for each answer, she said, "I'm fine, none of your business, and I have no idea. You look cranky this morning. Hangover?"

He shook his head, turning to scan the great room and walkways with his frown still in place. "He woke me out of a dead sleep. Something's wrong. Destin's upset."

"Um." A blush heated her face. "This bond thing

lacks in privacy, Rune."

"I told you, I have no control over it." His anxious hazel eyes fixed on her. "What happened?"

With a sigh, she opened the door further and stepped aside, a silent invitation Rune accepted. When he was in the room, she closed the door again and turned so he could see her back.

"What is that?"

She faced him with a frown. "What does it look like? We were kissing and he caught on fire."

"He burned you?" He stared at her, eyes wide and face twisted with the same kind of horror Destin had worn.

"For gods' sake, it's not like he did it on purpose. Calm down. He didn't even notice he was weaving fire until after I showed him the burn."

"But he hurt you," Rune said in a strained voice, taking her arm and turning her to look at the mark again.

"Oh, please. I've burned myself worse trying to cook. I'm fine, Rune. I heal fast, remember?"

"It doesn't look as though it's healing. And what's the dark color?"

She grinned. "Watch." Closing her eyes, she focused on the memory-image of the handprint in the mirror and continued her work.

After a moment, he began to laugh. "Holy Mother…why?"

"Because he's too good at denial. Last night I asked him why he tried to kiss me at the sanctuary, and he asked if I was drunk. Can't pretend I don't light his fire now, can he?"

Rune laughed again with a gleam in his eyes and

reached to touch the mark.

She knocked his hand away. "Keep your paws to yourself," she admonished, moving to the mirror to judge her handiwork. Black now outlined Destin's handprint, the fingers decorated with fine scrolling and the palm emblazoned with ancient Earth Keeper runes.

"What does it say?"

"Prince of Fire," she answered with deep, inexplicable satisfaction, letting the red of the burn begin to fade again.

With a wicked chuckle, Rune leaned closer, studying the mark. "How is this possible?"

She gave him a look of utter disgust. "Did you hit your head again? I'm a changeling, Rune."

"I've never seen a changeling work such detail. Is it permanent?"

"It's called a casting, like a human ink tattoo, but it's not permanent. Most changelings can do it."

He straightened, eyes shrewd. "Oh? Can they make a casting so intricate? So fine and detailed?"

She folded her arms. "What are you getting at?"

"You're not a normal changeling, Lia. I've seen you color your skin, change your hands, grow sharper teeth, all in a blink. You shift shapes just as easily and I'm starting to suspect there's no animal you can't become. How are you able to do all of this?"

She stared at him, stared at the knowledge in his eyes, and sighed. "So that's how he figured it out. You helped him along."

His forehead drew a puzzled crease. "Des? What did he figure out?"

She chewed on the inside of her lip then shrugged with sharp aggravation. The prince was bound to tell

Rune anyway. "My sister is the Vessel of Power. Being around her every day of my life made changing as easy as breathing. I've never had to think about it. I just do it. It wasn't until—" She stopped, pressing her lips together. "Never mind. Your prince figured out the Vessel was a person and he was so sure I'd been exposed to her. Now I know why." She glared at him.

He didn't seem to notice her anger, his handsome face shocked. "The Vessel's…your sister? Mother of All, that's…not good. So very not good." His eyes unfocused, head tilting to one side in what looked like a listening posture. "Did you give Des her location?"

"Of course not."

He cursed under his breath and headed for the door with urgency in his every motion.

"What are you doing?"

"What I'm feeling from him is disturbing. I think he's about to do something rash."

Alarm tightened the skin across her bones and coiled like a snake in her gut. "What do you mean rash?"

Rune didn't answer and Lia followed on his heels with a chill running down her spine that had nothing to do with the weather. Rune didn't pause at the bottom of the stairs, heading straight for the front doors, but Lia took a moment to grab a monk's woolen overcoat before she followed him out into the icy morning. It was still, the quiet before a storm, the sky grim with clouds.

"Wait, Rune, where are you going?" Lia called when he sprinted in the opposite direction from the sanctuary. Then she realized what his destination must be and cried out a wordless denial. Fear lent wings to her feet as she ran after him toward the livestock barn. They burst into the dim space, startling the sheep, the donkey, and Rune's pretty little mare. The sheep bleated and circled in their pen but the horse whickered a soft greeting.

Lia ignored the mare, rushing through the barn, hoping her eyes were deceiving her. "No," she whispered at the absence of Destin's stallion. "No, no, no. He left? How could he leave? You're still here," she protested, spinning to meet Rune's pained gaze. "He left you here? I didn't tell him how to find her. What in the gods' names is he thinking?"

Rune folded his arms and hunched in on himself as if he'd begun to feel the cold. "He's thinking he's a menace, unable to control his weaving. He's afraid he'll harm us, if he stays."

"That's stupid," Lia snarled, pacing around him in savage strides. "Why in the name of the Earth Mother would he think that?"

"Because he already did harm to you. He burned you, Lia. He's never lost control that way in his life, not even when he was a boy. He caught his room on fire once," he muttered, spreading his arms. A warm current of air brushed by her, stirring the hay in a circle at his feet. "But after his father was done with him, he was the perfect fire weaver. He's not accustomed to being out of control. For him, it's weakness. It makes him less."

Lia stopped pacing, standing in front of him with hands on hips and a frown, his warm air stirring her clothes. "Just because he wants me? Horse dung. There's no such thing as total control, especially with the elements. Do you think the Earth Mother gave you your gifts just so you could put a leash on her and bind her to your will?"

Rune flinched as if she'd slapped him, but his voice was even. "This isn't about me. This is about a man raised under a hard hand, whose own mother surrendered to death rather than face the king. Control is all Des has."

It was Lia's turn to flinch. "He has you," she said in a low voice, folding her arms around herself.

"I couldn't deflect the king any more than his own mother could. Lady Myst was not a strong soul and I was just a child." He spoke matter-of-factly, but his features twisted into lines of guilt and sorrow, eyes dark with pain. "Des didn't have a choice. He believed what his father taught him at the end of a fist. I just thank the gods he didn't become a replica of the king. King Stern would have enjoyed causing us pain."

"Do you think he'll give up hunting my sister?"

Rune sighed, eyes sliding closed. His face seemed to age a decade. "No. He'll see it as a way to restore himself, his self-worth, and restore his control. He must retrieve the Vessel to be the son the king wants him to be."

Lia had to clench her teeth to keep them from chattering, though she wasn't cold wrapped in wool and standing in Rune's warm currents. "Then we have to go after him. Where are your things?" When Rune blinked at her with trouble in his eyes, she frowned. "You are coming, aren't you? You're not going to let him leave you behind?"

"Of course I'm coming. But we need provisions and gear. I doubt he'll return to the ship. Uncle Storm would expect that, if our uncle has even left a ship to return to by now. So Des will travel over land and we don't have enough provisions to follow."

"I don't need anything, but Yel can get you whatever you need."

"And what of Cleave? We can't just abandon him."

Lia narrowed her eyes. "You're trying to slow me down, aren't you? Give your soul brother a head start. Well, I'm leaving now, with or without you. You'll have to catch up." She shrugged out of the woolen coat and began yanking on the sleeves of the dress.

"Wait, Lia, I'm not trying to slow you down. I agree with you. We need to stop him."

She continued struggling with the dress, muttering curses under her breath. "How do people wear these things?"

"It has a clasp in the back. Lia, stop undressing and listen to me." He clutched her arms and gave her a little shake, meeting her gaze with intent hazel eyes. "I said I agree. Retrieving the Vessel was always a fool's errand, but now I know it's your sister, it's imperative she never, ever fall into the king's hands. If she's anything like you, she might resist him for a while, but—"

"She's not like me," Lia whispered, a lump forming in her throat. "She's sweet and kind and just about helpless. She believes in the good in everyone and your king will break her until there's nothing left."

A crease formed between his eyes, his hands sliding down her arms to wrap around her cold fingers. "I don't understand. She's the Vessel. How is she helpless?"

"She holds the power of the gods but she can't use it. She was born half elemental and half changeling, but without the special abilities of either one. If you want to help me, we have to leave now, Rune. Before your blasted prince gets too far ahead of us."

"I have a responsibility to the boy. I can't just leave Cleave behind. But I have an idea you aren't going to appreciate, though it'll quicken our pace." There was a furtive gleam in his eyes.

"What's the idea?" she asked with sudden suspicion.

He was right. She didn't like it. But in the interest of speed, she agreed.

After they'd gathered necessities from the monks and bid them goodbye, Lia, Rune, Cleave, and the pretty brown mare headed for the pass down the mountain, leaving the slower donkey behind in the barn. As she stepped into the rocky cleft with Cleave riding the brown mare behind her, Lia flicked her ears and sent Rune a warning look over her shoulder.

"I said nothing," he responded with laughter in his eyes. Then he shifted forward and patted her neck. "Though you do make a beautiful mare and a comfortable ride."

She nipped at his dangling leg, bucking just enough to rock him without tossing him off her back. He yelped and grabbed hold of her mane, thighs tightening around her. Then he snickered without a trace of remorse.

She snorted and tossed her head. When she was human again, she'd have a few things to say about what was acceptable behavior for her rider. He was heavier than she'd been expecting, but he seemed to know how to shift his weight to work with her instead of being a burden.

On the way down the mountain trail, she went slower than she wanted, hampered by the strange, numb sensation of hooves on stone and the disconcerting tendency of those hooves to slide. Nickering horsy curses, she made her cautious way down the trail, only pausing once at the location of her rockslide to stare at the utter lack of blocking stone and stomp her foot in aggravation. Rune chuckled but said nothing. She snapped her teeth at him anyway.

He dodged her bite and patted her neck again. “It was an amazing piece of work, love. How did you manage?”

She thought nasty thoughts at him, remembering how much effort it had taken to drag each boulder into place. *All thrice-damned day,* she snarled in her mind, stomping past the site. *I’ll bet it didn’t take him more than a candle mark to clear it.*

Rune coughed. “Quite a bit less, actually.”

She sent him a jaundiced look over her shoulder. *Are you reading my mind?*

“Somewhat,” he muttered, eyes sliding away to the long drop. “You’re thinking very loud just now. What shape did you assume to move those rocks? The image you’re sending me is…odd.”

You don’t want to know. She wasn’t sure she knew. It was something with lots of muscles and opposable thumbs.

“Incredible. You can change into something that’s not even a real animal?”

She gave an uncomfortable mental shrug. She was used to the ease and versatility of talent her sister had bestowed on her, but shifting into something unnatural was considered an abomination among changelings and it wasn’t something she enjoyed doing. *Where will he go, Rune? He doesn’t know where Ettie is.*

"At a guess, I'd say he'll retrace your steps, since you were with the Vessel at some point. He knows you followed us to sea from the port at Churling Bay."

Her stomach tightened with worry, but she tried to keep her mind from dwelling on it. If Rune plucked Ettie's last known location from her thoughts, he could send the information to the prince on a spirit weave. She considered him a friend, but she knew where his loyalties lay and wasn't willing to trust him with her sister's life. *It doesn't matter. I can track him. We'll catch him before he finds her trail.*

Rune said nothing and she concentrated on getting down the mountain without tumbling. When they reached the foothills, Lia looked over her shoulder. The brown mare stepped with dainty precision, ears forward and eyes calm, the picture of equine grace and serenity, but Cleave's face was pale and pinched.

Lia twitched her skin and tail. *Curse it, Rune, the boy looks like he's sitting on a pile of blisters. I'm not slowing down for him, you hear?*

"Let's stop for a rest," Rune called to Cleave as if he hadn't heard her. As if she was just a simple beast of burden. She laid her ears back and stomped her foot in warning. As he slid from her back, he ran a soothing hand along her neck. "We'll rest while you find Destin's trail. I assume you'll change form to track him?"

She curled her lip at him. *Lame excuse. When I find his trail, I should just keep going.*

"But you won't because you love me." He smiled his charming smile and tugged at her forelock.

Grumbling, she shook him off and headed for a concealing rock formation. She didn't care if Rune saw her shift, but Cleave seemed to have less tolerance. When she'd appeared as a horse, his eyes had gotten so large she was afraid they'd pop right out of his skull.

A moment of privacy behind the rocks and she reemerged as a great, shaggy wolf, nose already to the ground. Yes, the prince had been there. Her nostrils filled with hot ginger. She almost started drooling and panting. Keeping her eyes down as she passed Rune, she thought to him, *I'll scout his trail. Be ready when I get back.*

His only response was a wicked chuckle. Yes, this bond thing really was lacking in privacy.

Destin's scent, mixed with the musk of eager stallion, led her straight down the path toward the road. He hadn't turned off anywhere, yet. Loping along with hot ginger filling her head like a fog, she had the strongest urge to keep going, to increase her speed and chase him down, to hunt him like prey. Reining in her animal instincts and slowing to a stop was more difficult than it should have been.

Panting to disburse the heat of her run, she closed her eyes and lowered her head, his scent forming a picture in her mind of the prince bent low over the stallion's shoulders, riding the animal as if devils were on their heels. *Destin,* she thought, and a shudder ran through her from nose to tail. *You shouldn't have left.*

Then she lifted her head, snorting and shaking her whole body before turning back the way she'd come.

Chapter 15

Living with a changeling had its ups and downs. Especially since the changeling was an irritable female with no patience and a one-track mind. *So like my cousin,* Rune thought. It had been difficult and dangerous just getting her to stop for the night.

Rune watched her pace in borrowed clothes beyond the small fire and sighed. She needed rest. They all needed rest, but she was being stubborn about it. Cleave hunched close to the fire, radiating misery and guilt, shooting her woebegone looks every once in a while. She either ignored him or didn't notice, still agitated over Destin's ability to outrun them. He had a faster horse, he was alone, and he probably wasn't resting either. But Rune knew better than to mention any of those things to Lia.

"At least eat," he admonished, tossing another stick on the fire. She shot him a look full of feral hostility and he smirked. "If you don't eat, you won't have strength enough to catch him."

She muttered something under her breath he was sure he didn't want to hear. Her stalking stride didn't falter for a moment. "Try again, Rune."

With a rough sound in his throat, he said, "As I've already explained, I can't pinpoint where he is. A bond doesn't work that way."

"But when he thinks about where he is or where

he's going, you can pick up those thoughts, right? You read my mind easy enough today."

"You're also not a spirit master. He's had much more practice keeping me out of his mind than you have. Before, he'd always kept me out for privacy's sake, but now he has another reason, doesn't he?"

Rune tried not to sound bitter, but it seeped into his tone anyway. He knew his bond brother had left him behind for his sake, for his safety, but that couldn't eliminate the sense of rejection and abandonment. They'd been together their entire lives. There'd been no question Rune would leave the palace with Destin, even if he did believe the search for the Vessel was a fool's errand. But now they were separated, and Rune was doing what would have been unthinkable back at the palace. He was trying to thwart his bond brother.

Lia slowed to a stop, studying him with unreadable gray eyes. "Second thoughts?"

"Regrets," he answered with a shake of his head. "I should have knocked him over the head a long time ago. Now he's going to believe I'm betraying him. Especially if he senses me rifling through his thick skull."

"All right," she said with cool calculation, rounding the fire to crouch by his side. "We don't want to tip him off. I can track him well enough anyway. But you'll still get a stray thought here and there without trying, won't you?"

He sighed, staring at her with an ache in his chest. "I was so certain you loved me for me," he murmured, lifting a sardonic eyebrow.

Her brows pulled together in a quick frown. "I'm not using you." When he just looked at her, she grimaced. "Fine, I am using you, but she's my baby sister, Rune. What would you do?"

He thought about it for a moment then laughed without humor. "I probably would've killed him. Why didn't you?"

She blinked, looking away. She seemed to notice Cleave's silent presence and rose to her feet, pacing again. "That's not important now."

Not for the first time, Rune wished he'd left the young sailor with the monks. "Tell me more of your sister," he said to distract her from the brooding thoughts he couldn't hear anymore but could read on her lovely face. "Does she look like you?"

"No, she takes after her father. Pale skin, blue eyes, and strawberry-blonde hair. With ringlets, for gods' sake," she said with a roll of her eyes. "The girl's never had a bad hair day. It's sickening."

Rune pursed his mouth to keep from smiling. "You don't have the same father?"

Humor fell away from her as if sheared off, her eyes darkening. "No." For a moment she said nothing more, pacing with a forceful stride. Rune was about to apologize for prying when she continued, "My mother met a man, an elemental, and fell in love, I guess. He didn't stick around. Pretty obvious when Ettie was born she wasn't my father's. My father was…well, I was about to say angry, but that's not a violent enough word."

Rune's gut clenched. "Violent?"

Her gray gaze flicked to his and then away, her expression hard. "We knew Ettie was special, but it wasn't until the Earth Keeper and Ephemeral showed up at our door we found out how special."

Cleave made a choking sound, eyes bugging out.

Rune couldn't blame him. "You've seen Ephemerals?"

"Well, just the one." Lia shrugged as if this was a modest achievement. "Ettie has seen more. She spent a lot of time with them and the Earth Keepers when we were growing up. Learning how to be the Vessel, I guess."

"What did they look like?" Cleave blurted, eyes round and gullible as a child's.

She grimaced and waved a dismissive hand. "All sparkly and see-through like the stories, but I think it's mostly for show. I was more impressed with the Keeper. I've never seen anybody so solid before, so…I don't know, there. He said more without words than any person I've ever met."

"They're also called the Wise Ones," Rune said, watching her with an equal measure of disbelief and envy. The two ancient peoples rarely showed themselves to the younger races any longer. They'd taken on a kind of mysticism making for great fairytales and legends. But it was hard to believe in the existence of creatures from such stories without seeing them in person. More than one elemental had declared them dead races, if they'd ever existed at all. He recalled the king had met with the Earth Keepers at least once, but he'd never seen one himself.

Lia settled into a cross-legged position next to the fire with easy grace, staring into the flame. Her gray gaze looked far away. "I suppose they're wise. But I didn't like how they looked at my sister. I know they helped her and she liked having them around, but the look in their eyes scared me."

"Why, did they seem interested in her power for themselves?"

She scoffed and shook her head. "No. They're old enough to know better. It wasn't greed, it was…" She swallowed, hands fisting in her lap. "They looked at her like she was already dead and just didn't know it yet," she said in a flat tone. Then she shuddered hard. "I've been protecting her most of my life and I'm afraid it's a losing battle."

With those stark words, she surged to her feet and stalked away into the darkness. Cleave met Rune's gaze in mute misery.

Rune shook his head and got to his feet. "Rest," he told the young sailor. "She won't wait through the night to travel again."

Following Lia's path out of the light, Rune moved through the scrub and sparse woods until his eyes adjusted to the dark. Still, he almost stumbled over her, her slim form merging with the night and the young tree she leaned against. "Lia." She ignored him, face turned up to the night sky. He put a hand on her shoulder as much to orient himself in the dark as to comfort her. "Destin would never harm your sister."

"Everything could harm my sister. She's so vulnerable, Rune. And so dumb about it," she hissed. "Whatever the Keepers taught her, it wasn't to protect herself. For some reason, she doesn't see the evil in anything or anybody. Only the luck of the gods has kept her in one piece."

"It must be more than luck. She's the Vessel."

"That doesn't make her invincible. She's just as fragile as the rest of us."

"So we'll find her. We'll protect her. Perhaps we

should go straight to her location and head Destin off rather than trailing behind him."

She shrugged, dislodging his hand and turning to face him. Nothing of her features showed in the dark, just a faint gleam of her eye. "If I knew her location, I wouldn't tell you. The prince might pluck it out of your head. But I don't know where she is. When I left her with Mama, I told them to find a safe place to hide."

"You have an idea where, though." He'd felt her certainty and resolve before she'd shrugged off his touch.

She was silent and still, as much a part of the darkness as any night animal. In contrast to the description of her sister, he could sense her capacity for violence, knew how tough, self-reliant, and dangerous she could be. But he knew other things about her that made her just as vulnerable as her sister. When he shifted away and changed the subject, it wasn't out of fear. "You seemed to know the monks well. How did you meet them?"

"Mama, Ettie, and I stayed there a lot when we were growing up. They're the guardians of the sanctuary of the Vessel of Power. Not that they did much guarding," she added in a sour tone.

"But not your father?" he asked, hoping she'd speak of it without him prying it out of her.

She was silent for a long moment then sighed. "The first few years of Ettie's life were hard on us. Father was furious when he learned Mama had been with another man, and made her life a living hell. Then he started to see how special Ettie and I were. I was changing so much it was freaky and things just seemed to happen around Ettie. Father tried to put a stop to it, tried to force us to be what he wanted, but it just kept getting worse.

"Then the Ephemeral and Keeper showed up and explained Ettie was the child of prophecy, born of both races; elemental and changeling. The new Vessel of Power. It was the last straw for my father. He waited until the ancients left and then beat my mother almost to death."

Rune's chest constricted until he could barely breathe, horrified as much by her flat, distant tone as by the words. "Lia," he croaked, but she wasn't finished.

"I tried to stop him. He turned on me instead. I took it for a little while, but then I just… I think it was when he screamed at Ettie, when it looked like he'd start on her, too, I lost it. She was wailing like kids do when they're scared or hurt. She just wanted it to stop. So I stopped it. I don't know what I changed into, but it was big enough to throw my father through the wall and out of the house. He disappeared that night. We never saw him again. The Keeper took us to the sanctuary the next day."

"Lia, I am so sorry." He tried to touch her.

She flowed away. "It was a long time ago. I don't need your sympathy."

"I know, but I need to give it."

She made a derisive noise but he didn't respond, watching her shadow. Then she sighed and stepped closer.

Rune wrapped his arms around her and rested his chin on her head. "Thank you. Now I understand why it's so difficult for you to trust an elemental. Your father must have hated us with a black passion. He would have tried to teach you the same."

Resting her forehead on his collarbone, she nodded. "Mama won't talk about it, won't tell me about Ettie's father, so all I can do is guess. I resented her for it, resented her and Ettie both for how they'd wrecked our family. At least that's what my father believed and I believed it, too, for a while. I think my mother stayed with him out of guilt, trying to make amends for what she'd done. I think the way I acted was part of what made her feel that, what made her take my father's attitude."

"You can't blame yourself. How old were you?"

"I was ten when he disappeared. Ettie was five. Thank the gods she doesn't remember much of it."

"You were both only children. Your parents were adults who knew what they were doing and should have been looking out for you. That's a parent's duty, to raise their children in love, not hate and violence."

"I think that's why I trust you, Rune," she drawled, patting his chest. "You're a hopeless optimist."

He chuckled. "I know you meant that as an insult, but I thank you anyway. My parents despair I'm too cynical."

Her head shot up and he imagined incredulity on her shadowed face. "Your parents sound scary. Almost as bad as my sister. Do they do things like walk in front of galloping horses and throw coins at thugs on the street?"

He winced. "They're happy, Lia, not suicidal. No wonder you're worrying yourself ragged. She sounds like a menace."

She pulled out of his arms and threw her hands up in the air. "She just doesn't think things through. She's too cheerful to think about the bad stuff, about how things could go wrong."

"That's astounding, after what you've been through. And considering what she is."

"Oh, yeah, Ettie's a real gem," she grumbled, but with an undertone of dry humor. "And don't think I don't know what you're doing. I heard that ragged comment. You're not as sneaky as you think you are, royal."

"But has it succeeded? Will you return to the fire and eat? Rest a while?"

"Only if you tuck me in and read me a bedtime story, Mama."

"May I kiss you goodnight?"

"Pervert."

"Darling, you flatter me."

She did eat a little and curled next to the fire, though Rune doubted she slept. On the other hand, he slept like a stone until she jostled him awake before dawn. She drove them without mercy until they were flying down the road again. To save time, she stayed in wolf form, adjusting her size to monstrous proportions in order to carry him. Riding a wolf had to be one of the strangest experiences of his life. After he got used to the disconcerting roll of her running gait, it exhilarated him.

Sugar, the mare, was less thrilled about running with a predator, but she adjusted with amazing aplomb, as if somehow she understood the great beast wasn't a wolf at all. She had a great deal of heart, but she wasn't Wind. Rune had to remind Lia again and again to slow down, to take rests for the horse as well as her companions. As the day wore on, she grew less and less tolerant of it.

The sun sank, painting the clouds in shades of vermillion fire. Rune was hunting for a gentle way of broaching the subject of a stop for the night, when Lia stiffened and skidded to a halt so hard Rune almost flew over her head. Sugar passed them before Cleave could slow the mare and come around.

"Lia!" Rune growled as he struggled to right himself. "What the devil…?"

Predatory anger whispered along their connection with the thought, *company. A group up ahead. They smell hostile.*

Rune twitched and looked at the empty road ahead of them. "Hostile has a smell?"

Shut up or I will bite you. The feral edge to her thoughts seemed too capable of it, so he held his tongue. *I see burn marks. I think Destin went through them. Some of them smell wounded. He didn't stop them though. They're still moving, heading the same direction.*

"Is it my uncle?"

How should I know? Could be him. Some smell like brine. But could just be a group of travelers who didn't like your prince's attitude.

"We need to find out."

No, we need to get past them and stop your blasted elemental prince.

"What is it?" Cleave asked, not privy to Lia's half of the conversation.

"Lia smells trouble ahead—" was all he had time for before she launched into an all-out sprint. He yelped and grabbed fistfuls of her shaggy coat to keep seated. "Are you mad?" he bellowed in her ear.

She ignored him, their connection writhing with

focused determination. Not a good sign.

"Gods curse it, Lia, they won't just allow you through!"

Hold on tight. When I say go, give me an updraft.

"An updraft? What—?" They rounded a turn and the road suddenly bulged with people bristling with weapons. Rune shut his mouth and clenched his jaw, breath coming hard and fast.

As Lia had said, the group was facing away, heading along the road in Destin's path. They didn't notice the gigantic wolf bearing down on them, and Rune had time to identify most of them as hired mercenaries, but the two riding horses at the front of the group were elementals. One of whom was Uncle Storm.

The rear guard caught sight of them and began to whirl. Eylee'ai launched herself into the air. For a moment, Rune thought she meant to jump over them all. Then the shaggy coat in his fists twisted and changed in some fundamental way. Her body under him grew less solid and he nearly let go in surprise. *Now, Rune, GO!*

Wings snapped out to either side of him and thrust down in a powerful beat, but he could tell his weight would drive her back to the ground. He shifted his hold so he had one hand free and the other buried in her bronze feathers. With a sweeping gesture he called wind and gave her the updraft she'd demanded, thrusting them toward the sky.

An arrow whistled by his ear and he ducked with a hiss of alarm, glancing down. Several of his uncle's entourage notched bows with more arrows. Rune wove air in a fast-moving funnel around them, whipping up dust and debris to obscure their line of sight.

The archers let fly anyway, but Lia banked to the left and spun on a wingtip before lifting her head to the sky and pumping her wings hard. The ground receded below them with shocking speed. The people shrank until they were splotches of color on the strip of brown road running through greenery.

"Lia? Lia! What are you doing?" he called, fighting to keep his seat and his grip. Their vertical assent threatened to spill him back to the earth. He'd never realized before how slippery feathers could be. "You can't leave Cleave behind!"

They're elementals. He's one of them. He'll be fine.

"That's absurd! Lia, fly straight before I fall." When she leveled out, he continued, "My uncle isn't known for mercy or forgiveness. If he doesn't kill Cleave outright, he'll clap him in chains."

She didn't answer him in words, but her turmoil rushed across their connection, a jumble of anger, dismay, guilt, frustration, and longing. He understood more about the last emotion than she would probably appreciate. Protecting her sister wasn't the only reason for her need to reach Destin. Though she tried to bury it deep, Rune caught glimpses of her fascination for his soul brother. It gave him a pang of dread and surge of hope in equal measure. He'd never seen two people more suited for one another, but the circumstances did not bode well for a happy ending.

Rune shook off the nebulous dread and focused on the problem at hand. "Little sister, you know it's wrong to leave Cleave to Storm. He's only a boy. I know you need to stop Des, but we shouldn't just sacrifice—"

She cut him off with a shrill raptor's scream, piercing right through his ears into his brain, stunning him silent and thoughtless. *Who are you calling little?* Her disgruntled thought carried with it a kick of resentment, but she didn't argue his point. Instead, she folded her eagle wings and dove.

Rune lost his stomach and ability to breathe somewhere close to the clouds and wondered, as he watched the ground rush toward them through tear-blurred eyes, if his heart was going to vacate his body as well. It was rattling hard enough to break out of his chest.

"Lia!" he shouted through clenched teeth, but she didn't slow her descent. They plummeted toward the earth, his uncle and the mercenaries expanding like a bad dream. They had surrounded Cleave. He sat on Sugar, hands in the air, facing the king's brother.

Just before they smashed into the group, Lia loosed another soul-shuddering raptor cry and opened her wings with a snap. Rune nearly fell off again, struggling to secure his seat as Lia make a grab for Cleave. The mercenaries were shouting, ducking, and scrambling in disarray, but Rune couldn't be sure his uncle would be as disorganized. With more haste than finesse, he called wind and encircled them in a cyclone.

The combination of raptor and cyclone must have been too much for Sugar, even with her sweet, gentle temperament. She reared, whinnying in shrill fear. Lia back-winged in a frantic lurch and Cleave screamed.

Oh gods, I'm hurting him...

"Fly, Lia, fly! Lift us out of here!" His command sounded callous and self-serving, but his uncle's red flame swirled around them. Whatever injury she'd given Cleave, being burned alive was a worse fate. Arrows thrummed, though none were flying true through Rune's windstorm.

Lia swept her wings down in a powerful beat, but Rune could tell their combined weight was too much for her. She wasn't going to be able to get off the ground. He focused and gave her another updraft of air. Then he almost fell off yet again when she expanded under him, growing large enough to heave them all upward.

This is not comfortable. Her mental voice was thick with warning and strain. Rune wasn't sure what she meant but assumed it wasn't good. They needed to get out of there as fast as possible. Lia was making headway, ascending into the sky, but the ground was receding too slowly. The cyclone turned into a maelstrom of fire, blazing ominous red. Rune closed his eyes, gathered his strength, and concentrated.

The cyclone blew outward, scattering fire with it into the surrounding fighters. Rune didn't expect his tactic to do much damage, hoping instead for a distraction long enough to get away. With the cyclone gone, he put all his efforts into a sustained gust of wind under Lia's wings.

She responded as if they'd practiced this maneuver a thousand times, tucking Cleave close to her underbelly and balancing their combined weight as she snapped her wings out to their fullest extent and rode the updraft, adding a powerful beat every few moments to increase their speed and ascent.

Rune had just begun to hope they'd gotten out of arrow range when a shaft of crimson fire struck Lia where her left wing connected to her body. She shrieked, the wing collapsing in and sending them into a horrible, tumbling spin. Flames scorched Rune and he beat at her burning feathers and his blazing pants leg.

A moment later, the sky filled with arrows.

Chapter 16

Destin closed his eyes, slumping lower in the saddle. His once tireless stallion plodded along the road like a weary workhorse, head drooping almost as much as Destin's. He'd run Wind too hard. Neither of them had had enough rest. He needed to get far enough ahead of his uncle, though, before he stopped.

The memory of the path he'd blazed through his uncle's forces still sent a chill down his spine. He'd meant only to scatter them, shake the ground under them, and create a chaos of fire to open the road for Wind to streak by. He didn't have the time or the inclination to fight Uncle Storm. Eylee'ai was on his trail.

The thought of the changeling chasing him had struck tinder along his bones and created a raging firestorm. He'd cleared the road with one white and merciless sweep. He hadn't stopped, instead taking advantage of the escape route.

Guilt gnawed at him. He knew he'd injured some of them, maybe even killed a few. Granted, they had planned to do him harm, but they were only following his uncle's orders. His uncle should have been his sole target, but he'd lost control of his fire.

The now familiar hollow sickness rose inside him again, shortening his breath. His father had always accused him of weakness, of having a vast inner flaw passed down to him by his frail mother. And here he was, revealing his weakness at last by losing control over the one element he'd always taken such pains to master. Even worse, he'd become a real danger to those around him.

The memory of his red handprint on Eylee'ai's smooth skin sent a surge of illness rising into his throat. He had to stay away from her, her and Rune both, or he would hurt them again. His only hope was retrieving the Vessel and taking it to his father. He would do one thing right in this entire calamity, fulfill his duty to his father and sovereign. King Stern would praise him for once and perhaps even help him restore his control.

Destin buried the knowledge that the Vessel was a girl. It was easier to think of the Vessel as a thing, a prized object. He told himself he had no choice.

In the middle of his rationalizations, sensation struck him, pain and fear washing through him like a tidal wave. "Rune!" he shouted and jerked around in his saddle, gazing back the way he'd come. Fire flared in the distance, small red blasts streaking the sky at intervals. His uncle was trying to burn something out of the sky. Destin feared he knew what that something was. "Brother," he whispered and groped blindly for their bond. The sensation of falling was so strong he had to grip the saddle with both hands. There was pain in his leg, a blur of fast approaching forest, fear but not for himself. *Lia...*

Destin wrenched Wind around, ignoring the stallion's snort of protest and stomping of hooves. *Rune!* He called through their bond. *Rune, what's happening?*

Arrows, was Rune's distracted, disoriented

response. *Fire. Crashing!*

Destin dropped the reins and reached, but the distance was too great. He cried out at the impact, rocking in his saddle at the shock of sensation and fear.

For a moment, a terrifying blankness erased their bond, a dark nothingness worse than anything Destin had experienced before. Then a trickle of pain lifted the crushing weight from his heart.

Rune? Rune, answer me! Are you all right?

Depends on your definition. There was a surge of panic across their bond then an enormous sweep of relief. *Be easy, soul brother. We're alive. See you soon,* Rune added with a thread of wry humor before he severed their connection.

Destin sat still for a long moment, taking deep breaths to calm his nerves and absorb the pain from Rune's exclusion. For the first time, his cousin had shut the door on their bond. Always before, Destin had been the one to barricade himself in and refused Rune entry, citing privacy. He wondered if Rune had been hurt by his unintentional rejections through the years.

He wondered if hurting people had been his habit all along.

Rune had said they were alive. He knew his cousin was traveling with Lia and Cleave—he'd eavesdropped a bit on Rune while he slept. Rune's mental tone had been tense but not as worried as he would have been if either of the others had a serious injury. And his last comment indicated they'd be following him again soon. They were alive, well enough to travel, and he assumed out of his uncle's clutches.

All of which meant he needed to keep moving. But he continued to sit, staring back the way he'd come with a longing so intense it radiated pain through his chest.

He wanted to be with them.

His hands clenched on the reins. His longing was not just to be with his lifelong companion and friend. He also needed to see Lia, to assure himself she was whole, to place himself between her and his murderous uncle. They were both in danger, and it was all he could do to keep from spurring Wind into a full gallop back to them. *I would only put them in worse danger,* he thought, swallowing past a stricture in his throat. Bile rose as he pictured again the burn in the shape of his hand. He could not help them.

Clenching his jaw hard enough to make his face hurt, he turned Wind back around and urged him forward. The only thing he could do was continue on. Get the Vessel. Return to his father. Try not to destroy anything or anyone in the process.

He reached a crossroads and checked the weathered road marker to be sure he was on the right path. Churling Bay was at least a two day journey up the road. Eylee'ai had been there. He was certain people had noticed her. She was, in his opinion, unforgettable. He would trace her steps, find out where she'd come from, and at some point discover when she'd last been with her family. From there, he would track the Vessel to its current location. It wouldn't be easy, but he would succeed.

Failure was not an option.

****

"Amazing," Rune said for the millionth time.

"Would you quit?" Eylee'ai snarled, pushing his face away from her healing shoulder. "I'm not doing this to give you a thrill, you nutty royal."

"But it's not even scarring," Rune marveled, avoiding her hand to lean close again, nose almost touching her skin as he watched the healing process. "And the arrow wound in your side only scarred a bit. Amazing. May I see it again?"

She smacked him. He didn't seem to notice.

A throaty chuckle sounded from somewhere beyond Rune in the dimness of the tent. "I have never seen an elemental so taken with a changeling. Are you certain he is not your beloved?"

Lia would have glared at the teasing older woman if she could've seen her beyond Rune's head. "He's not my anything. You can have him."

That got Rune's attention, head coming up and hazel eyes widening with furtive alarm.

With another chuckle, the healer leaned in and rested a hand on his shoulder. "You hear that, boy? I'm not as quick to change as this young thing, but I wager I've got a few tricks you haven't seen yet."

"Ah, that's tempting, Healer Brees'na," Rune choked, easing away from her grip. "But I should see to Cleave now." He bolted out of the tent like lightning.

"Amazing," Lia drawled to the healer's soft laughter.

"Alas, he is too fast for me to catch. I suppose I must content myself with that old chieftain of mine."

Lia made a disparaging sound in the back of her throat. "You wouldn't want him anyway. He's annoying."

"So it is not his mark you have cast so passionately upon your back?"

Lia twitched, staring at the smiling woman with

wary alarm. "Um. I didn't know you'd seen it. Why do you describe it that way?"

"As passionate? It's in the splay of the fingers, in the intimate placing of the mark. It's quite beautiful and intricate. The casting must have taken much time and emotion to create. What do the symbols mean?"

Caution held her tongue as she met the gray gaze of the changeling healer. She was grateful for the rescue of the nomadic tribe who'd whisked the three of them away through the forest like tree spirits, hiding them from Rune's searching uncle and caring for their wounds. But a full explanation of her casting would only raise even more dangerous questions than the ones brightening the other woman's eyes.

She'd already put herself in jeopardy by letting the healer see the casting and watch how fast she could heal. She tried not to let other changelings know the extent of her abilities. It sparked jealousy. Or they might see her as an abomination they had to eliminate. She'd dealt with the whole range of changeling reactions before and wasn't thrilled with the light of curiosity in Brees'na's angular face. Nomads were wilder and less apt to judge, but still…

"It's, uh, symbolic of fire," she hedged, shifting against the bedding. "Burning desire," she mumbled, her face flaming with embarrassment.

The older woman smiled gently. "I would love to meet the man who inspired such an exquisite fever. He must be something."

Lia blushed harder. "How do you know it wasn't a woman?" she asked to deflect the conversation.

"The handprint is large. I guessed it was male." She paused, smile fading into a look of warm concern.

"You're traveling with two young men who aren't family. They care for you, but it worries me to see a young woman without the protection and support of her family. Why are you alone, child?"

Because I am my family's protection, she couldn't say aloud, mouth twisting a little. "You're kind to worry, but you don't need to. I'm used to being on my own and can watch out for myself."

"The wound in your side and burn on your shoulder say otherwise."

Lia turned her face away to hide a flare of anger. She knew the woman meant no offense, but Lia's independence was a source of pride and having it questioned triggered her temper. "The world is a dangerous place," she said in a wooden voice. "I've been hurt before and will be again. But I'm still free. I'm no one's prisoner or slave or whore. The man who gave me these wounds and the people with him…" She turned her head to meet the healer's gaze again with steady intensity. "Stay out of their way. He's going to keep moving on up the road because there's somebody he wants more than me, but if you get in his way, he'll go through you. Got it?"

Brees'na's full lips curved in a faint smile, but her tone was respectful. "We will heed what you say. I admire your strength, young Eylee'ai. I cannot speak for my mate, but I would be delighted to welcome you into our tribe. Though you bear it well, you need not be so alone."

Lia stared at her for a stunned moment. "I…oh." Other changelings had expressed concern about her solitude, but none had invited her into their lives, into their families as this woman had just done. "I'm honored. But there's something I have to do. And I do have a family. I'll be with them soon."

The woman's sharp eyes narrowed. "Does this something have to do with the person your attacker is seeking?"

"Well," Lia stalled and thought fast. Not fast enough, though.

"That person wouldn't happen to be the man whose hand is cast upon your skin, would it?"

Her blush gave her away.

The healer sat back with a noncommittal hum, her angular face unreadable. She was silent for a moment, tugging on one of the small braids in her silver-streaked brown hair. Then she sighed. "This is hard. It's clear you are going toward danger instead of away from it. My instinct as a mother is to protect you, but since I'm not your relation, it's not my place. Is there anything we can do for you?"

"You've done plenty," Lia argued. "You put yourselves at risk to get us to safety and patched us up. It's more than I would have asked for. I can't accept anything else."

The woman pursed her lips and glanced down at the blanket draping Lia's naked form. "Not even covering?"

"Ah." Lia looked down at herself and squirmed a bit. Their provisions and possessions, including her borrowed clothes, had been strapped to Sugar and were now lost. "Well, I would be grateful for anything you might have on hand. Cast-offs would be great."

"And your friends?"

Lia looked at her blankly. "They're wearing clothes."

"Both are wounded and can't heal as fast as you. The baby-cheeked one should not be traveling."

Lia flinched and wallowed in a moment of guilt. When she'd snatched Cleave off the horse's back, she'd dug her talons into his shoulders. Their wild escape had only made those wounds worse. "I can't stay," she muttered, mind whirling with images of her sister in royal clutches.

"But they can."

Lia thought about it. "Rune won't. He'll insist on coming with me. Cleave, though…he needs a healer's touch and lots of rest. After that, he should go home."

"He is already under my care and protection. Seeing him safely home is a small enough thing to ask."

An enormous weight lifted from her shoulders. She took a deep breath and let it out on a sigh of relief. "Thank you. For all you've done. You've been wonderful and I can't tell you how much I appreciate your help."

"You are one of us," Brees'na murmured, reaching out to stroke a gentle finger under one of Lia's gray, changeling eyes. "We don't leave our young stranded. Now," she continued with a smile curving her lips, "let's discuss clothing. My daughter has outgrown many of her things. Before she grew large with child, she was about your size and if I may brag, she has a keen eye for color."

"Uh-oh," Lia said without thinking and made the woman laugh. Nomads were famous for their bright, revealing apparel and outgoing, sensual natures. She didn't have a problem with it, but she was in the habit of blending with the crowd, not standing out and attracting attention to herself and her vulnerable sister.

"Don't worry. We will find something to suit you. When will you be leaving us?"

"As soon as possible," Lia answered, glancing down at her shoulder. She'd leave right now if the healer would let her. Her shoulder hurt, but not enough to keep her down. The arrow slice in her side still throbbed with a dull, angry pain and would slow her down more than the burn, but she could still travel.

Destin had a solid head start on them by now. She'd been so sure she was catching up, but they'd lost whatever ground they'd gained in the nomad camp. And Destin now had his uncle nipping at his heels. Urgency gnawed at her, tightening all her muscles and driving her after the elemental prince. *He can handle himself,* she thought in quick denial. She didn't need to help him. She'd seen how capable he was of dealing with his uncle. She was only worried about what would happen if he found her sister.

"What is his name?"

Lia looked up, startled. Was the woman reading her mind? "Uh, who?"

Brees'na gave her a slow smile. "The man you are chasing."

Lia cleared her throat, gaze sliding away to study the sparse interior of the tent. "Destin." She thought it would be safe enough to say that much.

"Another elemental, I would guess. Such an ill-luck name."

Lia frowned. "What do you mean?"

"To name a child Destiny is to tempt the gods to take a hand in his life. Perhaps his parents believed they could avoid divine notice by omitting the last letter." She shook her head and clucked her tongue. "Foolish.

Elementals are reckless. To be noticed by the gods is a hazard no child should face."

Lia stared at her, ice forming around her spine. She had no doubt the gods had touched the life of the elemental prince. He'd been chosen to search for the Vessel of their divine power. Some might think of the quest as glorious or heroic. Lia knew better, the gods' notice was going to be hazardous for them all.

Brees'na leaned forward with a crease in her brow. "I'm sorry. I didn't mean to frighten you. I'm sure your man will be fine."

"He's not my man," Lia said, her mind still occupied with Destin's name. Could so small a thing have caused all of this? The audacity of two parents believing they could write their child's future in his name. Had that triggered divine judgment? It didn't seem possible. Maybe it'd been the final insult, the right circumstance at a time the gods had already decreed for their test.

"You've claimed him, Eylee'ai. If he is not your man now, I wager he soon will be," the healer declared with a throaty chuckle.

Lia's face burned again and she grimaced. Maybe the casting hadn't been such a good idea. She thought about getting rid of it. That would be smarter. Less conspicuous. Less obvious. The memory of Destin's hand in the small of her back sent quivering weakness through her muscles, and she stared up at the tent canvas with a bewildered sigh.

She left the casting on her skin. From a trunk full of clothing Brees'na brought her, Lia chose a skirt and top the color of his eyes. It bared her midriff and exposed the casting for all to see. *Gods be merciful.* At least she had sense enough to cover the foolish outfit with a long cloak she found at the bottom of the trunk.

A few hours later, she stood over Cleave’s cot, shuffling her feet. His eyes snapped with accusation and his jaw set in a stubborn line.

“I’m sorry, but you can’t come,” Lia said.

“I can ride,” he protested, struggling to sit up. “Lady Lia, I won’t hold you back. I swear.”

Rune leaned past Lia and pushed the boy back against the cot. “Stay down, Cleave. You’ll tear your stitches.”

Lia decided not to point out he’d already held her back. “You’re a sailor. You belong on a ship with your own kind, not stomping through the countryside after a crazy prince.”

Cleave glowered at her. “My prince is not crazy. And he is my kind. So is Lord Rune—”

“Gods’ help us,” Rune interrupted with a sigh. “You aren’t able to travel and we need to leave now.”

“But—”

“Cleave,” Lia said, touching his hot, damp forehead. “You’ve been very brave. I’m sure your prince appreciates your service, but it’s time to go home now.”

“But what about you, lady?” he asked, a brightness in his eyes like the prelude to tears. “Won’t you need help? I could protect you.”

Lia pressed her lips together to hold in a bark of laughter. Good gods, the poor, deluded boy thought she needed looking after.

Rune came to her rescue. “I’ll be at her side, Cleave. We’ll protect each other.”

Cleave slumped back against the cot and turned his

face away. "All right. I said I wouldn't hold you back and I won't. Gods be with you both," he whispered. "May the Traveler guide your steps."

"Thanks, Cleave. Safe journey to you, too," Lia muttered and hurried to escape.

When Rune joined her outside the tent, he gave her a disapproving look and shook his head.

"What?" she asked in startled defense.

"The boy is in love with you. You could have at least not acted as though you were happy to be rid of him."

"I… that's not…I didn't! Oh, gods." She folded her arms and glowered at the ground for a moment. Then she heaved a sigh and turned back toward the tent.

Rune caught her arm. "Never mind. There's nothing you could say that would ease it for him. He'll recover in time."

Lia hesitated then sighed again and let Rune draw her away. The horrible, guilty truth, she was happy to be rid of him. She'd liked him well enough and wouldn't have minded his company any other time, but he'd slowed her down when she couldn't afford the delay. The entire world couldn't afford the delay.

The other part of her guilt was more selfish. She was relieved not to have a constant reminder of what she'd done, how she'd hurt him when she'd been a monstrous bird of prey. This guilt had roots far back in her past, roots she didn't want to explore. *I'm a selfish toad,* she thought as she walked away from Cleave's tent. The fear she might be an abomination danced at the edge of her thoughts before she buried it. She didn't have time for self-doubt.

They said their thanks and swift goodbyes to the

tribe members who'd rescued them before stepping out of the camp and into the thick woods. Lia led the way, Rune limping along behind her. They were quiet for a while, moving through the greenery at a slow but steady pace in deference to Rune's burnt leg.

Then Rune cleared his throat. "Out of curiosity, why are we walking?"

"I don't want to change where the tribe can see me."

"But they're all changelings."

"They won't understand." Lia glanced over her shoulder. Rune wore a quizzical frown. "They've seen how fast I heal and Brees'na knows about my casting. I don't know if any of them saw what form I was in when we crashed, but it wasn't a natural shape and size. This tribe is pretty easygoing, but they won't take it well if they find out just how much of a freak I am. I don't want them deciding not to help Cleave because of me." *Or deciding to hunt us down.*

"You're no freak, Lia. You're gifted. The gods gave you great power."

She said nothing. He was an elemental and wouldn't understand the changelings' respect for the natural order and their revulsion for anything that warped it. This belief was the fundamental difference and rift between their races. Elementals used nature for their own means, warping the natural order every time they wove the elements. Rune wouldn't see how her "gift" would cause changelings to revile her.

He must have sensed something of her feelings or thoughts. His tone turned defensive. "Being near the gods' Vessel made you what you are. They gave you the right to use their gift. Why else would you be able to do what you do?"

"Maybe they give us abilities to see if we'll misuse them, if we are responsible enough to have them in the first place."

He was quiet for a moment. "So you believe you shouldn't shift into an eagle form because it's a misuse of the power they gave you?"

"Eagles don't grow that big. But I'm going to change into it anyway. It's the fastest way to get where we need to be. At least an eagle is a real beast and not some monster."

He drew in a sharp breath. "Lia, just because your father named you a monster doesn't make you one."

She spun so fast she almost slammed into him. "How did you…?" She glared at him, hands fisting at her sides. "Don't do that, Rune. You don't have the right to dig around in my head."

"I didn't," he said, hands raised and eyes soft with sympathy. "I guessed."

"We're not talking about this." She spun back around and stomped through the greenery, anger and furtive panic driving her onward. *I'm not thinking about this,* she told herself and stared ahead.

When she judged they'd gone far enough away from the tribe, she stopped, shrugged off her borrowed pack, and narrowed her eyes at her companion. "Fix your eyeballs over there and don't even think about looking."

He raised his eyebrows with a smirk. "All of a sudden you're shy?"

"You're supposed to be my soul brother. Brothers aren't supposed to see their sisters naked. And they sure aren't supposed to drool if they do."

He made a haughty face and fixed his glance to where she'd pointed. "I beg your pardon, I have never drooled. And being related to your soul doesn't rule out admiring the view."

She snorted, stripping out of her new clothing. "You don't admire. You fantasize. Pretty sure that's gross."

He grumbled under his breath, but she ignored him, tucking away her clothes and placing the pack at his feet. Then she stepped back and morphed, expanding her raptor's body until she could carry his weight.

Ruffling her feathers and lifting her wings, she shook herself and shifted her feet, assessing the feel of this new body. Though she was enormous for an eagle, the form was light and agile. Crouching low, she allowed Rune to slip onto her back, then shook out her wings again and turned her gaze skyward. An odd hunger burned in her avian breast for the blue and white expanse, for the open freedom of the sky.

Leaping upward and ignoring Rune's yelp of dismay and yank on her feathers, she pumped her wings and rose through the trees to burst into sun and sky with a cry of triumph. Every animal form had its amazements and advantages, but flying had always filled her with such joy. The thrill of aerial acrobatics was only part of her pleasure. With the earth and all of life's complications at a serene distance, she could just be. The empty sky held no worries or fears, just open freedom and peace.

For a moment, Lia allowed herself to feel peace, rising through the air toward blue and white serenity, thinking nothing but how the air flowed over her wings and through her feathers like a caress, like a welcome.

But Rune's weight pulled her thoughts back to earth and her beleaguered family. With a mournful cry, she hovered on the wind and looked down again, orienting herself to the lay of the land. Her eagle's keen eyesight traced the coast and spotted the port where they had landed. Smoke rose from there, thicker than she would expect from a human habitation.

Your royal ship is burning, she thought at Rune with an inner grimace. She hoped the crew had made it off before it had gone up in flame. Rune didn't respond. She wondered if he wasn't able to read her thoughts in this form or if he just didn't have much to say about it. He'd predicted this would happen when they were still at the monastery.

Focusing her sight further along the coast, she caught the wind and flew toward Churling Bay and her wayward prince.

****

The Vessel of Power stared out at the night and sighed. It was time. She'd been preparing for this all her life and wasn't afraid. She was surprised to feel melancholy about it, though. Leaving her mother was the hardest part.

Merr'et, Ettie to everyone who knew her, rose from the edge of the cot and glanced back into the shadows of the one-room cabin. Her mother lay motionless on the other cot by the fire, her weary face looking even more haggard by the dim light of the dying flames. Hyloa'ki was not made for this life of running, hiding, and constant fear of discovery. They had both relied on Lia much more than they'd realized, understanding after she was gone how she'd shielded and guided them, providing them with a sense of safety.

You rest, Mama, she thought, the sight of her mother's face blurring with her tears. *I love you.*

Turning away, she stepped to the door and opened it with slow care. The hinges squeaked just a little, but her mother didn't stir. Slipping out into the night, she closed the portal and took a deep breath.

Her life was about to change. Her dreams had led her to this point. The Keepers and Ephemerals had done what they could to prepare her, but only she could move into her future. She could do it willingly or be dragged kicking and screaming. Either way, her future had arrived and she had to face it.

Taking another deep breath, she stepped away from the cabin and onto the little forest path leading to her fate.

Chapter 17

Churling Bay was a bustling town, sitting on the border between elemental land and the nebulous changeling territories, a space occupied by humans as well as changelings and elementals. Lia had brought her family here to hide with the idea that the border would be one of the last places an elemental would look for the Vessel.

It was also a great location to listen for rumors coming out of their nation. She'd heard the elemental king had given his son the task of searching for the Vessel only days before the prince appeared, like a bad dream, in the town. Destin hadn't announced himself as royalty, but he'd been recognized. Knowledge of his presence, an exciting first in Churling memory, spread like wildfire.

Striding along the wooden walkway of the busy thoroughfare with Rune by her side, Lia remembered her feelings of shock and foreboding when she'd realized the prince had come. Most of her life she'd known the day would arrive, the search for the Vessel would begin, but she hadn't expected to witness the start of it. Watching the prince begin his search in the town where her sister hid had been an uncomfortable experience.

Didn't take him long to find his way back here either, she thought with a grimace. She'd at least expected his new search to take a while, expected to have some time to avoid the searcher and hide her sister where no one would find her. Avoid or kill, she'd made that decision when she'd seen the prince in Churling Bay. He was too close too soon. His death would have extended the search for years.

Instead, she was now wandering around Churling with another royal elemental, tracking down a man who was very much alive and getting closer to finding her sister by the moment. The gods had a strange sense of humor. The sly God Effrenu, master of chaos, must be snickering his divine rear off.

"Why this tavern?" Rune asked as they turned into the entrance.

"You don't remember it? You and Destin were here last time you were in town. This was where I heard about you."

He frowned, looking around the dim interior. "We visited a few. I don't recall this one."

The proprietress, a big, beefy woman with a gaping smile and shrewd eyes, lumbered over. "Welcome, good sir," she rumbled, no doubt reacting to Rune's refined air. Lia ducked her head, hiding her face in her hood and edging behind Rune. "Can I get you and yer lady a room, or would you be lookin' for a meal?"

Rune didn't hesitate, jumping right into the role of a lord about town. "Bless you, dear lady, but I'm searching for my companion. He and I were separated on the road and I've only just arrived in town. I assume he arrived before me. He is about this height, dark hair, scar on his cheek…"

The woman's massive chest rose on a sharp inhale, her eyes widening. "Aye, I know the one. Rumor is he's a prince." Her voice rose at the end.

Rune ignored her curiosity. "You've seen him, then. Have you any idea where he is?"

"He ain't here, sir. He keeps askin' about a changeling," the woman answered with a deferential air, her gaze darting to Lia in her nomadic clothing. "A changeling and her family."

Lia almost bit through her tongue to keep from demanding what the woman had told Destin. She held herself still and willed Rune to do it for her.

"A changeling? That's odd. Perhaps he means my traveling companion and is searching for us in turn. Did he give any indication where he was headed from this location?"

The proprietress focused her attention on Rune with an ingratiating smile. "He didn't right say, sir, but if y'give me a bit to think on it, I might 'member what I said to 'im."

The woman was looking for a bribe to sharpen her memory, but Rune had lost all his possessions on the road. The only coin he had was his face. He turned on the charm, smiling at the beefy woman as if she was the only female in existence. He clasped one of her thick hands and raised it to his mouth. "My dear lady, I would give you the world if I could, but I happen to be in a bit of a rush. I would take it as a great service if you would tell me where you might have directed my friend."

He was handsome, quite charming, and the woman's face turned ruddy in response, but she must have had plenty of experience with handsome and charming before. Her smile turned shark-like.

Lia sighed, reaching into the little pouch of coins

she'd pick-pocketed off a traveler on their way into town. Before the tavern owner could repeat her demand in more direct terms, Lia held out the coin between her first two fingers. The woman's experienced eyes fixed on the money through the dimness with practiced intensity. "Maybe this'll help," Lia said in a low voice, still careful to hide her features in the hood. She didn't want the woman to remember her from the first time she'd been here. It wasn't likely, since she hadn't spoken to the proprietress, but the less she triggered the woman's memory the better.

"Yer a gracious lady," the woman simpered, plucking the coin from Lia and tucking it away before they could blink. "Let's see now, I do 'member tellin' the young man the place down the way did more changeling business than m'self. They're a lusty lot, they are, beggin' yer pardon, lady, and ol' Trig and Sal do brisk business in beer and bed bouncin'." She guffawed once then sobered when they didn't laugh with her. "If yer into that sort. My place is quieter, no doubt, but I dish up the best grub in Churling. Care to try some?"

Rune gave her a gorgeous smile and Lia backed to the door. "You've been very helpful. If you see him again, will you tell him I'm looking for him? Thank you so much." He followed Lia out onto the walkway. Slipping an arm around her waist, he leaned close and whispered, "Where did you get the coin?"

"You don't want to know," she answered, elbowing him away and looking down the street. "She was talking about Red Satin, a tavern and sex shop just down the way there. She's right, there are plenty of changelings there, both client and staff. Destin ought to find lots to keep him busy."

"Sex shop?" Rune kept pace, staring down at her with a lifted eyebrow.

"You'd rather call it a whorehouse?" she asked with an impatient look. "There's a side entrance we should use instead of marching through the front door. I don't want to give him any warning."

"Lead on," he said in a bland voice, a smirk curling his mouth.

Lia ignored his peculiar sense of humor, leading him down the street and into a narrow alleyway, dank and dim even in the light of day. Rune muttered something unappreciative under his breath, but she continued to ignore him, stalking straight to the side entrance. There was a short hallway beyond, the small door to her left leading down into the cellar while the door on the right stood open to the kitchen. Taking a deep, fortifying breath, Lia stepped into the steaming kitchen with Rune on her heels.

"Hey! You ain't allowed…Lia?" The cook's red, sweating face crinkled with surprise. "That you, girl? Where you been? Trig's fit ta crack yer head."

"I'm not back, Bean. You don't see me," Lia told him as she wound through the cramped kitchen past two workers staring at her with wide eyes and open mouths.

"Whad'ya mean? Got me a load here and you go runnin' off ta gods know where."

Lia paused, meeting her former boss's gaze across a wide table. "Pretty sure I'm not coming back, Bean. You'll have to do without me."

His brow furrowed, eyes lifting over her shoulder to Rune. "You got yourself in trouble, little girl?"

Lia smiled at the irony. "Don't be stupid, Beanie, I am trouble. And I'm not here right now," she added with a pointed lift of her eyebrows, tugging the hood of her cloak around her face. Without waiting for his reaction, she headed for the door into the salon.

Rune followed right behind her, clearing his throat. "You were employed in a sex shop?" he whispered over her shoulder when she paused at the door.

"Shut up, I worked in the kitchen," she muttered, shooting him a glare. "Past this door is a set of rooms where clients pick a partner to take upstairs. It's got more cover than the dining room, so we'll start here. If we don't see him, we'll work our way to the front. Anybody looks at us, just act like my jay."

"Act like your what?"

She paused in the act of easing open the door and sent him an impatient look. "My jay, my fancy boy."

His handsome face altered to an odd expression. "You want me to be the whore?"

"I need to cover my face, not be recognized. Working girls don't get paid if they cover the goods. Don't worry, you're pretty enough. They'll just think you're new." She patted his arm and pushed the door open enough to slip through. Rune spluttered but followed without another word.

The rooms beyond the door oozed decadence and indulgence, plush with lots of satin furniture and curtains, sultry colors, and secluded nooks for the illusion of privacy. Lia had planned to use these nooks as cover, slipping from one room to the next while hiding from both staff and her prince. She hadn't expected to find Destin nestled in a nook with one of the house's most popular girls.

Lia shoved Rune behind a lacy curtain, pressing against him in a parody of passion. Then she stiffened in Rune's arms, staring through the lace at the couple smiling at one another, at Destin's arm across the woman's shoulders and her hand pressed to his chest. The prostitute was practically sitting in his lap, face glowing as she gazed at him.

"Rune."

"Lia."

"He's being charming."

"It appears so."

"I didn't know he could do charming, Rune. He's never even smiled at me."

"He's attempting to gain information."

"She wants to give him a lot more than information."

"Well, it's not as though he would…" Rune stopped talking when Destin rose and drew the woman to her feet. The prince wrapped an arm around her waist and the couple strolled away, bodies so close not a breath could come between them.

"They're heading for the stairs," Lia said through gritted teeth.

"Oh?" Rune's tone rang false, edged with discomfort.

Lia glared at him. "The beds are upstairs, Rune. It looks like your blasted prince is taking a little break from his gods-forsaken search."

He grimaced, arms tightening a fraction around her. "That would be unusual. He's never paid for a woman before."

"With the look on her face, I'm pretty sure he's not gonna pay now," she snarled, pulling away from him and trying to swallow past the acid in her throat.

"Lia, I'm sure he's just doing what he must to get the girl to talk. Do you know her? What could she tell him?"

"More than I want him to know," she muttered, swallowing hard again as her stomach rolled and burned. Bad enough the man had found the one place that would know too much about her. He just had to find the one person who couldn't be trusted to keep her mouth shut. Britty didn't know the meaning of the word secret. It wouldn't take much more than the prince's shockingly gorgeous smile to get her to jabber anything he wanted to know.

So there was only one good reason to take her upstairs. It wasn't to talk.

Lia's chest constricted and she blinked back the sting of tears. *Stupid.* She should know by now kisses from a man didn't mean a thing, especially when that man was an elemental. Did she think he'd just pine away for her, burn in celibate misery, when he could take what was offered for free? Britty was pretty, obliging, uncomplicated, and human, not a monstrous changeling who defied him at every turn and threatened his precious mission.

Her mind flew to the casting on her skin and she flushed under a wave of humiliation. She must have made way more out of his flaming touch than had been there. She'd never been good at reading men, at least when it came to sexual attraction and relationships. She'd been too busy looking after her family to gain much experience.

Rune rested a hand on her shoulder. The sympathy in his touch doubled her humiliation, catalyzing it to anger. She shrugged him off, sending him a murderous look. He made a quick retreat, expression wary. “Lia, he’s not—”

“Come on,” she growled, grabbing his arm and tugging him in her wake. “We’re going upstairs.”

“I don’t believe it’s such a good idea.”

At any other time, she would have snickered at his nervous tone, but fury burned away her humor. “Don’t be an idiot. I’m not taking you up there to bed you. We came here to stop the prince, so let’s stop him.”

“Right.”

Later, she’d find his relieved expression funny. At the moment, she was too focused on avoiding notice and getting to the second floor. Ducking away from the curious looks of the staff, she plastered herself to Rune’s side and turned her face into his chest, muttering directions so he could navigate to the stairs. It worked, but only because he looked about to make a sale and no one wanted to interrupt business. If they spent much more time here, though, someone was going to approach him or question Trig or Sal about the new guy.

This was the excuse she applied to her sense of urgency when they topped the stairs and started down the long hall on the second floor. She pretended it had nothing to do with what the prince might be doing with Britty in one of these many rooms, even as she thrust open the first door to look in.

“Hmm,” Rune said over her shoulder at the display inside the room.

None of the occupants noticed, so she shut the door without comment and moved across the hall. That room was empty but the next one earned her a shout of outrage and a curse. "Sorry," she called, shutting them in and moving on.

The next room had them both wincing and she skipped the door beyond that, trying not to hear the somewhat scary noises coming through the barrier. She opened the door across the hall and paused, blinking at the tangled, erotic sight within.

"Educating," Rune mused behind her.

She shut the door again, a blush heating her skin from head to toe. "Holy Mother," she muttered under her breath and motioned with a stern hand for Rune to start opening doors himself instead of waiting for her to do all the work. He complied with a grin that was much too accommodating and wicked. "Pervert," she called after him.

They found the right room at the end of the hall, next to the back stairway. But she didn't find the prince engaged in sex games. She didn't find him at all. Instead, a fully-clothed, teary-eyed Britty sat alone on the edge of the bed, pouting at them when they entered. "Guess he was right about you bein' here," she grumbled, glaring at Lia. "I thought he was just tryin' to get me in a room." She sniffed, lower lip quivering.

Lia stared at her. "He's gone?"

"Went out back," Britty said in a snappish tone, jerking her chin at the stairs just beyond the door. "Paid me not to say nothin' to you." She caught sight of Rune and softened in the blink of an eye, a tentative smile growing as her lashes fluttered. "But I don't take kind to bein' played. Least, not like that," she added with a wink at Rune.

Rune didn't hesitate. Sinking to one knee at her feet, he took her hand in both of his and gazed at her with a remarkably genuine expression of concern. "Say it isn't so, flower. He used you? Just to slip by us? That was unkind, and he must be ice through and through to resist your loveliness."

Britty was putty in his hands. Lia watched in silent disgust and reluctant admiration while he charmed the girl half out of her mind and unleashed her tongue in a barrage of information.

Destin had been there for just hours, spending most of the day hounding the staff, until Britty came along and sugared him up. He was so serious and scary with the scar, but she knew how to loosen a man and he was so much tastier when he smiled. They talked and talked and he wanted to know everything about her, about her life and who she spent time with and what she did when she wasn't bouncing.

Sure, he asked about Lia, said she was a thief who'd stolen something from him and he was just trying to find her and get back what was his. Of course she told him what she knew about Lia. Why wouldn't she? About how she was too proud to work the beds and stayed in the kitchens, even though she had a family to feed and could have made a fortune upstairs. How her family had to live in a little shack on the edge of town where they kept to themselves, maybe because they were ashamed to live so poor, but who knew because Lia never spoke of them, never brought them by.

Unable to stand it any longer, Lia broke in. "Did you tell him where we lived, Britty?" She may have had a smidge too much hostility in her tone.

Britty paled, eyes wide and fixed on Lia. "Y-yes. Wasn't no secret."

Lia pinched the bridge of her nose and tried hard not to curse. She failed several times.

"Well, you didn't say it was a secret!" Britty wailed.

"Hush, pigeon," Rune soothed, patting the woman's hand. "Lia isn't angry with you. She and Destin just don't see eye-to-eye."

Britty leaned closer to him, still staring at Lia with wary eyes. "I caught on to that. She steal from him?"

"No," Rune answered while Lia hissed another foul word and began to pace.

"Shoulda known, way he rabbited. Funny thing, though. Whenever he said her name, he'd get hot."

Lia skidded to a stop and braced herself on the nearest solid object. "Hot?" she squeaked without looking at the other two.

"Not hot like mad, but he'd feel hot all'a sudden, like a bad fever. Ain't that just the oddest thing?"

Lia couldn't move. The base of her spine tingled as though ghostly fingers had just brushed over the casting of Destin's hand. Deep, relentless heat spread weakness and consternation through her muscles.

Rune chuckled and murmured, "Very. Did you reveal anything else about Lia, my sweet?"

"Don't know much more, y'know? Kept to herself, she did." Britty sighed. "Fine lookin' man, scar and all. Kissed like he was born to it. Wish he woulda stayed."

Kissed? Heat transmuted to ice in the space of a heartbeat. Lia glanced over her shoulder and caught Rune's eye. "Time to go," she said tightly and headed for the door.

"Ah, duty calls. I regret I must leave you now, flower. Until we meet again?"

Britty's giggle set Lia's teeth on edge. She was grinding them when Rune joined her at the top of the back staircase. "What a sick display," she said over her shoulder as she started down. "Sick and scary. Is there anybody you can't charm out of their head?"

"Well, I couldn't charm you, darling. And believe me, I tried," he purred.

She rolled her eyes. "I was planning on killing you both. You talked me out of that."

"That wasn't charm. That was panic. He didn't bed her," he added.

"We didn't give him enough time, did we? A prince's work is never done." The bitterness of her words nearly curdled her tongue and she swallowed hard against the burn of acid in her throat. "Doesn't matter. We have work of our own to do."

She slammed out into the alley and paused to take a deep breath of the dank air. *Doesn't matter,* she repeated to herself, picturing her little sister.

"Lia, he didn't want her. He wants you." Rune's hazel eyes were dark and earnest in the dimness of the alley, his hand warm on her shoulder.

Lia pressed her lips together and clenched her hands into fists, trying to ignore a surge of affection and dismay. Pervert or not, he was a kind man, sweet in a way that unnerved her. She was getting altogether too attached to both royals. Stiffening her spine, she said in an even tone, "That's special. Pretty sure he'll get over it, though, when I yank my sister out from under his greedy fingers. Let's go, Rune."

He sighed when she turned away but he said nothing else, just walked at her side and radiated pitiful melancholy. She added irritating to the list of things describing him and did her best to ignore his morose silence.

"We rented a little place on the edge of town," she said into the quiet between them. "I took a job at the Red Satin to pay for it and to get news. The place is full of gossips. I heard about your prince the moment he took to port. Didn't think me and my family would make the gossip chain, though. I didn't even know anybody knew I had a family."

"Mysteries are intriguing. You kept too much to yourself. It incites curiosity."

Lia sighed. "Figures. It's too late to fuss about it now."

She led him through the back alleys of Churling, a path she'd mapped out when they'd lived there. On the way, she mused about her decision to bring her family to the port town. Had it been a mistake? She'd decided getting news of the world and the search was worth the risk of exposure, but maybe she should have just secluded her family in the middle of nowhere, no contact with anyone.

But was it possible? Someone would have known where to find them. Even if only the Earth Keepers and Ephemerals, who seemed to know everything. The Vessel was meant to be found. She'd as soon stop a hurricane as keep her sister hidden from the world. Hadn't Destin proven this already?

Chest constricting with worry, she increased her pace. She knew her family was no longer at the little hut, but a sense of impending doom darkened her vision anyway. Just the fact Destin had no trouble finding where they'd been living distressed her to the edge of panic. But he couldn't know where they'd gone from here, could he? How would he follow their trail? She tried to reassure herself it was impossible. Her mother and sister knew better than to tell anybody where they'd gone. But she couldn't quite get over the lurking sense of disaster.

The Vessel was meant to be found.

She bit her lip hard enough to draw blood when they approached the ramshackle little place where she and her family had stayed. The air of disuse and abandonment calmed her a bit. No one was here. Not her family, not Destin. Rune ducked inside but she didn't bother, pacing instead before the slumped stoop. The prince wasn't here. Where would he have gone? They hadn't given him enough time to inspect the place, so what had he found to make him leave so quickly?

"Rune," she called, still pacing.

He reappeared, handsome face tense with the same foreboding chilling her bones. He said nothing, his hazel eyes filled with the same questions running through her own mind.

"There was nothing here to find," she said with force, trying to deny their fears. "He's not a bloodhound. He can't sniff them out." She jerked to a stop. "Unless he hired a tracker."

"He hasn't had time," Rune responded in a low voice.

"We can't assume that." She swallowed past the stricture in her throat and edged toward the door. "I'm changing. I can at least catch his scent and figure out which direction he took. If it's back into town, we'll just keep on him."

Rune nodded but didn't look reassured. Pressing

her lips together, she ducked inside the hut and paused, letting her eyes close on a prayer for the gods to have mercy on her baby sister.

Chapter 18

Destin ducked low over Wind's heaving neck, avoiding a low-hanging limb as they sped along the trail in the woods. Lia and Rune drove him like a flail, pushing him to greater speed and recklessness. They would be on his trail by now, following him into the woods. But he had hope he'd succeed in spite of them.

Hope in the form of a note sat tucked in his belt, a note written in a flowing hand, written in Earth Keeper runes. Few people would even recognize the language, let alone be able to read or write it. It said only, "Follow the wooded trail." But since he'd found the note nailed to a tree behind Lia's shack at the head of said trail, it wasn't hard to deduce the meaning.

Perhaps it wasn't an Earth Keeper who wrote it. Destin had only seen a Keeper once as a child, sneaking a peek into his father's tent on the side of a snowy mountain to watch a historic, secret meeting between the elemental king and an Earth Keeper. His young eyes had seen solidity and a frightening amount of patience wrapped in a simple form of unremarkable looks. He'd also seen his father's veiled contempt and annoyance at being commanded to meet this plain person. He'd slunk away before the king could find and punish him for eavesdropping.

Did they even exist any longer? Perhaps it had been curiosity that led King Stern to make the mountainous journey and not an imperative command from an ancient race. Maybe that strangely solid, exotically modest being had only been a man and not an Earth Keeper.

But even if the note had not been written by an actual Earth Keeper, someone still knew the ancient language, which made them a rarity in this rustic territory. Destin thought of the monks, thought of their respect for his search with a surge of hope. There would be others who knew he must find the Vessel. There must be others who would help him.

The trail was narrow but easy enough to follow. Wind made good time, carrying him deeper into the forest, into an area of monstrous trees old before his grandfather was born. They stretched into the sky and wove together, blocking much of the light so the ground beneath thinned of brush, opening visibility far into the forest, despite the dimness under their thick arms.

Destin had no trouble spotting the girl seated on a rock when he flashed by.

Instinct drove Destin to pull the stallion to a halt and wheel him about. Guiding the gray at a slow walk, he urged Wind back along the trail, through the enormous trunks to the flat-topped boulder where he'd seen her.

The girl was still there.

He stopped Wind a few paces away and stared at her. Everything in him screamed he knew her, knew what she was. This was the end of his search. This was the Vessel of Power.

She smiled at him. "Hello Destin. I've been waiting for you."

He blinked. She didn't disappear like a mirage or

hallucination. She also didn't look much like a divine vessel. She was a young woman with strawberry-blonde hair glowing in the dimness and cascading around her shoulders in ringlets. Her eyes sparkled blue and merry. Her pretty face still carried some of the soft roundness of childhood but feminine curves, outlined by simple travel pants and tunic, pointed to maturity. She sat on the rock with slim hands folded in her lap, heels crossed and kicking at the stone, a small travel bag resting next to her.

She radiated a disturbing calm.

"You've been…waiting for me?" Destin repeated. Was she about to attack him? Bring lightning down from the sky, or open the ground to swallow him whole, or some other show of spectacular power?

Her smile widened a fraction as if something about him amused her. "You're the elemental prince sent to find me. Well, you found me. I'm Ettie. It's nice to finally meet you, Destin. You look just like you do in my dreams." Her smile faded and she tipped her head to one side, studying him with unnerving, thoughtful serenity. "You should smile more, though. Your soul needs more joy." With the cryptic pronouncement, she lifted her bag and slid off the boulder, looking at him with an expectant air. "Ready to go?"

"Go?" he asked. His thoughts were dull and muzzy as if someone had whacked him on the back of the head with something large and brutal.

"Well, you're supposed to take me to your father. I don't know the way. I figured you'd know how to get us there." She paused, a furrow forming between her sunset brows when he said nothing. "Um, do you know how to get home? I'm not sure how to do this if you're lost."

He blinked again, hard. She still didn't dissolve away. "You're Lia's sister," he rasped.

She nodded.

"The Vessel of Power."

She nodded again with a faint smile. Her blue eyes were crystal clear.

"And you're going to come with me willingly to the elemental king."

Her head bobbed in agreement.

He rubbed a rough hand over his face. "So, either you're insane or I'm dreaming."

She snickered. "Lia thinks I'm crazy, too. That's why she worries about me so much. She's way too serious, just like you." She glanced past him toward the trail. "If we wait around long enough, they'll catch up."

"You're going to come with me," he repeated like a man groping for solid ground and finding only mist.

She grinned. "Yes."

"Why?"

She shrugged. "I'm supposed to. I've seen it in my dreams for so long. It's the only thing that stays true." Her tone was wistful, expression admiring and eager as she looked at Wind. "Do I get to ride up there with you? What a beautiful boy," she crooned, reaching out to rub the stallion's nose. The daft beast nuzzled her and made happy, besotted horsy noises.

"You're going to kill me in my sleep, aren't you?" Destin accused, glaring down at her.

She laughed. It sounded like music. He would swear the trees swayed in rhythm to the sound over her head. "You're so funny. You look terrible. But we don't have time to rest, unless you want my sister to find us."

She winced, looking serious for the first time. "Oh, gods, she's going to be so mad at me," she mumbled, mouth turning down at the corners.

He stared at her young, worried face and shook his head. "I've lost my mind." Reaching down, he helped her mount before him, which she did with the competence of a seasoned rider. "This is absurd. You're not supposed to want to come with me."

"Why not?" she asked with such profound calm the hair prickled at the back of his neck. She settled in and patted Wind, mouth curling in a dimpled smile.

"Because…" He fumbled for a reason but the one that came foremost to mind was disloyal and possibly treasonous. He didn't even want to consider what would happen when he brought her before his father, what the king would do to her, because then he'd have to think about the right or wrong of it. He shoved the thought into oblivion.

"Just because?" She snickered. "Even my mama doesn't use that one anymore."

This family was bad for his equilibrium. At a loss, Destin asked, "Where is your mother? I expected to find you together, the way your sister spoke." Turning Wind, he guided the big stallion back to the trail.

Her slim shoulders slumped. "I had to leave her," she sighed. "She wouldn't understand what I had to do."

"Well, that makes two of us," he muttered.

She sent him a frown, looking too much like her sister for his peace of mind. "You have what you want, Destin. You found the Vessel of Power. Why aren't you happy?"

"This has been too easy, you're not acting right,

and the whole situation feels like an ambush. I'm waiting for trouble to show itself and that does not make me happy, little girl."

She smiled and corrected, "Ettie. I'm eighteen."

He stared at her and considered slamming his head into a tree trunk a few times. Perhaps then some part of this lunacy would begin to make sense.

"Can we go now? Before Lia catches us?"

Her name had its usual effect on him, striking tinder on his bones and sending fire rushing under his skin. He clenched his jaw and tried to suppress it, but Ettie gasped, eyes widening as she stared over her shoulder at him. For a moment he panicked, thinking he'd caught fire again and burned her, but a quick inspection showed no visible flame.

When he met her gaze, he was startled by the grimness of her features, an expression that made her look much older. "Destin, you have to let it go. The Great Mother gifted you with the ability to weave her elements, but you cannot control them. Control is an illusion. Let it go before it consumes you."

He stiffened. "I'm an elemental master. Control isn't an illusion, it's a state of being. Besides, there's nothing to let go, I'm fine." Having lied through his bone-white teeth, he kicked Wind into a full gallop to end the conversation. She bent over Wind's neck and shook her head but didn't speak.

It was an uncomfortable ride. Wind's gait was as smooth as ever and the girl seemed to know how to move with the horse as naturally as though she was born to it, but Destin was uncomfortable all the same. Her gods-forsaken, sunrise-colored ringlets blew in his face, tickling his nose and obscuring his vision. Her hair also carried a scent similar to her sister's. It kept Lia at the forefront of his mind and destroyed his concentration, wreaking havoc with his control.

Fire became his constant, terrorizing companion.

The sun was considering the horizon when Ettie called over her shoulder, "You're too hot."

"We have to stop," he said at the same time, jerking Wind to an uncoordinated halt. Clumsy with urgency, Destin almost fell off the restless horse. The moment he stepped away, white fire erupted around his hands and raced up his arms, incinerating his shirt sleeves. With a shout of dismay, he stumbled back, staring at his flaming limbs in horror. "Gods! What is this?"

"Oh, Destin, I'm so sorry."

The regret and sorrow in her voice took a moment to penetrate. He tore his gaze away from the white fire writhing along his skin and looked at her. "What?"

"This is what happens to people who come near me. Any ability they have is intensified. It gets worse the more time you spend with me. I can't do anything about it. I'm really sorry."

"You are doing this?" His voice was weak, breathless. His world was shocked and spinning into chaos.

She shook her head, blue eyes dark with pity. "No, you are. I've just made you stronger. Fire won't be contained. The more you try, the worse it'll get. Let it go, Destin."

"I don't..." He shook his head, watching in disbelief as the flames rose higher. "That's insanity. If I let it go, it'll burn down the whole forest."

"You are making this happen by trying to bottle

what's inside you, crush it into nothing, but you can't. It's like trying to bottle a flood. It can't be done. All you can do is let it flow and channel it to where it'll do the least damage."

"Senseless," he groaned and stumbled away, keeping his arms out in front of him and praying he didn't set any trees alight. "There's a river. I can feel it. I'll douse the fire with water."

"Destin, no!" she called behind him, but he ignored her, putting all his concentration into dampening the flames as he edged around trunks and ducked under branches. His lurching journey seemed interminable, every moment dancing on the edge of explosion while fire raged inside him like a wild beast. Finally the liquid voice of the river called to him and he stumbled toward it.

Between two great knots of tree roots, a hard-packed mud path led him into the water. Falling to his knees and turning his face away, he plunged his hands in the clear flowing liquid. Steam exploded into the air. Even with his face turned away, it stung his skin and made him cough. When the steam cleared he looked down at his hands in the water. There was no flame, but steam still drifted from the surface. The fire had moved from his arms across his chest and back.

Numbly he lifted his hands from the river and watched as white flame bloomed once again between his fingers. The riverbed shuddered under him. Water rose, swirled, and ebbed away. Destin stared at the river, at the ground beneath him, at the hungry fire, and knew with a sudden, black despair he was losing control of everything.

"Destin?" Ettie's voice was thin and high.

He looked over his shoulder at her. She had her arms wrapped around herself, eyes wide and face pale as milk, her slim form trembling. She was supposed to be the Vessel of Power, but she looked like a terrified teenager, vulnerable and lost in the woods.

"Go," he rasped, defeat roughening his voice. "Go find your sister. Get as far away from this place as you can." He was a master elemental of all five elements. When he lost complete control, it was going to be catastrophic.

"I can't just leave you here. You need help."

"Making me a stronger weaver isn't helping, Vessel! You must leave."

She hesitated, brow crinkling with indecision. Then she pressed her lips together and shook her head. "I can't." She sank down onto a tree's gnarled, exposed roots, huddling into a ball. "You don't know me very well, but I know you. I've watched you for years. I knew you were the one who would come looking for me and I was glad. You're a good person, funny and smart, and you'll make a great king someday."

The flames sizzled on his skin, the ground shifted under him, and he let out a broken laugh. "Neither one of us is going to see the sun rise."

A wolf howled in the distance and Ettie turned her head toward the sound with a relieved smile. "Oh, thank the gods. Here comes my sister. She'll fix you."

Destin groaned, tipped his face to the blazing sky, and silently begged the gods to stop torturing him.

Chapter 19

Riding a furious wolf was more excitement than Rune had wanted out of his evening. Lia's pounding gait was difficult enough for him to endure, but he could also hear her every violent thought, all the bloody things she planned to do to Des, after she shook the teeth out of her sister, paddled her rear, and hog-tied her. Lia now smelled her sister on Destin's trail, and only one explanation fit this set of circumstances. Ettie had defied logic and sanity by traipsing out of hiding right into the path of the one man she should be avoiding at all costs.

Rune patted Lia's shoulder in sympathy. Her sister was as nutty as a squirrel in autumn. No wonder Lia had always been so worried about her safety.

While I'm taking care of my sister, you are to hold that gods-cursed prince down until I can get to him. If you try to help him get away, I will skin you alive, Rune. I swear it.

He didn't take the threat seriously. Destin had the Vessel of Power, her baby sister. One step away from what he knew was her greatest fear, Ettie in the hands of the elemental king. Rune gritted his teeth at the thought, almost as disturbed by this turn of events as she. He'd been so sure they'd catch Destin before he could find Lia's family. Until he'd seen the empty shack and the pale tension on Lia's face.

You might want to ask her why she did it first, he thought to her.

Her mental snarl made him wince. *I know why. Ettie thinks she knows the grand design. She spent too much time with Earth Keepers and Ephemerals. She has dreams and swears they're the truth of everything. But she gets it wrong half the time and then I have to scramble to save her.*

Rune wondered what Ettie got right the other half of the time but knew better than to ask. Instead, he concentrated on moving with her as she flew along the twisting trail.

A moment later, her ear-piercing howl nearly made him lose his grip. He yelped then almost fell off again when she took a hard left into the woods. Out of the corner of his eye, he caught sight of the big, gray stallion bolting away down the trail without a rider.

Are we close, then?

Something's wrong, she responded, worry overcoming her fury. *She's afraid. Her and Destin both. I smell their fear.*

Rune gulped, head swiveling as he searched for the danger. The forest remained serene, dim and sleepy, until they reached the river. He barely noticed when Lia skidded to a halt and shook him off. He slid to the ground and stood staring at a thing that shouldn't exist, an elemental master weaving chaos instead of order. "Destin?"

His bare back was to them, sprouting white flame in angry flares threatening the tree canopy. The river heaved and lurched around his kneeling form in mad defiance of logic. The ground shivered under their feet. The trees moaned and creaked, battered by rampant gusts of air.

Rune reached out a hand and calmed the wind, but he could do little for the other elements. He stared aghast at his soul brother.

"Thank the gods you're here," said a light, feminine voice, but Rune couldn't tear his gaze away from Destin's bowed back.

"When I get through with you, you won't walk for a week," Lia snapped. Then she added in a lower tone, "What's wrong with him?"

"The same thing that was wrong before. I just made him too strong to hide it anymore."

This cryptic explanation drew Rune's attention and he glanced over with a frown. Lia stood next to her sister, fastening her skirt as she glowered at Destin's kneeling, flaming form. Ettie also watched the elemental prince. The sight of her nearly knocked Rune to his knees.

Lia had been right. Ettie was lovely and fragile, looking vulnerable enough to make the gods weep. She didn't have her sister's tough competence or fierce demeanor. Rune had seen kittens look more dangerous. But he still wanted to drop at her feet and beg for mercy. She was no great beauty, her features too soft and sweet, yet his breath caught in his throat, his muscles loosened, his mind fogged, and his chest constricted around a gigantic hole through the middle of his ribcage.

Lia grabbed her shoulders, shook her once, and then hugged her. "Where did you leave Mama?"

"She's fine," Ettie whispered, eyes closed and arms clutching her sister tight. "She's safe."

"She'd better be," Lia growled in a ferocious tone,

but when she pulled back her gray eyes were filled with tender worry. "Ettie, what were you thinking? Do you know where he was taking you?"

Ettie nodded and waved a hand in what appeared to be impatient dismissal. "You have to help him, Lia. He's, you know…" She made a little gesture toward the kneeling prince, her expression uncomfortable. "Burning up."

"Help him? What do you expect me to do? He tried to take you, sister. That makes him the bad guy."

Ettie rolled her eyes. "Lia," she sighed.

Lia grimaced and glanced over at Rune. "Can't you stop him?"

Rune pulled his gaze away before he met Ettie's eyes. He wasn't sure he'd be able to speak if she looked at him. Watching his soul brother weave wrongness into the elements, he answered, "He's stronger than I. In a duel, he'd decimate me. Best I'm able to do is slow him down, calm the air and settle the water a bit. I've never seen this before. I don't know how to stop him, Lia."

"Kill me," Destin said in a dull voice without turning around.

Rune jerked as though stabbed and stepped several paces forward. "No," he blurted, denying both the idea and the despair behind it. "No, Des. Don't be a fool. No one's dying."

Destin lunged to his feet and spun around, meeting Rune's gaze with blazing fury and pain. Holding his arms out, he shouted, "Look at me!" White flame flared across his skin, billowing around him in a corona. "The pressure keeps building, Rune. Soon I'm going to crack and when I do, this piece of land is going to be a burned out hole with nothing alive inside it. If you don't kill me, everyone dies."

"Lia, fix him!" Ettie cried, her voice squeaking with urgency.

"What?" Lia looked horrified. "How am I supposed to do that?"

With a frantic flutter, Ettie reached around her sister and touched the casting on Lia's back. Lia twitched as though she'd poked her with a stick.

"Are you serious?" Lia gasped, eyes round and shocked.

"Like I said, he's burning up." With an awkward shrug, Ettie edged past her sister and hurried back the way they'd come. "Come on, Rune. We have to leave now."

He blinked at the sound of his name on her lips, odd and compelling. But he shook his head and refused to look at her. "I won't leave him. Des, be strong. We'll think of something—"

"Leave," Des growled, his gaze sharp and commanding, a prince still even in this extremity.

"I won't."

"All of you. Leave." His glance flickered to Lia and Ettie before settling again on Rune. "Hurry."

Lia made a hissing sound and stepped to Rune's side. She muttered, "I can't believe I'm doing this," before she grabbed his arm and said, "Go with Ettie. I might be able to help him but in case it doesn't work, please make sure my sister is safe."

Rune looked down at her with incredulous dismay. "I'm not leaving either one of—"

"Rune." Somehow Ettie had approached his other side without him realizing. She touched his arm and sent a shock straight through to his soul, her clear, blue eyes dragging him to a place where he had no will. She leaned close and whispered, “Rune, they need privacy.” Then she tugged at him as though that was enough.

And somehow, it was. His fear slipped away, a vast peace wrapping around him tinted the same glorious blue as her eyes. His feet moved without conscious decision from his clouded mind. He followed her into the woods and left his best friend and prince behind.

****

Destin watched his soul brother go without even a farewell and his control slipped another fraction. Flame roared into the sky, blazing his pain and sorrow to the heavens.

“You took my sister.”

He dragged his attention away from the spot where Rune had disappeared and met Lia’s narrow gray gaze for the first time. He’d avoided looking at her, knowing what would happen when he did. As predicted, despite the danger, despite the fear of losing his grip on his abilities, the sight of her drove molten heat through his center and filled him with a need so intense it was pain.

Her outfit only made it worse. If she’d borrowed again, it had to be from someone at the Red Satin. It was all provocation and little cover. The top was a greenish-gold cloth wrapped around her neck and crossed over her breasts. A skirt of the same material clung to her hips and though it hid her slim legs, it rode low enough to be almost immoral.

But as usual, she moved as if unaware she even wore clothing, stepping down to the water’s edge. Folding her arms, she tilted her head and watched him with a steady gaze. “You have nothing to say for yourself?"

"Does it matter?" he asked harshly. "She's safe and I'm about to explode. Get out of here, Lia."

"I'm supposed to help you. I can't do that if I scamper away with my tail tucked between my legs."

"There's nothing for you to do here," he said through clenched teeth, trying to wipe images of anything tucked between her legs out of his mind.

"Ettie thinks there is."

"Your sister's a lunatic."

"Pretty much," she agreed with a nod. "Still, she tends to be right half the time. So if you're not going to say you're sorry for taking her, we should agree I get to hit you later."

He'd ask about the state of her sanity if the situation wasn't so urgent. "What does she think you can do?"

She sank her teeth into her lower lip and sent flashes of fire curling down his body. "Let's talk about Britty first."

"What?"

"Britty. The bird you smiled for and charmed and put your mouth on. Remember her?"

He shook his head and waved a flaming hand between them. "Lia, we have a situation here. This isn't—"

"Did you or did you not kiss her?"

"To silence her! No one would speak of you except that chatterbox. But I couldn't keep her on topic, so it was either kiss her or strangle her. Now, focus! How are you supposed to help me?"

Her eyes narrowed further, lovely features sharpening into a predatory expression that caught at his breath. She took a deliberate step forward into the river. "Did you want her, Destin?"

He didn't hear her words at first, attention riveted on her bare foot in such imminent danger. "Get out of the water," he rasped. "It's not safe."

"Did you want her?"

"What?" His eyes shot back to hers, confusion spinning reality into unfamiliar vistas.

"Did you want her like this?" She spun on her toes, giving him a clear view of her sleek back, keeping her gaze on him over her shoulder.

Shock drove the air out of his lungs and rocked the ground beneath his feet. There was the mark he'd put on her body, but it had transformed from an ugly burn into a delicate work of art. Of passion. He recalled his desperate need when he'd touched her supple curve, splayed his fingers, and pressed her close. The Keeper runes named and exposed him, Prince of Fire. Why had she kept the print of his hand on her skin? Was she mocking him?

"No," he said in a voice hoarse with impossible strain and desire. "I've never wanted anything so badly." When she spun again and stepped toward him, eyes dark with promise and mouth in a sultry curve, he backed deeper into the heaving water, fire cascading off his torso and hissing into steam. "Lia," he groaned, "this isn't helping. What are you doing?"

"Destin, stop trying to control everything. You're allowed to feel, to want, and need. You're hurting yourself by holding it in. Let go." She stepped further into the water and held out a hand. "Let go with me," she murmured in a husky voice guaranteed to drive him mad.

"That's your solution?" he croaked. "That's insanity. My weaving has nothing to do with…"

She twisted and tapped the mark on her back, lifting her eyebrows at him.

"But I'm unable to touch you. I'll burn you again."

She straightened with a strange look of discomfort. "I have an idea. But maybe you won't like it." She shrugged one shoulder. "Either way, it should take care of the problem," she muttered and lifted a hand. Her skin darkened and took on a gleaming, subtle hardness. This effect spread until her entire form was shimmering ebony. "Touch me?" she asked, reaching her fingers toward him.

"What?"

"It's dragon-snake skin. They love fire. Am I monstrous?" She asked the question with defiance but her gaze flickered and her shoulders tensed.

Monstrous? Not possible. No matter how she changed, it was still her and gods she was beautiful. He shook with the need to touch her, ached all over with the need to stroke her sleek, midnight skin. Unable to find his voice, he stepped forward and lifted a tentative hand. Fire wove between his fingers, and he kept it from licking her with a lurch of anxiety. Would he burn her again? How would he stand it if he did?

She closed the distance, brushing fingertips to his, and he held his breath. She didn't jerk back or scream. Instead, she slipped her fingers between his, pressing palm against palm, cool velvet to his fiery touch.

"It doesn't hurt?" he whispered, watching his flame dance across her dark skin.

"No," she breathed. "It feels amazing."

He searched her features. Her eyes were heavy-lidded, lips parted on rapid breaths, the pulse in her throat beating even faster than his own. “Lia,” he growled, closing his fingers around her hand and pulling her closer. “What do you want?”

“I want you to touch me,” she whispered, drawing their clasped hands to the small of her back. “There. Everywhere. I want your fire, Destin. I want…” He splayed his hand over the mark on her back and she gasped, clutching him as her legs buckled. “I want you.”

Fire billowed and roared around them as he reacted to her words, enveloping them in white light and heat. She didn’t flinch or run. Instead, she pressed against him and his flames, running her dark hands over his chest with an absorbed look on her face. The cool silk of her touch drove him past any pretense of control, any thought of restraint. Groaning her name, he wrapped his arms around her, slanted his mouth across hers, and let go.

The ground beneath them bucked hard, sending them to their knees. The river surged into a wild dervish of air, met a column of fire, and burst into steam, all three elements swirling into the sky and dissipating. Destin didn’t notice, all his attention and suppressed energy channeled in another direction. He was absorbed in the feel and taste of her, his fierce, relentless little changeling.

His fire had burned away their clothing. Her cool-silk skin and supple curves sliding against him both satisfied and tormented. He explored her with greedy hands, barely noticing when her skin returned to normal. He learned the arch of her throat, the graceful sweep of her back, the luscious curve of her bottom.

She arched like a cat when he stroked her sides and quivered when he circled her hip bones with his thumbs. He discovered the backs of her thighs were so sensitive she writhed against him and whimpered at the slightest stroke. Any touch to the back of her neck made her purr like a cat and melt into him.

He wanted to know every part of her, every finger-length of her body, every seductive response, every sound and taste, every want and need and thought. He relinquished the addiction of her mouth and raised his head, needing to see what he'd already learned by touch. But they were still kneeling in the river and rushing water covered most of her. With an impatient jerk of his head, he called rock from the riverbed beneath them. Lia huffed and tightened her hold when the rock thrust them above the surface of the water, but she said nothing, watching the liquid sluice away from their bodies with a hungry light in her eyes.

Fingertips tracing drops of water down his chest, she smiled, a slow and sensual curve of her mouth sending blood pounding hard and hot all through him. "My beautiful prince," she whispered. "If I'd known this was waiting for me, I would've stripped you that first day."

He shuddered under her touch and pulled her fingers away when they trailed down past his tense abdomen. "If you'd wanted to kill me, touching me like this would've done it."

"No dying," she purred and nipped him on the collarbone. "I'm not through with you yet."

"Lia," he growled in rough warning and kissed her again hard, just to keep her clever mouth busy. Lifting her against him, he lowered her to the rock then leaned up to take in the sight of her. The view drove the air from his chest and shook him to his bones.

Perfect. How could one woman be everything he wanted when he hadn't even known what he was looking for? Somehow she was what he'd always needed, this gorgeous creature with her sleek body and her steady gray eyes seeing all the way down to his soul.

Still trying to catch his breath, he leaned down and tasted the skin between her breasts, eyes sliding closed at the feel of her frantic heart beating under his lips. When his mouth brushed over her, she whimpered and dug her nails into the nape of his neck. His whole body tensed with urgency but he wouldn't be rushed, exploring her front with as much attention as he had her back.

He found a stunning mix of strength and softness, sleek muscles tightening under smooth skin, enticing curves quivering under his lightest stroke, a maddening banquet of luscious female. She fit his hands as though tailor made, each curve so right and perfect. He couldn't stop touching and tasting each part of her, reveling in her silky feel and lush flavor, her wild responses and erotic little noises driving him out of his mind with need.

She touched him in kind, writhing beneath him with staggering enticement, but the cool stroke of her fingers pushed him too far. He caught her wrists and slid up her body until they were face to face, quick breaths mingling and eyes locking. "Lia, if you don't stop teasing me—" he growled but she nipped his lower lip and silenced him.

"Look who's talking," she panted and hooked her

legs around his hips. "I can't take anymore, Destin."

"You can't take anymore?" he asked in a rough purr, shifting his hips until he pressed against her center, gritting his teeth at the delicious feel of her.

Her eyes slid closed on a moan. "Oh, I'd really like to take you."

"Will you?"

She opened her eyes slowly as if her lids were almost too heavy to lift. "Yes. Oh, yes."

He moved with deliberate care, dying by degrees at the unbearable hot slide but loving the sensual, dazed pleasure in her eyes and the softness of her features as he sank deep. When he was buried within her, he went still, closing his eyes and resting his forehead against hers, gulping for breath and shuddering at the exquisite burning feel of her, a pulsing pleasure so intense it was terrifying. They fit together as if made for one another, aligned with such seamless perfection it hurt to think of ever moving, ever separating from her.

She shifted under him, legs tightening and hands stroking over the taut muscles of his back. "Let go with me, Destin. Please," she whispered, her lips clinging to his. "Let go."

With a fierce groan, he did.

She made him wild and joined him, sharp little nails digging into his skin, teeth marking him hers, as they rocked together in savage abandon. When she threw back her head with a sharp cry, every muscle squeezing tight around him, he exploded in a cascade of impossible pleasure. Only the gods knew if he'd survive it, but he didn't care. If death was the price, he was willing to pay.

Chapter 20

Lia watched the stars winking in the twilight sky. She must have done stupider things than have sex with her enemy. She just couldn't think of any at the moment. She'd never done anything so foolish that had felt so good, though. Or so right.

Her body hummed with delight lying next to him, absorbing his heat, feeling his breath in her ear. His arm pillowed her head, a hand splayed on her ribs, the weight of one leg draped over her. A piece of river rock bit into her shoulder blade and the night had cooled, sending goose bumps chasing over her skin, but she didn't want to move. She couldn't leave his arms.

"You've killed me," he rumbled in her ear, slow and filled with gravel.

She shivered and stroked his arm, enjoying the textures of rough hair and warm muscle. This prince had the most beautiful male form she'd ever seen, all those taut muscles and golden skin unfairly hidden by his royal clothes. "Well, it was about time, don't you think?"

His deep sound of amusement sank into her like sunlight. She turned her head, needing to see what humor looked like on his too-stern face. But he met her with a kiss, lips nibbling hers so tenderly her heart spasmed in her chest. His hand stirred on her ribcage, fingers making little exploratory patterns on her skin.

The man was an artist with his hands.

"So fierce," he murmured against her mouth. "Yet so silky soft all over."

She yearned to arch under his hand, beg for more, and plead with him to show her she was everything he wanted. It scared her. She edged away, needing to slow the frantic beat of her heart, needing to put some safe distance between them. "I still get to hit you for taking my sister," she announced, annoyed when her voice sounded achy and breathless instead of strong and confident.

"I didn't agree to that," he responded, lips curling at the corners.

"Agree or not, you took her and weren't at all sorry. You need to suffer."

He cocked an eyebrow, fingertips sliding just under her breast, making her breath hitch. "Getting a power boost nearly forcing me to explode wasn't punishment enough?"

"Since that ended in sex, which is a whole lot more reward than punishment…no. Not enough."

"Mmm." He leaned in, nuzzling against her cheek in a disconcertingly sweet gesture before his tongue slid across her lower lip and sent heat spiraling down to pool in her abdomen. "Good point."

"Stop distracting me," she whispered, swallowing a moan when his teeth scraped her skin and his warm hand cupped her breast. "You deserve a serious beating."

"A beating? The bargain was to hit me once or twice."

"I didn't agree to that."

His chuckle vibrating on her skin sent a warm,

gooey sensation through her chest. A thin slice of panic followed. *Uh-oh. So not good.* Falling for this enticing elemental prince would be the most idiotic thing she'd ever done in her life.

He pulled back, meeting her gaze with steady green-edged gold, his mouth not smiling but relaxed. His hand went still on her skin. "What if I end the search?"

She stopped breathing and stared at him, panic twisting up a notch. Was he serious?

"Lia?"

"Sorry, I must have dozed off. I just had the most bizarre dream. You told me you were going to stop chasing the Vessel. Isn't that strange?"

He sighed and turned his face into the spill of her hair, resting his forehead against her temple. "Your sister isn't as fierce as you. I've held baby bunnies with more fight. And she has no sense of self-preservation." He lifted his head, a frown darkening his brow. "She needs a keeper. How could you allow her to just roam about?"

A bubble of incredulous laughter rose in her throat and she swallowed it with difficulty. "Why are you yelling at me? You're the one putting her in danger."

"The whole world is dangerous for her," he grumbled, his arm tensing beneath her head, hand flexing on her breast. "She's fragile. Breakable, Lia. She wouldn't survive—" He broke off, shifting against her, mouth thinning to a grim line. "My father would shatter her. Why would the gods choose her to carry their power? It's a miracle she lasted this long."

She smiled at him, feeling just a little giddy and ridiculous. "Welcome to my world," she drawled, patting his arm. "It didn't take her long to get to you, did it? What did she say?"

He scowled at her, fearsome and ruthless. A horrible urge to giggle took hold of her. "She told me I was taking her to the elemental king." He slid his arm out far enough to prop his weight on his elbow, looming over her to scold, "Didn't you teach her anything? Like how not to find the quickest way to die?"

A snicker slipped out and she pressed her knuckles to her smiling mouth. Mumbling around her hand, she asked, "So you're really giving up the search?"

"She's a menace, Lia. I refuse to bring her anywhere near other elementals. I wasn't even with her a full day and disaster struck. We'll find a place to seclude her, keep her from making any further messes."

She stopped trying to kill the sappy smile on her face, reaching up to stroke his cheek and lingering to enjoy the contrast between smooth skin and raspy growth on his jaw. "Destin," she sighed, fighting the urge to say words she had no business uttering to a prince. Emotions she had no business feeling for a prince. She managed to swallow them. "Where are our clothes?"

His fierce, stern expression altered to something close to discomfort. "Ah. I burned them."

"Oh, blast it. I liked that skirt."

"Mmm." His gaze traveled down her torso. His hand slid over her flat stomach and his thumb did another mind-bending swirl over her hip bone. "So did I."

She sucked in a breath with a helpless quiver. "You're very good with your hands," she gasped, fascinated by the intensity on his face. When he looked at her, when he touched her with such absorbed deliberation, he made her feel beautiful. He hadn't answered when she'd asked if she was monstrous, but he'd stroked her scaled skin without hesitation, no revulsion in his eyes when he'd looked at her altered form. *And, oh gods, his fire.* The heat had driven her senseless with ecstasy.

He lifted his head, meeting her gaze with a faint curl of his hard mouth. "You're the most responsive female I've ever touched."

Her eyes narrowed. "Touched a few have you?" she growled.

His lips twisted in a smirk, hand gliding down her thigh. "Jealous?" he purred, doing things to her flesh that made her vision blur. "Now you know what I've gone through. Do you have any idea how you appeared in my cousin's clothing? Do you even know what you do to men with just the way you move?" His mouth flattened, eyes glittering. His hand stilled and gripped her thigh in possessive demand. "Who touched you, Lia? Who else has laid their hands on you?"

She blinked at him, her mind slow to function. "Nobody," she murmured, wiggling a bit to entice him to continue his magic on her skin.

He frowned at her, hand pressing to hold her still. "Nobody? I hope you don't dismiss me so easily when you're through with me."

Through with him? Was he joking? "No, I mean I've never had sex before." She spoke without thinking then winced at what he might infer from it. What he might guess about her reasons for choosing him. "Never had time," she rushed on, looking past him at the starry sky. "I was too busy taking care of my family and hiding. Most of the men I knew were either monks or, you know, scum."

He made a choking sound like a strangled laugh and rested his forehead on hers. "I'm no monk. I hope I'm not scum. And you were no virgin."

"Yes, I was." He lifted his head and gave her a skeptical look. She rolled her eyes. "Changeling, remember? No need for awkward deflowering or virginal hysterics. But I can get all weepy and accusing if you want me to."

"I doubt that," he said with a snort, eyes gleaming with humor. "And by the way, there's always time for sex."

"Who are you, Rune now?"

He tipped back his head and laughed.

It was the most wonderful sound, deep, rough, and musical. His grinning, delighted face was so beautiful her heart cracked and shimmered to pieces. Nothing on earth could have stopped her from reaching for him, from pulling his head down and tasting the humor on his lips. With a sinuous twist, she freed her legs and locked them around him, then shoved until she rolled him onto his back.

Lifting her head, she whispered against his mouth, "Do you have time now?"

"Absolutely," he growled, hands flexing and muscles turned rock hard beneath her.

She smiled to feel his flesh flash hot against her skin. "My Prince of Fire," she breathed, rubbing against him in sensual delight.

His hand slid down, finding the casting in the small of her back and pressing possessive heat into her skin.

She gasped, writhing as the strength ran out of her limbs.

"You touch me and I melt," she whimpered, watching his eyes blaze fierce and molten gold.

"You touch me and I burn," he husked then showed her just exactly what he meant.

****

Rune woke, blinked, and stared into the most heart-stopping blue eyes he'd ever seen. Framed by long, sun-tipped eyelashes, they glowed clear and true, like a cloudless sky or the finest crystal.

"Rune? Are you all right?" Ettie asked, hovering over his reclined form.

"I'm not sure," he lied. He knew very well he was not all right. He was far from all right and most of the way to all wrong.

For one thing, he didn't know how he'd come to be lying in the sunlit grass. There was an enormous gap in his memory, where the entire night and a bit of the morning had disappeared, if he was measuring the light in the sky correctly. Even more wrong was his sudden, scary fascination for this woman-child. He'd always been attracted to older, experienced women, not young, tender things barely out of childhood with innocence written all over them. Getting lost in those blue eyes was the most benign of his sins. His fingers tingled with the urge to tangle in those sunrise-colored spirals of hair, to discover their texture and weight, to bury his hands in them, throw them into disarray, and pull her close. He slammed mental doors on those thoughts, careful not to look at her mouth or anything below that tempting curve.

But the greatest wrong was leaving his soul brother

to die.

Rune lurched to a sitting position, breathing hard around a sudden, agonizing constriction in his chest. "Des," he gasped, clutching at his heart and reaching with desperate strength through their bond.

"He's fine," Ettie said. "They're both fine."

A truth he discovered for himself a moment later when his mind collided with Destin's tranquil surface and plunged into deep, peaceful lassitude. Destin roused enough for an irritable mental grumble and lazy shove. Then he subsided back into the kind of wordless bliss Rune hadn't suspected his cousin even knew existed, let alone could experience.

Retreating with haste, Rune sat with his hand over his heart and his jaw hanging down to his knees, staring dumbfounded at nothing in particular. "Well," he wheezed. "He seems quite happy for a dead man."

"I'm glad," Ettie murmured at his side.

He turned his head to look at her, drawn by the reserve in her tone. She was looking down, hands in her lap. Under his regard, she pulled her legs in and wrapped her arms around them, resting chin on knees. Her eyes remained downcast.

Rune drew in a sharp breath, recognizing guilt. "Ettie? Is there something you'd like to share? For example, how I could leave my soul brother when he's in danger, or why I have this enormous hole in my memory? Or perhaps you'd like to explain how my cousin is still alive and more relaxed than he's ever been in his life?" He blinked. "And how do you know they're fine? Where are they?"

"Well," she started then hesitated, flicking him a deep blue glance from under sunshine lashes. The look pierced him somewhere in his chest and alarmed him on several levels. "You're not going to like this. But try not to be mad, all right?"

He clenched his jaw and breathed through a sudden stricture around his ribs. "Just tell me."

"You weren't going to leave Des," she said, eyes skittering away and cheeks turning pink. "You're too good to let him die alone. But they couldn't do what they needed to do in front of you. So I, um, I sort of used our bond to get you to come with me. I'm sorry, I didn't know you'd be out so long but it was a good thing, you know, because otherwise you'd have felt what was going on and it would have been really embarrassing. They wouldn't be too happy—"

"Ettie," he interrupted, a little dizzy and lost. "Start over. What bond?"

She cleared her throat, face darkening to a rosy color, arms tightening around her knees. She didn't meet his gaze. "You and I, we're, uh…we're soulmates," she finished in a rush then rocked a little in place, features tense.

Everything in him went still. After an endless frozen moment, he repeated, "Soulmates," in a flat tone.

She nodded, nibbling on her lower lip. "This went better in my dreams," she sighed. "I shouldn't have used the bond. It wasn't fair to you. But I didn't think. I just did it because I had to get you away from there. I like Des and I knew Lia could fix him but not if we were there and…and I couldn't stand it. You were in danger and I couldn't stand it."

He stared at her while she rocked a little more and continued to not look him in the eye. "Soulmates?"

"Um, yes. I know you need time to get used to it

and to me. You don't know me like I know you."

"And how is that possible?" His voice held a thin edge of hysteria, but he couldn't help it. *Soulmates?* Was she mad? He was a spirit weaver. He'd know if he had a gods-blessed soulmate. Wouldn't he?

"I've seen you in my dreams all my life," she said in a quiet voice to the ground. "Both you and Destin. I've watched you live and love and laugh. That was hard for me because I wanted to be there with you. Just talk to you sometimes. But I'm glad you had each other and your parents are very sweet." She smiled a little, flicking him a quick glance through her lashes. Then her expression sobered and her eyes fell again. "I never liked Destin's father, though."

"Not many do," Rune muttered, feeling dislocated and strange. "Are you saying your dreams are real?"

"Some of them are. It's kind of hard to tell which ones because the true ones show different times, things in the past, what's happening now, and sometimes the future. I knew you and Destin would find me. I'd seen it in a dream. It didn't go like this, though."

"Your sister said you don't have any abilities, you're half changeling and half elemental without the talents of either."

She shrugged. "She's right. I don't. I just see things."

"You said you used our…" He couldn't quite say our bond. That seemed to give it too much weight, too much reality. "You forced me to leave Destin against my will and placed me in a stupor all night. Only a spirit master could have done that. An old, experienced, and powerful spirit master."

She covered her face with both hands, shoulders

hunching. "I'm so sorry. I just couldn't think of what else to do."

Rune ran a rough hand over his face then pinched the bridge of his nose, trying to put his scrambling thoughts in order. The girl had to be as daft as a damselfly. The idea of him having a soulmate was mad, especially someone who was more girl than woman. But how else had he lost an entire night? Why else would he leave Destin? "How do you know Des and Lia are fine?"

"I saw it."

"In a dream?"

"Yes."

"Gods help me." He tipped back his head and stared at the sky. It was losing its sunrise colors and turning into a blue as pristine as her eyes. "All right. Let's pretend this isn't some sort of crazy fantasy of yours or a nightmare of mine. I know Des is feeling quite good right now. What I don't know is how it happened. How did he manage to find the control to stop the chaos weave?"

"He didn't. That's the point. That's how Lia fixed him, she helped him lose control."

He stared at her, opened his mouth, and then closed it again when he realized he didn't know how to respond.

She must have read the disbelief on his face. With a little frown and a quick gesture, she went on. "Des has been trying to squash his own feelings. You know he's been doing that a long time, pretending not to hurt, not to get angry or feel anything." She tipped her head, lifting her eyebrows.

He nodded to show he understood, swallowing the

urge to ask how she could know such a thing.

"He puts a lot of energy into that. Well, when he met Lia, he had a load of feelings to bottle up. You know. You've seen them together."

Rune nodded again without prompting, still holding back a flood of incredulity. She'd never seen Des and Lia together before last night. How could she know these things?

"It was too much for him to keep inside. Too much energy, too much pressure. It had to come out some way, be released somehow. It started with fire. He wove it without knowing he was doing it or why. Then I came along."

She shook her head, wrapping her arms around her legs again. "I can't stop what happens when people are around me. You'll see it yourself soon. You'll start being able to do things with air and spirit you never could before. It built up a lot faster than I expected with Des, though. He was so close to…" She shivered and rested her forehead on her knees. "But Lia helped him. She showed him how to stop trying to control everything."

"If she did, it'd be a miracle," Rune said, his voice rough. "So you're saying he didn't explode because she helped him direct all of his suppressed energy into something besides the elements?"

She lifted her head and smiled at him, stopping his heart for a moment. "Yes, that's it."

"Do I need to ask?"

"They had sex."

"Right," he muttered, turning his face away to hide his dismay. He had no issue with Des and Lia together, but he should not be having a discussion involving sex with this girl. Or any discussion within shouting distance of that topic. The matter-of-fact way she said the word disconcerted him to a worrisome degree. "So are they still at the river?"

"Yes."

"And where are we?" He glanced around at the pretty little meadow ringed by large, handsome trees. Wildflowers speckled the grass with a scattering of color, sunlight bathing their section of the meadow in warmth.

"Not too far. Wind carried us here, but I sent him back so they'd have clothes."

Rune's gaze snapped back to her, absorbing her serene smile with another pang of dismay. He opened his mouth to ask what'd happened to the clothes they'd been wearing and how she'd sent Wind anywhere then shook his head. Her answers tended to cause more questions and illicit deep discomfort. "We need to return to them."

She nodded as if she'd known what he was going to say and rose to her feet with a smooth economy of motion. His mouth went dry. He looked away and muttered a curse under his breath, rising and dusting himself off. He noticed with a little frown of annoyance that his once fine travel clothes were stained and frayed. He'd never looked this rough even when camping.

Then he glanced up and caught Ettie watching him. The look on her face and in her dewy eyes could have spooked the most hardened skirt-chaser. Rune had had enough success with women to recognize their signs of attraction. The soft yearning on Ettie's innocent face froze him solid with panic.

A moment later, the expression disappeared into a

hard blush when she met his gaze. Before he could remember how to breathe, she spun on her heel and moved away, waving a hand in a vague gesture at the trees. "This way," she said in a high, tight voice.

Rune moved after her, his mind still buzzing and muscles stiff with terror. Bad enough he was forming a sick sort of obsession with her. How could he deal with that and a girlish crush at the same time? *Gods help me. I'm in so much trouble.*

Chapter 21

Destin frowned, pausing in the act of tightening Wind's saddle strap. "There it is again," he said, wincing a little at the sea of agitation lapping at him through his soul bond with Rune.

"I feel it," Lia responded, ducking around Wind's head and moving to stand at his elbow. Her gray eyes darkened and her brow creased. "Are they in trouble? Can you tell if Ettie is still with him?"

He shook his head, clenching his jaw against a surge of concern. "I can't get through to him. He's not paying attention and there's too much flowing out to get anything in." He swung into the saddle and held a hand out to her. "But if I had to guess, I'd say she's with him. Only the Vessel could make him this strong."

She took his hand and swung in front of him with a lithe grace that captured all his male attention. She'd borrowed from him this time, and the sight of his clothing lying against her skin gave him a deep, possessive satisfaction. Her sleek form settling into the cradle of his body fogged his mind for a moment, triggering molten memories of their night together. With hungry instinct, he grasped her hips and shifted her closer, hissing in a breath at the feel of her pressing against his hardening body.

Lia glanced over her shoulder with a wicked little curl to her lips and a cool lift of an eyebrow. "Again, my prince? Wasn't last night enough?"

His fingers tightened before he forced himself to let go and reach around her for the reins. Her tone teased and he liked her possessive *my* more than he cared to think about. But the suggestion of an end to their time together bothered him. "This has been my constant state since I met you," he growled in her ear as he turned Wind and nudged him along the trail. "You think one night will do?" He inhaled the sweet spice of her, gritting his teeth at the tantalizing friction between them. "This ride will be pure torment," he muttered.

"The things we do for our family," she said, voice filled with laughter.

He smiled against the soft curve of her ear. A deep well of pleasure grew at his core, despite the agony of her bottom rubbing against him, a sense of euphoria to have her in his arms, to hear her laugh. It was a simple joy just to be with her. Her touch unlocked a part of him he'd never known before, showed him a freedom he hadn't believed possible. This wasn't just lust. This was some deep, internal release he was only just beginning to understand. He was fast becoming addicted to everything she gave him and everything she was.

That ought to scare him witless. It made him vulnerable in a way he'd never been before. Alarming when he considered who made him this way, a wild changeling with a prejudice against elementals and a sister whose very nature spelled trouble. He just couldn't seem to develop any serious concern with her soft laughter teasing his senses.

"Go faster, Destin."

"Death of me," he muttered but loosened the reins

and gave Wind his head. Then he leaned with her over the stallion's neck and tried not to burst into flame.

A short while later, when he caught sight of Rune and Ettie walking the trail toward them, an enormous wave of relief caught him by surprise. He soon realized the feeling wasn't coming from him. "That's odd." He pulled Wind to a slower pace and straightened in the saddle.

"But they look all right," Lia responded. "Why is Rune so relieved to see us?"

"Let's find out." He reined Wind to a walk as they neared, studying the two on foot. Ettie looked the same, wearing a sweet, welcoming smile, her appearance tidy and pack swung over her shoulder. Rune was limping a little and looked a bit worse for wear, but nothing out of the ordinary for what they'd been through of late. His face had lost its usual easy-going cheer, though, his features tight with anxiety.

"Good rising!" Ettie said when they met.

"Are you all right?" Lia asked, frowning down at her little sister.

"Of course." Ettie's reply was easy, her pretty face serene. Rune said nothing.

Lia glanced over her shoulder, meeting Destin's gaze for a baffled moment before she slipped from the stallion's back. While she hugged Ettie and whispered to her in a big-sister tone, Destin dismounted and faced Rune, remembering with a flash of pain his cousin had left him without saying farewell. For Rune's sake, he was glad he'd left. They'd averted catastrophe, but the danger had been real and his cousin's departure relieved him. Without a word, though? That wasn't like Rune.

The silence between them stretched. Rune didn't

meet his gaze, staring at the ground instead. "I wouldn't have left you," Rune muttered.

"Never mind. I could feel your panic. Did you run into trouble?"

Rune's head snapped up, brows pulling together. "I wasn't…how did you…?" Comprehension flooded his features and he turned to look at Lia's sister with narrow eyes and tight mouth. "So it's begun, then. Her being the Vessel is a bit inconvenient, Des."

"Tell me about it," he snorted, disturbed by the level of resentment on his soul brother's face.

"The girl also has a talent she may have been hiding from her sister."

Lia turned from her conversation with Ettie to frown at Rune. "What are you talking about?"

Rune didn't answer, eyes never leaving Ettie.

Lia sighed. "Now what did you do, Etts?"

Ettie flushed a deep pink, her serenity disappearing in a flustered babble. "I didn't mean to. I mean, I did, but I didn't think it through and I didn't know it would last so long. He was out all night, but he seems fine. Doesn't he look fine?"

Lia grasped her sister's shoulders and gave her a shake. "You knocked him out? You can't even squish a spider and you—"

"No, no," Ettie said with a quick shake of her head. "I didn't hit him."

"She wove spirit," Rune clarified.

Ettie sent him a look of pure consternation, but Lia shook her again and regained her attention. "You did what?"

"I can't do it with everybody," the girl protested, her face turning an even brighter shade of pink. "Just him."

"And why is that?" Destin asked in a flat tone. If she could weave spirit so strongly, they were in trouble. It explained why Rune had turned and walked away from him in a crisis, but it also implied many alarming things about the might of this Vessel of the gods.

Ettie nibbled on her lower lip and looked away from them, not answering.

"She claims to be my soulmate," Rune answered, his face expressionless. He sounded mildly annoyed, but a spike of distress flared across their bond. No wonder Rune had been panicking all morning.

"I know you don't want to believe it," Ettie said in a low voice, her face still turned aside. "But it's true."

"Soulmate," Lia repeated with hard emphasis. "Why am I hearing this just now, sister? Or did you decide this when you saw his pretty face?"

Ettie's features crumpled into tragic hurt. She looked at her sister with big, wounded eyes. "I didn't decide anything. I never get to decide anything. I've known he was my soulmate most of my life, but…" She trailed off, turning away and folding her arms across her chest.

Lia snarled a curse and began pacing, the fierce aggression in her stride startling Wind from his lazy grass-nibbling. The big gray blew a nervous snort and sidled away. Rune did a similar maneuver, amusing Destin.

"You've seen him most of your life," Lia repeated her sister in a growl, shooting Ettie a look of violence. "So you've also seen Destin. And you never told me? How much did you see, Merr'et? Did you know he was the prince? Did you know when they started the search?"

Ettie nodded without meeting her sister's gaze, her face losing color.

"Well, isn't that just fantastic!" Lia shouted, throwing her hands up in the air. "I'm supposed to protect you, little sister! Don't you think I could've used that bit of thrice-damned information?"

"I couldn't," Ettie whispered, her lashes sparkling with tears. "You were trying to stop him and he was supposed to find me."

"Gods above!" Lia said through her teeth in a muffled shriek, stomping away from them. She paused at a fallen log and brutalized it with kicks and curses.

"Oh, gods," Ettie breathed in a broken voice. "She's so mad."

"Better the dead tree than you," Destin said, trying not to grin. Watching Lia throw a temper tantrum struck him as ludicrous and endearing. He glanced at Rune to find his cousin watching Ettie with a troubled frown. "Or you, soulmate," he added, lips twitching with humor.

Rune sent him a killing look that did little to disguise his terror. Destin suspected he was more afraid of the word soulmate than the threat of Lia's wrath.

He took pity on his cousin and changed the subject. "When Lia is finished decimating the forest, we'll discuss our next destination. We need to find sanctuary within a reasonable distance, somewhere Uncle Storm won't be able to find. After passing him on the road, I assume the monastery is out of the question."

Both of them frowned at him. "Sanctuary?" they said in unison. Rune flashed the girl a startled look, but she didn't take her eyes from Destin. "You're supposed to take me to your father," she added.

"That would be insane," he retorted, reaching for Wind's reins. "After what you did to me, what you're doing to Rune, I would be a fool to take you anywhere near other elementals."

Her blue eyes clouded with confusion. "But…"

"I don't know if you've noticed, little Vessel, but you're a menace to society. You're also your own worst enemy. I don't know how you're still alive, or how any of us are, for that matter. If we mean to stay alive, we need to seclude you. Preferably under lock and key," he added when she gave him a mutinous glare.

"This isn't how it's supposed to go," she protested.

"It is now." Destin glanced over at Lia. She paced alongside the mutilated log, muttering to herself with furious gestures. Smothering a smile, he handed the reins to Ettie without looking away from his fierce changeling. "Give me a moment with your sister. Then we'll decide where to go from here."

"Good luck," Rune mumbled behind him, tweaking his humor again as he approached Lia. The predatory violence in her sharp movements should've given him pause, had made Rune and Ettie nervous. Destin waded in with fearless abandon. If she wanted to take a swing at him, he'd consider it her due after saving his neck and giving him the best night of his life.

She spun to face him, features feral and eyes sparking with temper, but he caught the undertow of fear lurking beneath her anger. With a lurch in his chest, he didn't wait for her to yell or take a swing, tugging her stiff form into the circle of his arms. "Don't, Lia," he whispered into her hair. "Don't think about what might have happened. She's safe now and we'll keep her that way."

"I don't know how," she groaned, dropping her forehead against his collarbone and fisting her hands in his shirt. Her lithe form stayed taut with emotion. "Everything's against it, even my nutty little sister. How do I keep her safe from herself?"

"How about a good, strong rope, and a thick gag?"

She snorted. "Believe me, I've thought about it. Makes it hard to tote her around, though." She tilted her head and met his gaze with shadows in her eyes. Her hands flexed in the fabric of his shirt. "I need to get my mother, Destin. But I can't leave Ettie alone."

"Lia—" He began with a troubled shake of his head, but she cut him off.

"Our mother is just as much my responsibility as my sister. Plus if anybody figured out she's the mother of the Vessel, she'd become a target."

And a liability, Destin thought. Being a prince meant he had to think in cold facts and ruthless strategies, but it was getting harder and harder to be objective. He sighed and released her. "Do you know where she is?"

"No, but Ettie does." She shifted around him with a feral sharpening of her features. "And baby sister is gonna tell," she said in a louder voice, prowling toward her sibling with a distracting, liquid glide. "Right, Merr'et?"

Destin followed, paying more attention to the roll of her hips than the dark threat in her voice.

"I want Mama with us just as much as you do," Ettie defended then turned to Destin. "You're the elemental prince, Des. You can't just forget your duty and hide me somewhere."

"Watch me," he growled, annoyed enough to pull his gaze away from Lia's too-tempting behind. "My duty as a prince is to protect my people. There is no worse way to do that than to bring you into the middle of them."

Ettie gave him a pained, puzzled look, as though he'd begun speaking another language.

Lia intervened with an impatient hiss. "Where's our mother?"

With a sigh, Ettie faced her sister. "She's straight north from the wooded trail behind our old place in a little wood cabin facing west with a stone well sitting in a glade just north of it. She should be fine. I haven't been gone all that long."

Lia gave her such a black, accusing stare that Ettie dropped her gaze and paled, wrapping thin arms around her waist. "I'll go get her," Lia snapped. "You stay here. And stay out of trouble. If I hear you put so much as a toe out of line, I will truss you up like a pig. Are we clear?"

Ettie nodded without looking at her, pale cheeks gaining a red spot high on each cheekbone.

"Lia, how do you plan to—?" Rune started to ask, but Lia waved him off.

"I'll fly there and back. Won't be gone long."

"We could all go," Destin suggested.

Lia shook her head. "That would take too long. And no one can track me in the air." She hesitated, eyes darkening like an oncoming storm. "You'll keep her safe?"

"Strong rope and a gag," he said with a curl of his mouth. Lia responded with an easing of her muscles and a wry tilt of her head.

"But who'll keep us safe from her?" Rune muttered under his breath. Not low enough.

Ettie shot him a hurt look then spun on her heel and marched away from them. Rune watched her go with a troubled expression.

"We'll continue on," Destin told Lia, unable to resist touching her, clasping her arm in a sliding hold, testing the softness of her skin. "East on this trail until we can find a path north. Will you be able to find us?"

She flashed him a challenging grin. "I tracked you down once, didn't I?"

His hold tightened, tugging her closer in instinctive male response to her baiting. But he kept his expression bland, aware of the speculative stare of his cousin. "Took you days," he drawled, amused when her eyes flashed silver and narrowed. "Don't be so long this time."

"As my prince commands," she purred, shifting close enough to brush supple curves against him and burn all thought out of his head. Then she pivoted and stepped away. "Rune, don't watch or I'll strangle you."

"Not watching," Rune answered in an absent tone, as though this was a conversation they'd had often enough to become routine. And he wasn't watching her, his amused hazel eyes studying Destin. "About to burn down the forest again?"

Destin made a choked sound of surrender. "It's possible," he mumbled, his throat closing and tongue sealing to the roof of his mouth when Lia began to remove the clothing she'd borrowed from him.

Rune chuckled and clasped his shoulder, turning him away. "You'd better not watch either. One near catastrophe a night is my limit."

Destin could only groan in wordless agreement, doing his best not to remember the silk of her skin and irresistible taste. The shrill cry of a raptor startled him and he jerked around. An enormous eagle leapt into the air, huge wings beating down in a hard thrust. The air swirled, kicking up dust around his feet, as Destin watched the gorgeous, golden-brown creature coasting into the sky as effortlessly as breathing. “Gods,” he whispered, his heart lurching and soaring with her.

“Every one of them,” Rune murmured at his side. “May they all watch over her.”

Destin smirked at the pious statement coming from his irreverent cousin, but he couldn’t look away from Lia’s altered form until she slipped over the tree line and out of sight. Then he glanced at his cousin with a questioning frown.

Rune gave him a one-shouldered shrug. “When last she was a bird, our uncle shot her down.”

“What?” Ettie yelped. The trauma in her crystal blue eyes made Destin wince. Rune uttered a strangled sound at his side. “Was she hurt? I didn’t see a wound. Should she be flying again? Will she be all right?” She whirled, facing the direction her sister had taken. “Can you call her back, Rune?”

“She’ll be fine, Ettie,” Destin said, shooting his cousin a warning look. “She had no injury and flew well.”

Rune cleared his throat once, twice, staring down at the ground as though memorizing an interesting patch of grass. Destin could feel his distress, a volatile mix of empathy, guilt, and panic. “Your sister is a force of nature, in any form.” His voice held a strange rasp, a rough strain sending a flare of concern through Destin.

"She's more than capable of quelling trouble."

Ettie put her face in her hands with a muffled sound. "I didn't dream of her getting hurt. Why didn't I dream it?"

Rune swallowed hard, hands fisting at his sides, eyes still fixed on the ground. "Welcome to the real world," he said in a harsh, callous tone that didn't match the conflict on his face. "Where the rest of us mortals live without knowing what's in store for us."

She dropped her hands and stared at Rune, mouth pinched and lashes damp with unshed tears. "You don't have to be mean. I'm not asking for anything from you." Then she marched off down the trail, back stiff, Wind following after her like a lovesick colt.

Destin watched her go, giving his cousin a moment to settle. Then he asked, "Care to explain?"

"It's utter madness," Rune snarled, stabbing stiff fingers into his hair and clenching them as though he meant to yank all his hair out by the roots. "That half-grown girl is not my soulmate!"

"No, of course not." Destin stepped over to Lia's discarded clothing and scooped them up, packing them away with swift efficiency. "It's clear you felt nothing when she was upset. Not affected at all. Not one urge to hold her, comfort her—"

"I will punch you, I swear." Rune's response was muffled behind his hands. He rubbed them over his face hard enough to redden his skin then dropped them with a glower.

Destin gave him a crooked grin and clapped a sympathetic hand on his shoulder. "Driving males mad must run in their family. Gods preserve us."

Rune snorted but didn't answer. With a sigh and

shake of his head, he headed off down the trail after Ettie.

Destin paused, casting a longing glance at the point where Lia had disappeared from sight. An ache formed in his chest, an emptiness he suspected wouldn't ease until she returned to his side. He couldn't believe how much he missed her already, how much he wanted her back in the safety of his arms. He'd lied to Ettie. He didn't know if she'd be all right and wouldn't know until she was with him again. He needed her to be with him again.

Hurry back, Lia.

Forcing his rigid muscles into motion, he followed his cousin on leaden feet and rubbed a hand over the ache in his chest.

****

Lia found them at twilight, following Rune's mental directions and the faint flicker of their fire. They'd settled deep in the woods, north of the road in a hollow that would hide the light of their fire from anyone on the ground. They were visible enough from the air, though.

Dropping down through the tree limbs, she changed from her eagle form at the last moment, landing on light, human feet next to the fire. Ettie jumped up with a surprised cry and Destin made a wordless exclamation, while Rune only sat forward.

She ignored them all, pacing with restless, helpless anxiety. "Mother's gone," she barked, clenching and unclenching her hands with the urgent need to do something. "I found a note. She went looking, said to wait for her return. She didn't come back and I couldn't track her. She's in bird form. I can't follow her scent in the air. I called, circled, hunted, and waited but I never saw her."

"Oh, no," Ettie moaned, sinking to the ground with hands over her mouth. "I didn't think she'd leave. Why did she leave?"

Lia let out a growl of furious impatience, sending her sister a look that made Ettie cringe. "She's your mother. Of course she went looking for you."

"What are we going to do?"

"I'll go back in the morning, search again. It's all I can do."

Destin intercepted her path, holding out a handful of clothes. "Please dress so I can think straight," he said, expression rueful, gold and green fire leaping in his eyes.

"Oh." Realizing for the first time she was naked, she took the clothes and yanked them on. "I wanted to leave a note, but what if somebody else finds the cabin? They'd be waiting for us."

"Do you know what form your mother took?" Destin asked with quiet reason, though his eyes roamed over her with fiery intent.

Part of Lia responded to his look, but the majority of her mind was still focused on her lost mother, a first for them. They'd lost Ettie countless times, often because her sister had wandered off on some aimless mission, but Lia had always known where to find her sensible, careful mother.

She resumed pacing. "She's a wren. A common, little brown wren. When she's in form, she's invisible, a perfect replica." Her mother was the perfect changeling, not monstrous, always humble with her gods-given gift, changing only under special circumstances and adhering to the creature's natural form and behavior. "If she stays in form, we'll never find her."

Ettie made a distressed sound.

Rune shifted and asked, "Why a wren? She's been as much in contact with the Vessel as you have, so wouldn't she have the same ability to shift into anything?"

Lia pressed her lips together and thought about not answering, her stride lengthening. But she couldn't protect her little sister from everything. Besides, Ettie knew. She might not remember their father, but she knew. "Mother chose a wren because it's small, easy to hide, easy to escape, and doesn't attract attention. She's not a fighter, but she stopped being able to fly away when she had us. Then she put herself between danger and us, always."

The silence had weight, presence. She paced its length with grim strides, ancient regret and fresh anxiety tightening her muscles until she yearned for something to rip and rend.

"If you return, someone may see you. You stand out," Destin asserted in a bland tone.

She whirled to face him. His long form leaned against a tree in a casual stance, arms folded across his chest and ankles crossed, but the harsh lines bracketing his mouth and the narrow gleam of his eyes betrayed his predatory thoughts.

"Let them come. If they have my mother, they'll wish they'd never been born."

"And if they follow you to your sister instead?"

She glared at him. "Same thing. I'll tear them into little pieces."

"We mean to hide her, Lia. Not raise large

signposts pointing right to her."

She growled low in her throat and spun away, pacing again. "Welcome to my life, your highness. Trying to hide my sister has been like trying to stop an avalanche with a hankie and happy thoughts."

Rune snickered and she sent him a violent look. "Amusing image is all," he muttered, eyes sliding away from hers.

"That's why you shouldn't be trying," Ettie declared, chin at a stubborn angle as she looked from Lia to Destin. Little pink spots of conviction rode her cheekbones like a fanatic's flag. "It's my destiny to meet the elemental king. You can't fight the will of the gods. If you do—"

"What?" Lia snapped, cutting her off. "If we do fight your supposed destiny, what will happen? Have you seen it? What else have you dreamt about, little sister? What else haven't you told me?"

Ettie met her gaze, though her lower lip quivered and her blue eyes gleamed with unshed tears. "I've seen lots of futures, but only one comes out right. The others are scary, Lia, and bad. I'm sorry I didn't tell you about Des and Rune, but I was afraid if I told you it would change things. I don't dream everything. I don't know all the steps. I know where we need to go, but I don't always see how to get there."

A tear slipped down her cheek and she brushed it away, gaze faltering. She tucked her knees to her chest and hugged them, looking down with such misery Lia's fury melted.

"Well, whatever you've seen in your dreams, we're not taking you to the king. So get that thought out of your head, baby sister." Lia sighed, running rough fingers through her hair. "And we need to find somewhere safe to hide you. I'll scout around in the morning, find a good place. Then I'll fly you there. No one will track your scent in the air."

"What about Mama?" Ettie asked in a small voice.

Lia rubbed her burning eyes, chest tightening around a hard knot of distress. She didn't want to make this decision, didn't want to choose between loved ones. But she knew what her mother would say. "Mama knows you come first," she rasped in the darkness behind her stinging eyelids. She dropped her hands and swallowed past the lump in her throat, not meeting anyone's eyes. "I'll look for her after you're safe."

Ettie made a wounded sound. She hid her face against her knees, sunrise-colored curls spilling around her shoulders.

Lia sighed again and stepped around the fire, crouching next to her sister. "Don't worry, Etts. Our mother has had lots of practice hunting you down. She'll probably find us first."

Ettie lifted her head, meeting Lia's gaze with a crease between her watery eyes. Her face was flushed and damp with tears. "You think so?"

Lia patted her shoulder and gave her a reassuring smile. "Remember the time you joined a troupe of nomads? She figured out where you were about five heartbeats after we noticed you were gone."

Ettie snorted, wiping her cheeks dry with absent fingers. "I didn't join the nomads. They just had the most beautiful horses and I wanted a closer look."

"Uh-huh. We found you sitting at the chief's fire in the middle of his family like you'd been adopted, all wrapped in a nomad's cloak and eating their food. Just a quick stop before you looked at the pretty horsies?" Lia asked dryly, settling on the ground and bumping a teasing shoulder against her sister's.

Ettie snickered, limbs relaxing. "They offered me dinner. It would've been rude to say no."

"Sure," Lia chuckled, wrapping an arm around her sister with a rueful shake of her head. She glanced at their companions, meeting Destin's amused gaze with a roll of her eyes before studying Rune's bent head and stiff form with a curious frown. What was wrong with her witty friend? That quirky humor and sideways charm she'd come to rely on seemed to have vanished. "Rune?"

He looked up, hazel eyes dark and handsome face tense. His gaze flicked to Ettie and away. A spike of distress flashed across their bond and she remembered this afternoon's crazy news. *Oh, right, soulmates.* Rune didn't look open to the idea. He also didn't look like he wanted to talk about it.

Clearing her throat, Lia decided she wasn't ready to talk about it either. "Speaking of dinner, is there any?"

With a faint smile, Rune scooped something out of a pot into a bowl and handed it to her along with a spoon. His silence was disturbing. Strange how much she missed his annoying jokes and teasing remarks.

Mumbling her thanks and shooting Ettie a wary look, Lia took a bite of the stew. "Mmm, tastes good. Who cooked?"

Rune lifted a hand in wordless answer, his attention fixed again on the flames. Destin settled across the fire from her and Ettie, catching her eye with a raised eyebrow. Lia acknowledged his silent, rueful message with a faint grimace. She didn't know what to do about it either. She wasn't even sure she believed it was possible. Just the idea of soulmates was hard for her to swallow, but Ettie and Rune? If it was true, the gods must have wicked, contrary senses of humor.

A lightening of the mood would be helpful, but that was Rune's thing. Lia tried to think of a distraction while she ate. She knew one way to divert her sister, though she was a little uncomfortable talking about it in front of the two royal elementals. Then again, the silence had become heavy enough to be almost visible and she couldn't think of any other way to get rid of it.

With a muffled sigh, she put down her empty bowl. "So, I had some fun in the sea while I was away."

Ettie looked up, her face brightening. "Really? What did you become?"

Avoiding the stares of her other companions, Lia described the different animals she'd morphed into for her sister and answered her eager questions on how it had felt to be each creature, what she'd done in each form. As usual, Ettie delighted in her stories, eyes lit with wonder and face flushed with excitement. Lia grinned as she detailed her adventures. This was the greatest gift her sister gave her, not just acceptance of what Lia could do but undiluted joy in her ability.

At least in her sister's eyes, she was no monster.

Without thinking, she turned her head to find Destin across the fire. Flames danced gold in his steady gaze, the blaze casting shadows and light across his face in stark lines, the faint curve of his mouth deliciously predatory. His look offered so much more than acceptance. The heat and need in his expression turned her bones to water and terrified her to her soul.

She looked away with a gulp. She knew in her heart if she continued to be with him she'd come to depend on his acceptance of everything she was, his need for every part of her, even the monstrous parts. Then what would happen to her when he left?

She had no doubt he would leave. He was the elemental prince. His duty to his people dictated he return to his home, a place she could not go, where he would take an elemental mate, a thing she could not tolerate.

They had no future together, even if he wanted one, which she doubted. Sure, he might want her now. She was probably an interesting experience, surrounded as he was most of the time by elemental females, nothing more than a changeling novelty. It would wear off once he'd had his fill and remembered his royal duty.

Rune interrupted these bleak thoughts with a gentle hand on her arm. She jumped a little and met his concerned gaze, realizing he'd asked a question. "What?"

Instead of asking if she was all right, the question visible in his eyes, he asked for more details on her experience as a shark. She complied, enjoying the genuine interest mirrored on both his and Ettie's faces. She didn't know if they were soulmates, but they at least had an endless curiosity in common.

After a while, she ran out of details and they fell into a comfortable silence. Ettie yawned half a dozen times before she gave in and curled in a ball next to the fire, head resting on her pack and a blanket tucked around her. "Night," she mumbled.

"Goodnight, Etts," Lia said, watching her sister fall asleep with affectionate envy. Only Ettie could drift off as if she had not a care in the world. Never mind she held the vast power of the gods, was hunted at every turn, and had dreams that would make most people lose their minds. Lia sighed under the weight of her sister's faith and trust.

Chapter 22

Destin watched Lia with a knot in his gut. She stared down at her sleeping sister with such love and worry his insides twisted with aching sympathy. They couldn't hide her forever. His father would never stop looking for the Vessel. Ettie would be found. Destin knew what he would have to do, but it hurt to a shocking degree just to think it.

"Lia," he murmured, drawing her gaze across the fire. "Will you walk with me? I need to speak with you."

Rune threw him a curious look but he didn't acknowledge it, keeping his eyes locked on his changeling. Her earlier withdrawal made his heart thump with nervous dread. He hadn't tried to hide how he felt. Maybe he'd frightened her. Her reaction had been a clear signal to give her space, but he wasn't sure he could.

Her fine brow creased in a frown and his heart skipped a beat. Then she threw a swift look at her sister and nodded, rising with the liquid grace that made everything in him feverish and jumbled.

Climbing to his feet, he led the way into the woods, putting space between them and the pair at the fire. He didn't want either of them to overhear what he had to say. Lia matched his pace, moving through the dark terrain with enviable skill and grace. She said nothing, which didn't help his nerves. He wished he knew what she was thinking.

They'd climbed out of the hollow and moved beyond the faint firelight before he found the courage to speak. "Lia, after we find a haven for your sister—"

"You'll leave," she interrupted, startling him.

"Yes. I need to see my father, explain to him why the search for the Vessel is futile, dangerous. He must see reason."

"He won't. He wants the power of the Vessel, the power of the gods. He won't stop."

He shrugged. "I still have to try. Lia…" He shifted closer, unable to keep his distance any longer. Her face was hidden in the dark, but she didn't move away. He used his fingertips to see, stroking the silky skin of her throat with visceral pleasure, finding and measuring the quick trip of her pulse. "Come with me."

She vibrated with shock under his fingers before taking a step back, away from his touch. "What? Come with you to your father's court? Are you nuts?"

"Probably," he snorted, running anxious fingers through his hair. "You wouldn't need to see him, though. You could keep your distance."

"Destin, if I went with you to the elemental court, I would kill him. I would kill your father. Is that what you want?"

He went still. The knot in his gut grew, eating away at his insides. "So don't attend court. Remain in town—"

"You're not listening. The only way I would leave my sister is to end the search. Killing King Stern would end it. If you bring me with you, I would do everything I could to see him dead."

Something constricted his chest, making it hard to breathe. "I don't want to leave you," he said softly into the dark.

"So stay," she said just as softly. "Stay with us."

He ached all over with the need to do just that. He closed his eyes, hands fisting at his sides. "I can't."

"I know," she whispered in the night.

"I must make him understand, or this won't ever end for you and Ettie."

She said nothing.

The distance between them twisted like a dull blade through his insides. "Lia." Pain rasped in his voice, a plea he couldn't hide. "I need you. I need you with me. I'm the exploding prince. I can't do this without you."

"You know how to let it go now."

"I won't just bed random females," he growled.

"Good," she retorted, folding her arms across her chest. "But what I meant was you know what to do now. You don't need me."

He blew a frustrated breath. She was slipping away from him. "I'll return. After I speak with my father, I'll come to you."

"You can't. You'll lead them right to Ettie."

"That won't matter if my father listens."

"What if he doesn't listen?"

"Then I'll leave Rune with you. He'll tell you where I'll be. We'll meet."

She made a strange sound but said nothing, and he couldn't stand it. He had to see her face, had to know if she meant to push him away. White fire bloomed on his palm and gleamed in the tears beading on her lashes. "Lia," he groaned, fracturing apart.

"You're the elemental prince," she whispered, clutching her arms tighter around herself. "I'm a changeling. What possible future can we have?"

"I don't know," he said with a desperate tremor in his voice. "But I want to find out."

She blinked at him, wet lashes glittering like diamonds. "You do?"

"Yes," he gritted through clenched teeth, easing closer to her. "Yes, Lia. Don't end this." *Please. Don't leave me alone.*

Her arms loosened, features softening. Her gaze slid to the fire on his palm with a speculative gleam, striking tinder through every bone in his body. He sucked in a sharp breath, lust crashing into him like an avalanche. She reached up, winnowing darkened fingers between his in a sensual caress, trapping the fire between them. He groaned like a dying man, roaring need tightening every muscle in his body to painful hardness.

"Maybe we should strip first," she said in a husky voice, misty eyes dark with desire. "So you don't burn up our clothes again."

Beyond speech, he pulled her tight against him and kissed her with desperate passion, relief and need a molten flow through his veins. He managed not to set fire to their clothing, but it was a near thing.

****

Rune paced, clutching his head in desperate hands and cursing under his breath. His soul siblings were making love in the woods. He was happy for them, but he didn't want to share in their intimacy. Try as he might, he couldn't shut them out.

This wasn't just awareness, wasn't just listening in

like a voyeur standing outside the room. He experienced everything. And holy gods it was good, a complete mind and body immersion in duplicate. He was connected with them both.

Worse, far worse, was the temptation lying across the fire, enticing him to end his torment in her sweet, supple flesh. He cursed again, this time much louder.

Ettie woke with a yelp, scrambling to her knees and looking around wildly, her sun-kissed curls a delicious tangle around her shoulders. "What's wrong?"

Rune turned his back on her and snarled another desperate curse. "What did you do to me?" he yelled at her. "I can't stop it!"

"What? Stop what? What's going on?"

Rune pointed a shaking finger toward the distant lovers in the woods. "They're out there…killing me! Oh gods," he gasped, bending double at a savage shaft of pleasure. If they continued doing that, he was going to make an embarrassing mess. Bracing hands on knees, he panted, "Turn it off, Vessel!"

"I can't," she cried and did the exact opposite of what she should be doing, she hurried around the fire toward him. "Are you all right?"

He stumbled away as fast as he could. "Keep away! Are you out of your mind?" Proving just how scrambled his thinking was. Of course she was out of her mind. She thought they were soulmates.

"Rune, I can help."

He choked and sputtered but couldn't say a coherent word. What was she offering?

"I can't turn off the bond but I can make you sleep."

"No, never again!" He groaned, sagging to his

knees at the doubled sensations flowing through him. “Sweet Mother of All,” he breathed, almost past the point of being able to decide anything.

“Rune, you’re invading their privacy!” she snapped, as though he had a choice. “They won’t like it and I really don’t like it. You’re sharing my sister’s…” She flushed a light rose.

If he’d been capable of speech, he would have begged to touch her, to sink his entire self into her, begged her for sweet release. He shuddered with helpless need and watched her stomp toward him.

“I won’t let you do this,” she declared and clasped his hot face in her hands.

Past thought, he buried his own hands in her hair and tugged her closer, molding his mouth to hers with a guttural moan of pure pleasure. Then darkness dropped over him like a stone.

Ettie slipped to her knees beside Rune’s sprawled form, trying to control her erratic breathing and thundering heart. That was not how she’d wanted their first kiss to go, but she couldn’t deny it was intense. Until she’d knocked him out. Pressing a hand to her racing heart, she stared down at his flushed face and wondered what would have happened if she hadn’t made him sleep. Biting her tingling lip, she shivered at the memory of the primal look on his face, the melting heat in his eyes.

But it hadn’t been his desire. She had to remember that before she woke him and claimed their second kiss. With trembling fingers she brushed damp hair from his forehead, marveling at its texture and hating herself a little for feeling hurt and jealous. He hadn’t wanted to share such a thing with his soul brother and sister. She knew him well enough to know he'd been mortified.

But the look of agonized ecstasy on his face had said clear enough what he was feeling, something she'd never experienced herself. And he hadn't been feeling it for her or with her, a humiliating thing to watch. So she'd knocked him out again, this time against his direct order. He was going to yell when he woke up.

With a sound of disgust, she lurched to her feet, then yelped in alarm for the second time. A man stood at the edge of the firelight. As her eyes adjusted to the darkness, other figures formed out of the night behind him. She recognized one of the men from her dreams, the king's brother, Storm. A wolf moved next to him and morphed into a naked man with changeling eyes. They'd hired a tracker.

With a sigh, Ettie let her shoulders slump and stepped away from Rune toward Storm. She would have liked it better if Destin had taken her to the elemental king. She trusted him much more than this forbidding brute of a man. But she had no other choice now. Resigned and resolute, she stood and said, "I'm the Vessel of Power. Your king's waiting for me. Will you take me to him?"

They tied her arms behind her back. It seemed a little rude, since she was volunteering to go with them, but they ignored her when she told them so. They also trussed up Rune and carried him along. She protested this a lot more, but they continued to ignore her.

They hustled her out of the woods then tossed her into the back of a covered wagon, bruising her tailbone. They tossed Rune in after her and she winced at the thud of his body hitting the bed of the wagon. Muttering, she eased over to him and tried to inspect him in the dark. “Rune?” she whispered, but he was still unconscious.

“Ettie?” a soft voice emerged from deeper in the wagon.

Ettie went still, wondering if she was dreaming again. “Mama?”

“Oh, my baby,” Hyla sobbed and stumbled to Ettie, wrapping her in a tight grip.

“Mama! What…? How are you here?”

“I knew they would find you.”

“But you could fly away. Wait, you let them capture you on purpose?”

Even in the dark Ettie could read her mother’s deep sorrow. “I know you, child. You left our hut to find them. You set out to be caught. I knew it was only a matter of time.”

“You came here to…”

“To be with you. If you’re going to that devil, I won’t let you go alone.”

Ettie burst into tears, muffling her sobs against her mother’s shoulder. To her shame, she realized she cried more in relief than grief.

****

Rune woke with a splitting headache and cramping muscles. He soon discovered he was bound like a pig on its way to someone’s dinner table. “What in gods’ names?”

“Hi,” Ettie mumbled next to him. “Go ahead and yell. I deserve it.”

He squinted at her, noting the dejected slump of her shoulders and bits of forest debris stuck in her disheveled curls. Her hands were tied behind her back. “My head aches,” he stated, trying to understand what had happened.

"They tossed you in here head first. Your uncle doesn't seem to travel with nice men."

"My uncle." Rune groaned, rolling until his cheek pressed against the rough wood of what looked like a wagon bed. It jounced along underneath him in a steady rhythm.

"Uh-huh."

Rune rested in this new position with his eyes closed, feeling his muscles ease a bit, though he'd lost feeling in his fingers and toes. He decided he wasn't fond of being trussed. How had he gotten into this mess?

He hunted through his memory, trying to place his moment of abduction. No nasty men with rope, only a gorgeous young woman with a cool touch and a soft, seductive, deceitful mouth. "You forced me asleep again."

"Uh-huh," she repeated.

Then he recalled why she'd done it and groaned in abject humiliation. Perhaps being abducted wasn't so bad. Better than facing his two soul siblings with the knowledge of what he'd shared with them. "Gods above, that is so wrong," he mumbled against the wood. "Thank you for stopping me before I…" He probably shouldn't finish his thought. "I grabbed you." He lifted his head to squint at her again. "I'm sorry for that."

She shrugged and cast a furtive glance over her shoulder. "I'm not," she whispered without looking at him.

Rune stared at her lips, recalling their sweet taste and soft resilience with a stab of white-hot lust. For a dizzy moment, he forgot why he shouldn't be thinking of her that way.

"My daughter tells me you're the prince's cousin," a soft voice interrupted his fantasy.

He twitched, arching his neck and twisting to look behind them. A woman sat against the side of the wagon in neat serenity, hands folded in her lap and gray changeling eyes studying him.

"D-daughter?" he stuttered.

"Yes. I am Hyloa'ki. You may call me Hyla. Lia and Ettie are my daughters."

He stared for a dumb moment until his neck wailed a protest at the awkward angle. With a grunt, he shifted and struggled until he was upright and in a more dignified position. "A pleasure to meet you, Hyla," he said with smooth irony. "Though I wish it was under better circumstances."

She inclined her head.

Rune paused, studying her. Both daughters resembled her, though Lia took after her more with her dark hair, gray eyes, and the sharp, vixen angles of her face. "You're a changeling." She nodded again. "I notice you aren't tied. Is there a reason you aren't escaping? Or helping us escape? Or at least removing these ropes?" He tried to keep his voice even, but an edge of temper snuck in.

"I tried," she murmured, looking away with a lift of her chin. "The knots are too tight. And we aren't escaping because my daughter refuses to go."

He blinked at her. He had so many issues with what she'd said he didn't know where to begin. Looking at Ettie, he raised his eyebrows in mute demand for explanation.

She sighed, tossing her curls over her shoulder.

"Mother can't change into anything with claws or teeth that could cut the ropes. And she's keeping me company."

"Keeping you company," he repeated. He looked between the two women. "So madness runs in your family."

Hyla's mouth twitched, but she made no comment. Neither did Ettie, though she flashed him a sour look through sunshine lashes.

"I mean no disrespect," he said to the older lunatic. "You're the mother of the Vessel and my soul sister, Lia. You've been through a great deal, I'm sure, and undoubtedly those experiences have made you wise. But I do believe it would be in everyone's best interest if you left now to find my cousin and Lia. I would like a dramatic rescue to be in my near future."

She turned her head and studied him, mouth curling in the faintest of smiles. "Lia will be along soon enough. You're a spirit weaver? How did you come to soul bond with her?"

"Not by choice," he grouched and earned a quiet chuckle from her. "The gods must have decided I needed a lesson in humility. Lia is difficult." Rune glanced at Ettie, wondering how much she'd told her mother.

Ettie turned her face away, saying nothing.

"Hmm. You have faith in her, though," Hyla commented.

"Lia has a talent for heroic rescues. I just hope she's able to find us in time. The Vessel has value, but I haven't endeared myself to my uncle. I'm surprised he hasn't already gutted me and tossed me out with the trash."

They both turned to stare at him, Ettie with dawning alarm and Hyla with concern. "He wouldn't kill you. You're family," Ettie protested.

Rune lifted an eyebrow at her. "That ugly truth makes him more likely to kill me, not less. Uncle Storm has no love for rivals at court."

"But…" she sputtered then rallied. "If he was going to kill you, why didn't he last night? Why go through the trouble of tying you up and dragging you along?"

"Uncle Storm's favorite pastime, besides doing away with nephews and other pesky royal family, is gloating. I was asleep for my abduction, which would not be at all satisfying for him. I'm sure he's only waiting until I'm aware."

She stared at him with a slack jaw, the picture of astonished innocence. It made him want to smile, but his head still hurt and the ropes cut into flesh in several areas, including the healing burn on his leg. He was thirsty, in pain, and out of patience. "On the other hand, I despise waiting. If he's going to kill me anyway, why prolong it?" Rune struggled toward the end of the wagon.

"What are you doing?" Ettie asked. "Rune!"

He ignored her. With a last heave, he rolled off the edge of the wagon and landed with a bone-jarring thud on the hard-packed dirt road. Everything flared with red pain and nausea. He groaned, listening to the scuffle of horse hooves and the shouts of his uncle's men.

When the pain subsided enough, he rolled to a sitting position, just in time to watch his uncle approach on an ugly looking black gelding.

"What do you think you're doing?" Storm asked

from atop his horse, not bothering to dismount.

Rune spit a gob of road out of his mouth and wheezed, "Escaping."

Storm snorted. "Always the smart mouth." He turned to his men with a curt gesture. "Cut him loose and rig him to a horse. My nephew needs watching."

"Not in the mood for murder today, Uncle? Or are you saving me for something special?"

"I expect the prince to come after his prize. When he does, he'll need some incentive to behave himself."

Rune snickered, holding still while Storm's mercenaries cut the ropes. "Destin, behave? Good luck."

"I don't need luck, nephew. I just need you to scream and bleed." He wheeled his ugly gelding and rode away.

Rune blew out a hard breath and flashed a humorless grin at the men yanking him to his feet. "He's my favorite uncle. Great sense of humor, endless fun to be around." One of them muffled a chuckle, but he couldn't tell which. "How much is he paying you?"

They ignored him, tossing him onto the back of a horse and lashing his wrists to the pommel. One of the men mounted his own horse and took the reins of Rune's beast, leading it behind him.

Rune glanced at the wagon and sighed. At least his legs were free and his arms could regain circulation. And one of the hired thugs must have been sympathetic, because the rope around his wrists wasn't as tight as before. His chances for escape had improved. Now all he had to do was call in reinforcements.

He closed his eyes and concentrated. *Soul brother. Soul sister. A little help here?*

Chapter 23

Lia woke in a deep, blissful lassitude, her whole being aglow. She held thoughts at bay and just enjoyed the feeling, shifting and stretching with languorous delight against her hard-muscled pillow. Her muscles were limber and relaxed, with aches in places that made her smile, remembering all the delicious things they'd done to earn them.

Destin's clever hands quested over her skin, chest vibrating under her ear with a low, wordless rumble. She sighed in response, lazy fingers finding their own way across hard planes and muscled ridges. His heat soaked through her, melting her entire body into taffy.

"Good rising," he said in a sleep-husky drawl, a smile in his voice.

She grinned without opening her eyes. "Yes, it is," she answered with a slow writhe to reacquaint herself with all her favorite parts of him.

He made a sound deep in his chest like the purr of a great cat, hands drifting down over the curves of her rear end. When his fingers teased the sensitive skin of her inner thighs, she gasped and shivered, contentment dissolving in a flood of rising heat.

"Could be a great rising," he suggested with a wicked chuckle.

She was about to beg him to touch her again when she made the mistake of opening her eyes. The sight of the cheery, sunlit forest jumpstarted her mind. "Oh, gods!" she yelped and lurched up to straddle him, staring at the bright sky through the trees. "Look how late it is."

"No wonder. We hardly slept last night." His fingers tensed on her hips as he shifted under her, growing harder and hotter by the moment. His eyes glittered with gold fire through his lashes.

She moaned with regret and scrambled off him before he burned away her resolve yet again. "We don't have time…"

He surged after her, catching her close and growling against her mouth, "Always time for this."

She lost herself in his kiss, arms slipping around his neck in a fierce hold. When he lifted his head, she panted, "Destin! We can't do this now. We have to get my sister out of here."

He rested his forehead against hers, breathing hard. "Right. The Vessel. Gods, Lia, how do you make me forget everything?"

"I was thinking the same thing about you, my prince," she said with a rueful, breathless laugh.

"Clothing." He lifted his head and gave her a stern look. "Dress so I can function."

She flashed him a cheeky grin. "You have to let me go first."

"Right," he mumbled again and relaxed his tight hold.

Lia dressed, watching him with furtive pleasure as he did the same. Gods, he was beautiful, sleek muscle and graceful power, dark and gold, her Prince of Fire. He dazzled her and filled places inside her she hadn't known were empty.

"Stop that," he said in a low warning growl without looking at her.

She turned away with a blush and a feral grin, leading the way back toward the campsite. "We shouldn't have the energy after last night."

"Only dead could I not want you, Lia. Stop discussing it," he berated in a rough voice. "It's not helping. Neither is the way you're moving your hips."

"So stop watching my hips," she retorted with a pleased smirk.

"Not possible."

They both came to a sudden stop, staring into the hollow. The fire had burned down to ash. All their belongings were still there, but Wind, Rune, and Ettie were not in sight.

"Destin?" she whispered.

"Rune would have warned us if something was wrong," he said.

"Unless Ettie…" Lia turned her head, seeing the growing alarm in Destin's gaze. "Knocked him out again," she finished and they plunged together into the hollow.

"Your sister's a menace!" Destin bellowed as he snatched a pack and began shoving things into it.

Lia was about to snarl agreement when the tracks caught her eye. She froze, grabbing Destin's arm and pointing at the horde of strange footprints in mute dismay.

"Oh gods, my uncle," he muttered, confirming the horrifying suspicion slicing through her chest.

Soul brother. Soul sister. A little help here?

"Rune!" Lia shouted her relief. "Where are you?"

Lower the volume, little sister, he grumped. *My*

head already aches. We're on the road. I assume heading into elemental territory, since we're treasured guests of dear, Uncle Storm. Ettie's all right and your mother is with her.

"He captured my mother, too?" Lia snarled in outrage, pacing to release a sudden surge of violent energy. Destin was more productive, packing and gathering their belongings.

In a way, Rune responded, his mental tone wry. *She let herself be captured so she could support your sister in her quest to meet the king. You ladies make my life so interesting.*

Destin caught her by the shoulders and began unbuttoning her shirt. She almost hit him until she read the grim resolve on his face. Wind was gone. The quickest way for them to reach the others was to fly, so she'd have to change shape. She shrugged out of the shirt and handed it to him to pack.

"Rune, where are you? Can you see landmarks?"

He didn't answer for a moment and she paused to meet the concern in Destin's gaze.

Yes, he said in an ominous tone. *Look for the royal encampment.*

"What?" she and Destin exclaimed in unison.

We've just topped a rise and there it is below. King Stern must be impatient to meet the Vessel. Your father is here, Des. You'll want to hurry.

With a sense of abrupt withdrawal, Rune was gone. Snarling a curse, Lia shoved the pants off her hips, but before she could step out of them Destin caught her wrists.

"Wait, Lia. We need a plan."

She tugged free and kicked out of the cloth,

meeting his intense gaze with a grim stare of her own. "You know my plan."

"I can't allow you to murder my father. And you wouldn't survive—"

"Stay, then," she snapped, furious urgency strumming along her muscles. "He has my family. I'm getting them back and nothing is going to stop me." She backed away from him, watching his expression harden with a sharp pain through her heart. Would he try to stop her? Wasn't it his duty as a prince, as a son?

"Fine," he growled through clenched teeth, eyes snapping fire at her. "We improvise. Let's go, Eylee'ai. Rune said hurry."

Relief and guilt flowed through her with the change. She was putting him in a terrible position, forcing him to choose between his family and hers. But even he had said the king should never possess the Vessel. He had to see her way was right, not just for Ettie's safety but for the safety of them all.

Destin watched his ferocious changeling morph into a glorious golden eagle, fists clenched as conflict shredded his insides to burning strips. How was he going to stop her? He couldn't hurt her, but he also couldn't let her kill his father, his king. And he couldn't let his father use the Vessel either, but King Stern already had Ettie within his grasp. He knew in his soul once his father tasted the gods' power, he would never let it go. How had this situation gotten so complicated, so out of his control?

Lia crouched, one huge clawed foot on their baggage, turning her head to pierce him with the unflinching stare of a bird of prey. Keeping his internal struggle off his face, he gave her a sharp nod and stepped forward. Knotting a fist in her feathers, he swung up and over her back, gritting his teeth as she launched with jarring force into the air.

He sent a gust of air under her wings, knowing his weight and their baggage would drag her back toward earth. He pinned her chest between his knees to keep his seat, his limbs vibrating with the great thrum of her avian heart and the surge of power in her muscles as they burst into the air over the forest. Then he forgot all about kings and Vessels.

"Gods!" he gasped on a wave of wonder and a swell of fierce joy. The world opened around him like a gift, the ground unfolding in a swirl of colors, the sky arching above in blue and white welcome. She carried him into the sun and wind in a rush of smooth power, leaving the ground and conflict behind.

Like a force of nature, like the goddess of all things possible, she showed him a freedom he could never have imagined. No fear shadowed his heart, only utter joy and near painful ecstasy like the sunlight had pierced him down to his soul, lighting him from within.

And all of a sudden, as if the gods had reached down and touched him, he understood. He understood everything. He knew why the gods had chosen this time to forge their Vessel, knew why he'd been chosen to search for her. The inexorable paths they'd all marched along and where it would lead them blazed clear in his mind. He knew what he had to do.

He also knew Lia would hate him for it.

With a choked cry he leaned forward and buried his face in her feathers, breathing in the exotic spice of her scent. How could the gods be so cruel? To give him this gift, this beautiful wild woman who unlocked him from himself and set him free, only to snatch her away again when she'd made him what they needed him to be?

"Am I just a tool?" he snarled into her sweet-scented warmth but received no reply from the gods. The answer was obvious, of course he was a tool, the blunt instrument of their will. He wasn't just a man. He was the elemental prince, named for Destiny, and he had a rather large chore to do.

He groaned, rubbing his face against her sleek feathers. Then he mouthed, "I love you," with a flash of despair and sat up into the wind. He would do what he had to do. If she killed him for it afterward, death at her hands would be better than living with her hate. Or worse, living without her.

****

Ettie's heart kicked hard in her chest at the sight of the elemental High King's royal tent. This was the moment she'd been dreading. She knew it had to happen, knew it was her unavoidable destiny, but she'd seen this man in her dreams. She knew his cruelty, his dark nature.

He terrified her.

A ringing filled her ears and her numb limbs couldn't resist the hard hands of the guards tugging her from the wagon and pulling her through the tent opening. Her mother whispered encouragement at her side, but the words were lost to her.

All her attention focused on the man moving toward her with a predator's stride, a hungry gleam in his dark eyes. Dreams had prepared her for how he'd look and sound, so much like Destin it hurt her heart. Like a shadow version of the prince, a mocking parody of Destin's inherent valor.

The dreams hadn't prepared her for the intensity of the king's stare, like a raptor sighting prey. She froze, mouse-like, and watched his mouth curl in a humorless smile.

"You would have me believe," he sneered with chilly royal arrogance, "this is the Vessel of the gods?"

Her voice wouldn't work. It took her a moment to realize, while she swallowed hard under his stare, he wasn't speaking to her.

The king's brother, Storm, shifted in the shadows. "So she claims, sire. Your son spent a great deal of time searching for her and your nephew was passed out at her feet when I found her."

"A girl," Stern spat, eyes glittering with black violence. "You're telling me a child holds the infinite power of the gods? Bring me Rune."

A moment later, a guard shoved Rune to his knees beside her. He didn't look at her, glaring at his sovereign. "For gods' sake, uncle, if you wanted to stop our search for the Vessel, you could've just sent a note. Or was this abduction just dear Uncle Storm's idea of a jest?"

"Show your king some respect," Storm growled and raised an arm to backhand his nephew.

Ettie gasped and twitched, fear choking the protest in her throat, but the king waved his brother away before he could hit Rune. "This girl claims to be the Vessel of Power."

"The world's full of lunatics." Rune sent her a swift, impersonal glance then shrugged. He lifted his bound hands with a pointed look. "Do you plan to imprison me for something, your highness? As far as I know, we were still doing your bidding. If you don't wish us to keep searching for the Vessel, I'd be delighted to head home."

"Why was she with you?"

Rune shook his head. "You'd have to ask the prince. We were separated on the road. When I reached him, she was in his company. I assumed she was a lost waif, the way Destin treated her. Could someone release me, please?"

The king flicked a finger at a guard who hurried forward to cut Rune's bonds. Then Stern turned his sharp, speculative gaze on her once more, his face granite hard.

It finally sank into Ettie's frozen mind that Rune was fostering their doubts about her as the Vessel. Maybe he was trying to protect her, but she couldn't allow it. The king had to be sure of his prize, or all their futures could unravel. "No," she wheezed, then swallowed hard and tried again. "I am what you've been looking for, King Stern."

"Is that so?" His dark eyes narrowed, voice turning silky with menace. "Then show me. Show me your great power, little grouse." He lifted his hands in an almost lazy gesture. Suddenly the air swirled with bits of rock and earth, the projectiles spinning and then whistling toward her at a terrifying speed.

Ettie yelped and ducked, covering her head as stones and dirt pelted her arms and flew around her like angry insects.

"Fight me. At least defend yourself, if you do hold the gods' might."

"I can't!" she squeaked.

"Stop it!" her mother cried, wrapping protective

arms around Ettie. "Don't hurt her."

"Who is this?" Stern snarled, and Hyla's comforting arms ripped away.

Ettie peered through swirling earth, gaping at the sight of her mother floating off the ground, limbs wheeling, face white and eyes wild. "Mama!"

"Easy, Uncle," Rune said in a mild tone and the stones froze in place, Hyla dropping to her feet with an audible gasp. He'd raised a hand in a warding gesture, weaving air to counter the king. "Don't want to be rude to guests, do we?"

Stern turned his predatory stare on his nephew. "You dare interfere?"

"Please! I can't fight you." Ettie held out both hands to the king, trying to head off any further violence. "The power is in me, but I can't use it, I just hold it. Please, you don't have to hurt anyone."

The king turned his attention back to her. "Then give it to me." The river of hunger in his voice scared her more than anything he'd done so far. His greedy lust for power was the kind that toppled kingdoms, shredded peace, and destroyed whole civilizations. She'd dreamt the future this man wanted, the entire world writhing at his feet, and she'd woken screaming.

"I c-can't," she whispered, voice thin and shaking with the mad beat of her heart.

"Not even to save your mother?" He gestured at a water pitcher and the liquid rose from it, forming daggers of ice that flew through the air, spinning in a dangerous ring around Hyla's neck.

Before Ettie could do more than cry out in protest, the king made another motion and snakes of virulent green fire slithered forward, twining around her in a cage of sickening heat. "Not even to save yourself?"

Ettie thought she was going to pass out. A strange buzzing filled her ears as her skin tightened with pain from the baking heat. Then cool wind swirled around her, a buffer against the king's fire.

"What are you doing?" Rune exclaimed, stepping toward his sovereign. "Are you blind? They're…" Rune slammed to the ground as if smashed there by an invisible hand. He let out a pained grunt, limbs straining against the force holding him.

"You're becoming tedious, nephew," the king said in an ominous tone.

Ettie stared down at her soulmate, horrified and guilty. He was distracting the king for them, drawing the royal's wrath. The green fire had dissipated, the ice daggers clattering to the ground.

Rune wheezed a laugh, shocking her. "It's my calling in life, uncle. And what is yours, torturing baby animals?" he sneered in a strained rasp. "These people can't help you."

Fearing for his life, Ettie babbled, "I can! I can help you, but I can't give you the power, at least not on purpose. I can't use it, it's just there and I don't know how it works exactly, but if you just…"

The king's black stare pierced straight through her, freezing her voice, her mind, even her heart and soul. *Give me the power of the gods.* The words sliced into her head like fingers of icy steel, wrapping around her thoughts and will, squeezing and vicious. The world disappeared in a red and black storm of pain, shredding her from the inside out. She couldn't resist the imperative of the king's spirit weave, but it was an impossible demand, one she couldn't fulfill. She hung helpless in a rage of agony, unable to even scream.

Then it ended. Ettie gasped and shook, numbly absorbing the return of the world. She was now lying on the ground, curled in a fetal position, her body like ice, cold and aching all over. Breath burned in her chest and her heart rattled like a broken toy. Rune lay on the ground in front of her, handsome face aghast, one hand stretching toward her. The king scoffed through the muffled roaring in her ears.

"Waste of time. Storm, confine them then find Prince Destin. He will tell me where my Vessel is or they all suffer."

****

It took Lia and Destin a short time to reach his father's royal encampment. The sun was still riding high in the apex of the sky when the colorful tents came into view. The king's tent stood out, twice as large as the rest, with the elemental flag rippling above it, the five elements artistically rendered on silver cloth.

Destin wondered when his father had decided to travel there, why his father had chosen this place. Perhaps he hadn't wanted to take possession of the Vessel in front of his whole palace court, in case it didn't go as planned.

Then Lia banked and Destin adjusted his grip, looking down with her as they circled high above the camp. He knew what she was looking for, though the distant figures below were hard to make out. If he was lucky, King Stern would be nowhere visible and he'd have a chance to talk Lia out of doing anything rash.

But the gods had taken his luck away along with his choices.

After a moment of circling, Lia screamed a raptor's

cry of triumph and folded her wings, plummeting toward earth in a hunting dive. The ground rushed toward them with terrifying speed and Destin cursed, realizing he had no time to be gentle.

He shoved into Lia's mind with a spirit master's implacable will, pushing aside her startled, hasty resistance and forcing her into a deep sleep.

He was falling with a limp woman in his arms.

Calling wind in a fierce rush to slow their descent, he cradled Lia to his chest and prayed for her forgiveness. His wind kicked up a wild dust devil as he neared the ground, battering the archers who had him in their sights and obscuring his view of his father. He ignored them all, settling on the ground and letting his wind die. He knelt, laying Lia on the ground before removing his shirt to cover her bare form.

Still ignoring the soldiers, he watched his father approach.

"Destin," King Stern said on a note of surprise.

"Father." He didn't rise from Lia's side, nor did he bow. He studied this man who'd given him life and wondered for the millionth time what his mother had seen in him. Destin's gentle, frail mother had wed this man, cleaved her life to his, and borne him a son. Why?

It was a rather burning question for Destin, one he'd spent a great deal of time trying to answer. He was almost an exact physical replica of his father; except for his youth, the color of his eyes, and his scar. King Stern was hard and cruel, merciless and unforgiving, his black eyes reflecting the dark nature of his soul. His people feared and respected him but did not love him.

Watching the king study him with cold calculation, Destin finally realized a great truth. He was also never going to love his father, no matter how hard he tried. He was never going to win his father's approval or affection. Stern was capable of neither. Destin was not going to be able to save the king from his fate.

With a sad curl of his lips, he met his father's gaze. Something moved in those dark depths, an emotion that could have been unease, and a muscle twitched under one eyelid.

Then the king glanced around at his soldiers and archers. "This is your prince. Lower your weapons, fools," he barked. While they complied, Stern returned his attention to Destin, face expressionless. "My brother spins a fanciful tale and you drop out of the sky with some unclad female, looking like a peasant. Shall I assume your search for the Vessel has not gone according to plan?" The icy contempt in his tone would once have made Destin flinch and scramble to make amends.

Now, he only snorted. "Since the Vessel is in your hands, I'd say it went exactly according to plan, Father."

The king's eyes narrowed. "And who is this?" He flicked a finger at Lia.

"Someone to whom I owe a debt."

"A debt?" his father repeated with a dubious sound. "She's a changeling, yes?" When Destin nodded, the king waved a dismissive hand. "Then we'll settle your debt in coin when she wakes. Take her away," he ordered his soldiers.

Destin surged to his feet and the ground surged with him, jumping under his splayed fingers. Soldiers cried out and stumbled. Destin locked eyes with his father and stated with quiet, deadly conviction, "No one touches her but me."

The king's eyebrows rose. "It seems you also have quite a tale to tell, Prince Destin. Bring her then, if you must." He spun on his heel and stalked toward the tents without looking back.

Destin took a fortifying breath and bent to lift Lia in his arms. She was limp. He began to worry he'd damaged her somehow. He'd never forgive himself if he'd harmed her.

A soldier at his side said with respect, "This way, your highness." Destin followed where he led, surrounded by an entourage of soldiers. They stopped before the king's tent and the soldier held the flap open for him. Destin ducked inside.

It took him a moment to adjust to the dim interior. Heavy fabric partitions broke the inside of the tent into chambers, leaving the center open as a makeshift throne room and audience chamber. A high-backed chair sat in the center with a low table in front of it.

King Stern stood, an arm draped over the chair, watching Destin while servants scrambled throughout the tent.

"I'll need a cot and blankets," Destin told one servant as she zipped by. She paused to bob a curtsey, wide eyes flying across his bare chest to the woman in his arms, before she scurried off again.

"Quite an entrance, son," Stern drawled. "Now put the girl down and explain yourself."

But Destin kept his father waiting until after the servants brought a cot for Lia and blankets to cover her. They also brought a wash basin, towels, a change of clothes for him, plus a chair and enough food and drink to cover the low table.

When he'd tended to Lia and the servants disappeared, Destin began to wash and asked his father, "So where is the Vessel?" He tried for a casual tone, hoping any tension would seem natural, considering the subject matter.

"You've changed," the king said.

Destin glanced over his shoulder and met his father's suspicious gaze with a mild lift of an eyebrow. "Yes," he responded, splashing water on his face then grabbing a towel. "Have you met with her yet?" He knew his father would have wasted no time inspecting his acquisition, but he needed to know how it had gone and if Ettie was all right.

"I have. I'm not convinced the girl is the Vessel of Power. She seems daft."

Destin pulled on a shirt with a short, humorless laugh. "So she is. And you'll see soon enough what she can do."

"Tell me now. She's weak, afraid, soft in mind and body. She did nothing to defend herself or her mother, or even that lazy cousin of yours. How is she the Vessel? She seems to have no power."

Destin stiffened, turning to face his king. "Did you harm them?" he asked softly, wondering in a distant corner of his mind if he was going to kill his own father after all.

Stern's upper lip lifted in a contemptuous sneer. "Do I see fear in your eyes, son? Don't concern yourself, I didn't clap your cousin in chains. And I haven't harmed anyone yet." The king lowered into his chair and hefted a goblet. "Sit. Eat. You look as though you haven't seen civilization in a year."

Destin clenched his jaw and sat, pouring some

wine to give himself time to think. The king had spoken casually, but Destin knew he didn't make idle threats. He wouldn't think twice about injuring Ettie. Glancing over at Lia's sleeping form, he took a thoughtful swallow of wine. "You're right. Ettie is weak and helpless. She carries the power but is unable to use it." He met his father's sharp stare. "Harming her will do you no good."

"Then how does it work?"

Destin shrugged. "I don't know."

The king sat back in his chair, face settling into lines of dark discontent. "Tell me of the search."

Destin obeyed his sovereign, giving him an edited version of events. He touched on his uncle's attacks but gave them no weight, as if they were the usual competitive interference between royals. He left out his near catastrophic power overload and the fact that they'd been on their way to sequestering Ettie instead of bringing her to the elemental king. He didn't mention Lia at all.

When he expressed some aggravation that Uncle Storm had stolen the Vessel from him at the last moment, his father chuckled. "My brother is as devious as he is useful. But he did admit to the theft. And the girl?" Stern gestured with his goblet at Lia.

"Ah." Destin curled his mouth in a wry smile. "She's the reason Uncle Storm was able to steal anything from me. I was distracted at the time."

"Celebrating your triumph a little early?" the king asked in a dry tone. Destin tipped his head in acknowledgement. "So what debt could you owe to some frill you bounced in the woods?"

Destin smiled and said nothing.

"Perhaps I'm better off not knowing," his father said with a little snort. He called for a servant and ordered her to show the prince to his own tent.

As he rose, Destin said, "I'd like to see the Vessel and my cousin. Do you object?"

"Do I have reason to object?" the king asked with a narrowing of his eyes.

"I won't be stealing them from you, if that's what you're asking," Destin replied with just the right amount of self-depreciating humor.

His father relaxed and nodded. "I will see you looking like a proper prince at my dinner table."

"Of course, Father," Destin murmured, lifting Lia and following the servant out of the king's tent. The young woman showed him to a smaller tent not far away and bobbed acknowledgement when he asked her to wait outside for him.

Then he ducked into the interior and laid Lia on a bunk, tugging the blankets away from her with soft curses and shaking hands. She was so still. He checked her pulse, checked her breathing, both regular and strong. He called her name, patted her cheek gently then less so, but she didn't respond.

He was afraid to spirit weave again, afraid he'd hurt her with his blindness. He needed Rune. Feeling for their bond, he called to his cousin.

Where's our rescue? Rune responded, his mental voice so clear and strong he could have been standing next to Destin, speaking in his ear.

Destin winced. "On hold," he answered, looking down at Lia. "I'll explain when I see you in a few moments, but I need you to make sure Lia's all right. Without waking her," he added.

Rune was quiet a moment. Then his furious mental voice blared like a shout. *A spirit weave? Who did this, the king?*

Destin clutched his head and gritted, "Stop bellowing. I wove her to sleep. She was about to commit suicide by elemental king and about a hundred archers. Please, brother. Did I injure her?"

Another pause. *No. She's just deeply asleep. Now come here and explain.*

Destin winced again, this time because Rune's tone had been too quiet and serious. Taking a deep breath, he tucked the blankets around Lia, brushed strands of dark hair from her cheek, and rested his forehead against hers for a pained moment.

Then he thrust to his feet and stalked to the tent opening. He asked the servant to stay and watch over Lia, to be sure no one disturbed her. The young woman nodded with a furtive smile and a strange light in her eyes. Destin set off to find his angry cousin and their wayward Vessel.

Chapter 24

Rune paced, more furious than he could ever recall being in his life. He was furious and afraid, not for himself, but for his thick-skulled, hopeless cousin and the stubborn, helpless young woman crouched and shivering inside the tent.

He aimed all his fury in another direction, toward the elemental king, the epitome of evil, the worst uncle ever.

After the morning's humiliating, gut-wrenching audience with the king, they were sent to this tent, Rune confined with the women as an afterthought to keep him out of trouble. It was amusing, since Ettie was the very definition of trouble. Even after the king scared the sass out of her, she still refused to consider escape and her mother still wasn't trying to change her mind. So Rune waited for Lia and Des to come to the rescue.

But now that wasn't going to happen because his dutiful cousin had stopped Lia from doing what needed to be done, kill their king. Blind and faithful, Destin was going to let his power-hungry father destroy him and everything else.

Rune was not in a reasonable frame of mind. So when Des ducked through the tent flap, he couldn't rein in the violence coursing through him. He pounced, slamming his cousin against the tent pole then tripping him to the floor and driving a knee into his chest.

"What did you do?" he roared.

Des didn't defend himself, a sure sign of guilt and atonement. He coughed with a pained expression and patted Rune's knee. "Easy, brother. That hurts a bit."

Scowling, Rune lifted his knee and shoved hard on his soul brother's chest before lunging to his feet. "Bonehead," he snarled and resumed pacing.

"I know," Des said in a soothing tone, sitting up and leaning back on his hands, ankles crossed in a casual stance. He turned his head toward Ettie and her mother, where they sat huddled at the edge of the tent. Des gave Ettie one of his rare warm smiles. "Hey, little sister."

Ettie reacted as though he'd just rescued her, her tense form relaxing and her entire face lighting with a smile of such happy affection Rune's legs turned to jelly. "Hi, Des," she said softly, edging over to his side and resting her head on his shoulder.

Rune stared, dumbfounded and a little numb.

"Ettie?" Hyla said in a warning tone.

"Mama, this is Prince Destin. He's the one who's going to save us," she announced without lifting her head from his shoulder.

"Pleasure to make your acquaintance, my lady," Des said over Ettie's head, his smile turning wry. "Though, save may not be the right word."

"What is the right word, cousin?" Rune asked, stepping closer and crouching down to glare at Des, avoiding Ettie's gaze.

"Well, it's complicated," Destin sighed, shifting a little and glancing down at Ettie with a faint frown. "It appears Ettie was right all along. She did have to meet the king."

Ettie tipped her head back and gave Des a saucy grin. "I knew you'd come around."

"You don't know everything," Des retorted with a mock scowl.

Rune smacked his leg hard. "Don't you dare be daft like her! Speak sense. Now." Ettie frowned at him, but he ignored her, focusing on his irritatingly calm cousin instead.

Des smirked and said with a note of irony, "Control is an illusion. I learned this when I almost exploded. I believe it now and I believe it to be the lesson we all need to learn. We have to have faith and learn to let go, to live life as it happens rather than trying to force it into whatever form we think it should be."

Rune shook his head. "That's beautiful, really. A lovely philosophy. Now explain why you fouled a perfectly good rescue."

"Lia's way would've gotten us both killed."

"You don't know that."

"I know it would've ended badly, any way we played it." Destin's expression hardened, gaze sharpening. "Let's cut to bare bones. We must keep my father from using the power of the gods. Agreed?"

Rune nodded, a kernel of hope blooming in his chest. Perhaps Des was beginning to see the light after all.

"How do you suggest we do that?"

Rune struggled with it, knowing what he had to say but afraid it would wound his cousin, or trigger him to play the dutiful son and holler treason. To his surprise, Ettie raised her head from Destin's shoulder and nodded once, her sky blue eyes compelling.

Rune sighed. “The man must die, Des. Please tell me you see that.”

To his shock, Prince Destin didn’t even twitch. “And who should kill him? Should I murder my own father and king?”

Lurching to his feet, Rune spun away from the thought, knowing in his heart it was wrong, not only for his soul brother but for their people. How could they honor and respect a man who slaughtered his own father to take the throne?

“So should Lia do it?” Destin pressed. “Should a changeling kill the elemental monarch?”

Rune snarled a denial under his breath, looking past his urgent need to see the king defeated. A changeling killing a royal elemental might trigger hostilities between the two races to the point of war, even with Destin on the throne. “So throw him in a dungeon. Or banish him into exile.”

“How do you imprison a master of all five elements? How do you keep such a powerful man from going wherever he wants, taking whatever he wants?”

“So what, then?” Rune growled, throwing his hands up in exasperation and turning on his cousin. “What’s the answer, Destin? We can’t kill him, trap him, or exile him. What are we to do?”

Destin grinned. “Nothing.”

Ettie laughed and the tent brightened, as if the sun had slipped in through the cracks.

Rune blinked and shook his head. Her laugh seemed to be slipping through his cracks as well. “What do you mean, nothing?”

Destin told him.

Ettie laughed again. Hyla sighed and put her face

in her hands. Rune stared at his cousin for a long time.

Destin waited with a curl of his mouth, a gleam in his eyes that could have been humor or triumph.

"You've gone mad," Rune concluded. Then he flopped on to the ground next to his insane cousin with a sigh, ignoring Destin's low laughter. "Well, at least your plan is simple. I can handle doing nothing." He paused, slanting Des a sly look. "I feel sorry for you, though."

"And why is that?" Destin asked through his chuckles.

"How are you going to tell Lia?"

His soul brother fell dead silent. Rune smiled, enjoying his moment of petty revenge.

****

Lia woke to unfamiliar surroundings and groggy confusion. Where was she? What had happened? She was lying in a tent lit by a brazier flickering with low flames. Judging by the darkness under the edge of the tent, night had fallen. A neat, plainly dressed young woman sat on a stool close by, humming as she sewed something in her lap.

"Excuse me," Lia whispered. "Where am I?"

The woman jumped a little then rested a hand on her chest. "Goodness, you startled me," she said with a smile. "You've been asleep quite a while. You're in Prince Destin's tent. He's been waiting for you to wake," she added in a lower voice, eyes sparkling.

"Prince Destin's tent," Lia repeated, staring at the woman with suspicion. "How did I get here?"

"He carried you," little-miss-helpful answered with a giggle. "He's so strong and he wouldn't let anyone else touch you. So romantic," she breathed and scampered away before Lia could stop her.

"Gods above," she muttered and sank back on the bed, rubbing at her aching temples. Her head hurt and her limbs were heavy, sluggish. Letting her hands fall to her sides, she stared at the dim tent roof and tried to remember. What had happened?

The last thing she remembered was being in the woods. Then Ettie, Rune, and her mother had been captured. She and Destin had flown to the king's camp. Lia sat straight up, clutching the blanket to her chest. Staring at nothing, she fought to breathe.

"Lia?" Destin's low, husky voice floated through the dim tent.

She dragged in a breath, but her chest still hurt like someone had punched a hole through her ribs. "You," she said in a strangled voice. "You did that."

"Yes," he confessed, his tone heavy. "I forced you to sleep. I'm so sorry. But I couldn't take the chance you might die or be condemned as a murderer of our king."

Out of the corner of her eye she caught his shadowy form approaching. She dragged another breath into her aching chest. "My sister, my mother."

"Both are fine. I won't let my father harm them."

"How can you stop him? Can you keep him from using her?"

He was silent.

She turned her head, studying the mute dismay on his usually impassive features. "You're going to let it happen," she whispered in horror. "Mother of All, he'll be a monster. How could you?" She stopped herself. "Was this your plan all along?"

"No, Lia—"

"And I believed you, talking about keeping fragile, little Ettie out of your father's hands. Stroking me and lying."

"I never lied."

"No? Then why is she here? How will you keep her safe?"

"Please, trust me."

"Trust?" she hissed, brushing off the blankets and rising into a predatory crouch. "You broke into my mind, elemental prince. Trust is dead." She grew claws and lunged, catching his throat in a fatal grip. "Maybe you should be, too."

He held her gaze, mouth curling at the corners. "Well, it's about time, don't you think?"

Those were her words, after their first time together. Furious he would use it and twist her up inside with the memory, she snarled and flexed her claws. He didn't fight, even when she pierced his skin. But try as she might, she still couldn't kill this thrice-damned prince.

With a cry of frustration, she shoved away from him and leapt from the bed, prowling the tent like a cat in a cage.

"Lia, please listen," he said, still sitting next to the bed.

"Listen to what? To you being the good little prince, the dutiful son, making excuses for your monstrous father? He will destroy everything, don't you understand?" She whirled for the exit. "If you won't stop him, I will."

Before she could reach the tent flap, air whirled around her in a rush, plucking her off her feet and carrying her to the center of the tent. "You are not going out there unclad, Eylee'ai," Destin said in low growl.

The air slowed, letting her feet touch the ground and brushing over her in a silky swirl before fading. Lia gasped, bare skin tingling from the sensation as if he'd stroked her all over. Infuriated by his interference and her own unwelcome response, she glared at him.

He turned his back with a quiet groan. "Merciful gods, Lia, put on some clothing." Then he headed for the tent flap without looking at her. "I'll send in Pepper to assist you. Please just… I'll take you to Ettie, just don't do anything rash." He lifted the flap and murmured something. The young woman she'd met earlier ducked in with a dimpled smile and scurried over to a long chest.

Destin paused in the opening, meeting Lia's gaze with grim authority. "Don't harm the girl. I'll be right outside waiting." Then he ducked out, ignoring Lia's wordless snarl.

"Well, that was an odd thing to say," Pepper chirped. "Why on earth would you hurt me, my lady?"

"I'm not your lady," Lia snapped. She took a deep breath and covered her face with shaking hands, trying to think. She could ignore Destin's warning and slip out the back of the tent, but then what? She would have little time to find the king or her family. She wouldn't be able to do both before Destin discovered she was gone and alerted the camp. She could just fly away and wait for another chance to rescue them, but the thought of Ettie and her mother in the clutches of the elemental king made her shudder. She couldn't leave them.

Dropping her hands with a sigh, she glanced at the wide-eyed servant. She would stay and bide her time, maybe play the prince's own game of deception and deceit. Her chest ached as if a hole still gaped through it.

"What should I call you, then?" the servant girl whispered, holding out a long-sleeved dress.

"Just Lia." She studied the expression on Pepper's face. "Why are you looking at me like that?"

"You are…" The woman gestured at Lia's bare body. "You stood unclad before our prince. Were you not shamed?"

"Shamed? What's the matter with you? It's just skin," Lia retorted, snatching the dress out of the woman's hands. Turning it back and forth, she grumbled, "How do you put this thing on?"

Pepper giggled then cleared her throat. "The underclothes are first. Let me help you."

With Pepper's assistance, Lia managed to pull on all the pieces of an elemental lady's formal wear, though she refused to let Pepper fuss with her hair. Ignoring the woman's crestfallen expression, she headed for the tent flap, kicking with absent irritation at the hem of the dress.

Destin stood outside under a blazing torch, between the guards flanking the tent. The light danced flames in his eyes, cast stark shadows across his face, and gleamed on his scar. He met her gaze and bowed. He wore just as fancy an outfit, a high-collared black jacket with gold embroidery and piping. It looked almost as restrictive as the thing she was wearing, though he seemed more comfortable in it.

For the first time, he looked every inch the prince, regal, dark, and handsome.

She scowled at him. "How do you people wear this

stuff?"

His mouth curled in a way that squeezed her heart, despite what he'd done. "Eylee'ai of the changelings, you are the most beautiful thing I've ever seen, no matter what you wear."

Pepper made a whimpering, swooning sound behind her, but Lia folded her arms across her chest and refused to be flattered. "Where's my sister?"

"This way," he murmured, waving his hand in a polite, courtly gesture for her to accompany him.

She walked at his side between a row of tents, not hiding her calculated interest as she studied the layout of the camp and its military strength. "A small army, right on the border. How peaceful and diplomatic of your father."

Destin hummed agreement. "He's not known for his diplomacy."

"So invasion? Is that his plan? Get the power of the gods and conquer the known world?"

"Perhaps in time. Right now he's still not sure Ettie is the Vessel." He was watching her as they walked, his tone even, his stride smooth and easy. As if they weren't talking about the end of the world. As if he hadn't betrayed her, betrayed them all.

Lia clenched her hands into fists, locked her jaw, and continued walking. She would let him take her to her family. Then she'd decide how best to make him pay. Maybe she couldn't kill him but she could still make him suffer, make him bleed, make him hurt as he'd hurt her.

Destin made a low sound as if he knew what she was thinking. But he said nothing, only walked at her side to a non-descript tent flanked by more guards.

They bowed to the prince and lifted the flap for him. Destin waved Lia ahead of him.

She entered the tent, bracing for whatever was inside, afraid for her family. She expected tears at least, fear and anguish at their imprisonment. She wasn't sure what she'd do if they'd been hurt in any way.

She did not expect to find them seated around a table, eating a hearty dinner as if they were home. Only Rune looked disturbed, sitting with his head in his hands until he caught sight of her. "Oh, finally," he groaned. "Please stop being angry. It's killing me."

"Lia!" Ettie jumped up with a bright smile, their mother rising behind her. They converged on Lia and she hugged them both hard, a lump in her throat.

"You're all right?" she whispered, looking between them anxiously and blinking the sting of tears from her eyes.

"We're fine," Hyla soothed with a gentle smile, brushing Lia's hair back from her face and behind her ear as she'd always done. The gesture made Lia's eyes sting even more.

She turned to Ettie, studying her sister's fragile features. "The king didn't hurt you?"

Ettie gave her another reassuring squeeze. "He's a big bully, but we're all right. And Des is here now, so he'll protect us."

"Oh, yeah?" Lia asked with another surge of fury, turning to stare at the prince standing in silence at the entrance. "How does that work?"

"Stop," Rune protested, drawing her attention back to him. He'd risen from the table, moving toward her with a pained look. "Lia, please listen. Des has a plan. I'll admit, it's completely insane—"

"Thank you, brother," Destin muttered. "Very helpful."

"—but I think it has promise."

Lia shook her head. "Any plan involving my baby sister in that man's hands—"

"But I have to be," Ettie interrupted with an anxious look. "It's the only way to stop him."

Lia looked around at them all, seeing the resolution on each of their faces, even her mother's. "Have you all gone crazy?" she snarled, stepping away from them.

"He's going to blow himself up," Ettie declared. "Just like Des almost did. The gods will have their justice."

Lia stared at her sister in disbelief. "Is that one of your true dreams, Etts, or just another fantasy you thought up?"

Ettie flinched but didn't look away, her solemn face older somehow. "My dreams don't matter anymore. It's out of our hands and in the gods'."

"My father taught me control, Lia," Destin said, drawing her attention like a magnet. The calm force of his green-gold gaze held her prisoner. "Control is all he knows, all he believes in. Even if he knew how to let go, he never would. He believes it's weak to surrender. He will fight to dominate until his last breath, but he can't control the power." He pointed a finger at Ettie. "And that is what will kill him."

Now she understood what they wanted to happen, the death of a ruthless king at the hands of the gods. But believing it was another matter.

"That's nuts. Even if it works out your way, what kind of damage will he do until then? And how are you going to stop him from killing half your people when he does explode?"

"I think I know how. If you'll listen," Destin said in a diffident tone most unlike her self-assured prince.

Thrown, she blinked at him then glanced around at the others. They watched her with expectant faces. "Fine," Lia muttered, crossing her arms over her chest.

"Will you sit?" Destin asked with another one of those courtly gestures, both annoying and impressive.

Lia sat at the table and listened. Destin explained what he thought they should do with his power-ravenous royal father. When he finished, she drummed her fingernails on the tabletop and thought it over for a while. "Too risky," she concluded. "Too many things could go wrong. I'll just save us the trouble and kill him now."

In the middle of the ensuing babble of protests from her companions, a soldier stepped into the tent. "Prince Destin, our king requires you dine with him."

The prince nodded acknowledgement and the soldier retreated with a bow. Destin stood and paused, looking down at Lia with a thoughtful gleam in his eyes. His mouth curled in a hint of challenge. "Will you join me?"

"Oh, you want me to kill him now? Sure, let's go," Lia responded, rising to her feet and moving toward the exit.

Destin caught her arm with a muffled chuckle. "You can't kill him, Lia. You'll start a war between our people."

His touch burned and she jerked away with a warning glare. "More excuses?" she accused.

"More truth," he said with a quiet calm that annoyed her to no end, though he had a point.

Folding her arms across her chest, she grumbled, "I could kill him so no one would know it was me."

"Breeding suspicion and chaos, leading to war. Why don't we just eat dinner instead?" He tipped his head toward the exit and raised his eyebrows, mouth still curled in amused challenge.

He looked like he was enjoying this. Lia turned to Rune in disgust. "This is what you put up with all those years?"

"I drank heavily," Rune explained.

Lia snorted then ducked through the tent flap. "Let's go, your highness. Introduce me to the elemental High King."

Destin drew alongside her and led her down the row of tents. "One thing you should know…" He hesitated and cleared his throat. Then he continued without looking at her, "Father believes you are just a girl I bedded. I thought it safer for you and Ettie both if he didn't know you were sisters."

She mulled it over then decided she didn't care what the king thought of her. "Smart," she responded. "Thank you."

His head whipped toward her, as if she'd surprised him. "Lia, I really am sorry for forcing your mind. It was a snap decision I regret—"

"It's done."

He paused. "But you don't forgive me."

"Trust is earned," she said with finality, not looking at him.

His steps faltered a fraction before he paced her again. "I see," he murmured.

Lia tried to ignore the ache in his voice and the trip of her heart, focusing instead on the huge royal tent.

"Well, this should be interesting," she whispered. She was going to come face to face with the man who'd caused her family such torment. And she didn't even plan to kill him. Of course, what she planned and what happened weren't always the same.

Destin seemed to have similar thoughts. He caught her elbow at the entrance and bent to mutter, "Nothing rash," in her ear.

She hid a shiver of reaction, pulling out of his grip and retorting, "No promises."

The guards acted as if they didn't see their clash of wills, holding open the tent flaps with servile patience.

Lia took a deep breath and stepped inside to meet the elemental king. She stopped short at the entrance, shocked by the resemblance the king had to Destin. She'd never given it much thought, assuming they'd look similar as father and son. But if it weren't for the few strands of gray, the age lines at the corners of his eyes, and the dark eye color, the king and Destin could have passed for twins.

Not a good comparison for Destin. Lia hated his father on sight.

The king said unsmiling, "You brought company," and stared through her with his black eyes as if she were nothing.

Destin introduced them in a flat tone, face as expressionless as his father's. Lia looked between the two of them and pressed her lips in a grim line. Oh yes, this was going to be a very interesting dinner.

To make sure she started off with just the right tone, she flashed her teeth at the king in a parody of a smile and said, "So, your highness, do you park armies on the border a lot or is this a special occasion?"

Destin shot her a sharp glance. She ignored him.

King Stern studied her a moment with those glittering dark eyes. “How amusing,” he said still unsmiling. “Only an ignorant changeling would consider this small camp an army. Do you drink wine?” He waved at a servant to pour.

“Gosh, no, I’ve never had it,” she lied through her razor-sharp smile. “The sex shop I worked in only served beer.”

The servant choked and sloshed the wine, but the king’s only reaction was a slight lift of his eyebrows. Destin’s muffled sigh sounded resigned.

“Charming,” the king said without infliction. “Sit. I assume you know how to use utensils.”

“Father,” Destin chided.

“Oh, I’m sure I’ll figure it out as we go along,” Lia said with a fake laugh. “I mostly like the sharp, pointy ones.”

The king paused next to his chair, giving her a narrow stare.

She blinked at him with wide eyes. “You know, to stab the meat,” she added and reached for the nearest knife.

Destin slipped it out from under her fingers, placing it some distance down the table. The servant seemed to be choking again. Lia pouted at the prince, but he only set a goblet of wine in front of her with a pointed look.

“Father, I spoke with Ettie today,” the prince changed the subject.

The king settled in his seat with a last mild sneer of disgust at Lia before seeming to forget her existence. “And what did my Vessel have to say?”

Lia nearly bit through her tongue at the king's use of the possessive but managed to keep quiet, easing into a chair next to Destin. The king was willing to talk about the Vessel in front of a stranger. Either he was overconfident or thought she was too stupid to understand. Mistakes she was very willing to let him make.

"Quite a bit," Destin answered his father. "It appears you made an impression."

The king nodded with arrogant certainty and signaled the servant to fill his plate. "Go on."

"She confirmed not being able to use the power herself. Like a goblet that holds wine for others to drink." Destin filled his own plate with food. Lia didn't touch a thing, holding her goblet and watching the royals.

The king grunted. "Do you believe her?"

"I do. She doesn't have a face for lies. Too innocent, too inexperienced."

The king nodded again and waved for Destin to continue.

"She also explained how she believes the power works. It's not an extra ability you pluck out of her, like being able to see the future." Lia tensed, but Destin moved on, "She increases your own abilities. With the Vessel, you will become an even more powerful elemental, Father."

The king paused, resting a forkful of food on the edge of his plate. His black eyes glittered with avarice, but he spoke with the jaded disbelief of a man too used to having people tell him what he wanted to hear. "She said all this to you?"

"After your warnings, a sympathetic ear seemed

just the thing she needed to confess. You may confirm all this with her if you like," Destin said in an offhand tone, eyes clear and calm, his movements smooth and steady as he ate.

Lia didn't want to admire him for his composure, or his subtle manipulation of his father. She didn't want to see how his sense of purpose and conviction had changed him, made him stronger, steadier, more. For the first time, she could picture him as king and it alarmed her for reasons she didn't want to explore.

The king made a reserved sound in his throat. "And how is this transfer of power achieved?"

"It appears to be involuntary and requires proximity. From what she has said, it will take time."

"How much time?" the king asked, a crease forming in his brow.

"She believes it's different for everyone. No way to tell how long. But it will happen as long as she's in your sight. Like standing next to a fire, it warms you whether it wishes to or not."

"Is it permanent?"

"I don't know and neither does she." Destin paused, studying his father with a thoughtful frown. "She's afraid of you, though. I don't know how it will affect the transfer." Then he lifted a shoulder in a dismissive shrug and took another bite of his food.

The king didn't dismiss it, chewing it over along with his dinner. Lia's stomach rolled and she swallowed a sudden nauseous surge of hatred.

"How sympathetic were you?" the king asked his son with sickening calculation.

"What do you mean, sire?"

"Does she trust you?"

"I believe so."

"Then you will bring her in my presence to give her the illusion of safety. Between her fear of me and her trust of you, she'll be effortless to control. Then we shall see what the Vessel of Power will do for me."

It was too much provocation for Lia. "Oh, are you talking about the myth, the thing holding the power of the gods?" she asked brightly. "I love that bedtime story."

Destin gave her ankle a hard kick under the table.

She turned her head and smiled at him with a flutter of her eyelashes. "Can I have the knife back?"

"No," he said without looking at her.

The king looked between them with a slight curl of his upper lip, a faint sneer of disgust. But he spoke as if there'd been no interruption. "Be ready to break camp in the morning, Destin. We head for the palace tomorrow."

"Yes, Father," Destin said, laying down his fork and pushing back from the table.

Lia bounced to her feet, more than ready to go.

The king remained seated, staring through her again with those cold, black eyes. "And son, don't bring your little changeling whore in my presence again."

Destin gave his father a fluid bow before turning to the exit without another word. Lia turned with him, smothering a smirk. On their way out, she gave the servant a saucy wink for good measure.

Once outside, Destin measured his steps to hers, quiet for a long moment, watching her out of the corner of his eye. "You didn't kill him," he said in a thoughtful tone.

"I thought about it hard."

"I noticed." He cleared his throat. "I'm sorry I didn't defend you against his insults."

She glanced at him in surprise. "Don't be. He thought just what we wanted him to think. And I don't have to see him again, so it went great."

His sudden smile was too warm and magnetic. "You're amazing."

She looked away, flustered. "No, I'm a forgettable whore he doesn't see as a threat. I didn't expect him to pull up stakes and head for your palace," she changed the subject, skin heating under his intense regard.

"It doesn't change anything. Here or there, what we do is the same." He spoke as if he wasn't paying attention to his words, his gaze still setting fires inside her.

"More people, higher risk," she said through gritted teeth. How could he still affect her so easily, so deeply? What kind of weak-willed idiot would want someone so deceitful?

He said nothing else until they reached the Vessel's guarded tent. "Will you tell them what's happened? I have duties to attend." She nodded, watching him through her lashes and wondering if he'd ask where she was going to sleep. He hesitated but said only, "Goodnight, then," and walked away.

Lia refused to watch him go, clenching her jaw and ducking into the tent.

Chapter 25

For Ettie, the trip to the elemental palace was agony.

Riding Wind wasn't a hardship, especially with Des for company in the saddle behind her. He was a wonderful riding companion and he called her little sister like he'd adopted her, expanding her heart with joy. He was everything she'd imagined in a big brother, almost always patient, stern when necessary, protective and playful, affectionate and kind.

On the few days journey to the seat of the elementals, she and Des had long conversations about their lives. Des seemed fascinated by her changeling upbringing, her experiences as a Vessel with Earth Keepers and Ephemerals, and most especially anything to do with Lia. Ettie had fun surprising him with all she knew of his life from her dreams, and she questioned him with endless curiosity to fill the gaps her dreams didn't cover.

Spending so much time with Destin was a dream come true for her.

But she was still miserable. Part of it was the elemental king, his ominous presence always within sight and always like a terrible, dark sickness seeping into her flesh. He said hardly a word to her but terrified her all the same with his soulless, black stare. She and Des watched the king, waiting for signs his power was rising and staying close in case they needed to stop him from hurting anyone.

Even worse was the separation from her family. By necessity Ettie had to stay close to the king, traveling near his majesty and spending the nights in his luxurious tent. She could only catch glimpses of Lia and her mother in the distance, as the king had made it clear they weren't welcome in his presence. She'd never spent such a long time away from them before. She worried, fretting about their safety and well-being. But mostly she missed them, missed the comfort of her mother's love and her sister's fierce protection.

Destin helped by giving updates on her family through his bond with Rune. And that was the source of her greatest misery, Rune's deliberate withdrawal from her.

If he was her soulmate, would he be able to pull away so thoroughly? Lia's sharp words came back to her, *is that one of your true dreams or just another fantasy you thought up,* and she wondered. She'd watched Rune grow up, he and Des, watched them live full, exciting lives while she stayed isolated and sheltered from the world. Maybe she'd wanted to be with them so much she'd invented the whole soulmate thing. Their bond seemed so real to her, but maybe she was as crazy as they all thought and it was pure imagination. Then how had she affected him, drawn him away from Des, and put him to sleep?

She swung back and forth between hopeful belief and crushing despair. And she wasn't alone in her misery. Destin tried to hide his pain, but every time he said Lia's name he flashed hot and tensed. Ettie sympathized and worried for them both. She knew in her heart Destin was a good man who'd never hurt her sister, but she also knew how wary Lia was around men in general and elementals in particular. She didn't know if her sister could forgive.

"How do I earn her trust?" Destin had asked at one point. The edge of rough desperation in his tone had cut through Ettie like a ruthless sword.

"Just give her time," she'd answered with as much certainty as she could muster. "She knows she can trust you or she wouldn't let you near me." Ettie hoped it was true. She wanted them to be happy and thought they'd be perfect together.

She hadn't dreamt it that way, though.

As they came within sight of the elemental palace, a wave of amazed relief brought tears to her eyes and blurred the magnificent view. She was here at last, at the end of her lifelong journey, the end of her dreams. And it was glorious.

The valley before them rolled away in gentle, green undulations. A thick river snaked through the center, leading toward the ocean shimmering like a silvery mirage in the distance to their right. To their left, the land rippled into foothills, gradually climbing to a regal mountain range on the far horizon. In the valley, farmlands, small forests, and fields surrounded a city the likes of which she'd never seen outside of her dreams. It spread vast and gleaming on either side of the river, a colorful skirt for its crowning jewel, the elemental palace.

The structure stretched toward the sky in a many-tiered, arced, and shining display of earth elemental mastery. Sea colors swirled on its polished surface, darker gray-greens and blues at its base lightening to almost translucent turquoise at its peaks, the whole fantastic display shimmering in the sun like the ocean it reflected.

"Oh, Des," Ettie whispered. "Your home is so beautiful."

He made an absent sound and she turned her head. He wasn't looking at the view at all, eyes narrowed on the still figure of his father.

"It won't happen here," she reassured him. "It'll happen in the palace." He looked down at her with raised eyebrows and she grimaced a little. "Yes, another dream. But I'm pretty sure it's a true one."

"How does it all end, little sister?" he asked with a teasing note.

"Can't spoil the surprise," she responded, giving him a little grin before sobering. "Anything I told you might change what you do."

He rested his chin on the top of her head and looked down at the palace with her. "Anything you can tell me?"

She'd grown to adore his willingness to accept what she was without censure or judgment. She'd known when she'd seen him for the first time after her capture that he understood. She'd recognized the calm certainty in him, the knowledge and acceptance she'd known most of her life radiating from him in an almost palpable aura. He'd been touched, either by the gods themselves or the older races.

She grinned again. "I can tell you you're my favorite prince ever." He snorted in amusement. An image from the dream popped into her mind, "And you won't believe what my sister can turn into." She bit her lip in regret when a flash of heat ran through him.

His voice was calm, though, as if nothing had happened. "I believe your sister can do anything. So she was there?"

Ettie nodded, cursing her impulsive tongue. But he didn't ask for details, urging Wind forward with some subtle signal she could barely feel. She leaned over and patted the horse, smiling when he nickered and arched his neck. "I know," she whispered. "I'm happy to be home, too."

Destin shook his head, less surprised than resigned to the mystery of Ettie. Beautiful or not, this place should terrify her. This was the seat of the elemental king's power and she'd seen in her dreams what he did with that power, what he could do to her. Yet instead of being afraid, she acted overjoyed.

Because she's mad, Rune grumbled in his mind. He was so strong now Destin couldn't keep him out even when he tried. But he didn't try hard or often. He could feel his cousin's desperation even if Rune wouldn't admit to it. Rune was a constant visitor in his mind, yearning to be near Ettie with a soul-deep hunger Des understood all too well.

Because she accepts her destiny, Destin contradicted his soul brother without rancor. *She wants to be here because this is where she's meant to be.*

Gods above, don't you start, too, Rune snarled, his flash of fury burning like acid in Destin's mind.

With a wince, Des gave his cousin an ungentle mental shove in retaliation. *Mind your manners, cousin, and stop making a mess in here. I like my head just the way it is.*

Sorry, Rune mumbled with a hasty withdrawal of a good portion of his mental touch. *She just makes me...*

I know, Destin answered. He knew what Rune was going through. His soul brother's torment reflected his own. *These sisters will be the death of us.*

Rune was quiet for a moment then sent, *Lia is requesting an update.*

As always, her name drove a rush of fire and longing through him. He took a slow, deep breath. *Father is feeling it strongly but isn't quite there yet.* Rune withdrew on a wave of sympathy and understanding, giving him a moment of much needed privacy.

He took another deep breath, releasing it on a leaden sigh. He missed her. He missed the freedom and soul-wrenching pleasure he'd found in her arms, but he missed the fearless challenge of her just as much, her quick mind and wit. His world was gray without her in it, leached of vibrant life. Her absence hurt like a part of him had gone missing, aching with emptiness.

Lia was avoiding him. She ignored his efforts to speak with her, ignored his many requests to see her. The few distant glimpses he'd had of her across the campsite only underscored her absence and sharpened the ache within him. At this rate, he was as likely to explode as his father.

Constant contact with the Vessel had the expected effect, he'd taken to slipping out at night to relieve the barrage of power, the building elemental pressure. With Rune's help, he would clear his mind and send his tension, worry, and longing back into the Earth Mother, channeling the energy and letting it go. He measured his success by the continued lack of major catastrophe, but he dropped exhausted on his pallet each night and wondered how long this could go on.

How had one female changeling become so necessary to him?

He brooded as they descended into the valley. Word had been sent ahead. The road was soon lined by curious onlookers. They bowed on bent knee to their hard king, but when they saw Destin, cheers rose and impromptu celebrations broke out in their wake.

Ettie cast him a brilliant smile over her shoulder. "I think they like you," she teased, eyes sparkling.

"I think they think I brought you home to wed."

Her face clouded. "What?"

"They don't know who you are and you're astride a horse with me. An elemental lady of the court would never allow such familiarity if I hadn't declared my intentions to wed her."

She sputtered, expression collapsing into dismay. "Well, that's just…you can't let them think that! Get another horse, hurry…"

He smirked and patted her arm. "Too late, little sister. But don't worry, they'll understand soon enough."

She sent him a reproachful look. "I don't know the rules here. You're supposed to keep me from making a total ninny of myself."

He chuckled, tucking her head under his chin again. "You're always a ninny, Etts. That's what makes you special."

"Creep," she mumbled.

"Fluff-head," he insulted back with affection.

She pouted but didn't hold onto it long. Soon she was waving and smiling back at his people, admiring the town as they entered and swept through it. She marveled over different sights and squealed with excitement when they crossed the wide bridge over the river, clutching his arms and peering over the edge at the rushing water below them, eyes as big as a child's.

He had to laugh. "Peasant," he teased.

"But it's so great, Des." She peered wistfully behind them at the town. "Can we go back later and explore?"

"If there is a later."

The reminder sobered her a little and she shot the king in front of them a wary look. Even the threat of impending disaster couldn't subdue Ettie for long. As they drew closer to the palace and the entrance to the courtyard, she gasped and exclaimed like a child at a sparkler show. She went silent when they entered the courtyard, though, head tipping back to take in the rising spires and sweeping lines above them, eyes wide and glistening with tears.

"Ettie? Are you all right?" he asked in a low voice.

"Thank the gods," she whispered, eyes still tracing the graceful arches above them. "I'm finally here." Then she dropped her chin to look at him, face filling with a warm glow like a sunrise. "I want to see everything!"

He chuckled and shook his head. "You're going to run everywhere and poke your nose into everything until you get lost, aren't you?"

"Yes. Help me down, I want to…" Then she froze, eyes fixing on a point beyond them. "Oh! That's Rune's…" Her voice trailed off on his cousin's name as if she'd lost all the air from her chest.

Destin glanced over. Rune's parents, his aunt and uncle, were hurrying toward them. He grinned, a burst of warm affection rushing through him. In the hidden chambers of his heart, he'd always considered them his true family and parents. Before, he'd hidden the thought away out of shame and guilt, out of loyalty to his father and the wistful memory of his frail mother. But now, he swung down from Wind and opened his arms wide.

"Destin!" his aunt exclaimed, her face alight, and rushed into his arms. She was a little woman, but big-hearted and enthusiastic, squeezing him without mercy. His uncle was a bit more circumspect, approaching at a sedate pace and clasping Destin's arm with a wide grin. "Nephew, welcome home."

"Thank you," Destin replied, surprised to find his throat tight and voice rough with emotion. He looked down at his aunt's amber-colored head resting on his chest and chuckled. "Did you miss me?"

She tipped back her head and smiled at him, loosening her fierce grip and easing back a pace. Her hazel eyes gleamed with maternal warmth. "Of course we did. We were worried for you, too." Her smile faded as she studied his face. "You look worn. What's happened? Where's Rune?"

"He'll be along," he reassured her, turning to help Ettie down from Wind's back. Her trembling startled him, and he studied her, taking in wide eyes and pale face. She looked terrified, watching his aunt and uncle. When he realized why, he smothered a snort of sympathetic amusement. She was meeting the parents of the man she'd declared her soulmate. The poor girl was nervous.

The older couple eyed her. Destin cleared his throat and introduced them. "Aunt Vale, Uncle Reach, this is Ettie. She's very special."

His aunt lifted her eyebrows, a gleam of

speculation in her eyes, but his uncle gave him a look of mild censure. “You go on some mad search for power, and found yourself a girl instead?”

“Apparently,” Destin smirked, then grunted when Ettie’s elbow dug into his ribs. With a pained smile, he captured her elbow and added, “The girl is what I was searching for. Uncle, Aunt, meet Ettie, the Vessel of Power.”

They both took a step back, Uncle Reach slipping a protective arm around his mate. They stared at Ettie with similar expressions of fascination and unease.

Ettie gave them a sick smile and small wave. “Hi. Um, don’t worry, I’m not dangerous or anything.”

“She’s not, but the power inside her is, so I’m enlisting your help,” he informed his family in a brisk tone. “She needs to stay secluded as much as possible, no public venues, no crowds, no visitors.” When Ettie made a sound of protest, he gave her a stern look. “No tours.”

“Oh, come on,” she whined and stomped a foot.

“Put her on a lead if necessary. A rope and gag are not out of the question.”

“He’s kidding,” Ettie told the couple with a dismissive gesture of her hand and a strained smile. “He doesn’t actually mean tie me down.”

“I mean every word. She’s a menace. You remember the phase Rune went through, sneaking out at all hours?” He pointed at Ettie with a solemn nod. “This one is worse.”

“Oh, my,” his aunt responded with rounded eyes and amusement lurking around her mouth. “Won’t this be fun?” Uncle Reach coughed into a fist, brown eyes twinkling, looking much like an older, stockier version of his son.

"I'm not that bad," Ettie protested, her expression a little desperate. She clasped her hands together and looked between them earnestly. "Really."

"Of course not, dear," Aunt Vale soothed with a dimpled smile and a gentle pat on Ettie's arm. "He's only teasing. You must be special to him. My nephew is usually quite contained." She flicked a quick, speculative glance at Destin.

"Oh, no you don't, auntie," he said with a crooked smile. "Save the matchmaking look for your son."

She huffed a little with a crease in her brow. "Young man, what a rude thing to say in her company. Lady Ettie, I do hope you aren't offended."

"Oh, it's just Ettie, please," the girl said with an easier smile, her expression warming. "And he didn't hurt my feelings at all. I don't want him either."

Uncle Reach snorted a laugh then managed to turn it into a protracted clearing of his throat, head swiveling to search the crowd. "So, where is our wayward boy?" he asked in a gruff voice.

"Keeping Ettie's family company," Destin answered, lifting his own gaze over the milling crowd to make sure his father had entered the palace. "The king required only the Vessel in his presence," he added in a flat tone.

Their expressions souring, his aunt and uncle exchanged a quick, enigmatic look before they both turned to stare at the entrance to the palace. Their faces had become blank. "And is our king satisfied with the results of your quest?" Aunt Vale asked, her voice threaded with the faintest hint of ice. Just then, she reminded Destin of his mother, her sister Myst.

“So far,” he murmured with a humorless twist of his mouth. Their eyes swung back to him, but neither spoke, any questions concealed behind practiced polite masks. “Let’s get out of this press.”

He handed Wind’s reins to a groom with a word of warning about the horse’s temperament, gave the beast a solid thump of affection, and then led his aunt, uncle, and Ettie out of the crowd. Using quiet corridors, they moved through the palace to the side wing where Destin had spent some of his fondest childhood days.

Uncle Reach and Aunt Vale chose to live in a quiet, out of the way nook, as far from palace intrigue and courtly demands as they could. A suite of well-lit rooms cupped a small courtyard where his aunt often puttered with her garden. He and Rune had spent hours holding mock battles in that sanctuary, climbing trees and playing a wild variety of boyhood games.

It hadn’t been so long since he’d last visited, but somehow, it all looked new to him, smaller and warmer than he recalled. Ettie exclaimed with delight over everything, showering his family with compliments. When she started reminiscing about some of his more colorful childhood exploits in that place, he hushed her and asked for refreshment.

They were just sitting down in the airy living room for some tea and a bite to eat when Rune strode in, calling for his parents. He froze at the sight of Ettie, and she lurched to her feet like a deer about to bolt for cover.

“Rune! There you are,” his mother cried, rushing over to squeeze him even harder than she had Destin. He patted her absently, eyes fixed on Ettie. Vale must have noticed his stiff tension, pulling back and looking him over with maternal concern. "What's the matter?"

He muttered something Destin couldn't hear and endured a rough hug from his father, but his gaze never left the young woman quivering at Destin's side.

Rune, breathe. You're frightening your parents, he sent to his soul brother, trying to hide his amusement.

Oh my gods, I forgot what she does to me, Rune answered back in the dazed mental tone of a sleepwalker.

Destin started to grin, then lost all humor when Lia and her mother eased into view behind Rune. The sight of his changeling drove the air from his lungs. She wore simple slacks and tunic like a field worker, dark hair twisted in a loose bunch at the nape of her neck. Her boots were scuffed, clothes and skin streaked with grit from the road, mouth in a grim line and eyes chilly, and she was still the most beautiful thing he'd ever seen.

His gut tightened and heat sizzled its way up his spine. "Lia," he said, and the room fell silent and still. He started toward her, but she shifted backward, chin lifting and eyes narrowing in clear warning. He paused, aching in every part of him.

Putting his hands behind his back to keep from reaching for her, he cleared his throat. "Lia, Hyla, it's good to see you both. Won't you come in? I'd like to introduce you to Rune's parents, Vale and Reach. Aunt and Uncle, may I present Eylee'ai and Hyloa'ki of the changelings, Ettie's family."

The polite words flowed well, even if his voice ran rough at the edges. But he couldn't pull his gaze from Lia, couldn't stop searching her eyes for something, anything to give him hope. After the first silent rebuff she refused to look at him, hands fisted at her sides and lithe form tense, shifting back and forth as if waiting for the perfect moment to make a run for it.

"It's a pleasure to meet you both," his aunt said with a gracious smile. "Please, come in, refresh yourselves. Dear, will you make them comfortable?" she asked her mate, then shifted closer and slipped an arm through Destin's as the changelings followed Reach into the room. When they were out of earshot, his aunt gripped his arm tighter and whispered, "What on earth is going on here?"

"Long story."

"Shorten it," she retorted, staring from her frozen son to the changelings and back to Destin with appalled insistence.

He sighed, watching Lia move around the furniture and settle in a seat with mind-bending suppleness. "In short, then. Ettie believes she and Rune are soulmates. It's probably true. Lia and I…were…"

"Destin!" his aunt hissed in shock, not letting him finish. "And you brought her to court with you?"

The insult smacked him hard enough to pull his attention away from Lia. He gave his aunt a grim look and removed her arm from his. "You surprise me, Aunt. I never believed you'd jump to conclusions or judge. Is it because she's a changeling? Are you assuming she's just some piece of fluff I found on the street? She's worth more than every simpering court lady in this place, and I would make her my queen tomorrow, if she'd have me. She deserves your respect."

"Oh!" Several emotions chased across Vale's pretty features before settling into suppressed glee. "Well, then. That's something else entirely, isn't it?" She glanced from Rune to Ettie and Lia with an eager light in her hazel eyes. "My, aren't they both beautiful? I always did want daughters," she added in a thoughtful murmur, patting him on the arm. "Don't worry, Destin. Leave everything to me."

He barely controlled a wince, watching her glide away with a sense of impending catastrophe. Now might be a fine time to escape. "I need to keep an eye on the king," he said, but no one was paying him the slightest attention, his aunt chattering away as she dragged her son to a chair.

With a last look at Lia's stiff form and wary eyes, he blew a hard breath, turned on his heel, and left.

Chapter 26

Destin's departure was like a storm slipping over the horizon, releasing Lia from some insistent pressure. She should have been relieved. Instead she was a little lost and ill.

He'd looked tired, drawn. Their days on the road had been kinder to him and Ettie, since they'd been at the head of the caravan, but he was still dusty and disheveled. His intent gaze had held an edge of desperation, as if she had something he needed.

But he was the prince and he was home, in the seat of his power, in this massive structure. What could he possibly need from her? She was just an uncivilized changeling from nowhere important. There had to be about a hundred elemental ladies lining up to be with him.

She needed nothing from him, either. It didn't matter she'd wanted to take his face in her hands and kiss away the shadows under his eyes, wanted to feel his arms around her again. Want wasn't the same as need. What she needed was to stand strong and not be a weak-willed ninny, giving him yet another opportunity to betray her.

And then there's these people, she thought, glancing between Rune's parents. Sweet and obnoxious, like their son. Reach had pressed her into a seat with gentle insistence, while Vale forced food and drink on her, both carrying on conversations pretty much all by themselves. Lia sat with a tiny plate of cheese and fruit balanced on her knees, cradling a fragile cup of fragrant tea, and wondered how to escape with her dignity intact.

Her mother appeared to be enjoying this genteel torture, smiling serenely and murmuring responses to the overbearing couple. But Rune sat with a fixed expression, hands clutching the arms of his chair and eyes looking everywhere but at Ettie. Her little sister huddled over her tea and oozed a cloud of pure misery.

Lia sighed. They didn't have time for this. "Rune," she said, interrupting his chattering mama. "How much do we tell them?"

His desperate hazel eyes swung to hers as if she'd become a lifeline. "Everything."

She lifted her eyebrows, but he said nothing else. "All right," she said, passing a sour smile between his parents. "I guess, since your son has lost his silver tongue, I'd better do the talking."

She explained their plan as concisely as she could, watching their faces go from disbelief to horror before settling into grim resolve. When she was finished, neither uttered a word of protest.

"What can we do?" Vale asked in a low voice.

Lia blinked. "I just told you your king's going to die. You don't have a problem with that?"

"He caused the death of my sister and abused my nephew."

Lia stared at the ice in the little woman's eyes for a moment. Then she nodded grimly. "Good enough. There's not much we can do until the king's ready, and we don't know when it will be. But when he is, we'll need your help."

She discussed it with them for a little while longer, discovering Rune had gotten his spirit sensitivity from his mother, though both of his parents were strong elementals. When the crisis arrived, they were going to need every ounce of strength to prevent the king from using spirit against them all. In Lia's opinion, it was the most dangerous of the five elements.

In a lull in the conversation, Vale turned to study her son for a moment, then glanced at Ettie with a faint smile. "Rune dear, you've hardly said a word. Don't you think it's time you told me just how it is you managed to become soulmate to the Vessel of the gods' power?"

Their heads shot up, both pairs of eyes staring at Vale, wide and dumbstruck. Lia sighed and looked toward the exit. If she made a break for it and abandoned her family, would it be so wrong?

Lucky for her, she had no idea the level of torture she'd have to endure the rest of the day. There were the emotional outbursts from her sister, servants trying to bathe her, maternal advice from both Hyla and Vale, and dress fittings, for gods' sake.

By the time a servant arrived to announce the king's summons, she was at the edge of mayhem, ready to shred the next person to come within reach. She also entertained the idea of hunting down the prince and throttling him. It was his fault she was stuck with these crazy people and trussed up in another dress. She should have just skewered the king when she first met him and been done with it.

But when they gathered in the corridor to follow the servant, Ettie took one look at Lia's dark blue gown and turned white as snow. "Oh," she breathed, locking eyes with her sister. "I—I think it's time."

Lia's stomach flipped and she tensed. "You dreamt this?"

"You wore that," Ettie whispered, shivering in her own new gown of pale yellow.

"Good," Lia growled, spinning on her heel and stalking down the corridor. "Let's get this over with."

The throne room was huge and overdone, in Lia's opinion. Massive stained glass windows rose and arched overhead, filling the space with disorienting, colorful light from the sunset. Hundreds of people milled about in a place that could fit double the amount, sitting on tiered seats along the walls and wandering the large space in the center of the hall.

At one end, monstrous double doors stood open. At the other end, an ornate throne dominated a raised dais. The throne looked like it was made of the same stone as the palace, deep blue-green and warped into strange lines.

It took Lia a moment to realize it was supposed to be an artistic representation of the elements, on which the king sat with enormous, smug arrogance. He wore a gold outfit and a hat Rune had called his headdress. Though it looked less ridiculous in reality than it had in drawings, it still didn't impress her.

Much more impressive, to her, was the dark picture of elegance Destin made, standing next to the elemental throne. His outfit was simple, not flashy like his father's, black with gold piping, subdued and refined. He watched his father with quiet expectance and captured her eye like a cool dark spot at the center of a light storm.

She couldn't tear her gaze away.

The king smiled with all the charm of a hungry snake and waved an imperious hand at Ettie. Destin moved down the steps toward them with a smooth, effortless stride, sending Lia's heart skipping. She caught his glittering gaze and pressed her lips together, trying to stay focused. He looked calm, but his eyes were bright with veiled fire.

She stepped closer to him as he took Ettie's arm to escort her to the king. He paused, head tilting toward her, his gaze magnetic. Mindful of a great many eyes on them, she stared past him at the monarch. "I won't be sorry," she muttered.

"Sorry for what?" he responded, voice too warm for her comfort.

"For this gods-cursed dress I think I'm about to shred. Ettie says it's time."

His long form tightened in reaction, but he only inclined his head with a faint smile and drew Ettie away. He was doing a good job playing the polite prince. Holding Ettie's hand, he guided her to the stairs with courtly grace and bowed to the king. Then he turned, standing close to Ettie's side as the king rose to his feet to address his subjects. Lia watched her sister tremble and clenched her jaw, grateful Destin was there to support her.

"Lords and ladies of the elemental court, I bring glad tidings. A new era is about to begin, my people. My divine destiny has arrived, and a golden age will follow, an age of prosperity and triumph for all elementals. I have found the key to this glorious future, an offering from the very gods themselves. I present to you the Vessel of Power."

The sick toad was gloating. Lia glanced between him and Destin and decided she'd been wrong. They looked nothing alike.

The crowd reacted with a rush of sound, an outcry of surprise and then celebration. High King Stern stood above them, a blade-sharp smile on his face, dark eyes glittering like a madman's. He stood triumphant, victorious, but the storm grew in him, the wild pressure filling his skin and straining to burst out. The gods' power mounted, and he appeared unaware of the danger.

The elemental prince turned, staring at his father. Then he moved Ettie to one side, shifting between her and King Stern. He climbed a step and said something to his father in the uproar.

The king's smile sheared off his face, eyes snapping down to his son. "What did you say?" Stern snarled, voice echoing over the crowd. Silence fell like a smothering blanket.

"I challenge you, Father, for the elemental throne," Destin announced with all the calm of a man commenting on the weather. "You are unfit to rule."

The palace floor shuddered under Lia's feet in an ominous rumble, and she stared at the two elemental masters with a sudden wrench of alarm. Ettie, in a rare moment of self-preservation, skittered back from the two men, shooting Lia a wide-eyed glance.

"You dare?" Stern growled, looming over Destin with violent, paternal outrage. "You dare?" he shouted and backhanded his son.

The sight of a father's hand striking her prince filled Lia with a red tide of rage, a tide so huge and compelling it wiped her mind of all thought. She darted forward.

“I wouldn’t do that,” she hissed, stalking toward the king with murderous intent. “It puts me in a very bad mood.”

“Lia, no…” Destin started, holding out an arm to block her, but his father barked an incredulous laugh.

“The changeling whore? I’ll chain you both and lash the skin from your backs!”

Lia was changing her form before he finished speaking. Fury flooded through her and expanded her skin in a flash of heat and light, like the scorching breath of a vengeful deity. This wasn’t part of their plan, but Lia was beyond rational thought.

He was evil. And she would end him.

She grew, vast and black, scaled and deadly, unaware at first what she was becoming. Her flesh settled in perfect alignment, strong and sinuous, just the right tool for divine judgment. Vicious claws and teeth made for regicide, skin tough enough to withstand any element, agile wings and limbs ready for anything. Her vision sharpened and gained extra edges, extra colors, like looking through crystal or the eyes of a goddess.

Or in this case, the eyes of a dragon.

The king stumbled back, shock on his face, a protective cyclone forming around him. The crowd screamed and scattered. But Destin placed himself in her path, staring up at her with bright, fearless eyes and arms outspread to halt her attack. “Outside!” he shouted above the cacophony, ignoring the sudden wind tearing at them. “We must get him outside!”

Thwarted, she roared her displeasure and stomped a clawed foot on the stairs, gouging ruts in the stone. But Destin moved toward her instead of away, casting a grim look over his shoulder at his father. The king stood in a pulsing corona of green flame, face contorting with rage. The palace shook, the air shrieked, and Lia had a sudden image of them all being crushed under a mountain of sea-colored stone.

She hesitated, snaking her huge head around to find Rune and his parents. All three nodded. As weavers of spirit, they swore they would prevent the king from using that element. For the rest, she and the prince needed to get the explosive monarch as far away from his people as possible, before real catastrophe struck.

Unfurling her wings with a snap, she crouched low in wordless invitation to her prince. He bounded up her side and swung over to settle between her neck ridges, as if he mounted mythical creatures every day of his life.

Destin called down to his raging father. "You want us? Come and get us!" His legs tightened against her and Lia responded to the cue. She smashed through the obnoxious stained glass windows with an inner grin, then worked her massive wings, looking back down into the throne room.

"Ah, gods above, Lia, you're magnificent," Destin groaned, his hands spread and burning on her black scales. "But you could have gone through the doors!"

She rumbled a dragon laugh, watching the king shoot up from below on a cyclone of air and green fire. Tilting and spinning on a wingtip, she thrashed her barbed tail at the High King and launched herself into the sky. The grace and power in this form thrilled her down to the core, the world brightening and opening in new dimensions of sight, sound, and smell. How could such beauty and magic be abomination?

But the elemental king didn't allow her much joy in her new form, chasing them with a conflagration of rage. If she rose high enough, she could deprive Stern of water and earth. With Rune, Vale, and Reach suppressing spirit, she and Destin only had to contend with fire and air.

Not an easy thing to do, she discovered, when facing an elemental master with the arrogance and certainty rivaling the gods'. On the other hand, she wasn't sure she could stay in the sky much longer. She shrugged off his fire with a dragon's disregard, letting it sizzle off her scales, but he battered her with air until she tumbled rather than flew.

"You can't escape me!" he screamed at them. "The gods have given me their power, and I am invincible! I will become a god, and you will be nothing!"

"You fool," Destin called back, his wind cutting through his father's and steadying her flight. "No one but them can wield their power! Can't you feel it?"

"I feel the rush!" the king answered with a wild laugh. "I feel the blessing of the gods. I am their chosen, and you will pay for defying me."

Lia slowed her headlong upward flight, wings straining and heart thundering in her chest. *High enough,* she thought and twisted aside, dodging a whistling blade of flame-edged air. Destin shifted with her as if they'd practiced the maneuver, his grip steady and sure.

Far below, a flood of people poured out of the palace, faces upturned. They were so small, yet her dragon sight brought each into incredible focus, right down to the texture of their clothing. Their expressions ran the gambit of emotions from awe to terror.

A hard gust of wind brought her attention back to the mad monarch, just in time to dive under a violent wave of flame. Destin gave a hoarse cry of pain and Lia bellowed in protest, fear striking through her veins like ice, darkening her vision. She spun and braced, trying to protect Destin with her body. Arching her neck, she craned to see how badly he was injured.

"Just singed," he called to her, easing her fear and stoking her fury. With a snarl she turned on the king, teeth and claws ready to shred, but the cyclone around him kept her at bay. Frustrated, she roared at the royal, raking through the shrieking wind with her claws, wings straining to the point of agony. The wind beat at her, tossing her to and fro as if she was only a toy. In a moment of anguish, she realized she wouldn't last much longer.

With a shout, Destin created his own whirlwind, a vast, swirling buffer against his father's chaotic weaves. At the calm center of the prince's hurricane, Lia righted herself and swept her wings in a hovering rhythm, muscles singing with remembered strain. Before she could feel relief at the reprieve, Rune's mental voice blared across her mind.

We've lost him! Something's blocking us from reaching the king. Lia, Des, I don't think it's him. Rune had never sounded so frightened. *I think I hear...*

Rune? Lia called, alarmed by his sudden silence. *Rune, answer me!*

Destin swore, a fast, vicious curse edged with desperation. "Lia, we have to keep him distracted. If he's blocked Rune from spirit weaving..."

The king laughed, a strident madness in its pitch. "Witness my transformation!" he bellowed over the shrieking winds. Green fire leapt and pulsed off his body in growing tendrils. His cyclone of air expanded, twisting and chaotic, smaller vortexes forming and smashing into each other, plowing into Destin's opposing whirlwind. "I will gain the pinnacle of the sky and remake the world! Every creature will quake before me and sing my divine name."

"It's slipping from his control," Destin called to her, his fiery hands braced on her scales. "We must provoke him to use it. The more he bends the power to his will, the more it's rebounding on him."

Lia glared over her shoulder with an impatient hiss. Did he think she'd forgotten the plan?

"Can you handle more wind? How well can you fly, my black beauty?"

Oh, I can fly. You just hold up your end, elemental. With a defiant bugle, she folded her wings and dropped like a stone out of the prince's hurricane. He clutched her neck with a breathless curse and she twisted her mouth in a dragon's grin. Snapping her wings open, she lunged upward again, dodging wild wind devils and gouts of flame in a circuitous path around the mad king.

After that first drop, Destin moved with her on the erratic flight as if he were born to it, shifting and leaning his weight with instinctive precision. At the same time, he sent daggers of white flame toward his father in a fierce barrage, though none reached the king, ripped apart by winds and green fire.

It was enough to pull Stern from his self-absorption and refocus his attention on them. Face stretched in a grin of insane delight, he answered his son's attack with huge spears of fire. "You are weak, my traitor son! By your new god's grace, you will see true power before you die."

Destin blocked a few and Lia twisted out of the path of others, her lungs burning for air and muscles aching, wishing the monarch would explode already. If he didn't, she'd drop out of the sky, the battle would go to ground, and their world would get a lot more complicated. Risking a swift glance at the king, she gulped at the blazing tendrils snapping around him with a life of their own. Stern bobbed in the air as if riding a bucking beast, face filled with lunatic joy or agony.

Then a strange sound whispered across her dragon senses, like the voice from Rune's spirit weaves on a higher level, as though she were hearing the sound of creation. If this was what Rune had heard, no wonder he'd been afraid.

Lia spun and braced, allowing green fire to splash and roll off her scales. Destin created another protective whirlwind around them, shouting a question which she ignored. She stared at the High King, shock rolling down her spine.

The man was glowing. He bulged like an overfilled sack, limbs moving in awkward sweeps as though he'd lost feeling in them. Her dragon vision perceived veins writhing under his skin, swelling with light, power rushing into him from some unknown source. The strange sound grew, distant music or a chorus of voices in perfect pitch, a divine language no mortal should hear.

"The gods come to me, my brethren!" the king shrieked, black eyes glazed and staring past them at something even her dragon senses couldn't perceive, his fire shooting in all directions. "Can you hear them? They're calling my…my divine name…" His face twisted from agonized joy to confusion.

The distant chorus converged for a heart-stopping moment in a word like the crack of an immense whip. *Trespasser.* A perfume drenched the air, the scent like an overflowing field of wildflowers baking in summer sunshine, and the air shimmered before Lia's eyes. She back-winged away in frantic awe.

King Stern's eyes bulged with stark horror, then disappeared in a terrible green light. A spasm twisted his long frame, snapping all his limbs out wide and quivering. His fire and cyclone paused, suspended with him as if frozen in time.

Destin's whirlwind dissipated and he said into the sudden calm, "You were right about one thing, Father. Your divine destiny has arrived. May the gods have mercy on your soul."

Then the air crackled around them and pressed, like a giant's hand. A prickling sensation skated across Lia's scales, sharp, painful, and alarming. The king's fire consolidated around him, solidifying and brightening like a green sun about to be born. The air filled with the scent of ozone.

"Oh, Lia," Destin breathed, pressing tight against her. "It's time to go."

On a sudden shaft of pure terror, Lia snapped her wings closed and dove.

All around them, the sky cracked and sizzled, thunderous and terrifying. Lightning slashed bright lines across the entire heaven, a net of ominous light with the king at its center, streaks of force tearing the very fabric of reality. The sky ripped apart in the roar of a many-voiced god, vast and unbearable, slamming into Lia with a force she could never have imagined.

Everything went shrieking white and then all disappeared into darkness.

Chapter 27

Destin blinked his eyes open and became aware of two disconcerting things. One was the ground rushing toward them at an appalling rate. And the other was the limp woman tangled in his arms.

"Lia!" he called, pulling air around them with the strength of panic. The battle with his father had tired him, but imminent death was a strong motivator. "Lia," he said again, pressing his face to her throat. Her pulse throbbed with life against his lips and he gasped in relief, tumbling them to the ground.

Panting, he hauled himself to a sitting position and dragged her onto his lap, cradling her close and running his anxious gaze over her. They were both scratched and bleeding from the hard landing. And Lia was out cold, scaring him witless.

"Lia, honey, don't do this to me," he rasped, brushing the hair from her face. "Come on, you need to wake now. Come back to me." He shifted her closer, kissing her closed eyelids and stroking her cheek. "Please. Please wake."

A remote part of him sensed people running toward them. He and Lia had careened to earth near the bank of the river, not far from the palace. Shouts and cries of alarm sounded in the distance.

When she remained still in his arms, Destin cursed. Then he shook her once and barked, "Lia!"

She groaned, cracking her eyes open and giving him a pained stare. "What?" she answered in an aggrieved tone.

He sucked in a breath, letting it out on a shaky laugh and rocking her against him. "There you are. You had me worried."

She grunted, lifting a hand to her head, eyes closing again. "Head hurts. Is it done?"

"Yes," he said with an ache in his chest. He had no doubt the king was dead. The gods had torn open the sky to exact their justice. Now he had to find a way to live with the consequences. Then he cleared his throat, setting his complicated grief and guilty relief aside to deal with later. "You interrupted my speech. You botched the plan."

She sighed and made a face without opening her eyes. "He hit you. I got mad," she confessed in a mumble.

He grinned, murmuring, "Temper, temper." She rewarded him with a smirk. "You were amazing. I don't think my people will ever forget the sight of you as a glorious black dragon, straight out of ancient mythology, smashing the throne room. Why?"

"It needed redecorating."

"Why a dragon?" he chuckled, ignoring the people rushing to them, wishing this moment would go on forever. She was letting him hold her, trusting him. Giving him what he needed.

"Don't know. It just happened. Doesn't your head hurt?"

"You folded your wings around me, protected me. I think you received the worst of it."

"Great," she said, opening her eyes again with a

pained wince. "Who are all these people? And when are they going to shut up?"

He lifted his head, frowning around him. Silence fell.

"You're handy," she muttered, patting his chest. "I'm gonna go back to sleep now."

With that his fierce little changeling, now a legend to his people, lay her head against his chest and passed out again in his arms.

****

The next few days were the busiest of Destin's life. The rending of the sky had frightened his people, and panic ran rampant through the elemental kingdom with rumors of the wrath of the gods and the end of their world. He soothed and explained, over and over, from his father's advisors and court subjects to the clerics, that the god's justice had been meted out. The crisis was over.

The Vessel still represented a danger. He kept Ettie out of sight and far away from his people in a remote spire of the palace, for her sake as well as theirs. Fear could cause people to do terrible things, and Ettie couldn't defend herself. He allowed only her family and Rune's to visit her.

Rune spent more time with her than anywhere else, appointing himself protector of the Vessel. From his disgruntled reports to Destin, he did more containing her than fending off danger. Ettie complained, she didn't appreciate being cooped like a pretty bird in her tower. Rune had reluctantly acknowledged his soul bond with Ettie after his mother confirmed it, but they still edged around one another with the wary caution of those standing next to a rumbling volcano. Destin surmised being soulmates did not mean instant joy and harmony.

Destin sympathized, since his life held little joy and harmony. The royal council had conferred and all agreed Destin should be crowned High King. All except Uncle Storm, who'd fled the moment his brother died. Few of Destin's court protested his crowning, since his challenge of King Stern had been within elemental statutes, the king's death had been an undeniable show of godly decree, and the people liked him.

But Destin, groomed his whole life for this fate, now found kingship a heavy burden. He agreed to wear the mantel of monarch but refused any ceremonial coronation. He would do his duty, rule and protect his people, but his future loomed gray and lifeless as ash, not worth celebrating.

He would be alone on the throne.

He hadn't seen Lia since the gods had slapped them out of the sky. The elemental palace was a huge and convoluted structure allowing her to avoid him with ease. He could have accepted this, given her time and space. He'd imagined courting her to build her trust in him again. He would make her a changeling advisor, a liaison between his people and hers, a position demonstrating how much he valued her and guaranteeing time spent with her. His people would come to accept her, their fearful awe changing to familiarity and approval of her as his queen.

But she slew all his plans.

She was determined to take her sister back into changeling territory, to the secluded monastery. She wanted to leave him. She ignored the protests of Rune and his family, ignored Destin's increasingly desperate invitations and messages. As the new king, he could summon her into his presence, but that would be about as helpful as cutting off his own foot. Lia would not take such an order kindly.

So Destin resorted to conspiracy and ambush, in the faint hope she'd resent it less than a royal demand. He enlisted his aunt's help, who issued an invitation to Lia to dine with them in their home. It was there he waited for her while his aunt and uncle made themselves scarce, his heart thumping with dread and nerves.

When she strode into the receiving room, he lost the power of speech, feeling more like the village dunce than the new High King. She'd refused to wear any more dresses, scandalizing his court and amusing him. Today she wore a cream blouse and brown slacks finer than a field worker's but still simple. She'd confined her hair in a thick, dark braid, sharpening her features, turning the faint smile on her lips to something cool and regal. His world filled with rushing heat and need, numbing his mind.

The smile disappeared when she saw him. She jerked to a halt, body snapping taut. "What are you doing here?" she spat.

"Lia," he managed, "Please—"

But she cut him off with a gesture and a hiss. "Never mind. I know what you want, King Destin, and you can't keep her. Go away." Then she stalked past him into the courtyard.

Taking a fortifying breath and clenching his hands into fists, he followed her into the sunshine. "Lia, listen to me. You can't hide Ettie any longer. News is spreading of her existence, and soon the whole world will know what she is. She would be safer here."

"Safer?" she snapped, spinning to face him. "She's a prisoner! And you were the one who said she should never get anywhere near your people."

"I have a royal retreat, a place in the foothills—"

"Bah!" She flung out her arms in furious denial, turning to brace her hands on the edge of a bubbling fountain. "A place for elementals. In case you forgot, we aren't elementals, your majesty. We don't belong here."

"You're wrong," he said, easing toward her. Gods be merciful, he could smell her now. Her seductive spice made his entire body tighten and hum with need. "You belong here with me. We could protect her together, Lia."

She shook her head, making another furious sound of denial. "With you? As what, your pet changeling? Gods, Destin, your court already looks at me like I'm some kind of monster. I'm surprised they haven't formed a mob and beaten down my door."

"You're no monster and no one's pet." His voice grew hoarse and he had trouble drawing a full breath. "You are the fierce champion of the Vessel of the gods, and they are stunned by you. You could slay me, mount the throne yourself, and they wouldn't bat an eyelash. Lia, I can't do this without you."

She went still, eyes fixed on the gentle rush of water from the fountain. "That's not fair, Destin. And it won't work. Pretty lies won't change my mind. You can't keep Ettie here."

"Then take her," he gritted, clasping her arm and turning her to face him. "Hide her in some faraway place. I'll send a whole army to watch over her. Just don't leave me, Lia."

She gasped as if he'd burned her and pulled away. He glanced at his hands in a flash of alarm, but the fire roiling in his gut and racing under his skin wasn't yet visible. "Don't do that," she breathed, eyes wide and silver with dismay. "Don't touch me and play with my head. I can't stand it. I can't believe you."

His throat closed, hope fading like mist in the sun. Desperate and aching, he sank to his knees at her feet, letting go of the last of his pride without a qualm. He had nothing if she left. What was pride compared to that?

"I've never been more serious in my life," he told her, his voice rough. "Lia, I need you. If you leave, I'll do my duty, lead my people, but I'll be stone. Have mercy, Eylee'ai, I beg you. Save me. Free me. Consent to be my queen."

She stared at him with shocked gray eyes, motionless. She didn't appear to be breathing. "You…" she wheezed, then paused to suck in a harsh breath. "Get up, you idiot!" she said, voice shaking. "You can't do that. And I don't believe you anyway…"

He captured her hands in his, pulling her closer. "Let me prove it," he whispered, fire raging through him, need blinding him to everything but her. "It would be my very great pleasure."

Her legs buckled and he caught her, tugging her onto his lap with a wordless murmur of delight. "Destin, you're a royal, an elemental," she protested in a strained voice, sleek form trembling in his hold. "Your people won't let you."

He brushed his mouth against hers, stemming her words. "They'll love you," he breathed, touching his tongue to her bottom lip and shuddering at her moan. "But not near as much as I do."

Then he slanted his mouth over hers and let go. The water in the fountain turned to steam in an instant, a billowing cloud swirling around them, dimming the sun and dampening their skin. The stone under them rumbled and cracked, but neither noticed.

Lia had no resistance left, melting into him and kissing him back like a woman starved. The gods knew she'd tried to keep away from him, tried to protect herself and her sister. No one had made it easy, not her family or Rune's, and certainly not Destin, with his sweet, pleading messages and little courting gifts. These she could have resisted, but seeing him, seeing her own suffering reflected in his beautiful eyes and face, hearing his voice rough with the same longing piercing her down to her bones, she shattered.

She needed this so much. He gave her a wild passion her body craved, an acceptance her heart ached for, and an affirmation of all she was and could be with him.

Lia drove her fingers into his hair and clenched hard, desire warring with panic. She couldn't do this. How would she survive it if he betrayed her again? With a desperate groan, she pulled back, meeting his fire-streaked eyes on a shudder. "Wait, stop," she panted, aching all over.

"You're killing me," he gritted, long fingers flexing on her hips and driving fire all the way up her spine.

"Des, just…wait." He rested his forehead on hers with a broken sigh and she shivered, closing her eyes against a rush of longing. This man was everything she wanted, everything she needed. He said just what she wanted to hear. "Did you just say you loved me?"

"Yes," he whispered, breath feathering against her skin, hot ginger spicing the air she inhaled.

"That's not possible."

He made a sound like a muffled laugh. "Why? Because you're a changeling and I'm an elemental?"

"You're a king! I'm nobody."

He nipped her bottom lip hard and sent heat thundering through her in a weakening wave. "Don't say that again," he growled against her mouth, hands pressing her closer. "You're the woman who changed my life. You showed me freedom. I didn't know it existed, didn't know how cold I was, how alone, until I met you. You light my world. You make me whole, Lia, and I do love you, madly. Stay. Stay with me."

If it was a lie, it was the best one ever told. His voice shook with conviction, husky and seductive. It was exactly what she wanted to hear, exactly the same emotions etched in her own heart. Belief budded and began to open like a fragile flower, warming her right down to her soul.

"Des, I want to. I want to believe you."

"Trust me, sweet Lia. I'll spend the rest of my life proving it to you."

She quivered, tightening her hold on him. "It'll be a short damn life if you're lying," she muttered. "You're death will be bloody and painful and really horrible."

"That's my queen," he answered with a grin.

She sputtered, the concept just as shocking as the first time he'd mentioned it. "And that's just insane. Me? Queen? Have you lost your mind?"

"Yes. You make me mad all over. And if you don't tell me you love me and kiss me again, I'm going to burn down this palace."

She smirked. "Promise?"

"Lia," he growled, one hand anchoring the back of her neck and the other pressing heat and wild need into the casting on her skin. Her King of Fire.

"Yes," she gasped, surrendering with a twinge of terror and a vast flood of hope. "Yes to everything. I love you, Destin. You're mine now, gods help you."

Then she proceeded to claim him, with savage joy and fierce determination, for all the gods to see and anyone else who cared to look, right there in his aunt and uncle's garden.

Epilogue

Ettie watched her sister and Destin ascend the steps to the elemental thrones and sniffled. "Oh, Rune, isn't she beautiful? She even wore a dress."

"Des hounded her into it. They fought so hard they hurt my head, then they reconciled, enthusiastically. I had to leave the palace." His needling tone had the effect he wanted, irritating the stuffing out of her. Ettie did her best not to frown. This was her sister's wedding day, and she should have her happy face on. Everyone else did, with the exception of the young sailor, Cleave; the poor fellow looked heartsick.

"You're right," Rune continued. "She looks magnificent. Queenly, in fact."

Ettie sighed and tried to focus on the royal couple. They were magnificent, as matched and tuned to each other in this as they had been battling the old king. Des wore black and gold, Lia white and silver, their hands linked and movements in accord. They paused at the top of the steps, facing the newly formed double throne. Still made of the same sea-colored stone and depicting the elements, it now stretched into two seats with a dragon crouching on the backrests, one stone claw on each and vast wings outspread behind. It showed a merging of two races and two destinies.

The pair looked at one another and smiled with such intimacy tears stung Ettie's eyes. Then the elemental king and changeling queen turned as one to face their people, regal and fearless. A matched set, so different from one another, yet so fitting. Ettie's heart overflowed with joy. And if a little bit of envy lurked in there, too, she did her best to ignore it. "Perfect," she sighed with another sniffle.

"Aren't they?" her mother murmured at her other side, face lit with pride and love. Beyond Hyla, Vale and Reach watched the royal couple with just as much parental approval.

This part of Ettie's life, at least, was everything she could ask for. Her mother and Vale were now the best of friends, and Rune's parents had welcomed Hyla, Ettie, and Lia as if they'd become family. Destin was Ettie's big brother in truth instead of just in her heart, and her sister had found a place where she belonged, where she flourished.

If Ettie could just stop being the Vessel of Power, her life might fall into place, too. Instead, she was trapped in a tower, visited only by obnoxiously blissful family and an even more obnoxiously resentful soulmate. As if it was her fault they were soul-bonded.

"Your happy face is slipping," Rune muttered. "Feeling sorry for yourself again, Vessel?"

Ettie gritted her teeth. How did he do that? She'd been careful to keep a smile on her face, but he always seemed to know what she was feeling. She wished she was a spirit weaver, too, wished she could feel more than just their bond. Then maybe she could figure out how to get past all those thorny barriers he put between them.

Not that she wanted to get past anything of his right now. All she wanted at the moment was to smack him. So what if he was right and she was feeling sorry for herself? He didn't have to rub it in or sound so scornful about it. "Why do you have to be so mean?" she hissed. "I'll bet you stomp on kittens and kick puppies, too."

"Only on holidays," he said. "Your sister's watching."

Ettie tore her gaze away from his much-too-handsome profile and plastered a smile on her face, giving Lia a little wave. "Don't you make me cry on their wedding day."

"You already were," he said softly.

His odd tone snagged her attention and she looked at him again. His shoulders were stiff, hands held rigid at the small of his back, jaw tight, and mouth in a grim line. He kept those beautiful hazel eyes turned away. Was it his usual resentment or something else?

"Does that bother you?" she whispered, trying not to hope too hard.

He shifted in place, a muscle flexing in his jaw. "Why should it? Little girls cry all the time."

She swallowed an angry snarl and clasped her hands together to keep from hitting him. She'd always considered herself gentle, until she met Rune. Now fantasies of doing him bodily harm appeared more often than the ones involving kisses, sweet words, and nakedness. He thought she was way too young for him and reminded her of it every chance he got.

Stupid, he was not even a handful of years older.

She opened her mouth to blast him, then froze as a familiar sensation rolled over and through her. "Oh," she breathed and the world brightened.

"Ettie?"

For once she couldn't spare Rune any attention. One of her true dreams was becoming reality and she stepped forward, entering it with a glad heart. It had been far too long since they'd visited her.

A commotion erupted in the back of the throne room, cries and exclamations rolling forward through the crowd. Ettie walked to the base of the steps for a clear view of the pair of beings moving at a sedate pace through the center of the parting onlookers. One strode with the inexorability of a mountain, solid and brown from head to toe, his dark eyes as calm and fathomless as an endless chasm. The other didn't stride at all but drifted, a swirl of air and light made form, flowing in insubstantial loveliness next to her earthy companion.

They were the elder children of the gods, the Earth Mother's son and Sky Father's daughter. Ettie's old friends and mentors; the Earth Keeper and Ephemeral who'd changed her life.

"Etts?" Lia whispered in a breathless voice behind her.

"Oh, don't worry," Ettie responded, shooting the king and queen a reassuring smile over her shoulder. "They're just here to see me." Then she realized how that might sound. "Um, but I'm sure they're happy for you. It's a big day for us younger races, you two getting together and all. They just need to give me a pep talk."

The approaching elders laughed. The Keeper sounded like a distant avalanche and the Ephemeral tinkled like wind through chimes. "Still dreaming?" the Ephemeral asked, or thought at her. Ettie had never been sure if she heard the speech through her ears or her heart. Either way, it always sounded like movement and magic.

Ettie shrugged and gave them a rueful smile. “Enough to see this, anyway.” Then she noticed Rune at her elbow and jumped a little, wondering how long he’d been standing there. “And I met him,” she said in a listless tone with a twitchy gesture at her soulmate. “Rune, your highnesses, this is Joy of the Ephemerals and Peace of the Earth Keepers.”

“Joy and Peace?” Rune muttered with a lifted eyebrow.

“Not their real names,” Ettie amended as the royal couple descended the steps to join them. “His name I can’t pronounce and hers is, I don’t know, a secret, I guess.”

“We are deeply honored,” Destin said and bowed to the elder races. “I am—”

“We know you,” the Earth Keeper interrupted, his words slow and patient, voice deep and rumbling. He bowed in return. “It is our honor to attend. May this union be blessed and your dynasty bring peace.”

Lia edged forward with a little frown creasing her brow, slipping a protective arm around Ettie. “Thanks, that’s nice. You’re the same ones, aren’t you? The ones who told us about Ettie being the Vessel?” Her sister tensed, her eyes narrowing and face sharpening like a predator sighting prey.

Ettie winced. Lia blamed them; after the elders branded Ettie the Vessel, their lives had shattered. “Lia, it’s all right,” she hurried to intervene. “They’re here to tell us we did well. Right?” she prompted the elders, sending them an urgent look. Gods knew they didn’t need Lia going all dragon on the two ancients. It would be bad for diplomacy.

“Children learn slowly,” Joy breathed like a gentle

wind. "Growth takes time."

Ettie swallowed a groan at the cryptic answer, flicking a glance at her sister. Thank the gods, Lia didn't pounce, though she looked ready enough. Ettie returned her attention to the elders to find them watching her with expressions she'd seen far too often. Affection mixed with sorrow, pride fused with pity.

Lia's arm tightened around her and Ettie knew her sister had read their expressions, too. "What?" Lia barked.

The elders glanced at her, then looked at each of them in turn. "You did well," the Earth Keeper said. "You have faced your challenges with bravery and forbearance. The first trial has passed and the gods are pleased."

"First trial?" Lia and Destin said in unison.

Ettie grimaced and muttered, "Wish you'd just stopped at you did well."

"She is the Vessel of the gods' might," Peace said in his inexorable voice.

"A river does not cease to flow, moving ever onward," Joy added, her airy form brightening as if a sunbeam had struck her.

Ettie nodded, trying to hold onto patience. "Until it becomes the ocean, I know, I remember."

"You grew up with this?" Rune murmured, shifting closer and slipping his fingers around her arm in a light hold. "No wonder you lost your mind."

She wanted to respond, but her throat closed. This was the first time he'd touched her by his own choice. He didn't seem aware of it, eyes on the elders, a frown creasing his brow and body at a protective angle. She held still and tried to remember how to breathe.

"So you're here to tell us this is just the beginning," Destin translated, easing forward and putting an arm in front of his mate. At first, Ettie thought he was being protective, until she felt the thrum of violence running through her sister.

Rune's long fingers tightened and Ettie quivered a little before she could control her reaction. "Don't kill the messengers," she said huskily, then cleared her throat and glanced at the royal couple, careful not to move. If she didn't bring his attention to it, maybe her soulmate would keep his hands on her all day. A girl could dream. "I didn't stop being the Vessel just because we passed the first test. You knew there'd be more. That's why you stuck me in the tower, Des, and why Lia wanted to take me away again. Not just because I'm a danger to your people. I'm a lodestone for every power-hungry maniac out there. That won't stop until…well, until I…"

"Die," Rune whispered, his clasp now hard, his lean form shifting close enough to radiate heat all along her side. She turned her head and met his gaze. His hazel eyes darkened, grim lines bracketing his mouth. For the first time, his mental touch slid along their bond like a caress. *I won't let them near you,* he avowed, his mental voice strong, determined, and so terribly seductive. *Ever.*

Ettie whimpered, knees buckling and muscles turning to water. Only Lia's bracing arm kept her from melting in a puddle at his feet.

Rune must have known what he was doing to her, but he didn't let go, eyes lifting to glare at the two ancient beings. "Stop this. She's not some toy for you to toss around."

"She is the tool of the gods," the Earth Keeper mused with slow finality. "Not my own. You think it cruel, but you are proof of our Mother's mercy, young one."

"And our Father's pride," the Ephemeral gusted. "His children learn and grow strong."

"A second trial is coming. What form will it take?" King Destin asked in a commanding tone, a sovereign demanding truth.

But these were the Ancient Ones. They merely smiled and turned to Ettie. "We remain your guides and your friends," Peace rumbled with deep, solemn affection.

"Thanks," Ettie whispered, eyes stinging.

Then Joy rose in a sudden swirl, bursting in a shower of sparks to the delight of the crowd. When the light diminished, she was gone. Peace bowed to them, turning and striding back through the hall with slow inevitability, as if time and obstacles were inconsequential.

"So that was Peace and Joy. They're always like that. A little fun, a little creepy." Ettie shook her head and glanced at her companions. "Where were we? I think you two were going to give your royal speeches. Then we get dancing and food, don't we?"

"Etts, those were the Old Ones," Destin said, pointing after the elders like maybe she'd missed which direction they'd gone.

"Uh-huh. I would've invited them to stay, but I don't think they dance."

"Baby sister, they just said more will come for you," Lia growled in her big-sister tone.

"Sure. Hey, the cook promised there'd be cake.

There's cake, right?"

Rune shook her arm. "Ettie, we don't know what it'll be."

"Me either, but I hope it's chocolate."

"The second trial, little Vessel. Is it war?"

"Don't know, I'll let you know just as soon as I dream it." When they continued to stare at her with nearly identical expressions of frowning concern, she threw up her hands. "What do you want me to say? I'm the Vessel and everybody wants what's inside me. I get it. But I'm not going to crawl in a corner and cry about it every day, worrying about what might happen. I'm going to laugh and love and be as happy as I can, because there's no point to life otherwise. And I'll make sure you all do the same, because you deserve it."

She paused, measuring their reactions. Lia's concern morphed into her usual sibling tolerance and long-suffering. Destin wore a crooked smile, eyes golden-warm with affection and amusement. Rune stared down at her and shook his head, baffled humor lighting his eyes. She relaxed a little, trying out a tentative smile. "So…I really could use some cake."

Lia snorted and looped an arm through Ettie's. "That's my baby sister, loony Vessel, and sugar freak. Yeah, let's eat and dance our feet off. Who's going to listen to speeches anyway, after those elders upstaged us?"

Ettie laughed and the vast hall brightened like the dawning of a new day.

A word about the author…

Sci-Fi/Fantasy romance author Michelle O'Leary resides in Marquette, MI, which graces the shore of pristine Lake Superior. Born and raised in Upper Michigan, Michelle is a child of nature, enjoying all things outdoors.

Originally published through a small e-publisher, Michelle became an independent author publishing her work through Amazon Kindle, CreateSpace, and Smashwords before being accepted into The Wild Rose Press family. Her titles include *Vessel of Power*, *The Huntress*, *The Third Sign*, *Last Chance* (Sunscapes Trilogy), *No Such Thing*, and more.

Michelle is a mother first, a dedicated chocoholic, a contented Michigander, and a delirious word lover. She loves all feedback and is always happy to hear from readers!

http://molearyauthor.wix.com/michelleoleary

A note about the author

Thank you for purchasing
this publication of The Wild Rose Press, Inc.

If you enjoyed the story, we would appreciate your letting others know by leaving a review.

For other wonderful stories,
please visit our on-line bookstore at
www.thewildrosepress.com.

For questions or more information
contact us at
info@thewildrosepress.com.

The Wild Rose Press, Inc.
www.thewildrosepress.com

Stay current with The Wild Rose Press, Inc.

Like us on Facebook

https://www.facebook.com/TheWildRosePress

And Follow us on Twitter
https://twitter.com/WildRosePress

www.ingramcontent.com/pod-product-compliance
Lightning Source LLC
Chambersburg PA
CBHW050026030726
47506CB00001B/146